Revenant

Book Five of the
Chronicle of the Seer
Pentalogy

Florian Armas

Cover design by Kimber McLaughlin

ISBN 13 978-0-9939772-9-9

For my mother

Table of Contents

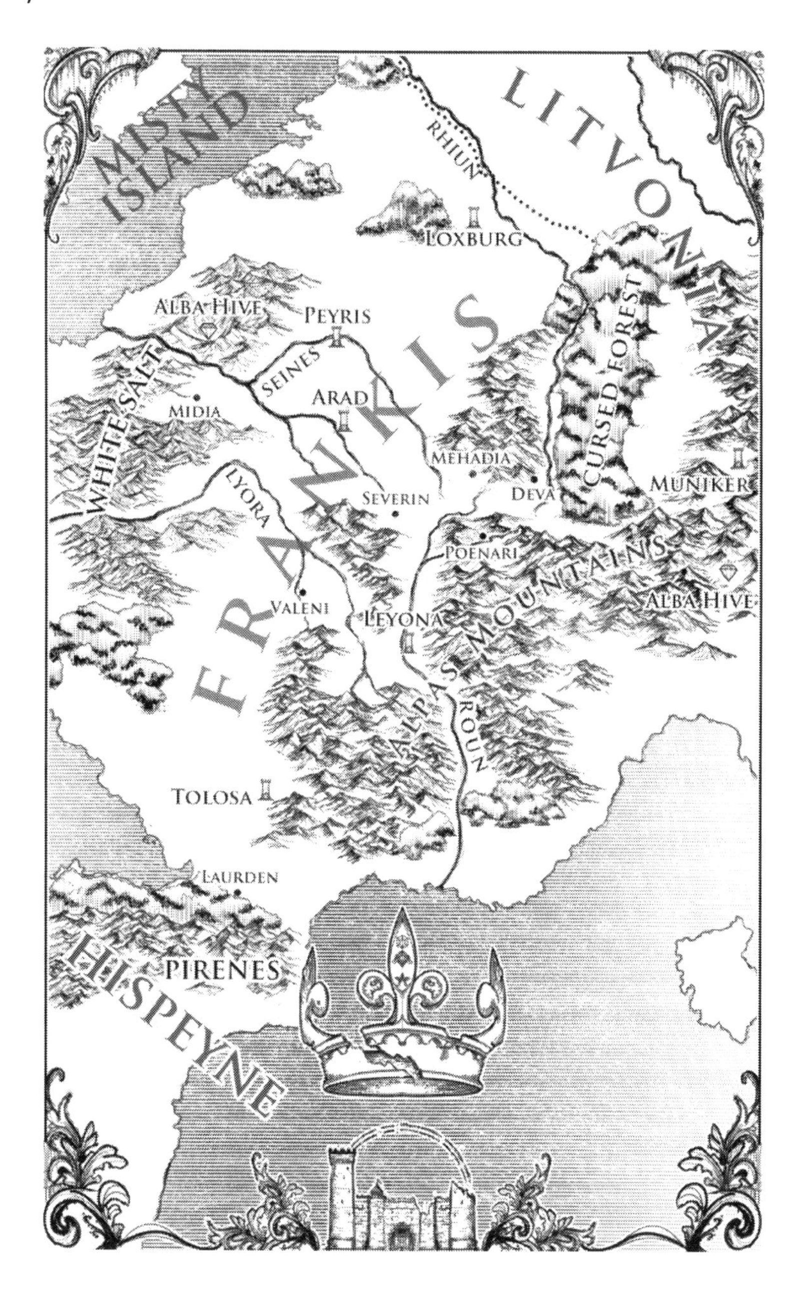
MISTY ISLAND
LITVONIA
RHIUN
LOXBURG
ALBA HIVE
PEYRIS
SEINES
ARAD
WHITE SALT
MIDIA
FRANKIS
CURSED FOREST
MEHADIA
DEVA
MUNIKER
LYORA
SEVERIN
POENARI
ALPAS MOUNTAINS
ALBA HIVE
VALENI
LEYONA
ROUN
TOLOSA
LAURDEN
PIRENES
HISPEYNE

Chapter 1 - Aliana

The passage sloped further downward, and the girl's feet padded noiselessly in the last shreds of light gleaming from the torch that was now partly hidden around the corner. Another turn in the long tunnel, then another one. It grew darker. The walls and the floor became nothing but hints, then the darkness became full and dense, even the faint noise of the air flowing from a hole several hundred feet away seeming to vanish. She did not dare to bring a torch with her; light is such a traitor when you try to escape. She waved her hand in front of her face. She could see nothing. Tense, the girl closed her eyes and let her mind wander, hoping for a hint of White Light. From the Vision she had had two days ago, she knew that this was the right night. But then it was her third Vision about the *right night*, and the other two had gone wrong. She was not the only Wanderer having Visions, and the whole Council was against her; the most experienced Wanderers were reading the future trying to prevent her escape. Every time, she went unchallenged out of the Hive, only to find a squad of Wanderers waiting patiently to take her back. They were all serious in the torches' light, but she knew that they were mocking her.

The tunnel was dark and damp, and she moved with the silence of a snake, only her fingertips trailing along the right wall making the faintest sound as they brushed the harsh irregularities of the walls. She did not really need to touch the wall for guidance, it was more to calm her mind. *But this time is different,* she thought and shook her head. *The Serpentist will try to escape too. I can't let that happen.* A strong stench of old, rotten corpses came from her right, and she wrinkled her nose. *The deepest tunnel; there is only death there.* There were many stories about monsters waiting to feed on trespassers. She did not believe those stories, yet she did not try to use that path for escape. Perhaps because it was longer. Or perhaps she didn't want to accept her fear. Eyes wide and unseeing, she stopped listening to the darkness. It was soundless, but that meant almost nothing to her. They never waited for her in the tunnel. The damp smelled so rotten. Unconsciously, she rubbed her fingers – they were sticky – then wiped them on her shirt, a cursory gesture. Sticky fingers meant a clumsy dagger in your hand, and this night was meant for fighting. She walked further until another flow of air touched her face, from her right again. There was nothing wicked in it this time, and she breathed deeply. *This is the right one... Splendra, the Serpentist will be somewhere at the end of the tunnel, ready to leave the Hive by the same path. She was once a powerful Wanderer. The Third Light of Frankis.* This tunnel was even longer, but close to its end some traces of light filtered in from the full moon above the mountain. The light leaked into the passage from two narrow cracks, small things, barely enough to admit a hand; she knew that. After a while and several curves, the light became darkness again. At the end of the tunnel, she peered round the corner. A great space opened out below her, a ring of smooth walls, partly carved blocks, partly of natural stone. She raised her head and smiled at the moon and its slow dance with the sparse clouds. *So far, so good.* There was a small exit in the ring, not a proper gate, just a thirty-foot-long tunnel. It looked so small after her long march through the darkness. Hanging on the wall, a few extinguished torches spread the faint scent of burned wood and resin from the evening, when a few people had passed through. At its outer mouth, she found a place not touched by the feeble moonlight and leaned against the cold stone. Dressed all in black, her body seemed one with the dark stone behind her. Her auburn hair was hidden too, under a heavy black hood, cinched around her head; there were no hats in a Wanderer Hive. Patiently, she waited. The scent of wildflowers, coming from the gentle slopes of the mountain, was pleasantly intoxicating. She paid no heed to it, and suddenly tensed, hearing steps, then relaxed; her Vision had been accurate. Her features were indistinct, but the faint moonlight caught the gleam of her teeth as she grinned.

"Going somewhere, Splendra?" the girl asked, without moving from her hide, forcing her voice to sound older.

The former Third Light of the Wanderers recovered quickly from the shock of being discovered; it took her no longer than a heartbeat. An experienced warrior, survivor of many fights, she did not try to move or run, and she recalled the voice, feeling the words and the tone, down to the slightest inflection. Her opponent was young and inexperienced; perhaps not even a Wanderer, just a novice who was trying to prove herself. Frozen in place, Splendra listened to the night, trying to figure out the girl's hiding place; the tunnel had distorted the sound. *The girl is alone... I will send her young soul to the Serpent. What a pity that I no longer have my Maletera, to make a new convert to the great god. Dochia took it with her, and she never returned. Soon, I will have an answer to my questions.* Tense and alert, Splendra raised her right foot, feigned a step forward, but returned it to the same place. She did it again with her left foot. And again, with her right foot. The faint sound mimicked cautious walking. She stopped moving and let out a long hiss of feigned panic. To her right, a shadow emerged from the wall. Unseen in the darkness, the woman smiled, her dagger tight in her hand. Then she sprang, and her blade arched in a split second, aiming for the girl's neck. There was a scraping sound, and the physical reaction of hitting something solid when her arm stretched to full length. Too late she realized that her dagger had hit stone. It came to her as an afterthought when she was already lying on the ground. Splendra was too experienced to react, she knew that she was dying; the other's blade had grazed her heart. She recalled that sometimes a Vision could be misleading. Hers was, at least.

Careful, the girl pressed her boot on the hand of the fallen woman, which still gripped the dagger. She pressed harder, and the woman's fingers loosened, releasing the weapon. "You were a strong Wanderer once, the Third Light of Frankis, before the Serpent enslaved your mind with that cursed tool: Maletera." There was a touch of regret in the girl's voice, but the dead woman could no longer hear it. "Because of that, I will clean your dagger and keep it."

Slowly, she cleaned her own blade too and turned, ready to leave the place. Before she could take her first step, the semidarkness flowered into full light. There were two torches in front of her. And three women.

"This is your third attempt to escape," Drusila, the First Light of the Frankis Wanderers said, her voice cold, but not angry.

"There will be a fourth one soon." The girl's voice was defiant, but she did not resist being disarmed by Satia, an old Wanderer who was her tutor. "The Serpentist tried to escape too." She pointed at the body. "I suppose she was able to trick your sentries."

"In three weeks, you will have the Rite of Passage. Is it so hard for you to be a Wanderer?" Drusila asked, ignoring the stinging words. Two Wanderer sisters had been found wounded and unconscious, just a few minutes ago. *Why did no one have a Vision about the Serpentist's escape? Splendra did not kill them... Was she still a Wanderer in her heart? How strong is that cursed Maletera?*

I am only seventeen; my rite should happen next year. "Perhaps not, but nobody asked me if I wanted to be one."

"Don't act like a spoiled child; you know the importance of your appointment as a Wanderer. You have read Dochia's letter. In two months, you will leave for Nerval. She needs your help in the Sanctuary. The nomads will soon invade the continent."

"They've already invaded..."

"Yes, and they came in the past too, but this time is different. They have Talant artifacts, tools to see at a distance, tools to communicate at a distance, over hundreds of miles. They can alter people's minds. The nomads' minds have been altered too. Now, when they take a village, they gather the young men and women as slaves, and kill everybody else. Half of the people on the continent will die. That's why we call their invasion a Fracture."

"Perhaps, but you could ask, instead of stealing me from my family."

"There was a dangerous situation when we intervened..."

"Oh, that I know well, Drusila. Quite a strange situation. I still wonder how much you were involved in it, but you will find an excuse, even for the worst things. You always have a good excuse for bad things," the girl said bluntly and walked away.

"Come with me, sister Aliana," Satia, the woman who had disarmed her said, her voice gentle, almost motherly. "I know that you have good eyes, but it's easier to walk with a torch. I can share mine with you." She placed a hand on the girl's arm; Aliana seemed mollified and did not resist. They walked together. They did not speak. Not yet.

Behind them, Drusila smiled. *You are a rebel, Aliana, but you will become a powerful Wanderer and help Dochia defeat the Serpent God, his high priest, Meriaduk, and heal the Fracture. Or so we hope. Here, well, we have different hopes, the kind that you must keep well hidden.*

They were some distance from the tunnel when Satia squeezed the girl's elbow gently, before releasing it. "You took a great risk..."

"I knew that I could beat Splendra," Aliana interjected, with her usual aplomb.

"Perhaps, but we have something in our Mentor book. When two ways are available to tackle a problem, the one with less risk should be chosen. Do you think it a useless teaching?" Satia's tone was not unkind, but it was uncompromising.

"No, but I had a Vision that I could escape this night."

"It could have been another Vision and another night. Was it worth risking your life and the possibility of Splendra escaping?"

"How are the wounded sentries?" Aliana's voice was thin and uncertain. "In my Vision..." she added quickly, but this time Satia reacted even quicker.

"Your first Vision foresaw your escape. It went wrong. Our sisters were not harmed badly, but they were wounded. Your Vision about them could have gone wrong too, and they could be dead."

"I am sorry, Satia. It's just... It's just that things are not fair. I should be with my family, not here."

"That I understand, and I am sorry for your trouble." Satia placed her hand on the girl's shoulder. "But sometimes, there are greater needs. Dochia needs your help to stop the Fracture. It's long past midnight, but I am expecting you at early morning training. There still is a weapon that you haven't mastered."

"What weapon?" Only the best Wanderers in the Hive were able to match Aliana in a fight. "Why not try to enhance my White Light?"

"There is a time for everything. The weapon's name is patience. It's a powerful one, and some of the younger girls master it better than you do. Now, I have something for you." Quietly, Satia opened the door of Aliana's bedroom, and let her enter first.

In the doorway, the girl stopped abruptly. "A Peregrine Raven," she whispered, then sprang forward as abruptly as she had stopped. In front of the bird, she stopped again, and stood stiffly, like a knife stuck in the floor. Astonished, she looked at him – a Wanderer's bond was always with a male raven –and their eyes locked. Since she was a young girl, Aliana was attracted by these intelligent birds.

"I think that you two will be good friends," Satia said, softly.

"But I haven't passed the Rite." Aliana could not take her eyes from the raven. She wanted to touch him, to feel him, but that was not allowed before the bond was made. If the bond were successful, the raven would become more than a friend or a brother, it would become her twin soul. "How can I...?"

"If you enter the Rite, you will pass it. I have no doubt about that. You hate to fail more than you hate the Rite or the Wanderers," Satia laughed. "And you will enter, because Dochia needs you. I will leave you now; remember that we have training early in the morning." With a glimmer in her eyes, Satia nodded to the raven, and left the room. With her skilled Light, she had felt the empathy flowing between the girl and the raven. It was a good start.

Alone with the bird, it took a while for Aliana to find words. "They teach us about the bond and mind-binding during the last week before the Rite. That will be in two weeks from now. I don't know..." She moistened her lips. "Do you have a name?"

The raven took his time to study her, before saying, "Of course I have a name, one given to me at my birth, but I am afraid that it's too hard for you to pronounce. You must find a new one for me. I must say that this is a peculiar situation."

"You have already passed the Rite. If I fail..."

"The name you give me will be forgotten, and I will receive a new one, if there is another Wanderer who..."

"It's not fair on you," Aliana interjected, with genuine concern, and she moved closer, but stopped herself from ruffling his feathers. She moistened her lips and stepped back.

"They seem sure that you will pass the Rite. Perhaps it was a Vision, or perhaps they trust you." The bird's voice sounded faintly amused under its seriousness. "For three days, I watched you training, and I feel a strong mind under that ... exuberance. It seems that your mouth is as fast as your hand. Perhaps even faster." The bird laughed, and the sound felt almost human. It felt warm too.

"I will call you Fortitude."

"That's an ... interesting name." Slowly, the raven turned his head and looked at her with one eye.

"If you don't like it..."

"It's just that I need to know why I deserve that name."

“Well, Satia told me that I lack patience, so you will be my Fortitude.”

“I have no objection, it’s an honorable name; from now on, my name is Fortitude.” Solemnly, the bird nodded three times, and Aliana nodded back at him. “If we pass the test of mind-binding, of course, but at least we did not fail the naming test.” The peregrine raven could choose to reject the name and the Wanderer too. He decided that the girl was strong, and he liked her enough to try the mind-binding test. Their final trial.

Chapter 2 - Codrin / Aliana

Eduin did not feel at ease at the court of Arad. There was always a place of honor for him, but the closer he was seated to Saliné, the harder it was for him. Almost two years had passed since her stay in Laurden, and he still loved her. His feelings were now attenuated, seeming more like a pleasant dream, but they were still there. And every time Codrin looked at him, the night he had spent with Saliné flooded into his mind. The images were vivid and fresh, as if they had happened only days ago, and the warmth was still there, in his mind. He both wanted and hated that memory, but what he hated the most was *their* wedding, which was interrupted by Codrin just minutes before the priest could proclaim Saliné his wife. What he did not know was that Saliné did not feel at ease either, in his presence. Her feelings were different; she liked him, but she did not love him, and in a deep corner of her mind she would have preferred that he was not there. Eduin was a reminder of something she wanted to forget, but the Seigneur of Laurden and his son could not miss her son's first birthday. Eduin had saved her life, a thing that she did not want to forget.

This ball is no different, Eduin thought. It was his third day in Arad, and he had been invited to the royal lodge. Saliné sat between him and Codrin. Uneasy, she felt at times the need to enhance her words with gestures, just to calm herself, and their knees touched involuntarily. To an outside observer, nothing of their inner turmoil could be seen; both were people who knew how to make a conversation that had nothing in common with their worries. There was another young woman in the lodge, and he recalled seeing her somewhere, but his mind was too caught in the game of hiding behind polite words to remember her name.

"I think it's time to begin the ball," Codrin said; the orchestra started to play a short song that was just a signal for the dancers.

Eduin felt suddenly relieved and watched as they moved away. Turning his stare from Saliné's bottom, he met the severe eyes of the young woman whose name he could not remember. They were almost alone in the lodge; all the other people around them were servants. *Did she realize what I was looking at?* He cleared his throat before saying, abruptly, without looking at her, "Would you care to dance with me?"

"There is no need to invite a woman only for some social convenience." She laughed, her voice carrying a hint of irony.

Absorbing the tease, Eduin realized her beauty. "I like to dance, and what's more pleasant than dancing with a beautiful woman?"

A man with a lot of imagination. Pompous and lecherous. He looked at Saliné's lower body as if it belonged to him. "I am sure you will find plenty of them in Arad." *Saliné speaks well of him only because he saved her life. Well, at least that was a good thing.*

"Lanya," a man said from behind Eduin. "Would you dance with me? I've heard that the Queen has chosen The Spirited Forest for the opening. It's the first dance you had at court. And it was with me." Dunican made a swift theatrical gesture, pointing at his chest.

At least he has imagination. Lanya almost sighed. "Yes, Dunican, I like the spirit of the dance." *Isn't that strange? Codrin taught me to dance, but my first dance was with Dunican. It was during the month before Codrin went to Tolosa to find Saliné.* Lanya was eighteen years old now, and she saw Codrin as a father figure; yet deep in a corner of her mind, there were different feelings about him.

Lanya, Eduin thought, looking at her walking away. *Orban had a daughter with that name. It can't be this one; they would not allow his daughter here, after he killed Vio*. In a weird repetition, his eyes followed her body the same way they had followed Saliné, up and down, stopping at her bottom. He shook his head and saw the discreet smiles on the servants' lips. *Well, it seems that my stay at the ball just ended.* He nodded curtly at the servants and left the lodge, walking absently.

"Leaving already?"

Eduin started; he had almost bumped into his father. "Well," he shrugged. "I just made a kind of gaffe. It's better to leave now." They were close to the door, and he did not know that, seeing him leaving, Foy had walked quickly across the hall to catch him.

Under his frown, Foy looked thoughtfully at his son. "You are twenty-three already, and you are not here only to enjoy the ball. We were finally able to break the marriage negotiations with Laure's niece, the little harpy who happens to be the cousin of the new Duchess of Tolosa, and you are here to find a wife. Saliné and Codrin helped us with the negotiations, and they promise help for ... the next step too. If you are not able to gather yourself, I will announce my decision to you, and you may not like it. You have two weeks to find someone you like, and who brings political advantages. Laurden is a small Seigneury."

"Yes, Father," Eduin said, without looking at him. *I am behaving strangely, but at least I managed to hide my feelings for Saliné. Did I?* "I will have a little walk and return."

"Saliné has already presented you with two girls."

Has she? "Yes, Father, I am ... looking."

"Are you going for a walk?" a woman's voice asked, and they turned to see Idonie. Her voice and face were composed, but under that Eduin felt her uneasiness; he knew his cousin so well.

"Yes, would you join me? We have not walked together for a year at least." Relieved to have a way out, Eduin lent her his arm, and making place for her to pass through the door, he saw Julien, walking toward them, and stopping abruptly. *I am not the only one hunted by stubborn old memories that don't want to die.*

Outside, it was not yet fully dark, but the moon was up there, big and yellow, glowing like new fire. They walked in silence for a while, the filtered light seeming to warm Idonie up, until he said, "Now tell me what is bothering you."

"Why do you think that I am bothered?"

"You grew up on my knees, little cousin. I think I know you better than your parents."

"That may be right; sometimes I think that they did not know me. Perhaps they still don't know... That doesn't mean that they don't love me, even after I left our home without their approval."

"Well," he said and placed an arm around her shoulders, "your choice to become a Wanderer was quite a shock."

"I did not have much choice, or maybe I had, but I was too young to realize it." She became silent, old memories invading her mind and bit her lip, hoping that the pain would stop them. "Sometimes I hate being a Wanderer," she hissed and froze, unbelieving what she had just said.

"It's a position of honor and power," Eduin said carefully, and pulled her tighter.

"I should have not said that. Yes, I am a strong Wanderer, perhaps the fifth or the sixth in the Frankis hierarchy by power, but I had no vocation to be one. I wanted family and children. Since I heard the story of Saliné's grandmother, I wished to be like her and find another way out of my problems than joining the Wanderers. But," she sighed, "it was that, or marry the man who tried to rape me. I could not marry him."

"Perhaps there is a way to leave the Wanderers."

"The Oath is for life. Nobody forces a woman to become a Wanderer, but once the Oath is taken, there is only one punishment for forfeiting it. You know that."

"People tell me that you are a good Wanderer, not just a strong one."

"Would that replace a child in my arms?"

He paused for a while before asking, "Is Julien bothering you?" They had grown together as children until Sava, Julien's father, had to leave for Leyona, having been appointed Chief of the Guard. Idonie was thirteen at that time, two years younger than Julien.

"He still loves me, and I still like him, but..." She shrugged, and he felt her uneasiness passing into his arm around her shoulders.

"I will talk with him."

"Don't... Don't be hard on him."

"He is my friend, and sometimes it is useful to be hard. In a friendly manner. Now, I think that we should dance. Our last dance was at the Solstice Party, two winters ago. No, at that one I danced with Saliné." His voice wobbled a little, then it recovered, but not fast enough to escape her attention. Idonie was a powerful Wanderer, after all. "Our last dance was three years ago."

"This is the Royal Ball. People are here to dance. I think that I saw you with Lanya."

"Ah, yes," he said a bit sourly, recalling her refusal. "We've talked a little."

They returned to the hall just before the last dance of the first suite, and new pairs were forming. Codrin took Lanya's arm. He whispered something into her ear, and the young woman burst into laughter; it strangely enhanced her beautiful face. Eduin turned his head, and he almost stumbled; his father was paired with Saliné, and they seemed caught in a serious conversation. *What is Father doing? He said that I still have time to...* When the dance ended, he wanted to catch his father, but Saliné gestured at him and Idonie, and he had no choice; he led his cousin toward the royal lodge.

When they reached the lodge, Codrin had a brief look at Idonie, as if trying to read her mind. *He had a Vision about me,* she thought. There was no way to guess what it was about but, in the break between dances, Codrin had caught in a Vision her lament about joining the Wanderers and her desire to have a family. He had learned about Julien too.

There were more people in the lodge this time, and several groups formed, one around Codrin, another around Saliné, and some changed places now and then. Suddenly Eduin found himself with only Idonie and Lanya.

"You know," Lanya said, looking at Idonie, "I just remembered your first visit here."

"Ah, yes," Idonie laughed, "I remember it too. I was seconding Dochia in a meeting with Orban. It was my first mission as a Wanderer, and your father had a terrible reputation."

"Are you Orban's daughter?" Eduin asked against his will.

"Yes," Lanya said coldly, then turned again toward Idonie. "You were sent out at some time, and I invited you into the garden. You told me about the orange orchards in the south. There was so much passion in your description, like you were dreaming with eyes wide open. You have no idea, but your dream became my dream, although you have an advantage over me. You really were in an orange orchard."

"Orange and lavender flowers are the southerners' pride," Eduin interjected, without knowing why. "They are beautiful."

"Everything is about beauty, isn't it?" Lanya's left brow rose, though whether in agreement, disagreement, or some polite irony he was not sure. "Beautiful flowers, and beautiful women to dance with."

"There is no sin in beauty." Eduin finally found his spirit. "But, sometimes, people who own beauty don't understand how lucky they are."

For the first time, Lanya seemed to show some interest in what he had said. "Beauty and intelligence are inherited. How one uses them, that's what really counts."

"There are ways and ways," Eduin agreed. "Should we discuss them in more detail during the next dance? It seems that the orchestra is ready. I have to confess that I don't know what dance they chose to open the second suite." He looked straight in her eyes and flashed his most seductive smile at her.

Lanya inclined her head slightly, before asking Idonie, "Does he always smile like this when inviting a woman to dance?"

"Only when he is asking a beautiful woman," Idonie said, bursting into laughter, and the other two followed.

From the corner of her eye, Saliné caught their merriment and smiled.

The flow of Light felt less fluid than usual and uneasy to Codrin, a heavy grey mist. There was fear and bitterness, and they flowed into him too. He could not understand that. There were no such feelings before in his trances, and he had learned a long time ago that new things don't usually mean good news. Ignoring the nausea, he stretched his mind further. He did not know that blood was running from his nose. It had happened before when he was using the Farsight of the Seer, but never during a Vision. A girl appeared in front of him, a dark silhouette, her face unrecognizable. *Sixteen or seventeen years old,* he thought, and tried to lock his eyes with those on the shadowed face. The eyes were dark blue, almost black. He knew no eyes like these.

The girl did lock eyes with him; it felt slippery, as if they were unable to control their stare. "I was kidnapped by the Wanderers. Help me."

What kind of Vision is this? Codrin thought. People could not interact through the White Light. *And the Wanderers don't kidnap children.* "Who are you?"

"I am..." The girl's voice vanished before she could finish.

"Who are you?" Codrin repeated.

"I am..."

I need to try something else. "Where are you?"

"...Hive."

"Which Hive?"

"...Hive."

Is the Light blocking her answers? *Or there is someone else hidden in the Vision?* "Where is this Hive?"

"Fran..." The girl answered faster than before, and Codrin guessed she meant Frankis.

"Why did they kidnap you?"

"They need me."

That's not a reason. "Why do they need you?

"Because of ..." The girl's answer was truncated again. "I can't talk..." Her voice became a wail, and she vanished from his Vision.

This was not a Vision, but I have no other name for it. The Wanderers may know what it is. I can't ask them. Codrin did not have much time to recover; he had hardly wiped the blood from his face when the next Vision appeared in his mind. There was a similar, not very fluid, uneasy Light, like in the previous one. But at least this one was comprehensible. It was a Vision. A boy, perhaps seven years old was lying on the ground, face down. There was a lot of blood around his head. *The boy will die in some future. I wish I could help him, but the place is unknown and the date too.* Then Idonie appeared in his Vision. She was trying to save the boy, in a strange way that he could not understand. He looked closer at her. *She is pregnant!* Codrin shook his head. *That's impossible, a Wanderer doesn't make children.* The Vision vanished, leaving behind a heavy headache. And an immense pain, the kind of pain he had not felt since the death of his brother. *There is a riddle in this, and a sense of urgency.* He pondered for a while. *For the girl. The boy will have the accident some years in the future. There is something strange about him.*

He opened his eyes to Saliné's worried face. Slowly, she started to clean the blood on his face and neck. She said nothing, waiting for him to talk.

"I had some strange Visions," Codrin said.

"You have not bled for a long time, and that was only when you used the Farsight. It must be something strong and important."

"My Vision merged with a girl's. That never happened before. She asked for help. The Frankis Wanderers kidnapped her."

"The Wanderers?" Saliné started, unable to hide her surprise. "I never heard of them kidnapping girls before. It's an honor to become a Wanderer, and few are chosen. What do you want to do? There must be a reason behind such a strong Vision that it made you bleed."

Rubbing his brow, Codrin pondered for a while. "I think that I will visit the Alba Hive. If the Vision is true, the girl must be there. I need to know more."

Alone in her room, Aliana sat on the floor, leaning against the wall. *I failed. Even the Seer could not hear my plea. I have no choice left. Why did they do this to me? I would have agreed to train and go to Nerval and help Dochia. I don't want to be a Wanderer. I want to have a family, children. I want to see my family.* Tears that did not fall came into her eyes, but she did not cry. She never cried. Images came into her mind, her family, and a young man she had not seen for a long time.

The door opened and Satia entered the room. "Aliana," she said gently. "It's time now." She stood in front of the girl, gripped her hands, and pulled her up. "You must not fail the rite of passage. It's important. Then..." Satia pondered for a while. "There are several paths in front of you. Today, you will choose one. I can't tell you more, you will figure it out."

Aliana did not fail her tests, and she was soon ready for the mind-binding with Fortitude.

"Are you ready?" Satia asked, her keen eyes moving from Aliana to Fortitude, and they nodded, the raven moving his head up and down in a way that, for a human, resembled the courting of a female. He would have been upset to hear that, but Satia was aware, and her face remained austere. Aliana wasn't, but her mind was too focused on the test to observe such small differences; the last thing she had in mind was to smile. "There is no need to be so tense; the Light is gentle; it never causes harm." *It happens sometimes, but only when you become a High Wanderer and try things above your power, which at that moment is strong. Strong power, strong effects. There is no need for you to know that now,* Satia thought. "I will open the Light for you. I know that you can open the Light," Satia added, amused, before the girl could voice her protest. "But you are not yet able to open the Light for two minds. You will know how to do it after passing the binding test. Be ready." Her voice was now harsh and demanding.

"Please, Fate, enlighten me," Satia prayed, touching her temples with both hands.

"Please, Fate, enlighten me," Aliana and Fortitude prayed too. She touched her temples with both hands, but the raven stayed immobile.

There was a burst of White Light, and Aliana found herself in the middle of an infinite red plain, the color of freshly spilled blood. "Does this have a meaning?"

"It always does, but you have to discover it. Sometimes, it takes years," Satia said, though she was not visible. "You are not allowed to walk; that will break the link, your Light is still weak. It takes a month to fully receive your power, and many years to control such kind of Vision. Now, it's all yours."

Aliana turned her head, trying to see if there was anything on the plain. There was nothing she could see, but she noticed that the 'grass' was not grass. It was a sort of glass, letting a flow of red liquid move at a low speed under Aliana's feet. She crouched and touched the glass; it felt a little warm. *The liquid must be warm*, she thought.

She stood up abruptly and looked at the boy standing in front of her, only a pace away. She could touch him easily. She wanted to do it. Thin and tall, and with that wide smile on his face. *It's exactly like when I saw him last time, three years ago, but he must be twenty now*. She stretched out her hands. The boy did the same, and their hands clasped. "Can you speak?" *Can you kiss too?* But she could not ask that question; they had never kissed before.

"Of course. I can do many things." He raised his hand and touched her face gently.

"But you are not him. You are Fortitude." She looked at the boy, who nodded. "How did you...?

"That was the first memory of yours that came to me, and I held it. I thought that it would be easier to make the bond like this."

Perhaps, Aliana thought, before saying, "I am here to make a bond with Fortitude, a peregrine raven. Please take your real shape. When I meet that boy again, I will talk with him again." *If I meet him again.*

There was a blur in her vision, and the boy vanished. The raven appeared and flew onto her arm. "Welcome, Aliana," he said. "Welcome to my world."

That's the word... "Welcome to my world, Fortitude," she whispered. *I passed the test.*

"The bond is now complete," Satia said, and the next moment, they were in the room again. The raven was Aliana's as much as she belonged to him. They were twin souls now.

Late in the evening, in front of all the Wanderers in the Hive, Drusila, the First Light of Frankis, stood in front of Aliana. The old woman carried the heavy Mentor book in her deep veined hands. She swept the hall with her keen eyes, before saying, "Today, Fate blessed us with a new Wanderer. Apprentice Aliana is no more; I welcome sister Aliana in our Hive. From now on, this will be your Wanderer name. The name you received at birth will be forbidden and forgotten." She raised the book in front of the girl. "You must take the Oath now."

Aliana raised her head, and their eyes locked. With a defiant look she said, her voice flat and cold, "I won't take the Oath."

There were whispers and gasps in the hall. Drusila raised her hand, and they all stopped. "Stubborn to the end. What do you want to achieve?"

"A chance to be with my family, a chance to have family and children. I will go to Nerval to help Dochia. I will agree to be a Wanderer for five years. Then I want to be free of my Oath."

The Oath is for life. Drusila pondered, her thick white brows drawing together. *In five years, she will become one of us. She is as strong as Dochia. Or even stronger. We can't afford to lose her. She must become the First Light of Frankis. In Nerval, Dochia will be her Wanderer Mother. The bond with Fortitude will work on our favor too.* "Five years," she said and pushed the Mentor book into Aliana's hands.

Close to the midnight, Satia came into Aliana's room again, and the severe teacher embraced the girl for the first time. "You have chosen your own path."

"Did you have a Vision about it?"

"Sort of. Tomorrow, you will leave for Nerval. Your life will be filled with wonders and achievements. And with danger. More danger than any of the Wanderers in this Hive had ever confronted." She pulled the girl even tighter to her chest. "You must help Dochia to stop the Fracture and save the Realm, Aliana. We are all counting on you." Her voice was motherly but cheerless.

"You are sad." Aliana pulled her head back from Satia's shoulder.

"Yes, this old woman is sad because you are leaving, and because she can't be your Wanderer Mother no longer, but Dochia is a stronger Wanderer, she can teach you better."

"A mother is not only about strength, Satia. Dochia is my friend, but you will always remain the mother who taught me to be a Wanderer."

Followed by a hundred riders, Codrin left Arad early in the morning, when the sun was not yet in sight. At noon, they stopped on the bank of a small river, and he went away, alone, trying to gather his thoughts; the Wanderers had their own world, and he had to be careful. There was a Fracture, and he was the Seer of the Realm. He had to work with the Wanderers. He wished Dochia were there, but he knew that she was faraway, in Nerval, the capital of the nomads. Though more than three thousand miles separated them, they worked together for the same goal, to stop the Fracture and save the Realm. Leaning against a tree, he watched his men eating and laughing; they did not carry his heavy burden. He did not react when a translucent silhouette materialized in front of him. *Is the Last Empress involved in this?* "Empress." He bowed slightly.

"Codrin," the Empress nodded. "It's not easy to talk about this, but you must let Aliana fulfill her destiny."

"So that's her name, Aliana. She must have the right to choose her path in life."

"She has chosen already."

"No, she was kidnapped, and she is too young to really choose right now. She is kept prisoner in the Hive. What's the difference between us and the nomads if we act like this?"

"She is important for the Realm, and she will help you to deal with the Fracture."

"Would it ever be possible for you to see the person behind a Wanderer or a Seer?"

"I always see the person, but the Realm is more important than our feelings. There will always be hard decisions to make. You need to defeat the nomads and build a new Empire."

"Empress, you build empires with strength and with people, not with marionettes. From up there in Mundi Chrysalis, we may be seen like small pieces in a chess game, but we are still human. Perhaps this has been forgotten in your world."

"What was done, was done, and I was not involved. This continent is large, and I can't be everywhere when decisions are made. You know that I rarely interfere to change the course of an event. My constant interference would make you *marionettes*. You have to decide for yourself."

"What was done can be changed. I will consider her destiny if Aliana is allowed to choose her path in five years. And there must be a sort of punishment too."

"Hanging the First Light of Frankis?"

"We are not yet there. I will ask them to free another Wanderer, Idonie, from her Oath. There is a good reason."

"And if not, you will do what?"

"I will take Aliana from the Hive."

"She has left for Nerval, and Drusila has already agreed to give her those five years to choose. The girl is stronger than you think; few can bend Drusila to their will. Five years for Aliana to decide her future, and Idonie is free," the Empress said abruptly and vanished.

For the first time, Codrin sensed some edginess in her voice. *I hope that I did not make an enemy.*

Despite the soldiers' angry shouts, Drusila stopped her carriage in the middle of the riding men. She stepped out and stood in the middle of the road, making them curse her. They took care to voice their anger inside their minds; it did not bode well to anger a High Wanderer.

"First Light," the driver whispered, while her guards went one in front and one at Drusila's side.

"Oh, shut up, Elka. This is not a war." *Not yet.* "And you," she gestured at the guards, "make room. I don't need you to pamper me." She closed her eyes, and opened them to see Codrin, who had dismounted in front of her.

"First Light," he nodded.

"Your majesty, let's spare the formalities, we know each other well enough. The guards are not needed either. I suppose that you want my head."

"I suppose that too." With his left hand, he made the sign to spread out, and his guards moved a safe distance away. "I am listening."

"What happened to Aliana... That was not a thing that I can brag about; it brought some misery to her and to her family."

"Some?"

"We all have our own definition of misery. Aliana is part of the Prophecy related to the Fracture. So are you and Tudor, your mentor. Everything almost crashed when Tudor was killed, and you almost died too. It was needed, no, it was vital for Aliana to become a Wanderer. She is... Stubborn is a weak word to describe her well, but there is no strength without stubbornness. That was the only way to keep the Prophecy alive. Three days ago, she left for Nerval to help Dochia; in fact, we left the Hive together. There was a certain need of secrecy and, because of that, she could not meet her family. There are two Triangles to defend her, both Wanderers and Assassins, along the road. The Third Light of Frankis and an Assassin Master are leading them. As you see, we took a lot of precautions, there are five nomad spies in Frankis, and one of them is a Khad's son. I have the feeling that you will meet him in battle. I was on my way to Arad to tell you. You don't trust me much, but at least you trust her." Drusila took Dochia's letter from her bag and gave it to Codrin, who took his time to read it.

"So, she foresaw this," Codrin said after a while. "There is an understanding between the Empress and me."

"Yes, she told me. It's ... unusual, but at the next Conclave, we will free Idonie of her Oath. It's rare for a Wanderer to forfeit it, and she is a strong woman, with a strong White Light. At the right time, she could have made a good First Light. It's not an easy loss for us to bear. Why?"

"She joined the Wanderers to escape marriage with a man who tried to rape her, but she did not ask me to free her, though she wants to make a family and have children. She never complained, but I have my ways to learn people's hidden sorrows and desires. It was my choice to let her go, and a kind of trade with the Empress." He looked at Drusila, but the old Wanderer said nothing. "I had a strange Vision about a seven-year-old child, lying bloodied on the ground, an accident perhaps, and whose face I could not see. Idonie was trying to save him in a way that was not revealed. She was in a kind of trance. The danger was not revealed either. I knew that he was not her son, but she was pregnant, so she was no longer a Wanderer. The whole Vision was strange, dark and sad, and I can make nothing meaningful of it right now, but it marked me. I hope that she will be able to save that child. I don't know why it feels important to me."

"Well," Drusila shrugged, "we all have our tests."

"Tests?"

"I imagine it was a test Vision. One day, you will learn if you passed it. Did you tell Idonie?"

"Not, I needed to talk with you first, and that accident will happen in six or seven years from now. We have plenty of time."

"I had once a Vision about a half-blurred face too. I realized its importance much later, in a small place called Valeni." Drusila's expression was almost a smirk. "It was about a young man killing Bernd, Orban's elder son, to save a certain woman, Jara, from being raped."

"Ah, yes, that was an important Vision indeed. That ... event started everything you see happening in Frankis right now. And what was your test?"

"I resisted the temptation to tell Orban about my Vision, for political gain, even when I did not know about the Prophecy at that time. Now, on the road here, I had a Vision about Litvonia. That fat man on the throne will die soon, without an heir. They will have a civil war between three contenders. Second and third Cousins." She shrugged.

"I don't like civil wars," Codrin said. "They bring only misery."

"They can bring opportunities too."

"Litvonia is twice as large and strong as Frankis. We can't meddle in the civil war. After that, yes, we may have an opportunity."

"It's the *after* that counts. The winner will be weak, and there will be two defeated parties hating the new King. They may be your allies."

"Hate doesn't make good allies, but let's wait to see when and how the Vision will be fulfilled."

The King of Litvonia died at the summer solstice, and many people hoped that such auspicious timing would bring a new beginning. The King was hated. Things changed indeed, faster than people had hoped. He was neither old nor young, had no children, and there was no established succession. As Drusila had predicted, three cousins disputed the throne, and a bloody civil war engulfed Litvonia. News arrived in Arad, and Codrin saw the hope of being able to unify the kingdoms before the nomad invasion. His first step toward rebuilding the Alban Empire.

"Alfrid the Pig has the best chance to win." Codrin was reading the detailed letter from his spy in Muniker. In front of him, lay the other letters, from the three contenders for the throne. They all requested his help. "Why do they call him Alfrid the Pig?"

"There is an old tradition in Litvonia to give bad names to your opponents. We have three contenders: The Pig, The Worm, The Snake," Verenius said. "They will never use the real name of the opponents, not even in official letters, as you can see." He pointed at the letters in front of Codrin. "They hire poets and troubadours to spread the bad words."

"Litvonia is a strange country. I think that I would prefer to be called a snake instead of a pig or a worm."

"Stranger than you can imagine," Verenius laughed. "They have official lovers, and a married couple finds it normal to go at a party together with their lovers. And perhaps even in bed after that, though I am not sure about the last part." His laughter was echoed by everybody in the room.

"Men," Saliné said, laughing too. "They only think of mistresses."

"I am sorry, your majesty, but Muniker is considered the Court of Love, and both men and women fight to win a place at court. Their troubadours sing many songs about that."

Codrin frowned for a moment before saying, "I remember something from my stay in Caravans Inn, in Muniker. Movil, the owner, was an unexpected friend. There was a couple, a Count and his wife, and their lovers. They have a fancy name for that, lemans, or something like that. All four shared the same suite. Such sort of decadency ruins a country from inside. We will not interfere in the civil war. At the end, we will see how weakened the Litvonian Kingdom is."

Life in Arad went on at the slowest pace Saliné and Codrin had felt in their entire lives. There was a sense of fulfillment and peace, and the most exciting events were the weddings. Lanya married Eduin, and Idonie married Julien. For different reasons, both Saliné and Codrin felt relieved.

The civil war in Litvonia ended two years later, late in the autumn. Helped by both Wanderers and the Circle, Alfrid the Pig became the new King, and Codrin planned his move to unify the kingdoms during the next year.

Chapter 3 - Dochia / Kasia / Aliana

Gresha's head was throbbing. It was almost midnight, and he fought hard to find a way out of this affair. After he had killed Iovon and taken over his band, he had tried to move away from the past, and enter the merchants' world. He was a sort of merchant, after all, but the real ones knew that he was selling stolen things. Iovon's trade was now his trade. He tried to avoid the bad ways of the past. Unfortunately, they did not want to avoid him.

"You will be rich, Gresha," Krisko said, and his wide mouth curled into an even wider smile. Three upper teeth were missing, offering a hideous black gap and dark red gums. The smile looked grotesque. It looked dangerous too. Krisko had lost his teeth in a fight against three men. His opponents had lost their lives.

You *will be rich*, Gresha thought, starting to realize that there was no escape. The subterranean world of Nerval had its own laws. They were simple and brutal. Krisko had helped Iovon in the past, but it was the band which really counted, and Gresha had to pay back the favor. A rich merchant and his family would be killed in three days, and he would be used as cover. "I will keep your merchandise in my warehouse for three days."

"Seven."

"Five. That's my last offer." Gresha turned his palms up.

"Let's have a drink." Krisko filled their glasses again. He used a different vadka bottle this time. Slowly, both men lifted their glasses and stretched out their hands until they reached the other's shoulder. They bent their arms until they formed a sort of chain, touching at the inner elbow. They drank the vadka in one shot.

This is good quality, Gresha thought, feeling the liquid burning his entrails.

"My men will come in three days."

"Fine," Gresha said, and stood up. He clasped a hand with Krisko and went out. The darkness felt heavy and dangerous. *I am alone*, he thought. *I could not avoid it.* This sort of business was best done alone, but he had not thought that they would finish so late. *I should have accepted faster. But then Krisko would have forced me to keep the things he will steal for two weeks.* His inner senses felt the shadow ahead of him before he could see it, and he slowed, taking out his dagger. He moved across the street. The shadow moved too, on a diagonal, coming closer. Some moonlight finally came through a thin gap in the clouds. *That's a boy*, Iovon thought, measuring the shadow, which was now only six feet away. "You'd better go. I don't like to kill children."

Before Gresha could finish his words or raise his dagger, the shadow sprang. He felt a strong kick in the groin and started to fall to his knees. A strong hand grabbed his arm, and his trajectory changed, projecting him into the wall. He slid down, was turned like a bag, and pushed down with his face in the mud. He felt the sticky substance sneaking into his nostrils and mouth. The sharp edge of a dagger pressed against his throat. "Still doing bad things, Gresha?" the shadow asked.

I know this voice... He tried to speak, but that only meant even more mud in his mouth.

"You've lost your voice." A rough hand went into his hair and pulled his head back a little. "Speak."

"Kasia?" he breathed.

"The vadka did not eat your whole brain, dear cousin."

"Kasia, you know that I had no choice with the Vicarius. I am glad that you escaped."

Without Dochia's help, I would have been dead. "Why are you glad, Gresha?" She pressed the blade harder to his neck.

"You know that I had no choice. The Vicarius came into our house to take you to the Sanctuary."

"Perhaps." The blade eased its pressure a little. "You will stop working with Krisko."

"He will kill me."

"And?" The blade pressed again, piercing his skin a little.

"You can kill me now, but you will leave ten families without food. And if you know about my deal with Krisko, you also know that I am trying to change things. You've always had a way to see things in the future. I knew that. Only your idiot brother thought that you could read what people were thinking, by looking at their gestures or face color."

"You are a smart man, Gresha. Iovon wasn't. Perhaps that's why he is dead, and you are still alive."

"You know that I killed him."

"Yes, I know. I wish I could have done it myself. My dear brother sold me to the priests." *Dochia played the Vicarius, and ordered you to kill him, but she told me that you already wanted to do that. For me.* She took the dagger from his throat and let him turn. "Now, listen to me. You will stop working with Krisko."

"He will kill me. He will kill some men you know. Their wives will become widows. They will be raped for many days by Krisko's men. Their children will become fatherless."

"The dead can't kill."

"Is Krisko dead?"

"No, but you will get your chance. He will come this way in five minutes."

"He always has three guards, and he is stronger than me."

"Then be stronger than him. I will take the guards."

"I don't know how you put me down, but you can't take on three men. Kasia, I am glad that you are alive, and that you escaped from those bloody priests. Don't die now."

"I am not alone. We will take the guards, and you will handle Krisko. He is no longer as strong as he was ten years ago, and you have grown up. You are twenty-two now."

He looked up and saw two shadows behind Kasia. They were not as small as her, but they did not look strong. "You came with two boys to take Krisko's guards. Go home, Kasia. This is not a game for children. I won't deal with Krisko again. I promise." His hand went to her face and touched it gently. "I always had a soft spot for you. Please, Kasia. Go home."

Silent, Kasia pulled him up, then bent to pick up his dagger from the ground. She pressed it into his hand. "They are coming."

He leaned against the wall, and Kasia did the same, next to him. The other two shadows crossed the street toward the house opposite. *They are women*, he suddenly realized. *What has happened to Kasia? Is she mad?*

The moon came out from behind the clouds. It was a full moon, as large as a chariot wheel. Four men advanced slowly down the middle of the street. When the silhouettes, leaning against the walls, became clear, they slowed even more. Daggers tense in their hands, two guards moved in front of Krisko, slightly to his right, on the other side of Gresha.

They are ready to take on the two women, Gresha thought, sliding his nervous thumb along his dagger's handle. *They are thirty steps away from them. Twenty.* One small thing flickered into the moonlight. Then another one, just a second later. One guard clutched his neck with his free hand and fell silently to the ground. The second one followed, a second later. Krisko and his last guard stood back-to-back, ready to fight. Gresha saw no flicker when Kasia threw her knife. He saw her hand stretching abruptly and the guard falling, a few moments later. Krisko was now alone. *Where did she learn that?*

"Gresha," Kasia whispered, and he knew that his time had come.

They will not fight for me. Why is Kasia doing this? Looking at the shadows made by the houses around them, Gresha advanced slowly along the wall, then he moved toward the center of the street until only five paces separated him from Krisko, taking care that the moon was behind him, the other man's face hard and angry under the moonlight.

"I knew that you were a dog," Krisko said, the dagger clutched tight in his hand. "I will have your skin. Look who I drank vadka with. Look at him. A little puppy wants to take me on. Come, little puppy, come and feel my blade. I will take your skin and put it to dry on the fence of my house. Your head will rest on a stake." Still speaking, he sprang forward.

"You talk too much, Krisko," Gresha said, pulling his blade out from the dead man's chest. "You thought I did not know that you talked to hide your moves." He turned toward Kasia. "I don't know how you knew it, but he was slow."

Kasia came and embraced him. "I knew that you had a soft spot for me. You were the only one protecting me in that house, even if you gave me to the priests. I will forget that. You didn't have much choice. Now, listen to me. In two days, you will go in the village of Naskiv. A man will come to sell his silverware. He can't come to Nerval; there is a death warrant on his head, so he will sell everything there. Some merchants know about him and always buy cheap because he can't come here. You will give him three hundred galbeni for everything he has. If you give him less, I will find you, take your skin and let it dry on the fence of my house."

"It's not easy to sell silverware."

"The Artisan of Baraki, the new Khad, is sick and dying. His son too. They were poisoned, but people don't know that. They were the best in Nerval. The four other men working silver are not skilled. That's why they killed the Artisan. Good silverware will become expensive. The man you will meet in Naskiv is even better than the Artisan. He was the Artisan of the Khad before."

In two months, Gresha sold his silverware for seven hundred galbeni. For many days he tried to find Kasia to thank her and talk to her, but she was nowhere to be found.

One day, late in the evening, she came to his house, dressed as a man. She brought a young, scared girl with her. "You will hide the girl and find someone in a village to take care of her. You will pay for her food and her clothes."

"What did she...?" Gresha measured the girl up and down; she was small and frail.

"Nothing." *She has the blood, and the priests want her in the Sanctuary to open another Maletera, but I can't tell you that.* "You like Mesko's daughter, Maja. She likes you too."

"I tried, but Mesko knows that Iovon robbed him. He will never..."

"Yes, I told him about Iovon. Go and ask again. Here is a list of places, dates and things to buy." Kasia gave him a piece of paper, then went to the girl and embraced her. "You are safe now." She embraced Gresha too and left the house.

From the window, Gresha watched Kasia walking along the street. Two young men joined her, but they could not fool him. They were the two women from the night he had killed Krisko. They moved like trained warriors; he could see that. What he did not know was that Mira and Irina were Wanderers, and Dochia's trusted guards. Gresha knew nothing about the Wanderers; few people in Nerval knew about the hidden order of Fate, the enemy of the Serpent, their god, and most of them were priests in the Sanctuary.

In a year, Gresha became rich, married and respectable, and almost each month, Kasia came with a boy or a girl, asking him to take care of them. He did not know that they were stolen from the priests. Not really stolen, as Kasia knew in advance when the priests would go to take the children from their families. There were the Wanderers' Visions, and news that Dochia gleaned in the Sanctuary. She was a priestess of the Serpent now. For half a year, no new Maletera was activated in the Sanctuary.

During the winter, Kasia had her rite of passage, and she was now a Wanderer too. Her entry into the order was still subject to approval by a Hive, but Dochia had no worries about that. Kasia had an issue though; there was not yet a peregrine raven for her.

There were no such magnificent birds in Nerval, but Umbra, Dochia's raven, was kind enough to train her on mind-binding.

❧

"You've grown a lot since the last time I saw you," Dochia said and embraced her. "And you are now a Wanderer. Aliana... The wild spring wind of Pyrenes. It matches a young girl I knew in the past."

"Yes." Aliana smiled and decided to hide that she had been kidnapped by the Wanderers. They had enough time to talk about this later, after their task in the Sanctuary was accomplished.

During the first week, Kasia and Irina were her guides. Aliana did not like Nerval; it was a dirty city. And dangerous. She could handle danger, but not the rotten smell on the streets; she had grown in the mountains. The only thing she liked was the Sanctuary. It impressed her from the first moment Dochia had sneaked her inside. *It would be a pity to destroy it*, she thought, looking at the high dome. She did not know that it was a small one. Then she thought better and asked Dochia; there was no way to destroy the huge building.

"We are not trying to destroy it; we want to close it. Soon, I will present you to my friend here. She is ... invisible. I know that it sounds strange to you, but Ai's magic is stronger than I ever could imagine."

"Dochia," Ai said in Dochia's mind, an unusual hint of agitation in her voice. "She is the one we need."

"What do you mean?"

"Aliana has the blood you and Kasia are missing."

"Are we able to close the Sanctuary now?"

"Not now. I have to know and trust her. Then the Sanctuary has to know and trust her."

"Do you trust Kasia and me?"

"Yes, but the Sanctuary is still taking time to fully trust Kasia. It will take a while."

"How long?" Dochia asked, with the eagerness of a young girl.

"I know that you will be disappointed, but it may take years. And we have the problem with the guards too. There is a secluded area that you've never visited. That's the place from where the Sanctuary is activated or closed. There are always ten guards there, and they have powerful weapons that stun at a distance. You know those weapons."

"We don't have that much time. Baraki may order the invasion any time, and the Sanctuary's magic is helping him. Many innocent people will die."

"The Sanctuary is not yet convinced that the magic it provides will bring a great advantage to Baraki. You must be patient."

Chapter 4 - Codrin

Codrin's plans to unify Frankis and Litvonia were ready when the Vision came to him. The nomads were invading the continent, starting from the eastern Litvonian border. The Seer's highest duty was for the Realm. In one week, his army left Arad, riding toward Rhiun River. Another week later, it reached the large river making half of the border between Frankis and Litvonia.

Down the hill, the bridge over the Rhiun was half visible through the mist. There was no single patch of mist hiding a large chunk of the bridge. The twelve-hundred-foot-long span looked like a snake cut into pieces of different lengths by long strips of mist, which resembled some snakes too. They were flowing slowly, seeming to eat the bridge.

Nine years ago, I crossed this bridge for the first time. It brought me a family and a kingdom. What will it bring me now? His thoughts went back to Arad. To Saliné. To his children. *I planned this war to take Litvonia, and instead of that, I am defending it from the nomads. I am defending the Realm, not just Litvonia.* He recalled his Vision about the nomad invasion. *That's a huge army*, he shook his head. *Perhaps three hundred thousand strong. Only riders. It moves fast. And I will meet Baraki. I will die in this battle, or I will fulfill my Oath of Justice.*

Arriving on the eastern side of the bridge, Codrin turned back: the mist was still there, hiding the bridge completely, and his riders seemed to emerge from a magical place. There were many whirlpools of haze, white and gray, and sometimes red. Their strange fluidity bothered him; it resembled the flow of time in his Visions.

At the head of his Guard, Codrin entered Muniker through the same gate he had left in a hurry nine years ago. He nodded at the captain, who stood stone-still in a military salute. *It's not the same man*, he thought, with a touch of nostalgia. They rode forward until the Caravan's Inn came in sight, and he stopped in front of it, making everyone else stop too. Vlad responded with a smile to his glance.

"Count Joachim," Codrin said to his host. "I want to stop here for a few minutes," he pointed at the inn, and dismounted before the Count could answer.

Inside the inn, Codrin and Vlad stopped in front of the counter, where an older Movil was still serving. The eyes of the innkeeper dilated briefly, and a large smile spread across his face.

"Your majesty," he bowed. "Vlad." At his words, all the people in the inn stood up abruptly and bowed too.

"You have a good memory, Movil," Codrin laughed and nodded at the standing people.

"I wouldn't survive these demanding merchants if I didn't."

"We are going to fight the nomads. If we return, we will come to eat here. You have good food, good wine, and good stories to share. I still remember them."

"Your majesty is a kind man. And a brave one. I don't have much Light, but my heart tells me that we will meet again."

From the inn, the road was wider, and there were more people on the streets. They did not look frightened by the foreign soldiers. They did not look pleased either. Alfrid, the new Litvonian King, waited for Codrin at the entrance of the palace, greeted him warmly, and they went into the Council Room. There were only five people there, one woman and four men; Codrin did not know that Alfrid had arranged to meet as few people as possible. The talk was well organized and precise. It was the woman who led it, Calista, the Second Light of the Litvonian Wanderers, the coldest Wanderer Codrin had ever seen.

Drusila is a sweet grandmother compared to Calista. Despite that coldness, Codrin enjoyed her swift mind, and soon understood that it made no sense to talk about the campaign with Alfrid; the woman was more aware of the military situation than him. She let the talk follow its course, and everything was agreed between Codrin, Edric, the King's brother, and Count Joachim.

"Our army will be ready in two days," Edric said. He glanced at Calista before asking Codrin, "Do you have a route planned?" The tone of his voice was a little insolent, but he was only nineteen years old. Ten years older, Alfrid was the elder brother in the family. There had been two more brothers, but they had died during the civil war.

"The Seer knows the day the nomads will pass the border. His army was prepared and came here in time. He knows their route too." It was Calista. Her eyes stayed on Codrin's. Her Light was probing him, as his was probing her. There were some dark waters in her eyes, but that was all that Codrin could glean. She learned nothing new; but she knew many things about him.

"The nomads will pass the border and take the road toward Drasdin and Kolugn, your richest lands. The traditional path of pillage. It's a ruse. They will turn south, ride a little through Silvania, and come back into Litvonia. In Baia. We must fight them north of the Jauras Mountains. There is a plain there that fits in my battle plan."

"The nomads fight better on a flat land," Edric said.

"Yes, they like open spaces. We need a plain that suits us better than it suits them. There are three hundred thousand of them, and they will not fight in a confined space. If we are waiting for them in the mountain passes, they will change route and traverse Dunaris a hundred miles west. There is no good place to fight them on that route. They will join the Arenian army coming from the east. We need to defeat the nomads before we go against the Arenians." There was a moment of silence, and Codrin realized that the size of the nomad army had staggered them. He let their fear grow, then explained what he had in mind. There were no more comments about his strategy.

At midnight, three shadows entered Movil's inn. They were expected. Two of them stayed in the main room to watch the place. Thais, the Third Litvonian Wanderer, went into a small room, followed by Movil. He placed a bottle of wine on the table, and two glasses. "Porto Wine," he said, knowing that Thais enjoyed the wine from the distant Hispeyne.

"Thank you, Movil." The Wanderer sipped some wine, then became silent. Caught in her worries, she turned the glass in her hand, this way, then that way. "There will be problems."

"When weren't there problems? With the nomads?"

"They always stir up trouble. Don't ask me about the battle; we never use the Light to learn its outcome. It's too dangerous; it can change the course of events in a bad way. It's what will happen after the battle that worries me."

"Can you be more specific?"

"Not much. A tough political decision has been made. Its outcome may result in the unification of the continent. Everybody who counts was involved: the Circle, the Wanderers. Here and in Frankis. It's both good and wrong."

"What else?"

"Hard to say, though it will save many lives. What kind of man is Codrin?"

"A great man who cares about the little man." Movil gestured between Thais and him with his forefinger. "His right-hand man is the son of an innkeeper from Litvonia. A competent man; I helped him find his first job as a Protector. A long time ago. I have many friends in Frankis. Codrin changed the laws there. Nobles who kill a commoner, rape a woman, or rob a merchant are now punished. Sometimes, he even hangs them with a placard on their neck: 'Born a Knight, dead an assassin,' or something like that. I wanted to visit Frankis just to see such a thing. I could never find the right time. At first, I thought that the nobles would revolt and kill him. It did not happen; all the three Duchies in Frankis are firmly behind Codrin. Now, what kind of man you think he is?"

"I can't say about the man; we've never met. But he is the Seer of the Realm."

"Ah, that is news. I feel relieved. There were rumors that Alfrid would become the Seer after winning the civil war. A strange thing, I must say."

"He has a strong Light, but he has never won a battle. There was never a chance for him to become the Seer of the Realm. Codrin is a skilled commander. Like his father was."

"That was my thought too, but the rumors about Alfrid were quite insistent. I found this insistence to be uncomfortable. I don't trust Alfrid. He may be jovial and not afraid to speak with a commoner, but it's all politics. He is rotten inside. I don't know where he will take Litvonia."

"It was a political game, and his Light is diminished since we have a Seer. And, yes, Alfrid is rotten. Partially. There is something good in him too, and he is a shrewd political player."

"Do you want to ask Codrin help you decide on this plan which is both good and bad?"

"Information helps," Thais shrugged. "This may help too. Spread the word that Codrin is the Seer of the Realm. He already knows where and when the nomads will attack us; that's why he is now in Muniker."

"After so many years of being your faithful servant, you still consider me an ignorant cousin. Not to mention how often I have to spoil you with my best wine. And all I've got from you is trouble. And tiny fragments of information."

"Then I will pay for the wine and curse your inn, so you lose all your customers."

"Please don't do that. This is the best inn in Muniker. Where can our good people find a replacement for this exquisite kingdom of steaks and wine?"

"There are so many good inns," Thais shrugged, and laughed. "You are always better than me at this game."

"Of course, you don't spend every day dealing with rich merchants who are even more spoiled than a High Wanderer. That good decision, which is bad, or bad decision, which is good, whatever… I have the feeling that it was voted for in your Council without much consideration. Just tell me what you want from me. Should I arrange a meeting with Codrin? He is a kind man."

"There is not enough time, I will leave early in the morning. I am planning… I am planning to add a little tweak to our plan. It will not solve the bad part, but it will mitigate some of its effects. I hope." Thais stayed silent for a while, playing with her wineglass. "Wish me luck, Movil. I need it. If my plan is discovered, I am a dead woman."

The army left the city, and this time, the streets were filled with people. The men bowed; the women cried the Seer's name; the girls threw flowers at him. Codrin felt a little embarrassed, but their enthusiasm was genuine, and he answered them with a smile or a gesture. This time, they took the Norgate, toward the north, and did not see the Caravan's Inn again, but for the next month there was always a long queue of customers hoping to find a free table at the inn and listen to old tales about two young men who came there a long time ago, looking to become Protectors. And each time, Movil ended his story with skilled words, to soothe the fear of the people in Muniker. "If there is one man who can save us from those savage nomads, it is King Codrin; he is not only the King of Frankis, but also the Seer of the Realm, the man Fate sent to protect us. He won his first battle at seventeen and has never lost one." And people went home with lighter hearts, praying for Codrin, the Seer of the Realm.

Chapter 5 - Dochia / Kasia / Aliana

The Vicarius was content. He could perhaps have been happy, but after so many years of serving the Serpent, he had forgotten how to be happy. He had everything he wanted, from good food and clothes to young women, but that did not make him happy. Walking slowly, he looked back again. Her arms pinned by two strong priests, who were at least two times her size, the girl was beaten and scared. That did not impress the Vicarius. It was her strong blood which impressed him. There had been a shortage during the last months of people with the right blood. Their network of spies brought information about girls and boys behaving strangely, but when the priests went to check, there was nothing to find. The strangeness usually manifested when they reached fourteen or fifteen years. Some children they found were indeed acting strangely, but there was no true blood in them; others had simply vanished, most of them taken by a swift illness that came from nowhere. It seemed that the blood was dangerous for some children, making them weak. Meriaduk was angry that he could not activate new Maleteras or other magical object s in the Sanctuary. He was troubled too; the Map could not be maintained well. Sometimes, he was doubting himself, thinking that he was falling the great god. The Serpent and the Sanctuary requested a lot of blood to answer the priests' requests. And if the High Priest of the Serpent was not happy, he made sure that his seven Vicarius were not happy either, not that they knew what it meant to be happy.

They turned the corner, the Vicarius lost in his own thoughts in dim twilight. He did not see the knife. It pierced his throat. He fell, snorting a strange word that no one understood. His last word. The guards fell a few moments later, and Kasia grabbed the girl. They ran, followed by Aliana and Irina.

"Stop!" Aliana shouted, and looked at the next corner of the street, surprised by her sudden Vision. Aliana was always different; she could have Visions about her own future, but usually they revealed small things, this one revealed a great danger that she could not fully understand, an imminent one. She stretched her mind into the Light, to learn more. "There are guards waiting for us. It was a trap. There must be guards behind us too." She tried to find a solution, but she did not know Nerval well enough and glanced at Kasia, who closed her eyes for a moment, imagining the city. The girl they had just freed from the priests started to cry, and Irina took her in her arms.

Think, Kasia pushed herself. *There are no side alleys. There must be a way out.* They were surrounded by tall walls protecting the rich houses. They were at the border with the slums, a dangerous place.

"Kasia," Aliana said in a low, urgent tone. The first guards had appeared three hundred feet in front of them, running, their swords up. The street was strangely empty, everybody locked in their houses; a Vicarius lay dead in the street.

"I am thinking. I am thinking." Kasia fixed her eyes on the house in front. The wall was ten feet high, and she had heard when the owner had locked the gate. *The wall is not well maintained.* "Climb!" She ran toward the wall and sneaked her fingers into a crack, high above. She pulled, found another crack with her foot. Stretched her free hand. It did not go high enough. Aliana made a support for Kasia's hanging foot with her palms. She reached the edge of the wall and climbed on top. Stretched her hand out for Aliana, who joined her fast. "Give me the girl," Kasia said to Irina.

The guards reached the wall just as the last woman jumped down the other side. They imitated her and helped the lightest man to climb. His weapons hindered him for a moment, and he nearly fell. Then he did fall, a knife protruding from his neck.

"Open the gate!" the captain shouted and banged his fist against the old wood. "Open the gate!"

It took a few minutes until an old man's man head appeared in the open gateway. "We have nothing to do with those women," he said, his voice trembling.

The captain pushed him down and ran inside. The courtyard seemed to be empty, and it was almost dark. "Where are they?" He kicked the old man lying sprawled in the dirt.

The man pointed to the back of the courtyard with a trembling finger; there was another wall, a hundred feet from them. He tried to speak, but slumped against a stone, unconscious. There was a small spot of blood spreading slowly over the stone his head had hit during his fall. Running, the soldiers trampled over his body. They stopped abruptly almost bumping into the captain.

"You three, search he courtyard. You," he pointed at the last two men, "see what's behind that wall in the back." His voice was calm now; he knew that the birds had flown. He did not know where, and in a few minutes, it would be fully dark. The moon was hidden behind the clouds. The second patrol entered, and the captain cursed them silently. They were lucky they had arrived late. They could blame him.

Before morning, the girl they had saved was placed in Gresha's care; the Wanderers were back in their home.

Leaning against the window, Dochia stared at them. *This is a difficult moment.* "I understand that you learned very late about the Vicarius taking the girl. The trap was set by Baraki; the Seer of the Serpent has the Light too. Meriaduk knew nothing. We can't command our Visions; sometimes, they come too late. I understand that you wanted to save the girl, but a Wanderer must understand risk. A Wanderer must know when to act, and when to ignore a Vision. If you had died today, our hope of closing the Sanctuary would have died with you. If we can't stop the Fracture, many people will die. Hundreds of thousands. And..." she pondered for a while, "there may be repercussions for killing a Vicarius. Think about this and go to sleep. Later, we will analyze everything that happened, and see what could have been done differently." *It is my fault; I gave them too much liberty, and they are still untrained. Nerval is not Frankis; the danger is different. This is no place for the untrained.*

"They killed a Vicarius," Meriaduk thundered and banged his fist against the table. "I will have a word with Baraki. That decrepit toad is unable to keep even our priests safe. A Vicarius..." He banged his fist against the table again. "Kill five men living on that street. Next time they will defend a priest when he's attacked. Kill old people; we need the young to work." Meriaduk stopped, struggling to contain his anger. It was good to scare his priests with a burst of anger, from time to time – the shock would make their poor minds more alert – but now he needed to think. "The Map has started to fluctuate. The Great Maletera, which controls all others, stops now and then. We. Need. Blood. The Sanctuary can't function without blood. All of you must go and find people with the right blood. All. You, you and you." Meriaduk pointed at Dochia, who was now an apprentice Vicarius, and other two Vicarius. "Come with me; we need to placate the Map."

This was the first time Dochia was allowed to enter the circular room under the Map.

"Put your hands on the red spheres," Meriaduk ordered, pointing to a panel filled with strange blinking lights, buttons and two spheres the size of a fist.

Dochia glanced at him, then at the spheres; there was a surge of Light in her and a surge of uncontrolled fear.

"You must fake pain," Ai spoke inside her mind. "Great pain. I must leave now. I can't stay for too long in this room. Meriaduk will know."

Dochia looked again at the spheres and touched one of them with a shy finger. Each sphere was mounted on by a stick as thick as thumb, which linked it to the panel below.

"They will not bite," Meriaduk laughed, but his eyes were tense, following her. It did not escape Dochia.

She placed her palms on the spheres and gripped them. The spheres started to pulse with light, and an undercurrent passed through her skin, as if the things were trying to communicate with her. There was fear too. There was no pain. She moaned, bent as if her body was tortured, and retracted her hands. She threw a guarded glance at Meriaduk: he seemed relieved by something she could not understand.

"Place your hand on the spheres again, and wait until I count to ten," Meriaduk ordered. "A former Wanderer of your power should be trained well enough to handle a little pain."

Dochia obeyed, and he started to count. She did not know that he was counting slower than usual. Contorting her body, she continued to grip the spheres. At ten, she pulled her hands back. A sudden intuition made her kneel, pretending dizziness, and two priests came to help her stand and walk out.

"The Map is working well again," Meriaduk said. *She could sustain the pain longer than any Vicarius*, Meriaduk thought, looking at Dochia as she walked away on weak feet.

Lying in her bed, Dochia started to recall everything that had happened in the strange Map Room. People with the Light could remember the slightest sensation; and there were plenty of them. *I had the impression that the spheres, or the Map, were trying to communicate with me*, she thought. *They did not really* speak, *they... They tried something else. I don't understand.* The memory was strange, as if something had played inside her mind. The sensation was physical, an undercurrent playing back and forth inside her skull. "Ai, where are you?" she called and waited.

"You feel strange," Ai said, a touch of amusement in her voice.

"Yes. What happened there?"

"You were in contact with the part of the Sanctuary controlling the Map. You have the best blood to communicate with the Map. The Map sensed it and probed your mind. There is nothing wrong, and it will not happen again."

"It probed my mind for what?"

"To understand you. The Map marked your blood as higher than Meriaduk's. From now on," Ai chose her words with care, "the Map considers you as the main authority in the Sanctuary. It will answer to you. It will answer to Meriaduk too."

"That means that I can close it, or at least make it hard for Meriaduk to look in some places."

"You can do that. But I wouldn't advise you to do it. The Map will ask for a reason. I know your reasons, but they are ... not convincing enough for it. And Meriaduk will know. He still is the highest authority in the Sanctuary. I know, it's a little confusing." There was slight amusement in Ai's voice, and she vanished, leaving Dochia a little more confused than she wanted.

In his office, Meriaduk was talking with Adex, his most trusted Vicarius. There was a bottle of wine on the table, and two young maids to serve them. One was sitting in Adex's lap, the other was massaging Meriaduk's neck.

"You may go," Meriaduk said, and waited until the maids went out. "I have a plan. We need to hasten Dochia's appointment as Vicarius. The last unfortunate death created an opportunity."

That bitch rose too fast in the ranks. "Other Vicarius may feel uneasy with such ... swift promotion."

You are one of them. "Don't act like a spoiled child, Adex; she will never be one of my trusted people. She was a Wanderer. I need her as Vicarius for one thing. Mordanek, the Great Priest, has set a certain level of blood to open the door of the Magic Weapons Room. I am talking about real weapons that kill at a great distance; magic weapons with great power, not these simple things, which can only stun people. Weapons that kill."

"So, it's true." Adex sipped some wine from his glass.

"Of course, it's true, I was inside with him and another Vicarius, who is dead too. Mordanek was our Great Priest, but he had a ... weakness. He did not want to use the most powerful weapons. Or he only wanted to use them to defend the Sanctuary. I don't have that weakness."

And you don't have the blood. "Powerful weapons can help our priests support Baraki in his crusade against the pagans of Fate. The victory will be theirs. That would make people even more obedient to the Sanctuary. How many soldiers can such weapons kill?"

"It depends on the weapon; there were a hundred types there. Mordanek tested two of them. The first one was able to send shots of ... light and kill five armored men in a row. They burned a hole, the size of a fist, in the men's plates and bodies. The second one was ... horrific." Meriaduk felt the need to sip some wine too. "It launched something that I can't really describe but it exploded. You know, like a log that explodes in the fire when it has too much water in it, but a thousand time stronger. It killed almost a hundred people. Unfortunately, the man who handled the weapon made a mistake, and shot at the wrong place, where our people were standing to watch the demonstration." *There were rumors that the shooter did it deliberately.* "We were unable to learn more about it, as Mordanek closed the Magic Weapons Room." He sipped some more wine. "That shot killed over fifty priests. It was a great loss, as they all had strong blood. Things were never the same in the Sanctuary after that. Even now, after so many years, we don't have the level of blood we had at that time."

Adex looked at his glass. "Entering that room... Is there something else that I need to know?"

"Yes," Meriaduk laughed. "The use of her blood will kill our new Vicarius. Sometimes, the Serpent requests great sacrifices." He raised his glass and emptied it in one shot. Adex did the same.

~

"The Serpent is giving you a great gift," Adex said, and placed a Maletera on the table.

Tihano looked at the small sphere and said nothing. He was accustomed to the priests. They said great words and did little. They prayed; but that was not hard work.

"Take it in your hand."

Tihano obeyed; he wanted to end the talk fast; the Vicarius would pester him until he got what he wanted. And Adex was worse than the others. Only Meriaduk was able to unnerve Tihano more. The sphere became warm in his hand. He heard a voice and turned his head; perhaps there was someone behind him. His vision blurred, and he saw the High Priest.

"You feel the power of the Serpent now," Meriaduk said in the man's mind.

Tihano gripped the sphere harder. He worshiped the Serpent, true, but he was a Toltar, a man of the wild steppes. A free spirit. With an effort, he unlocked his jaws. "What is this object?"

"Power."

"What kind of power?"

Meriaduk flicked his fingers, and the Map appeared in their vision. "This is the Great Map, and you can see the continent. What else do you want to see? Your Yurta?" 'Yurta' was the word for the tents the nomads lived in, and also for their camp. He did not wait for an answer, but slid a finger over the smooth surface, and rotated the red sphere. The Great River of the east appeared, then a great camp made of thousands of tents. For the last few hours, Meriaduk had rehearsed finding Tihano's Yurta. The image focused until a great tent appeared in all its splendor. Its beautiful ornaments were not overcomplicated but gave a sensation of power.

"That's my Yurta," Tihano breathed.

"Ah, but you doubted the power of the Serpent. Do you understand the power of my gift?"

Tihano pondered. Once the first shock has passed, he tried to understand. He was a practical man. If there was power, then there was power. If it came to him, he would use it. "When I touch the ... Maletera... I will see the Map."

"No, you will see me. I will bring the Map to you; it answers only to the High Priest. I will tell you where your enemies are. What they are doing. You are a great warrior; you understand this kind of advantage."

"Yes, I understand."

"The Great Horde belongs to you. This army is our main weapon, and you are the commander, the Tooth of the Serpent. We trust you to bring us victory. We trust you more than we trust Baraki. He is a man of many words; you are a man of action. There is one more thing. The sacrifice. The Serpent requests you to kill five hundred thousand unbelievers." Meriaduk made the sign of the Serpent with his fingers and closed the link abruptly.

Tihano shook his head. There was no pain, only strange things that he needed to understand. He was a practical man. *It's a waste to kill so many people. They need to work the land to make money and things that we can pillage again in ten years. We always kill some, to frighten them, but who would count the dead? Nobody.* He shrugged. After victory, the horde would split into small troops to pillage. There would be more than a hundred troops. There will be five priests. *Let the priests count; we kill only what we need to kill.*

Adex's stare was stern when his eyes met Tihano's. He knew the game well. "You should not boast about the gift until Meriaduk allows it. Secrecy is important. In a week, we will have the leaving ceremony for the Horde. There will be a smaller ceremony later, and you will receive great weapons. Weapons that kill at a great distance."

Great... They like this word so much. Everything they do is great, but it's us who will fight the unbelievers. It's us who will spill blood for the Serpent. And for pillage. Tihano understood that he had to please the Serpent, but pillage was more important for him than the god. Pillage kept his men close. "Thank you for the Maletera," he said, his voice flat.

The ceremony for the Great Horde started with a quarrel. Who would stand in the most important place? The Khad, or the High Priest? They argued; they shouted; they banged heavy fists on the table. The ceremony was postponed, then postponed again.

Nabal, the Last Emperor, materialized in Dochia's mind. "The bulls are too stubborn. We need to find a solution to please them both."

"Why are you coming to me?"

"I have a plan. A long-term plan. You will make a better High Priestess than Meriaduk a High Priest. It may take a few years, but... You understand. Now find a way to tame the bulls." He vanished as abruptly as he had appeared.

Well, Dochia mused, *who would have believed that I could be the High Priestess of the Serpent?* She shrugged and went out of the Sanctuary.

The plaza separating the Khad's Palace and the Sanctuary could fit fifty thousand people. Dochia climbed the stairs toward the palace and stood in the middle, from where the Khad was talking to his subjects. That was the place both Baraki and Meriaduk wanted for the ceremony. *Baraki has more claim to this place*, she thought. The guards looked at her and nodded; she was known in the palace. From the top of the stairs, she looked down. There were a hundred and one steps below her. That number was important for the Toltars and Rosins. A squad had a hundred riders. One more was a step toward infinity. The great steppes were infinite. The power of the Serpent was infinite. She looked left and right; the stairs were as long as that side of the palace. Two hundred feet. At the corners, there were two round landings, twenty feet in diameter, the Rondos. *It may work*. She went to one of them and looked at the buildings around. Then she did the same from the other one.

Everything was decided in the evening. The Khad would occupy the left Rondo, the High Priest the right one. In the middle would be the sacred place with the flags representing all the powers. The Serpent. The Khad. The Toltars. The Rosins.

She is clever, Meriaduk thought, looking at Dochia walking away, *but she doesn't know that she will die during the next ceremony, to open the Magic Weapons Room. How could she know that?* He shrugged.

It was cold that morning. For two days, a frigid wind blew from the north. The wind lost some of its power, and the air was crisp. There were no clouds. From the top of the roof, Aliana could see the land far away. She could see many things. The small mountains around Nerval. The walls. People walking toward the plaza for the ceremony. She could even see a corner of the plaza. She shivered and turned her head toward Kasia and Mira. She smiled. They answered with a brief smile too. The wind blew, freezing their lips.

Baraki and Meriaduk left the palace at the same time, the door was large enough. Tihano and Adex followed, then more tribal chiefs and Vicarius. They stopped in front of the flags to salute the people in the plaza. There were more than fifty thousand there, some filling the streets going into the plaza, some sitting on the roofs of the houses surrounding the place. In front, there were soldiers, a hundred from each tribe of Toltars and Rosins, and a hundred more from Arenia. The crowd erupted when the leaders saluted them. "Serpent! Holy War! Serpent! Holy War!" Under the flags, Baraki and Meriaduk seemed content. They still wanted to do something to eclipse their rival. Something small but good enough, but they feared disrupting the ceremony. It would mean bad luck. The tribes believed in luck as much as they believed in the Serpent.

When the shouts faded, the Khad and the High Priests turned and went toward their Rondos. The Vicarius split in two and followed them. In the middle remained only Tihano and Adex, a flag in each of their hands. Dochia counted as a Vicarius too, and she went with Meriaduk; there would be three Vicarius for each leader.

In the middle of the stairs, the priests lit the holy fire. People kneeled in the plaza; only Baraki, Meriaduk, Tihano and the

Vicarius were still standing. The priests raised their hands and started to pray to the Serpent. The plaza was silent now.

From the sky, a black point descended. No one saw it. There was a surge of Light in Baraki, and he turned abruptly. That was his good luck. The arrow pierced his upper arm and stuck into his chest. It was a dark red arrow. The priests continued to pray; the people were still kneeling. “Alarm!” Baraki shouted. The soldiers and the Vicarius turned toward him. They saw the red shaft of the arrow, and Baraki slowly falling to his knees. The Vicarius tried to run away; the soldiers ran toward the Khad. They collided with each other, and no one could move. The Rondo was a crowded place. There were blows. There were curses. But they could not move. The second arrow killed a Vicarius. And the third. And the fourth. They came one by one from the sky, thirty seconds between each flight. Dark red arrows.

Six hours later, in the palace, Adex looked at Baraki lying in his bed. The bandaged wound was not mortal, but he could no longer lead the Arenian army to war. Then Adex looked at Meriaduk, who shook his head; he would not use the Healing Chamber to heal Baraki. That red arrow came from the sky; it was a gift from the Serpent. Red was his color. The color of blood. Three Vicarius were dead, but there was no gift without sacrifice. The Serpent was a demanding god. West of the city, Tihano was leading the Great Horde, three hundred thousand strong, toward glory; he was no longer the second-in-command; he was the Commander, the Tooth of the Serpent.

The two surviving Vicarius and Dochia hurried toward the Sanctuary. Meriaduk had asked her to control the Map; he needed to contact and impress Tihano once more, and wanted to do it in front of Baraki. In the long corridor, the Vicarius walked behind Dochia; they had orders to keep a keen eye on her. They had eyes only for her. They had no eyes for the two silent women who came out from a room behind them. When they realized and turned, it was too late; the maces hit them in the forehead. The women dragged them into the room, closed the door, and the corridor looked peaceful again. There was no blood.

The ten guards of the Serpent Room were tough soldiers, and they had powerful weapons that could stun people at fifteen feet. They trusted their skill, honed over many years; no one tried to enter the room without Meriaduk's approval. Theirs was an important task, but they were relaxed. Three of them were sleeping. Four were playing dice. The other three were yawning. They were bored. It was always like this.

Some of them turned their heads when Dochia entered the room. They knew the new priestess, and the two who were closer to the door stood up to meet her.

"The ceremony has ended," Dochia said, "but we had a situation. The Khad was wounded. Three Vicarius are dead. Meriaduk is in the palace, looking after everything. He needs the Map. I tried to start it, but there is an issue here." She pointed at the long panel, across the room. "Speak to him." She gave the Maletera to the lead soldier. "These priests will help me." She made place for Aliana and Kasia, who were dressed as men.

"I don't know them," the soldier said, cautiously, but he did not try to stop the priests.

Kasia moved left, three paces away from Dochia. Aliana moved right. This time the soldier eyed them suspiciously.

"Speak to Meriaduk," Dochia said, pointing at the Maletera.

The moment the soldier gripped it and went into that inside world, the women sprang, knives up. None of the powerful stunning weapons were in sight. They were somewhere in the room; it was the safest room in the Sanctuary. The soldiers died before they could grab them.

In the palace, Meriaduk felt the call of the Maletera, and reached the soldier, but everything was gone before he could learn anything. "I have to leave," he said to Baraki, and hastened toward the door. Outside, he was already running, followed by his guards.

Dochia stopped in front of the panel; it was a complicated thing, with many flashing lights and buttons. "Ai, what should I do know?"

“You have to place a hand on the red horizontal bar and pull it down. All three of you at the same time. Only together you have enough blood to close the Sanctuary.”

“What changed your mind?”

“Meriaduk asked Tihano to kill five hundred thousand people as a gift to the Serpent.”

“I did not know that. When we close this,” Dochia pointed at the red bar, “you will come with us.”

“I can’t.”

“Please Ai, you are my best friend here. I won’t leave you behind.”

“I am glad to have been your friend, but I can’t leave the Sanctuary. I don’t have a body like you.”

“Whatever body you have…”

“Dochia, my body is the Sanctuary. I am its mind.”

Dochia’s jaw dropped, and it took her a lot of effort to ask, “But… What will happen to you? Is it safe for you to close the Sanctuary? I don’t want to harm you.”

“I will sleep. I slept for four thousand years until Mordanek woke me up. Pull the bar down.”

Chapter 6 - Codrin

From the head of the valley, Codrin looked down, matching the image from his Farsight with the one on the ground. Things look different when looked at from the sky. Even seen from his horse, the almost two-mile-wide field looked promising. Three miles down from him, a small river cut the field in two, its riverbed an almost straight white line, contrasting with the green around, before falling over a precipice, on the right. There was nothing spectacular; the precipice was only twenty feet high, and the water flow was small. On the left, a thirty-foot-high ridge towered over the valley. It was broken in the middle by the river. From his position, a moderate slope led down, ending a hundred feet shy of the river. The rest of the valley was a flat, six-mile-long field. Codrin took his spyglass and looked at the end of the valley, which was almost three miles wide. *It will accommodate their three hundred thousand riders*, he thought; the place should provide him an advantage without looking too obvious; the nomads were skilled warriors, accustomed to making war in wide spaces. Any trap works better when the enemy feels comfortable. There was a road too, the main road in the north-east of Litvonia, and he had seen in a Vision that the nomads would use it, though a Vision could change sometimes. He dismounted and hit the ground with his boot. It answered dully; there was solid rock under the thin layer of grass, and he rubbed some soil between his fingers, to feel the place. Thoughtfully, he glanced at the small, peculiar ridge that traversed the slope diagonally from the river in front to the forest behind them. The lower end of the ridge was less than a half mile from the precipice on the right. At the higher end, there were only five hundred feet between the ridge and the precipice. Sixty feet wide, and partially covered by grass, the ridge was irregular, and grew in height, from two feet, to almost five, before vanishing into the forest. The edges were surprisingly straight, as if someone had cut the land with a giant knife. It was a Talant artifact, built more than four thousand years ago. Eyes closed, Codrin tried to imagine how the space on and around the ridge would look when filled with soldiers. He let his Farsight fly down and looked at the place from the other side of the valley, from where the nomad commander would supervise the battle: the ridge was almost invisible.

"This will be our battlefield," he said, turning toward Alfrid, who was on his right. "Vlaicu, give the order to make camp here and around the small ridge on the right, then find me five hundred woodcutters. Vlad, send experienced scouts to see how well suited for riding the land across the river is."

"What do you have in mind?" Alfrid asked.

"To use the riverbed. We will build some wooden structures over it, and place archers inside them. We call them cazems in Arenia."

"It's water..."

"We will change the course of the river. There is a place behind the left ridge, where it can be done easily. Count Joachim," Codrin turned toward the Spatar of Litvonia, "Send some masons who know about fortifications to see how many men they need to change the course of the river in two days."

"They will destroy the ... cazems," Alfrid insisted. "A hundred men with axes, and all our archers will be killed."

"You will not find a single axe in their army. The nomads like to travel light, and for them the axe is an impure weapon. And," Codrin added in a tougher voice, feeling that Alfrid wanted to interject again, "in front of the cazems there will be rocks. They will stop the horses to ride over them."

In the evening, hundreds of thirty-foot-long logs were placed along the river and, leaning with his back against an old tree, Codrin surveyed the preparations. From time to time, he caught himself daydreaming, his thoughts going back to Arad. Thinking of Saliné and little Cosmin strengthened him.

"Dreaming?" a voice asked, and a translucent silhouette stood next to him.

"Even a Seer is allowed to dream from time to time."

"Change is coming."

"I will lose the battle," Codrin said, resigned.

"This is not about your battle, and the news is good. Dochia and Aliana were able to close the Sanctuary in Nerval. The Serpent lost most of his eyes and ears, and we were able avoid the Fracture. Not all battles are won in a battlefield."

"They are strong women, but that will not affect the battle here, only that..." He thought for a while. "Perhaps there will not be another invasion."

"Such a game can't be stopped with a snap of fingers. The nomads are stirred, and they will come in waves, again and again, for about ... fifteen years, but without the power of the Talant artifacts their strength is diminished. A strong and united Realm will defeat them again."

"The Realm is weak. The unification will take perhaps half a lifetime. Perhaps even more. Six hundred years and still ... nothing. It still helps to be a Seer."

"It may happen much faster than you think. There are some ... new evolutions. Without a Fracture, there is no need for a Seer."

Unable to control his reaction, Codrin turned to face her. He moved slowly and silently. Silent too, the Empress raised her right hand, palm up, her forefinger pointing at him. A small translucent pearl came out of his body and landed in her palm.

"From this moment, you are no longer the Seer of the Realm."

"Couldn't you have waited for another three days?" Codrin asked, bitterly.

"There are rules I have to obey. I am not alone there." She pointed to the blue sky.

"Perhaps you should improve the rules."

"The rules are not made to give you an advantage, Codrin; they must balance everybody's interests. The nomads are people too. We don't want them eliminated. We just need to make them turn their back to the Serpent and his vicious religion."

"This is what you think about me? That I want to kill all the nomads and their families in the steppes? And how can I do that anyway?"

"No, I don't, but the rules are not about what I believe about you."

"Do you know what will happen if their army changes course, and I am not able to see it? Three hundred thousand bloody riders are invading Litvonia."

"You must find another solution."

"If they avoid the trap, there is no way to defeat the nomad army; it's more than four times larger than mine."

"There are always ways."

"If they win, they will not spare a village on their way toward Muniker. They will kill everybody, every man, every woman, and every child that are not taken as slaves. You fear that I would destroy the nomads' villages, which are more than two thousand miles away from here. You don't care if the nomads destroy all the villages in Litvonia, and they are already here, ready to spill blood. Don't you have rules to avoid this carnage too?"

"Win the battle."

Biting against the curses crouching on his tongue, Codrin said nothing, just leaned his head back against the tree. The rough bark scratched his skin. He did not feel it.

"Baraki was wounded by Aliana and had to stay in Nerval. The Arenian army will not pass into Silvania. That is one burden less for you."

I will not fight Baraki. Is that good or bad? "I wish to meet her."

"She will return to Frankis," the Empress said hesitantly, and Codrin's eyes narrowed. "Seers are transitory, and from now on, you are the Pillar of the Realm. That's a burden for life. I trust you to win this battle, Codrin." She tapped gently on his temple before vanishing. Everything was happening in his mind, yet he physically sensed her finger touching his skin. It felt icy, and a strange shiver went down his spine.

Will I return to Frankis?

The first attack by the nomads was just a test. They sent a column of twenty thousand strong cavalry, which rode in a half circle, almost touching the left flank of the cazems built over the small riverbed, riding in parallel with them, and returning to their lines. Covered by grass, the cazems resembled some long mounds, but the nomads were cautious people. The archers hidden inside the cazems did not react. The battlefield fell silent, and through his spyglass, Codrin could see the nomad council gathered around their commander, Tihano. It was too far to see their faces – there was no more Farsight for him – but their meeting was long. *Bloody Empress.* Codrin shook his head.

"Once," Vlad said, "I followed three pairs of dogs gathering sheep for the night. It was a large herd, over five hundred head. There were two openings in the pen, and the dogs circled around the sheep in opposite directions, until they moved closer and closer, making a two-hundred-foot-long wooly carpet. Then an intelligent ram entered the pen. The sheep followed. The sight was strange; it resembled a giant hourglass, flowing sheep instead of sand. That's what will happen here. We are the dogs. They are the sheep and have to pass through the gaps between the cazems."

"I forgot to tell you that Vlad is a poet," Codrin laughed. "Yes, the riders' flow will be restricted at the entrances, between the cazems. The riders behind the front lines will be almost static; easy prey for archers."

"They may decide to charge in fifteen narrow columns and pass quickly through the gaps," Alfrid said.

"They may," Codrin shrugged, "but the result is the same; the longer columns need more time to pass the soldiers on our side of the river. That gives the archers plenty of time, and we will counterattack when the forward half of the columns cross the riverbed."

"How many nomads can our archers kill?"

"They will send some fifty thousand riders in the first attack. We may be able to put five thousand down."

"There are three hundred thousand nomads there." Alfrid shrugged, pointing north toward the enemy camp. "Five thousand dead means nothing to them."

"Don't be defeatist, Alfrid," his brother, Edric, interjected. "In most cases, armies don't destroy each other. If the losses go over a fifth of their numbers, they will retreat. Once I saw an army running away after losing less than a tenth of their strength. The nomads are tougher though."

"I wager they lose a fourth part of the horde before they retreat," Codrin said, "but the main purpose of the cazems is not to kill. We needed them to hinder the nomad's moves, to delay; they are the masters of swift attacks. Vlad's sheep." He became silent, studying the valley with an intense look. Commanders!" he shouted suddenly. "Be ready."

Down in the valley, a wall of riders was moving slowly, in a way resembling a giant grid sliding over the land; they were the best riders in the world and could ride in all sorts of formations. It gathered speed, flowing like a huge wave of horses.

"I bet that they will attack in one wave," a Litvonian soldier said.

"We need to wait, and from this moment, you should comment no more," Codrin ordered.

The nomads split with perfect precision, and fifteen columns formed, ready to pass at full speed through the gaps between the cazems.

"Five hundred feet, four hundred, three hundred, two hundred," Codrin counted, his voice loud and clear. "Now!" At his order, the drums began to beat, long, long, then short, then long again, and arrows started to fly from the cazems. It takes an experienced archer ten seconds to nock, aim, and let an arrow fly. That's what they did, in the beginning. When the nomad riders came a few feet in front of the cazems, there was no more need to aim; they could find a target with their eyes closed.

"Left wing, charge!" Codrin shouted, and the drums gave the signal again. Long, long, long, barroom, that meaning the left wing. Barroom, barroom – charge.

The cavalry of his left wing, fifteen thousand strong, moved as if they were not in a hurry, and Codrin waited, thoughtfully.

"More archers?" Count Joachim asked, sensing Codrin's hesitation.

"No. Go and tell the heavy cavalry to charge in parallel with the river on our side." There was a moment of silence; no one understood why Codrin had changed the plans, and he seemed lost in some inner thought. It took Joachim two minutes to reach the heavy cavalry. Fifteen thousand Silvanian Hussaris and Litvonian Teutons started their advance, making the ground tremble. They were slow in the beginning, but when they gained speed, they looked like an iron wall charging across the plain.

Down in the valley, the nomads changed direction in a heartbeat, forming fifteen circles that wove themselves back through the gaps between the cazems, trying to run away. They rode in parallel with astonishing elegance, and if not for the war and death coming, that unnatural ability of the nomads to be one with their horses offered a show to be remembered for a long time, and the grist of stories for even longer. In their cazems, the archers were ready for the nomads. When the Hussaris arrived, followed by the Teutons, they sliced through the remaining nomads as though they were just dolls, trampling them to the ground. Once the nomads retreated, the heavy cavalry joined the other riders on the left wing. The right now had no riders, apart from the much-needed couriers.

Joachim took his time to sense the new alignment of the army, before saying, "The right wing is now the real trap."

"Yes," Codrin smiled wryly. Even in his army, only Valer understood the new situation; then he turned toward the captains. "Count the dead," he ordered, and they all started to count, in a pattern Codrin had devised for them. They imagined a grid of hundred-foot squares and counted the dead in them. When they tallied up the estimates, they ranged from four thousand four hundred, to five thousand. "I would have expected more dead from two passes between the cazems and a heavy cavalry attack," Codrin said, his voice low. "Most people don't count accurately, and spread out on the ground, bodies look more numerous more than they actually are." There were now archers in view, spreading between the cazems, silencing the wounded enemy. "Vlad, take a few scouts and go to the cazems. We need to understand what did not work."

The second nomad attack hit both sides of the small ridge, and Vlad had to retreat fast. Fifty thousand riders attacked the center of Codrin's army, and fifty thousand more charged his right wing, which had no more riders. In the center, the armies met under the clear sky. The light was clean and pure; the battle seemed a profanation of both land and sky. From above, it looked as if two blocks had crashed into each other. There was a clear line between the smaller riders from the steppes and the tall Litvonians and Frankis. There was a difference in colors and weapons too. Here and there, the contact line shredded into fragments, and the riders mingled, looking now like a rough curve with strange protrusions. The numbers favored the nomads, and they pressed. Some parts of the line became islands of men surrounded by nomads. Blow by blow, the islands shrank, the battle line changed again, more protrusions and more islands. In twenty minutes, the nomads managed to gain more than two hundred feet. Some of them, at the back, forced their horses to climb the small ridge. Some horses and riders fell; some gained the ridge and moved to trample the foot soldiers. Only the hedgehog of spears at the lowest end of the ridge remained intact.

The second column of fifty thousand nomads went between the small ridge and the precipice, and there were no riders to stop them. Some foot soldiers climbed down into the precipice; some climbed the ridge. Most of them retreated fast toward the forest, way before the clash could happen. Unopposed, the nomad line advanced fast.

Under his helmet, Alfrid was breathing heavily; the nomads had almost surrounded him and his five hundred-strong Guard. His best soldiers. An arrow came and put down the rider on his left. Then another one. Then the one on his right. He panicked, feeling that the world was void of air. He glanced right, then left. They were half surrounded by the nomad beasts, who were about to separate them from the Frankis Guard. He had feared the nomads since he was a child. He feared them even more now. There was a space on his left. Alfrid turned his horse abruptly and tried to run. He could not go far, but he still tried to run. Stunned, his soldiers almost stopped the fight, and the nomads advanced further on the flanks.

Edric turned his head. It took him a split second to understand, and he turned his horse too, riding until he reached Alfrid. With the side of his sword, he swiped at his brother's helmet. Alfrid did not stop, so he hit him again. Harder. "Fight!" Edric growled. "You are the King of Litvonia. Defend your kingdom." He stretched out his long arm and grabbed Alfrid by the ornament of his helmet. Edric was a strong man and made Alfrid turn slowly. "Fight," he growled, and hit his brother again.

Codrin saw that the Litvonian Guard was close to being surrounded. He saw Alfrid running away. He saw Edric. Then he lost sight of them as two nomads attacked him at the same time. One died under his long sword, the other one was killed by Lisandru. "Valer," he shouted at the Black Dervil, who commanded his Guard, "we need to help the Litvonians. We need to reach them. Split our Guard in two and follow me."

They had to cut a path through the nomads. Forming a Triangle wedge with Lisandru and Pintea, Codrin fought like a madman. His Guard followed. Everything would be lost if the Litvonian Guard were crushed. It took a minute, then two, then five. The will of the nomads separating the two troops of Guards were crushed too; they have never met two-sword devils fighting like this. Half of them turned back; half of them fell. Codrin reached Count Joachim, who bowed perfunctorily. Then he reached Alfrid, who was too paralyzed to fight. "Edric, Joachim," Codrin shouted, "take command of the Litvonian army."

Tihano rode ahead of his left wing and led it to attack the foot soldiers between the ridge and the precipice. The middle of the battlefield was crammed and stationary; victory would be decided on the flanks. His first wave of riders was already crushing the foot soldiers on the left. They rode fast and entered the gap between the small ridge and the precipice. Some of his riders jumped onto the ridge behind the hedgehog of spears. In a few minutes, the spearmen were all dead.

From the opposite flank, the Duke of Homburg followed the nomads crushing the foot soldiers. He looked at the center and saw that Codrin had stabilized it. That was the moment when he started to believe that the Seer's strategy could work, and he smiled for the first time that day. Slowly, he unsheathed his sword. "Teutons, Hussaris, ride with me!"

In front of his men, Tihano had a good view of the battlefield; it rose gradually in front of him. Between the ridge and the precipice, it resembled a trapezoid, its shorter base at the edge of the forest. A man of the large steppes, Tihano did not know what a trapezoid meant, but he knew that if his men were able to reach the forest, they could bypass the ridge and attack the enemy from behind. That always meant slaughter, and after slaughter came the pillage of an undefended land. He passed the lower point of the ridge, rising on his right, and looked up again: his men were now close to reaching the forest. This was his battle to win, and he goaded his stallion with his spurs, pushing him to a gallop. The riders behind him did the same.

The Duke of Drasdin had the best spearmen in Litvonia, his Hedgehogs. He was proud of them. Hiding behind a large oak, he was following the advance of the nomads up the slope. The infantry could not offer much resistance and they were falling back. Many men went down the precipice on the right. They did not fall; the slope was abrupt, but it allowed a man to climb down fast using his hands and feet. They threw down their swords first, to free their hands. Behind the Duke, his spearmen lay down in the grass or stood, hidden by the trees.

"Stand up!" he shouted. "Lazy Hedgehogs, stand up and be ready. The savages are coming."

The men picked up their spears, some fifteen feet long, some ten. They did not rush; such long weapons were not easy to handle in tight spaces.

"Shorties, form your ranks," the Duke ordered.

The soldiers with shorter spears and heavy armor formed three rows at the edge of the forest, keeping their weapons vertical.

"Show your beautiful heads to the nomads."

The spearmen walked three feet out of the forest. The retreating Litvonian soldiers no longer stepped back toward them;

they gave up the fight and went to the right, hustling to climb down into the precipice.

"Longies, form your ranks. Make the Hedgehog."

Forming three ranks, the men with long spears came out of the forest too, placed their spears at an angle against the ground and let rest them on the shoulders of the men in front.

"Breathe and wait."

The Teutons and the Hussaris moved down. Gathering speed, they turned right toward the rearguard of the nomads, who were pressing against the center, led by Codrin. Fifty thousand nomads were riding up to attack the heavy cavalry from behind. The Duke of Homburg mimed attacking the rear of the nomads in the center, then went toward their left wing, commanded by Tihano. The incoming nomad riders were reaching the cazems, and arrows flew, delaying them. Homburg's men entered the place between the ridge and the precipice at full speed, a mass of giant horses and steel. Like a wave, they crashed into the lighter nomads from behind. On faster horses, the nomads tried to evade and fight back. They were the masters of evasions and swift counterattacks. But there was no place to ride and evade the advancing cavalry. In front, the riders were already grouped tighter than they were accustomed to fight, with Drasdin's Hedgehog stopping them. The trapezoid became a trap. The Teutons and Hussaris used their mass and speed to herd the nomads like sheep. A few horses fell into the precipice. Then more. The tighter the space became the more nomads fell into the precipice. Some of them died in the fall, some were killed by the foot soldiers waiting for them.

Tihano tried to turn his horse and fight. His knees were already touching the legs of the two riders flanking him. They were flanked by other nomads, all trying to turn. "Flip!" Tihano shouted and turned in the saddle, sitting backward. He could no longer control the horse, but there was nothing to control in that tight space. The rest of nomads turned too, but what could they do against the wall of hard steel coming against them? Tihano was right in his assessment of the battle; it had turned into slaughter.

The upper end of valley was filled with fires that evening. People were singing. People were dancing. People were mourning. It was always like this after a battle. And this was a battle like no other for many centuries back. It would be remembered as the Trap of the Seer. There were stories to tell and pass on to their children. In a generation or two, they would become legends.

Chapter 7 - Thais / Codrin

The tension of the battle was still in his blood. The day before had been a day of worry, a day of death, and a day of victory. Memories and feeling were slowly fading away, slower than Codrin wanted. No other battle had marked him so hard, but there had been no battle like this one before. Codrin rode slowly, half aware of his surroundings, half thinking of Arad. Of Saliné. Of his sons. There were reports from the scouts that a fifty thousand strong group of nomads had gathered some twenty miles away. They were gathering for an orderly retreat toward east, but Codrin did not want to leave that to chance, and he was looking for a narrow part of this valley to serve as a potential new battlefield. The nomads had been routed, but he would engage in battle on his own terms. If there were another battle. He missed his Seer's power, being able to hover over the land with his inner eye. It had been part of his life for so many years, and he felt naked without it. Even his Light seemed diminished. From time to time, they met companies of soldiers, combing the land. None of them had encountered a single nomad. They passed a company of sixty Litvonian archers, and Roderick, their captain, gave him the same answer; there were no nomads around. Codrin rose in the saddle and saw two large rocks straddling the river down in the valley. *That's a good place for an ambush.* With a gesture for his twenty guards to follow him, Codrin pushed Zor to a light canter. Cries burst out behind him; men were dying. Before he could turn, an arrow pierced his body, and the second, and the third. *Nomads*, he thought. Zor sprang forward and, for the first time in his life, Codrin felt completely helpless, though he knew his people were dying – he could hear their screams. Two more arrows pierced him, and he leaned forward in the saddle, all thoughts of fighting gone. His hands tightened around Zor's neck. He caught the smell of his own blood, branches scratching his back, then nothing.

"He's escaped!" cried Roderick. He was the only rider, and the closest to the point where Zor had vanished into the forest. Even knowing that Codrin was wounded, he did not dare to follow him alone, and the archers had no horses. It took thirty more minutes until a troop of twenty Litvonian riders finally arrived, led by Edric, the King's brother.

"Sixty of you and you lost him," Edric snapped, turning his horse on the place. "Where did he go?"

Codrin had lost a lot of blood. There was numbing pain in his body and dizziness in his head. He slid slowly form his horse, hit the ground on a patch of dried leaves, and lay wheezing; the forest around him was blurred through his stinging tears, until two women wavered into view against the lace of fluttering leaves and white-blue sky. They were on a small plateau, hidden behind a thirty-foot-tall ridge. Codrin did not know that Zor had ridden through the river for almost half a mile; he was a well-trained war horse after all, from a long and noble lineage.

"He is almost dead and in great pain," the young Wanderer said and unsheathed her sword. "I will give him mercy."

"Iantha, don't." Thais, the Third Light of the Litvonian Wanderers, stopped her.

"But the Council of Seven asked me to verify that he was dead. And to act, if not..."

"I am part of the Council. Three days ago, Codrin was the Seer of the Realm and, yesterday, he defeated the nomads. I understand that our order wants to unify Litvonia and Frankis, but Codrin does not deserve to be killed for the political advantage of a man like Alfrid, a coward who tried to run away from battle. We are not assassins, and we must act in a fair way. What's fair in this? And worse, we broke our own code and plotted to kill the man who saved the Realm from the nomads, a man who has never threatened us. Help me treat his wounds."

One by one, they pulled four arrows from Codrin's body, took down his ring mail and dressed the wounds. The last arrow was broken.

"This one doesn't look good." Frowning, Thais looked at the arrow, which entered his back and went out through his chest, the arrowhead half visible. "I hope that his lungs are not affected; I don't see blood around his mouth, so he may be lucky in this at least."

"You are a skilled healer."

"Let's hope that's true." Thais smiled, tiredly. "The arrow is broken; we need to cut the iron point from the shaft and pull it out of his back."

"Can't we pull it out by the point?"

"No. This is a war arrow, made to pierce armor. The shaft has a conic shape; it will do more damage if we pull it by the point. Now, let me see." Thais cut his clothes, and breathed out, relieved. "The arrowhead is fully out, and I can break the shaft." She did it carefully, breathed deeply, and gripped the remains of the shaft, a small stump protruding from Codrin's back. She tested her grip then, slowly, pulled the arrow out of his body. He gasped and opened his eyes for a few moments, then fell unconscious again. With an expert eye, Thais examined the wound. "Bandage him." She wiped her red hands on the grass and waited until Iantha finished with the dressing. "If everything goes well, he will be fully healed in a month. The wounds are not really bad, but he has lost a lot of blood. Five arrows," she shook her head. "We need to find a shelter for him, far from here, so no one will find him, friends or foes."

"Thais," Iantha said timidly; she was only nineteen years old and had passed her Rite of Passage only nine months earlier. "If he can walk again in one month, he will go back to Frankis. That will ruin our plan."

"No, he won't. I prepared a magic potion to block his memories. It's strong enough to suppress them for seven years. He will not be able to access them. Codrin will fully recover ... well almost fully, one year before the next invasion. It will be a slow recover; his memories will return to him in a few weeks. Or in a few months, these potions are hard to predict. I have the feeling that Codrin still has a destiny to fulfill. He is a strong man." *I pray that my Vision is right.*

"Where did you learn to make that potion?"

"It's a long story. I found it in a Talant book, a long time ago. The remains of a book, in fact; there were only thirty pages left. This is it." She took a small vial from her pocket. "Open his mouth." It took them less than a minute to make Codrin swallow the drops. *It's a powerful thing, and there was no way test it. Let's hope that it will work well.*

"You knew that Codrin would not be killed by Alfrid's men," Iantha said, tentatively.

My Vision was that they would find and kill Codrin two hours after the first attempt. We still have one hour to help him escape. "I had a Vision about the attack even before this bloody arrangement between the Wanderers and the Circle to kill him, and there must be a reason why it came together with the one announcing the next nomad invasion, eight years from now. That's why I changed the course of things. Let's see to his horse now; there are three arrows in him too." *And that's why I came here without my guards. People think I am still in south-eastern Litvonia, a hundred miles from here. Only Elagia and Calista know that I am the Juras Mountains. If another Wanderer had a Vision about my plans, I am a dead woman.*

She walked slowly in front of the stallion, and Zor shook his head nervously. "Let me help you," Thais said gently, tapping his mane. "Zor is your name, isn't it?" The first arrow was in his left foreleg, and it did not seem to be deep in the flesh, it lay at a narrow angle, almost hanging. Her other hand went closer to the arrow, and Thais felt the horse tensing his neck. "I have to do it." Her fingers closed on the shaft of the arrow, and she pulled it out. Zor snorted and shook his head, but he did not move. "You are a clever horse, aren't you?" She pressed a piece of cloth until the blood stopped flowing, then did the same for the other two arrows, though she had to use a knife to extract them. Zor never moved until she finished then, to her surprise, he came and nudged her shoulder with his muzzle and, without knowing why, she laced her arms around his neck for a while. She liked that warmth, but it was mostly to hide her tears from the younger Wanderer. *What's happening to me? The last time I cried, I was still a young girl. Things are taking a toll on me.* It was not easy for her to disobey an order given by the Wanderer Council of which she was part. In almost forty years since she had joined the Wanderers, she never disobeyed an order until now. There was the fear too; she had changed the future in an unforeseeable way. It was her choice and Vision against the choices and Visions of other Wanderers, some stronger than her. After a while, Thais mumbled an unintelligible curse, and moved away from the horse. He followed and pushed her, with his muzzle, toward Codrin. "I can't do anything more, Zor," she said, and a wry smile formed on her lips. "From now on, he is in Fate's hands, though I can't say how good her hands might be for him. He was her Seer, and she..." Thais pressed a hand on her mouth and stayed silent; her words were a blasphemy.

Zor did not stop, pushing her until they reached Codrin. He nuzzled Codrin's hair and snorted gently, then tapped the ground with his left hoof. Codrin felt the nudge and tried to lift his right hand. It rose an inch and felt to the ground again.

"Iantha, help me to mount him on his horse; he is a heavy man. Sorry, Codrin," Thais whispered, "this will hurt you."

"What?" an almost unconscious Codrin asked.

She ignored his mumbling and kneeled to take hold of his body, passing her arms under his armpits, then stopped abruptly. The horse came closer and lay down beside his master. "Zor, you really are a clever one." It was much easier now to put Codrin on his belly over the saddle. Then she tied him and tied on his ring mail and his famous swords too. *I will not leave you unable to defend yourself, but I wonder how much fighting knowledge you will have when you wake up. None, I suppose. You will have the mind of a toddler. No, that's wrong, his mind will not be affected, only his memory. He must be able to think. I hope. He will have less knowledge than a one-year-old boy, and the muscles of a well-trained adult. That's a strange challenge.*

Before leaving, Thais glanced at the sky, searching for the sun's position through the thin clouds. *Riders will arrive here soon*, she thought, recalling her Vision, *and I don't know to whom they belong, or if they will be the men I saw killing Codrin. Most probably Litvonian. Sometimes, my Visions are so sparse.* They rode at a slow pace through the meadow until they reached a small river emerging from the dense forest. She guided her horse into the water, and Zor followed her without hesitation.

Drops of water splashed Codrin's face, and a hint of consciousness returned to him. "Where am I?" he asked, though his lips did not move. He did not notice. His gorge and entrails were burning from the potion, and he tried to swallow. He could not and tried to raise his head. Pain stabbed through his neck, and his mind fell into the darkness. His head fell too, hitting Zor's body. It did not feel hard. For him it did not feel at all.

They passed over the small mountain chain and slept in a small overhang surrounded by tall rocks, on the other side. The next day, they passed another small mountain chain and arrived at the house Thais had seen in her Vision; a place she had visited once, a long time ago. It was isolated in the mountains, at the edge of a dense forest; the closest village was more than seven miles away, and it fitted well in her plans. The owner was a Wanderer Helper, but Thais was not coming now as a Wanderer.

"Anyone home?" Thais asked, and stopped her horse sixty paces from the door. With a careful look, she examined the house, without dismounting. *It's not large, but it's well maintained. And there are only two women living here. A few months ago, they lost a son and a husband. It could be an advantage, or it could be death, if the house is attacked before Codrin recovers.*

"Yes," a woman in her mid-twenties said, and an arrow appeared through the window. Then half of her head.

She must be Ildeko... She was not yet born when I visited the house. "I have a wounded man with me. Will you help him?"

An older woman came out, followed by the young one and a six-year-old boy. Saying nothing, the woman came and studied the unconscious man. *He is strong*, Pireska thought. *And young...* "Who wounded him?" She locked eyes with Thais, then assessed the women; they were in disguise, but she felt their Light. Like Cleyre, the Duchess of Peyris, Pireska had a power that few others possessed, and none of them was a Wanderer; she was able to feel one's Light, even when it was not used. *You are a Wanderer... Did I meet you before?* A Wanderer could feel one's Light only when its power was drained, and Pireska forced herself not to use it.

"Some robbers, perhaps. We did not see them." *And she did not recognize me. I was the twenty-three-year-old novice of her aunt, who was the Fifth Light, when I came here. Now I am... Who cares how old am I?*

"He seems well fed and has the look of a rich man."

"Rich?" Thais asked, involuntarily assessing Codrin; he was dressed in dark blue clothes as usual and wore no jewelry. There was no way to recognize a King under those simple clothes, yet they were made of the best quality material. Pireska seemed to have a good eye. That could be good. That could be bad too.

"Those are unusual swords," Pireska said again, pointing at Shadow and Flame. "And I never saw such a horse."

"I think that he is a hardened soldier, a captain, perhaps. Those are Arenian clothes and weapons. He must be far from home, but I know nothing more."

"What if the robbers come here?"

"There is nothing more on him to rob, and anyway, it happened half a day's ride from here. We came through the forest following the small river to the east."

That's a lot of caution. What are they afraid of? The old woman had another look at Codrin, this time with the eye of a healer. *He looks pale, but he breathes regularly. We need a strong man here. He can replace my dead son, Tudor. My grandson needs a father, and Ildeko needs a husband, but he will not remain here for too long; we are poor people.* "Five wounds. You tended them well." *But what are they afraid of?* she repeated. *The Wanderers always have ulterior motives.*

"I am a healer, and so you are. He has lost a lot of blood, and he has also lost his memory."

Frowning, the old woman looked at Thais, but said nothing. In fact, she was only four years older than the Wanderer, but a much harder life made her look ten years older. And she had seen many things in her life.

"He no longer knows who he is, but before losing his memory, he mentioned the name Marcus. That was the only word I heard from him. Once he is up, he may act like a small child who needs to learn how to speak, but he will learn fast. His mind is mature. His body is strong. The discrepancy between knowledge and body strength may create some problems, in the beginning. You must be careful."

Then he may stay with us after all. At least for a while. "That could be the name of his father or brother."

"I asked him his name." *You must use that name, just to let me to know who I have to look for him later. And using his own name may hinder the effect of the potion and help him to keep some memories. It will spoil my plan. It will attract unwanted attention.*

"The name of his horse is Zor," Iantha said from an impulse. She bit her lip, and glanced at Thais, who smiled, nodding to encourage her; there would be a small link between Codrin's past and future.

I like the name of the horse more, but I can't call a man by a horse's name. "Help us put him in a bed," Pireska said, and they worked together to carry Codrin inside the house.

"When Marcus wakes up, make him walk; it will help with the healing, and he may relearn how to walk faster. There may be some traces of memory left in him. Unused, they will vanish. Goodbye, Pireska, Ildeko," Thais said and mounted her horse.

How does she know our names? Pireska thought, looking at the two Wanderers riding toward the forest. When they vanished from sight, she returned to her house and sat close to Codrin, on the edge of the bed. "It's strange, but I have the feeling that I will like you, that you are a good man, and that you will care for my family. My aunt was a Wanderer, and there is some White Light in me. There is an aura of mystery around you. I feel it; it clings to you like a shroud. There is pride too. You are not a soldier; you are a man of power. It's written on your face, or I have become blind. A Knight, perhaps. I wish that my aunt were still alive to help me learn more about you. I don't like that name, Marcus, it's cold, the name of a man without heart. I am not even sure that it is your real name. There was a small spark of Light when the Wanderer said it. Let's call you Tudor, the name of my son. He was a good man. And people will not ask questions; few ever come here, but many know that Ildeko is married to Tudor. My son died nine months ago, killed by that bastard Count. You look strong, and maybe you will avenge my son, not that I really want this; life is more important than dreaming about evil things,"

Pireska said, caressing his hot forehead. She stood up and made a cold poultice of fine blue clay and water, then placed it on his burning skin.

"Will he survive?" Ildeko asked when she entered the house.

"Do you like him?" Pireska glanced up and smiled at the sudden redness on the cheeks of her daughter-in-law. "I think that he will survive and, if everything goes well, you will have a new husband and Ferent a new father. And I will have more grandsons. Children bring happiness and strength to the family. You are my daughter now, Ildeko."

The young woman sat next to Pireska and leaned her head on the other's shoulder. "I miss Tudor."

"Then his name will be Tudor."

Thais's potion kept Codrin unconscious for five days. Its purpose was to block his memories for seven years, but it helped him to heal too, something that the Wanderer was not aware of; the Talant recipe was more advanced than her mind and knowledge could understand; it came from a four-thousand-old book after all and belonged to a more advanced civilization. Codrin's waking was supposed to be gradual, so his memory would be fully blocked. As his body healed faster, he started to turn in his bed, and his elbow pressed into his worst wound. The burst of pain woke him abruptly, and he opened his eyes. It was late in the morning, but he did not know that. Four days had passed since he was wounded.

"You are safe now," Ildeko said in Litvonian, and smiled at him.

Codrin could not understand her, and his sight was blurred, but because of the sudden stimulus coming from the pain and her gentle voice, a spark of consciousness inside his brain raised a barrier against the potion, which worked better on an unconscious mind. He was fluent in four languages. In that moment, his mind clung to the Litvonian like a drowning man to a log and fought to keep it awake. His strong Light helped too. Strangely, Pireska could not feel its presence. He had no control over the fight, and the drug's advance could not be fully stopped, but he became Litvonian now, despite having no memories about it, and what that could have meant. Together with some basic knowledge of the language, a small part of his memories remained available to him, but his mind was not aware of it. Not yet. Even those memories he had to relearn. Codrin fell asleep, without realizing what had happened to him. A day later, he woke up again, and this time it was a natural, unforced process; most of the potion had vanished from his blood. What remained in his brain, was the part that will bring the memory back to him later. He stared at the young woman taking care of him, and tried to shift his body, to push himself up, but he couldn't. He worked his mouth, grunting and moaning, unintelligible words.

"Good morning, Tudor. Do you feel better?" Ildeko asked, wiping his brow with a wet cloth, and he started, then looked at the young woman as if seeing her for the first time.

The name sounded familiar to Codrin and, after a brief indecision, he blinked in acceptance. That familiarity warmed him and opened some links to the part of his memory that was not blocked by the potion. Litvonian words came to him, slowly, as if they were hurting his mind. "What... What ... hmm... What happened?"

"You were wounded."

"You were...?"

Ildeko frowned and turned her head toward the older woman, who nodded before saying, "He has lost his memory, and even the use of language. Don't press him." *The Wanderer told me that he would not remember anything for a few years. It seems she was wrong. That could make our task easier, but he may learn who he is and leave us too fast. We need him for those few years at least, to protect my grandson and Ildeko. I am old, and I am not afraid to die, but they deserve to live. This is a dangerous place, and he is not an ordinary man. Those swords hanging on the wall are good weapons. But how fast will he remember how to fight?*

"You..." Codrin repeated as if he were in a trance and blinked again. "Me...?" He pointed at himself, and the young woman nodded, biting her lip to stop a smile. His was speaking almost like a child, his voice thin, lacking control. She did not know, but that was the voice he had at fifteen.

"Yes, you were wounded," Ildeko repeated, still wiping his brow.

"Wounded... What is ... wounded?"

"This," Ildeko pointed at the bandage over his chest.

Codrin tapped the bandage with his hand and moaned because of the sudden pain. "Wounded," he gasped.

"Don't touch the bandage again, it will hurt you. There is a wound there, made by an arrow." *There are five holes in his body, but I will tell him later.*

"Hurt... Hurt... Pain."

"Yes, a wound gives you pain."

"Pain... What... What hurt you? Me?"

"You are still weak," Pireska interjected abruptly. "Let's eat something."

"Eat..." Codrin said, hesitantly. "Food..."

"Yes, soup." Pireska placed a spoon in Codrin's mouth before he could speak again. After five days of fasting, he was hungry and did not protest. He relearned the taste of soup, and he liked it; Pireska was a good cook. "I am tired. You can take care of him." She pushed the bowl to Ildeko and stifled a smile. She moved away from the bed and sat in her chair, watching how the young woman fed the young man.

I am... Hungry? The repetitive physical activity of eating let Codrin's mind wander free at a snail's pace, the slow crunching movements of his jaws helping to erase the stubborn fog still filling his head. There had been a battle; he remembered a strange mêlée of riders, though he did not remember the proper word to describe or understand what happened. *No*, he shook his head, and some soup ran down his face and neck. Ildeko was quick to wipe it a towel, but said nothing, and he smiled sheepishly. *It was not a... It was not like that. It was like what? Arrow... What is an arrow?* He moaned, even trying to think was painful.

"This is the last spoon," Ildeko said, and Codrin's eyes widened; he was completely lost inside his thoughts. "Now, you have to stand, a little bit of movement will help the healing."

Watching her, Codrin lifted his arm to feel his face, and pain shot through it. He glanced at the bandage on his left shoulder. "Wound." Then at his left upper arm. "Wound." There were two more bandages on his chest. This time, he stayed silent.

"You have five wounds, but only one is bad. This one." Ildeko pointed to the right side of his chest.

"Five..." *Numbers.* "Five..." He looked at the fingers of his right hand and flexed them one by one. *One... Two...* "Five." He stretched all his fingers in front of Ildeko. Then he stretched the fingers of his left hand. *Five... Five... Then?*

"Five," she nodded, and smiled at him. For the first time, he smiled back. Unseen in her corner, Pireska smiled too. "Let me help you," Ildeko said and grasped his palm. With her other hand, she pulled the blanket away and, with both hands, she pulled him up. Codrin did not resist, though he breathed a little faster from the pain.

Standing, he felt dizzy and leaned forward, ready to fall, but Ildeko helped him recover, and placed an arm half around his waist. Their eyes locked, and he felt that something was expected from him. He had no idea what they wanted.

"You need to walk, it will help you heal," Ildeko said, and smiled encouragingly at him.

"Walk..." He frowned. "What is walk?"

"This is walk." Pireska stood up and made a few steps through the room.

Codrin looked at her, then at his body. He was naked, but all social conditioning was erased from his mind, and he did not feel any shame at being naked in front of two women. "Walk... How?"

Pireska looked at him and shook her head. *This is a magnificent man.* She had seen him naked, lying in bed, but standing was a different thing. *He has lean muscles, and some would be tricked by this, but he is a highly trained fighter. Or a killer. What kind of man is he? Was it a mistake to accept him in our house?* She was an experienced healer, and had been to three wars to mend soldiers, in her youth. She had seen few men with such a body, and they were the best warriors. "Like this." Pireska pulled her skirts up, and raised one foot, then put it down three palm's widths in front of her. "Follow me." She raised her left foot and stepped again, then again until she arrived in front of him.

Frowning, Codrin looked at his feet again. Vaguely, he understood what she wanted, but did not know how to do it. Pireska gripped his free arm, then bent and pressed on the back of his right knee with two fingers. Unwillingly, he flexed his foot while she raised it and made him step a palm's width forward. He lost his balance and almost fell, but both women kept him standing. On her side, Ildeko pressed on the back of his left knee. This time, he stepped forward by his own will. He lost his balance again.

"Don't be afraid, we will help you." Pireska gripped his arm, firmly but gently at the same time.

"Afraid... What is ... afraid?"

"It doesn't matter. You will learn many words." Pireska shrugged and pressed again on the back of his knee. He stepped forward. After ten minutes of walking lessons, both women were more tired than Codrin, who seemed to enjoy the learning process. "I think that it's enough for today," she said, wiping her brow, and they helped him sit on the edge of the bed.

"Soup?" Codrin asked, and smiled at them, the smile of a joyful child.

"Soup." Ildeko nodded and burst into laughter. "And four eggs for us. You worked us hard. I wish I could make a steak."

After a week, Codrin was walking with the same confidence and skills as Ferent, Ildeko's six-year-old son. After a month, he was walking like an unstable teenager, but his mind was only two or three years older than Ferent's.

Chapter 8 – Ildeko / Codrin

That day, Ildeko went several times to the cellar, and each time she returned even more worried than before. “I’ve should have done the inventory earlier,” she said to Pireska when she was back in the house.

“Ildeko, you have too many things to do. It doesn’t look good, but we are not yet desperate.”

“You knew that we are low on food.”

“I didn’t want you to worry...”

“Soon, it will be autumn, and we have provisions for less than one month left. Tudor is eating more than I thought. He is eating more than all of us together. I know, he has started to help us with some simple things, he is guarding our hens and geese on the back meadow, but... Well, I am not the best hunter, but I need to go hunting. We need meat. We need to make provisions for the winter. We need to cut enough wood, and that’s hard work for a woman. I can’t cut enough wood to sell in the market. There is no money left. We can’t buy anything. It will be a hard winter.” Ildeko crashed in the chair, and leaning her elbows on the table, she caught her head between her palms, trying to hide her tears. “I don’t know if I can do it. To cut enough wood for a whole winter. We are tough women, but Ferent is so young. He won’t survive the cold.”

“He will. Soon, Tudor will be able to help you, and you are stronger than you think.” Pireska’s voice was sharp and unyielding.

"I can't put an ax in Tudor's hands. Remember how bad he cut himself with that knife. Well," she sighed, "we still have time to think about gathering wood, but tomorrow, I will go hunting."

"Be reasonable, it's dangerous for a lone woman. There are wolves and bears out there, and even worse, there are men. Bad men like those who killed my son. One glimpse of you, and they will stop their hunt and chase you like beasts. You are a woman who attracts a man's eye. If they see Tudor, they will leave you alone. Look at him," she pointed through the window; he was running toward the house. "He is strong and tall. They will keep some distance from such an unknown quantity. He looks dangerous."

"We need food."

The door sprang open suddenly, Ferent and Codrin running into the house, laughing like any other playing children of Ferent's age. Seeing Ildeko's face, Ferent stopped abruptly, and that made Codrin bump into him, sending the child down onto the floor; he was still not fully conscious of his strength or reflexes. At six, Ferent was beginning to know how to read his mother, and he understood that something bad was happening. She had red eyes from crying. Last time she had those red eyes, he had lost his father, nine months ago. He jumped to his feet, and ran to embrace her, placing his head on her chest. Accustomed to following Ferent, Codrin came closer too and stopped abruptly behind him. Frowning, he looked at the embracing mother and son, Pireska's eyes tight on him. There was something vague in his mind, a blurred trace of a memory from his childhood, and something in his heart that he could not understand. With a sudden impulse, he took both in his long arms. By instinct, he squeezed them gently, without breaking their bones. Stirred by emotions he had not felt since his father died, Ferent was comforted, but Ildeko froze, unable to speak. Through instinct, again, Codrin felt her uneasiness, and gently, without knowing why, he started to stroke her hair, and pulled her head on his chest. Unwillingly, Ildeko placed one arm around his waist, and Ferent felt happy, sandwiched between them, as had happened many times in the past, when his father was still alive. They were a happy family. Hearing Codrin's strong heartbeats calmed Ildeko, and she leaned against him. She was still at a loss for words.

"See, Mother," Ferent said in a cheerful voice, "We are good. No need to cry."

"Yes, we are good," Codrin echoed, without knowing why, but something strange was passing through his body. It felt pleasant in a weird way. It felt vaguely familiar too. He leaned his head over Ildeko's, and this time she did not freeze. He also wanted to call her mother, as Ferent did, but in some corner of his mind he knew the truth, though he was not consciously aware of it.

Tudor is acting like a child, Ildeko thought. *But it has calmed us... Under his childish mind, there must be some traces of sensibility still alive in him. He seems to be a kind man. He wants to help. Well,* she shook her head*, I am putting too much of my own desires in one incidental act.*

It was Pireska who broke the strange silence, and she coughed to gather her voice before saying, "It's time to eat."

At dawn, unseen, Ildeko left her room with the first light. In the storage area, she prepared her quiver and tested the bow that once belonged to her husband. Hers had been destroyed in the fight. At least she had to pay a lesser price, to stay alive for her son, but a week later, when Count Irvath let her go, almost unconscious and naked, she felt both dirty and mournful. She still remembered Irvath's words: "I hope you survive. The only reason I left you alive is because I want you in my bed again. Next time you will be more eager to please me; if not, I will kill your son." Her body was blue from the beatings and rapes. Irvath's wife, Elsebeth, a woman with a winter's cold beauty and even more vicious than her husband, raped her too, late in the night, after the men were gone. Sometimes the Countess played a gentle game, sometimes she was wild and liked to grope and hit her with a belt at the same time. Elsebeth enjoyed pressing a woman's head between her legs, and Ildeko was forced to do wicked thing with her mouth. She had to do them. She was buying the life of her son. In the end, the Countess stirred a storm in the castle, after *learning* that her husband had a new mistress. Ildeko was thrown out, dressed only in her boots while many men were ogling at her. It was freezing that day. Ildeko was lucky that an old man took her into his house, after one mile of walking naked through the snow. It was the image of her son that kept her walking and walking. And it was the Countess who ordered the old man to take the almost frozen woman in his house, but Ildeko did not know that.

Thoughtfully, Ildeko flexed the bow with skilled fingers. *It's a bit too strong for me, but I will manage. Soon, I will make another bow. I was lazy; it should have been done already. I am not good at making bows, maybe I should ask... I have no money; he will ask to spread my legs. I am not a whore.* She turned to leave the house and found Pireska in the doorway.

"Old women sleep lightly," Pireska said, her voice seeming cold and distant.

Ildeko walked fast and embraced her. "Sorry for not listening to you, but I have to go. I need to feed my child, to feed us. We are already eating less to have more food for Ferent and Tudor."

"I asked Tudor to be ready for a trip in the forest."

"No, he is too ... young-minded."

"Listen to me." Pireska took the young woman's hands between hers. "During the night, there was a spark of Light. I don't know exactly why, but I have the feeling that he *must* come with you. Please." She gripped Ildeko's hands strongly, trying to instill her will in her daughter-in-law, who she considered her own daughter. "And there is something more. I have followed Codrin these last few days; his reactions are bloody fast, and he is intelligent." *I followed him from that day when he embraced you and Ferent. That was another trigger, for a different kind of thing. Perhaps...*

"But he doesn't know what to do. Last time, he almost cut the tendon of his left arm with my dagger. It happened fast indeed. I can't say if it was an intelligent thing."

"Three days ago, a large boar invaded the backyard of the farm. You were away, and I did not want to scare you. It's not a big deal, we handle boars all the time, but Ferent and Codrin found themselves in front of him – I was inside the house and saw it too late. Sensing they were frightened and weak, the beast charged. Ferent cried and started to run. He was too slow. In a split second, Codrin lifted him with one arm, ran and threw him onto a branch in the cherry tree, which was some thirty feet away. He did that by instinct, and he ran faster than the boar, then climbed the tree in a moment. I think that his mind wants to grow faster, but it needs challenges. I don't know why. Sometimes, we wake up an unconscious man by burning strong resin in front of his nose, slapping his face, splashing cold water... Tudor needs a different splash: danger. I know; it's just a feeling."

"And if we meet a bear? They are aggressive now."

"His mind is better than it was a month ago, but still diminished, yet there are some instincts in his body, I think that he will manage something." *Or at least I hope so*.

In the small hall, they found Codrin pacing back and forth, a wide smile on his lips. He was already dressed in new clothes Pireska had adapted from her son's. She needed two pieces to make one for Codrin, who was so tall and broad in the shoulders. Ildeko looked at him and sighed.

"We are going into the forest." Codrin's voice was filled with childish expectation. "Where is Ferent?"

"He is not coming," Ildeko said. "He is too young."

"Young?" Codrin frowned.

"He is too ... small, we need to walk fast. There are wolves and bears out there."

"Small." He nodded. "I want to see a bear."

"No, you don't. Now listen to me carefully. You will stay close to me, and don't comment when I give an order."

"Yes, I will stay close." Codrin nodded enthusiastically, ready for an exciting adventure, and followed her outside.

Hiding behind a dense bush at the edge of the large rock overseeing the meadow, Ildeko placed her quiver and bow on the ground.

"What are you doing?" Codrin asked.

"We are here to hunt. See?" She pointed down at the herd of deer grazing two hundred paces away from them.

"Do you want to kill them all?"

"No, one is enough to feed us for a month."

"I don't like to kill them."

"We need to eat. People eat deer, hens. You like hen's meat, aren't you? I want that young stag on the right, but we must wait until they come closer. I can't shoot that far."

"What is stag?"

"A young male. Look at his horns; they are much smaller than the ones of the large stag on the left." She pulled three arrows from the quiver and placed them in front of her, on the warm stone.

Codrin looked at the arrows for a few moments, closed his eyes, and a dark shadow passed over his face. Ildeko saw it, but she said nothing, keeping an eye on him. "What are these things?" He pointed at the arrows. "I have bad feelings. I feel pain." Unwillingly, he stretched his arm to take an arrow, and Ildeko slapped his hand.

"Arrows. Don't touch them."

Codrin pushed her hand away and grabbed the arrow. He raised it fast and scratched her hand. He didn't notice. The arrow both fascinated and repulsed him. "Arrow," he said, using an almost adult voice for the first time.

"Put it down, slowly."

Codrin did not listen and pressed a finger on the tip of the arrow. The sharp iron cut him, but he did not react, just rubbed the blood between his fingers. "Arrows hurt..." He rubbed his fingers harder. "Arrows hunt..." His voice trembled a little. Without realizing what he was doing, he grabbed the bow. Ildeko tried to stop him, but he just turned his back to her, nocked the bow and shot almost without aiming. The arrow pierced the neck of the young stag. "Arrows kill..." he whispered and started to shake, dropping the bow, and falling onto his knees, crying. "It hurts..." His nervous fingers massaged his chest on the right, over the scar of the arrow wound that had almost killed him.

"Shh," Ildeko said. She took his head in her hands, pressed it against her chest, and he still cried, embracing her waist.

That night, Codrin went to bed with a high fever and slept badly. Pireska watched him all night, placing cold poultices on his burning forehead and chest. From time to time, images came to him, disparate strings of memories from his past life. It was a strange thing, but there were almost no people in his memories, only landscapes, and old things from when he was a child. And those few people were strangers that he had seen in his travels, sometimes only for a few minutes. Only once, he had the blurred image of a girl, who was turning fast, her hands glowing white. It was the last view of his twin sister before she was killed by their uncle, but he did not know that. It was only that blurred image and her name whispered in his mind. "Ioana..." He gasped in his sleep, and turned violently in his bed, throwing Pireska to the floor.

She said nothing, just stood up and massaged her bottom, then gripped his restless hand between hers. After a while, he clung to her palms and stayed motionless. "I still don't know if it was a good thing to send you to hunt, Tudor. It will heal a part of your mind, but I am afraid that the healing may hurt you even more. I have never treated such wounds..." She touched his forehead, and found that his fever had diminished, then stretched her mind for some traces of Light. Pireska could have been a Wanderer, if not for her brother. He hated the order and jailed her in a cave just before their aunt came to take her for training. She was kept prisoner for two years, and when her aunt finally freed her, it was too late to be trained. She never forgave her brother and hated him as much as he hated her; she had a reason, but that pitiful man had only bad feelings and stupidity. For years, she wanted to kill him, but her aunt forbade it, because she felt there was a purpose in what had happened. Pireska had cursed her *purpose,* but she was accustomed to listening to her aunt, who was the Seventh Light of Litvonia at that time. She spent her youth wandering across Litvonia and Silvania. During her mid-twenties, she found this house, and the man who became her husband. Four years ago, she had lost him to an arrow. Their region was dangerous, but they had nowhere else to go, even after the death of her son.

The door opened, and Ildeko came in. She looked at Codrin in the low light and found him sleeping like a child. "You must be tired, mother. Go to sleep, it's almost morning, and I am rested now. I can take over."

"No Ildeko, I need to stay and see all his reactions. My healing knowledge is limited in such issues, but I may be able to make a potion. Sometimes, a treatment for one disease may be good for another. It depends on symptoms and ... and on your guess."

"Tudor ... my husband... I feel strange using the same name for both... Why did you choose this name for him?" She gestured at Codrin.

"I don't really know. It was a feeling. There is something that I did not tell you. The women who brought him here, were Wanderers, and this man," she mimicked Ildeko's gesture, pointing at Codrin, "is not a commoner. They did not know that, or they lied to us."

"Mother, I may be young, but... His swords are unusual. His horse is unusual. His clothes are unusual. They are expensive things. And there are many old scars on his skin, despite his youth. He may be from Arenia, as the women said, but he speaks Litvonian too. He did not learn it from us. There was a book in his bag. It is written in Frankis. He is educated." Ildeko was educated too; the daughter of a wealthy merchant, she spoke Litvonian and Frankis fluently, and like most people living close to the Silvanian border, she knew Silvanian too. Both women knew how to read and write. Her father's caravan was attacked during one of the many local wars in the area, and all her relatives were killed. Ildeko was only fifteen and wounded too, and only Pireska's healing skills saved her life. From that day, she stayed in their house and grew up with their son who, later, became her husband. "I don't know where this will lead us, but..." She shrugged and passed a hand through her hair. "My husband was a good hunter, and there are only two or three men better than him in the county. But ... he would not have been able to make that shot. This ... Tudor, did not even aim, he just released the arrow. It hit the stag in the neck at two hundred feet. Then he fell into a trance, crying. At the end, he was like a stone, unfeeling. When I told him to carry the stag, he carried it. I told him to walk; he walked. I told him to stop; he stopped. There was no will in him. You were right that the hunt was important, but we must learn why, and why was he so affected."

"Perhaps we will learn. We will not try anything else for a while. I don't like to see him like this. Go to sleep now."

Close to the morning, half awake, Codrin had a Vision, though he did not know what it was. For him it felt like a strange dream. There were two sad women in his Vision. Their names, Saliné and Jara, told him nothing.

"You must become the Queen of both Frankis and Litvonia. There is no other way," Jara said at the end, and the image vanished from his mind.

Feeling that something strange and important was happening, Pireska watched him closely during his Vision; she gaped, pressing a hand to her mouth. *He has the Light.* She almost fainted from the shock, and gripped the edge of the bed, to stop her body falling. *Men don't have the Light*. When she recovered, she placed her palm on his forehead. "You can't hear me, but maybe the Light will carry my words to you. You are an important man, and your place is not here; but when you leave, please take Ildeko and Ferent with you. Make her a servant, or whatever you want, but save them. I will not bother you and die here in peace, knowing that you took care of them." She retracted her hand, and a few stray tears ran down her face.

In the morning, Codrin still remembered some parts of the Vision, but the dream was too strange, the women were unknown to him and, slowly, everything fell back to a lower level of his mind. During the following days, Codrin did not speak, or play with Ferent; he just ate and sat under the cherry tree in the backyard, holding an arrow in his hand, looking nowhere. The tree attracted him, though he had no memories of the time spent with Saliné under a much larger one, in the garden of Cernat's hunting house in Severin. Each day brought several new scratches on his hand, from playing with the arrow, but he ignored them, and Pireska took care of them, but she did not try to stop him playing with the weapon. A realignment took place in his mind that not even Pireska was aware of. It brought sadness and pain to him and, sometimes, he took his head between his hands and moaned. Pireska gave him some potions for the pain, but they had little effect.

During his seventh day of illness, Ildeko did not have time to gather wood from the forest, and she tried to split some old logs for the evening fire. They were thick, hard and irregular; she had already used up the easy ones. Codrin watched her for a while, then stood up and approached her, watching the movements of her ax, up and down. "Let me try," he said, and Ildeko turned, started by his sudden appearance. Their eyes locked, and he sensed her worry. "I will be careful. Just let me try."

Silent, she passed him the ax, and he examined it for a while. The thing felt strange and clumsy, but his hand did not feel much weight; it was like a large toy to him. He slid a finger along the edge and tested its sharpness, then mimicked hitting a log. After the fifth attempt, he picked up a log, and placed it in a vertical position on the chopping block. Unstable, the log fell even before he was able to raise the ax. Ildeko stayed silent, afraid of disturbing him. He tried again. The log fell again. Breathing deeply, he closed his eyes and recalled how Ildeko did it. She kept the log in place with one hand, before letting the ax fall. *It's dangerous...* He would have liked to let it go but, for the first time in his new life, he felt ashamed, and he wanted to help her. Tense, he placed the log again, and kept it standing with his left hand.

"Try to mime the hit first. Like you did in the beginning."

Keeping his left hand on the log, he swung the ax up and down, several times. When he felt confident, Codrin let it fall on the log, retracting his left hand at the same time. The blade chopped out a small splinter and sent the log flying.

"The first time I tried, I was no better," Ildeko said. "Try to hit the center. This is oak wood and splits easier through the center."

At the third attempt, he hit the center, but it was a weak blow, and the ax remained stuck in the log.

"Don't try to pull it out. Lift the ax and hit the chopping block with the log. Don't hit too hard."

Codrin did as she said, and the log finally split in two. In two hours, he split half of the wood in the warehouse. The heavy tool felt light in his hand, and he was not tired at the end. He was elated that he could do new things to help Ildeko and Pireska. Carrying some wood into the house, he realized that his headache was gone. Pireska watched him; he was walking now with the confidence of an adult man, but the next day, he still acted like a child, but no longer an eight-year-old boy. Ferent was the only other *man* in the house, and Codrin, not having any adult memories, was still imitating him. He had to create his own path toward adulthood.

The next day, Pireska took Codrin to see his swords. He looked at them with no visible reaction. The things were strange to him.

"Touch one of them," Pireska said, and he obeyed. It happened that he picked Flame, his short sword. Perhaps things would have moved smoother if he had chosen to touch Shadow, his sentient sword. Sometimes, Fate was capricious.

A week later, Ildeko took Codrin to cut hay. They had a huge workhorse and a cow, and Zor needed food for the winter too. There were many meadows around; it was only the amount of hard work which bothered her. They had two scythes with them, and the longer one belonged to her dead husband. Walking together sent Ildeko's mind back to the past when she still had a full family. She shook her head, trying to escape the sudden invasion of longing memories. She had a child to raise and could not afford weakness.

"Look at me," she said, and moved to cut the grass slowly, so he could understand and learn. It was not an easy skill to learn.

Codrin watched her, and frowned for a few moments, looking at the tool in his hands. Then he started to use it. His movements were fluid, nothing like when he had learned how to cut wood. Her eyes wide, Ildeko looked at him, unable to understand. She did not know that he had learned to make hay in the autumn he spent in Vlad's and Pintea's farm. Neither did he.

Chapter 9 - Saliné

The riders were in a hurry. Late in the evening, they had to wait patiently until the guards opened the postern and gave them a long look. They were known in Loxburg, and the main gate opened too. The riders rode like a storm, through the narrow streets, scraping sparks from the old cobblestones, the metallic noise chafing the nerves of a rather peaceful city, echoing between the walls. Scared by the horses, the few people walking on the streets leaned hastily back against the walls, and cursed, too afraid to move away from the walls; curses were safe to throw at hurrying riders, who could not hear them. At the castle, Iulius showed his Itinerant Sage conduct and was allowed to enter without his two guards. "I know the way," he said to the gatekeeper.

"Do you have news?" the man asked, hesitantly.

"I was supposed to bring the news directly to Duke Manuc, but... The nomads were defeated. It was something you might see once in a lifetime, or a few lifetimes. A sea of nomad dogs running home, tails between their legs. It was bloody too. I never saw so much blood flowing, the land was sparkling ruby into the sun, like the devil's wine, but more than seventy thousand soldiers died there. Mostly theirs, but we had losses too."

"Ah," the gatekeeper breathed with relief. "The King is a great man." His voice was sparkling now, stirred by an itch of desire to see that blood, and the running nomad dogs.

"Yes, he is. Keep the news to yourself, the Duke will want to make the announcement." Without waiting for an answer, Iulius walked away, but instead of going to meet the Duke, he went to a small suite reserved for important guests, where two women were waiting. The guards let him enter. Inside, the women were having dinner, and both turned at the same time when the door opened. They frowned at first, then they smiled. "Ladies," he bowed. "I almost killed the horse under me, and I am not in much better shape, but..." He breathed long and slow on purpose, keeping them guessing. "The nomads were defeated."

"Oh, Iulius, don't be so theatrical," Drusila, the First Light of the Frankis Wanderers, said. "We already know that. My Visions travel faster than your poor horse. So?" She looked at him with a stare that could freeze a man, but the Sage was too experienced to be frightened. Or perhaps he was, just a little.

"He is dead. Thais, the Third Light of Litvonia confirmed that to us."

"Go and tell the Duke about the nomads, then take time to rest," Maud, the second woman in the room and the Master Sage of the Circle, said. "You must be tired. There is a room and food waiting for you. One of the guards at the door will lead you there. Yes, my sister knew that you would arrive today." She waited patiently until her Sage went out of the room and turned toward Drusila. "I am not particularly proud about this ... event."

"Neither am I, my dear, but sometimes there are higher imperatives, and we were not involved in his death."

"Once we agreed to the plan..."

"We were *not* involved in his death. It doesn't really matter. We can start the next phase, toward the peaceful union between Frankis and Litvonia; one step closer to rebuilding the Empire. That's precisely the reason for which the Wanderer Order was founded, by the Last Empress. And no history book will record our work." Drusila shrugged and raised her glass. "To Codrin. He was a great man. It's strange, but I will miss him. Well, why should be that strange? We were born to serve the Realm, not a particular man, however great he was. I will still miss him." She sighed, looking at her glass, which trembled a little in her deep veined hand, stirring ripples into the red wine.

Maud raised her glass too, before saying, "To Codrin." There was a long moment of silence, each woman avoiding the eyes of the other. "We have to handle Saliné now. It will not be easy. My past attempts at taming her failed..."

"No, it will not be easy, but after a while, she will understand the importance of this new ... future. The net we have started to weave at the court in Arad should serve its purpose. It's a fine mesh, and each line will tighten around her at the right time. We will leave in the morning. In six or seven days, we should be in Arad. Eh," Drusila shrugged, "we are no longer fit for riding. Soon, I may no longer be fit for traveling in a carriage either. The news about Codrin will arrive there before us, and Saliné will be in a state of mind that will make her softening easier." She sipped some wine and frowned at a string of odd memories. "You know, when Calista, the Second Light of Litvonia, wrote to me about this plan, I threw her letter into the garbage. It was the month before our army left Arad for Litvonia. In the morning, I went to take it back. I was lucky that it did not leave the house. Night is a good counselor, and I realized that her plan might succeed, and there would be a bloodless unification. Well, apart from Codrin, but there will be no more wars, and they usually kill more than one man and a few guards. This was..." Drusila pressed her teeth on her lower lip. "This was the hardest decision I had to take in my whole life. There were two things I did not tell you. We could not see a future for the Empire Codrin and Saliné were building. Their son is weak, and he will die in his late thirties, with no children. That would have stirred a civil war and ruined everything."

"Their son... Is Codrin his father? There were some developments in Laurden, when Saliné spent that winter..." *When she escaped from my net.* Maud shook her head, trying to avoid an avalanche of old, bitter memories.

"Yes, he is Codrin's son. I had several Visions about that. There was another Vision about a second child, a daughter, but she would have died a toddler. Something did not ... work well between Saliné and Codrin. Two strong people, two weak children." Drusila stayed silent for a while, trying to bring together some disparate strings of thought. For the hundredth time. She failed again. "We don't know what, but it happens sometimes that great people make terrible children. The next thing: Calista's plans concerned Silvania too; that woman has a sharp, organized mind. If everything goes well, in five years the largest three western kingdoms will be reunited under a new Emperor. Frankis will diminish, and the Litvonian Wanderers and Circle will oversee the Empire, but I can live with that."

"And Arenia?"

"That will be a much tougher nut to crack. Codrin would have helped bring Arenia into the fold, but we can't switch kings like toys, and he was not a man to sideline. I may not live long enough to see the full unification of the continent. You are younger..." Drusila fell suddenly silent.

In the morning, before leaving Loxburg, Maud called Iulius to her room, and gave him a small vial. "You will stay here. You know what to do. It should happen three weeks from now."

A week later, they arrived in Arad in the evening, and went to the Council Room. Three years earlier, Codrin had surprised them, and made both women part of his council; they were the First Light and the Master Sage after all. But he did not make them part of the Council of the Realm. Drusila knew that of course, but Maud was not aware of it, and her sister kept it to herself. Sometimes, Maud could be too proud, and that was not politically wise. Not with a King like Codrin. They bowed to a pale Saliné, longer than usual, and waited until she gestured for them to have a seat. There was no need for words. Drusila took a sideways look at Idonie, who was sitting next to Jara. She could never forgive the woman for leaving the Wanderers, but she was more afraid of her strong Light; it could interfere in the new plans for the Realm.

The couriers had arrived in Arad the day before; Vlaicu, the Spatar of Frankis, had delayed sending them for a week, still hoping to find Codrin; they had not found his body. There were other bodies; the twenty soldiers guarding Codrin were all dead, all killed by arrows. Each day, two thousand riders from Frankis combed the northeast of Litvonia, still hoping. When the couriers arrived in Arad, Vlad's scouts were still searching in Litvonia.

The council continued, and there was a sort of slowness in everyone's reaction, as if time were dilated, but the kingdom still had to be governed. Both Drusila and Maud stayed silent up to the end, when Drusila coughed to claim their attention before saying, "These are not normal times, and we must be more cautious than usual. The Litvonian King is an ambitious man. His ambition and interest may extend into Frankis now."

"We took this into consideration, and Vlaicu was instructed to return with most of the army. Vlad and five hundred scouts will stay behind to ... continue the search." Except for a small wobble at the end, Saliné's voice was calm and controlled; the tone of a commander in a battle.

She is moving fast... "That was good thinking, your majesty." Drusila bowed and signaled that she wanted a private conversation at the end of the council.

"If there is nothing else," Saliné said, and nodded toward Drusila to stay, then waited until everyone else left the room before asking, her voice hastening with each word, "Do you have news? A Vision? Our scouts could not find him. We still hope."

What is in Calista's mind? Codrin's body should already have been sent here. There will be legal complications if we don't have the body. Drusila waited for a few moments before saying, in a low voice, "The news I have is not good. In my Vision, the King was wounded by arrows. I can't say how many." Drusila had had no Vision about what happened, but she knew from Iulius that two companies of archers were sent to kill Codrin. There was also the strange thing that each time she summoned the White Light, she was not able to have a Vision about Codrin's body, and she was a strong Wanderer, able to gain glimpses of the future when she was concentrating on a certain subject. This kind of forced Vision never revealed something important, but all she needed now was a glimpse of a corpse, even a rotten one, and a place.

Significant Visions came at their own will, and the Wanderers could not control them.

"Yes, all his guards were killed by arrows. We think that maybe the nomads took him prisoner."

"I don't want to give you false expectations. The nomads take prisoners, yes, but only young women and men to be made slaves. They don't take soldiers, and you can be sure their mission was to kill the King."

"Then?"

"In my Vision," Drusila sighed, "he was caught with one leg in the stirrup, and Zor was galloping. He was not ... moving."

"I see," Saliné said, her voice controlled; through her Light, she felt that something about what she was hearing was false, but there was nothing more useful in that feeling. "Tomorrow, we will have a new council. Pierre, the former Spatar of Tolosa, and Grandfather will make plans for ... any situation. A summons will be sent to the Duke of Loxburg. We need every good mind here."

The courier may arrive too soon in Loxburg and derail our plans. We'll see. "Yes, it's a good strategy to be one step ahead."

"I imagine that you are tired from the road."

"Well, I am no longer a young woman." Drusila stood up and took a few steps before turning. "Your majesty," she said with studied calm, her voice warm and soothing, "you need not punish yourself, or hold back sorrow. The kingdom is stable and has good men to stand for the Queen. It is all right to mourn."

Saliné nodded quietly, and no reaction could be seen on her face. *But I am mourning, Drusila, each moment I am mourning. There is no need for you to know that.* Alone, Saliné went stiff suddenly, and her face lost that hard-won composure. She leaned back against the chair. For a long moment she remained rigid and motionless, then she made a harsh, unnatural sound, as if something had been torn in her throat, and tears ran down her face. *Why are you trying to raise the pressure on me, Drusila?*

The army returned to Arad, the soldiers in sour mood and, for a while, they camped around the city. Their return after victory felt like a defeat. Some days passed, then a week, then two without bad news from the border, and Vlaicu started to send them home, but he still kept three thousand soldiers on duty.

Drusila came to Saliné's office, and after some banal exchange of words, she said abruptly: "I have a bad feeling, but no Vision yet."

"The Litvonians?" Saliné asked and closed her eyes for a few moments. "There have been no incidents at the border. Yet."

"The best time to strike is when your opponent is not aware, and we cannot keep our army forever around Arad."

"No, we can't. Can you force a Vision?" *Why can't I have Visions anymore?* It was a strange thing that all her past Visions involved Bucur, and after his death, nothing else came to her. She still had the Light, and her skills of reading people through it evolved, but there were no more Visions.

"I am trying, but my powers seem somehow diminished after the Seer's death."

Saliné flinched inside at the old Wanderer's words, but nothing transpired on her face.

"There is something else." Drusila made a brief pause as if searching for words. "I think that it is the right time for your majesty to know. Before the battle with the nomads, the burden of the Seer was taken from the King."

"The Empress... She left him alone in the battle."

"The King won the battle."

"And she let him be killed. Or kidnapped," she added quickly, without believing it.

"The Empress doesn't interfere in such ways, but..." Drusila made a brief pause again, "there may be a sort of realignment in the long-term plans for Frankis."

"Like Litvonia conquering Frankis," Saliné said, bitterly.

"Litvonia is stronger, but not strong enough to take Frankis. I wish I could provide more information, but I am afraid that I have only this vague feeling that something will happen, and we have to be prepared."

"Well, we have to live with what we have," Saliné said flatly, and nodded to the old woman that the audience was over. *The Wanderers always have ulterior motives.* She shook her head in anger, looking at Drusila walking away. *Should I send her away from Arad?* "Let's go to the council now; it seems that Iulius has come with some news from Loxburg." They walked together to the Council Room, both women silent and thoughtful.

"Your majesty, the Duke Manuc of Loxburg died in his bed of old age." Iulius bowed and gave Saliné the letter from the Secretary of Loxburg.

From his chair, Verenius had a brief, intense look at him, yet nothing could be read on Iulius's face. There was something that had raised a question mark, a feeling of repetition, but Verenius, while still being the Primus Itinerant, had been sidelined in the Circle's affairs by Maud. He had helped Codrin against her. She could not forget that. Or forgive, even when she gave Verenius the credit for unifying Frankis. It was a matter of trust.

"We've lost a great man," Saliné said after reading the letter. "Sava and Julien will represent the King and me at the funeral. It's in seven days from now."

"We will leave as soon as it's possible," Sava said. "If we ride hard, we can be there in three days. I was only fourteen when I met Manuc for the first time. He was still young, and it was a pleasure to witness his sword and speech duels with Duke Stefan of Peyris. Even strong men like them wither and leave us at some point."

Both Dukes left us at a very precise moment, Verenius thought. *Stefan was poisoned when they wanted to give Peyris to Bucur, to help him defeat Codrin. We have a crisis again. Something is rotten. With Codrin dead, those two foxes, Maud and Drusila, smelled blood, and perhaps some kind of revenge. They are trying to be less visible in the council. Drusila and Maud acting ... shy, that's a contradiction in terms. There is something that I am missing.*

"Yes," Saliné nodded at Sava, a lump in her throat. "Do we have other news?"

"The borders are quiet." Sava threw an encouraging look at her. As most of other captains had joined Codrin in Litvonia, he was left behind as the Spatar of the Kingdom, and it would take some time until Vlaicu would understand everything that had happened when he was away.

It was raining hard when Edric and his army crossed the bridge over the Rhiun into Frankis. Five thousand Hussars from Silvania had joined his army, and he had twelve thousand heavy cavalry, the hard men who had passed through the nomads as if they were toys. There were no foot soldiers in the army; Edric was in a hurry. Behind him and his guards, a carriage carried Calista, the Second Light of Litvonia, and Klavis, the Litvonian Chancellor, a sixty-five-year-old man, Chief of the Litvonian Circle, and the King's uncle.

In Arad, the council was gathered in haste. Vlad presented what the scouts had given him and placed the document on the table. "They have fifty thousand men, twelve thousand of them heavy cavalry, Teutons and Hussars. It seems that Silvania has joined Alfrid against us."

Pierre took his time to read it and pinched the bridge of his nose between thumb and forefinger before saying, "Autumn is upon us, and they will arrive here in two or perhaps more weeks. We have enough time to gather most of the army, perhaps only twenty thousand soldiers, too few to fight in open field. Anyway, it's hard to fight against heavy cavalry. A trap would help, but there are no good places on the road from Rhiun to Arad."

"Heavy cavalry doesn't work well against the walls of Arad, and Poenari is even stronger," Sava said.

"Yes, we will let them fight the walls. We will hit and run, the strategy Codrin used to rout me at the siege of Poenari. Sieges can be made long and bloody, and winter will come soon. It's hard to understand why they did not wait to invade in spring." Pierre stood up and looked at the map on the wall behind Saliné. After Codrin, he was the most experienced commander in Frankis, but he was now too old to lead an army into battle.

"They hope to find us disorganized, and perhaps some people from Frankis have already moved into their camp," Verenius said, struggling not to look at Maud and Drusila, yet they both stared at him. That did not escape Saliné. It did not escape Verenius either.

"What if we try a diplomatic approach?" Drusila asked quickly, before someone could react to Verenius's words. "We still don't know why they came."

"Is it so hard to figure?" Saliné asked. "They want Frankis."

"How? As Pierre said, Arad's strong walls and the coming winter are our allies. If we know what they want, we can prepare better. Let's send an embassy to their army. I am ready to go."

Saliné closed her eyes for a while. *She may be right about sending an embassy, but not her.* "Thank you, Drusila, but it's a long road. Cantemir will go. Pierre, Foy, can you go too?"

"I am not that old, your majesty," Pierre said, with a warm smile on his lips.

"If this old man can ride to see Alfrid's moustache, then why should I stay home?" Foy, the Seigneur of Laurden said through the general laughter. It was a sort of forced reaction, but everybody tried to play their own part to raise morale. Even Saliné smiled, her lips wry, a touch of sadness still visible on her face.

"When should they leave?" Drusila asked, struggling to look uninterested.

"When I consider that it's the right time," Saliné said, without looking at her.

"Of course, your majesty." Drusila bowed slightly. *Too much delay, and things may go sour for everybody. Everything hangs on a thin thread.*

Lost in inner thoughts, Saliné heard her answer without really taking it in, and she frowned before saying, "We owe a great debt to Manuc, but I can't send Sava to his funeral now. You were supposed to leave tomorrow. Cantemir, send the Second Secretary with Julien. Give them a fifty strong escort."

Three days of forced riding through the drizzle brought the Litvonian army to occupy the Tri Cross, where the main roads from Loxburg and Peyris met the one going from the border to Arad. Without knowing it, they followed the same road Codrin had taken on his arrival in Frankis, so many years ago. Comfortably seated in his large tent, Edric raised a glass of wine to his aunt, Calista. "So far, so good. Any news from the Frankis Wanderers and the Circle?"

"Don't act like a hasty child. These things have a pace of their own. The Wanderers can't send anyone until some sort of talks happen. The Circle's liaison will be here soon, perhaps even tomorrow. And our most important guest too."

"They did not send yet an embassy to salute us; Saliné seems to be ... stubborn, yet I can't wait to meet her."

"I doubt that someone can be more stubborn than you. She is one of the most intelligent women in both Frankis and Litvonia. We will not have an easy ride here."

"That will make things even more pleasant." Edric laughed, and stretched his long legs, then his whole body, like an animal just awake. "We occupy the most important military point in north-east Frankis. Arad's communication with Loxburg and the Seigneuries will be delayed. I will wait a few days and send messages to all the Seigneurs in the area to pay allegiance to Litvonia or else..."

"You will send them only after the Circle's liaison comes."

"Of course, dear aunt," Edric grinned. "I am a man who likes to collaborate with the enemy. If they betray my other enemy."

"Don't be childish." Calista slapped the back of his head but smiled. "The Circle's allegiance is to the Realm, they are betraying no one. And Saliné is not our enemy."

"Would you say the same, if Codrin were still alive and marching with his army into Litvonia, waiting for the Circle's ... liaison?"

"Of course, the Wanderers are working for the Realm too, but the thing is that ... he is there *without an army* while we are here *with an army*. In such games, once the snowball is rolling, you don't try to stop it, you ride it. It's a savage horse, I warn you." She frowned for a while and stayed silent. "I am still worried that we could not find Codrin's body." *Why can't I have a Vision about him?* Calista was a powerful Wanderer, even stronger than Drusila, only Dochia and Aliana were more powerful than her.

"Food for the wolves." Edric shrugged and stood up, then walked a few steps around the tent. "Not even that; the bones are still there, somewhere. I will leave you, now. I am itching for a fight, but as my dear aunt advised me, patience seems to be a good thing. Even for a stubborn young man."

"Better itch for a woman."

"Where do you think that I am riding? My scouts found an interesting peasant girl in a village not far from here. She is waiting for me."

"No fighting, or..." Calista raised her eyebrows at him.

"My dear aunt, when did I need to force a woman? She is waiting for me. Well, perhaps she is waiting even more for my purse but, on campaign, I think that my pride can live with that."

The new Duke of Loxburg left the city early in the morning. Thin and frail, he did not resemble his father. And while he was not an idiot, his mind did not match his father's either, but his weakest part was his will; it was completely subdued by Agard, the Secretary of Loxburg. Once the call to arms came from the Queen, it was Agard who pulled all the strings to assemble the army of three thousand strong men riding behind them. In his early forties, he was a competent man, both with papers and swords, the latter being a rare skill among Secretaries.

It was late in the evening when the scouts came shouting that the Litvonian army was already at the Tri Cross.

"We should return," the Duke said.

"We should change path," Julien said.

"We will camp on that hill," Agard said, pointing at the hill on the right. "We need more information, and we will decide our path in the morning."

It was a long night; the news had spread already: there were fifty thousand soldiers only ten miles away from their camp. Morning came slowly, and Julien asked Agard to gather the council and leave early.

"We are waiting for our last scouts," Agard said. "We can't leave without knowing what is happening around us. We..." He stopped abruptly when a scout entered the tent in a hurry.

"There is a Litvonian embassy at the foot of the hill," the scout said, struggling to calm his breath.

"How could they come so close to our camp without being spotted?" Julien asked.

"The road has many curves and goes through the forest," the scout said sheepishly. "And we were more focused on watching the hills, for a surprise attack."

"Are there any other enemy soldiers around?"

"No, only the fifty men with the embassy. We are not sure, but we believe that King Alfrid's brother is leading the embassy. There is a carriage too, but we don't know who is inside."

At the foot of the hill, the new Duke of Loxburg found himself in front of Edric and Calista. He had to crane his neck to look at Edric, who was a tall man. Introductions were made and the Duke found his mouth clenched.

"Duke," Agard said softly. With a strong hand, he gripped the undecided man's arm, and pushed him one step in front.

The Duke looked helpless at Agard, and moistened his lips before saying, "I, the Duke of Loxburg, swear allegiance to the Litvonian King."

"I accept your allegiance in the name of King Alfrid." A small grin flashed on Edric's lips. "There are some men who are not part of the Duke's entourage." He looked at Julien. "They will be our honored guests until some sort of understanding comes between Litvonia and Frankis."

"And if they chose to leave?" Julien asked.

"Ah, Julien, a Prince's invitation can't be refused. Did they not teach you that at the court of Arad? To prove that I am kind man, you are allowed to send a courier to the Queen."

Chapter 10 – Saliné

Struggling to contain her anger, Saliné started to read the letter again. She was in the Council Room, with Jara and Cernat. From time to time, she looked at Codrin's empty chair, as if hoping for a miracle to fill it again with the love she had lost. For mere seconds, her mind produced some sort of miracle, and she saw Codrin smiling at her. Mechanically, she smiled at his ghost too, a sad, brief smile. When she finished reading, she passed the letter to her mother. They all knew the contents; news was flying fast through the kingdom; Veres had proclaimed his allegiance to Litvonia. Eyes closed, Saliné recalled the last phrases of the letter: 'The Kingdom needs a strong hand, and only the King of Litvonia can provide it. We have a weak woman on the throne. We need a strong man.'

"These are not Veres's words," Jara said, her voice as weak as her face was white. She looked as if both her will and blood had left her at once.

"Oh, Mother, nobody will think him able to write such letter, yet those words have fulfilled their purpose. All Frankis knows that we've lost control over our *Grand Seigneur of Midia*. My brother and your son. Now, my hand is weaker, and many would think twice, if I want to confront the Litvonians. It looks like a lot of people are working against me behind the scenes."

"Do you think that I encouraged Veres?"

"With this?" she pointed at the letter. "No. But this chain of events was of your making. Codrin should have hanged Veres after we learned about his crimes. It's you who insisted on keeping Veres alive, marrying him to keep him under control. Look what your control has done. Not only is this weakening me in Frankis, but it's also weakening my position in any negotiations. It seems that there is coordination between different actors. The Circle, the Wanderers, and perhaps others. Someone helped Veres to take the lead in Midia. What do think happened to his wife? The one you promised to protect. Or to her father?"

"We don't know..."

"Veres is a sort of animal; you know what he can do when..."

"Saliné," Cernat interjected gently, "we are going nowhere. This is a problem indeed. Let's focus on how we mitigate it."

"This is betrayal, so I will do what Codrin wanted to do a long time ago, without Mother's interference."

"Saliné, jail him, but don't kill him. He is still your brother," Jara said.

"I lost my brother when he helped Bucur against me. When he killed Senal, who was your loyal Secretary. When he helped Aron to kill Mohor, who was your husband. That's if I ever really had a brother. In Severin, you always saw Vio and me as tools to be used for Veres's power. We were always traded for him."

"You are bitter now, but this recrimination doesn't help us," Cernat interjected.

"No, it doesn't. I will send Vlad to Midia. If Veres's wife, and her father have been treated well, he will bring Veres in Arad, and he will stay in jail until he rots there. If she was treated as Cleyre was at Eagle's Nest, Veres will be judged and hanged. I will..." Saliné stopped abruptly as the door opened, and one by one the councilors entered the room. She struggled to control her breath and, eyes closed, tried for a few times the Assassin Cool. It did not help much. "This is Veres's letter." She picked up the paper abruptly and waved it in front of her when everybody was seated. "It announces his allegiance to the King of Litvonia. Vlad, tomorrow take two thousand men and see what happened in

Midia. You will receive more instructions at the end of the council. This," she waved the letter again, "is not of my brother's making. I want to know who is behind it." She paused and exhaled. "This is not enhancing our position."

"Perhaps we should send an embassy to the Litvonians," Drusila said.

"It seems that they are not eager to send one either. We will wait. Even with this letter, time works to our advantage. They won't be able to take Arad before winter." She looked at Pierre.

"No, your majesty. I will offer my own head to you, on a silver plate, if they take the city from us. And with the coming winter, they will have to learn frugality. I am afraid that they will not enjoy it. In less than two months, their trip here will end with their tail between their legs."

"If there is nothing else," Saliné said and gestured vaguely, yet her hands carried a message, then waited patiently until some people left the room, including Maud and Drusila. "I have the feeling that we are being played, yet I don't know what for. Or how."

"There is a certain coordination between the Litvonians and some of our people," Cantemir said. "Alfrid could not do this," he pointed at the letter in front of her, "alone."

"No, he couldn't, and they have reached even into my family." Saliné slapped the letter in front of her and grimaced. "Idonie? Do you feel something? Your Light is stronger than mine." She turned toward the woman who was a Wanderer once.

"I don't see much," Idonie said, hesitantly. "And I don't see any siege of Arad. I don't have the feeling of a war coming to us either. It's strange. It's very strange. There are some nebulous negotiations coming soon. I don't know what for."

"Do you know when?"

"In less than two weeks, it's hard to know."

"It will already be the second month of autumn," Pierre said.

"We should not think only in terms of war," Saliné said, thoughtfully. "There may be more surprises, like this one." Her palm settled on Veres's letter, and she made it glide along the table with a twitch. "With such a large army close to their homes, some Seigneurs at the border may be forced to do similar things."

"It may happen," Pierre agreed. "A temporary thing. But at the end of the day, their lands are much closer to Arad than to Muniker. Once the Litvonians leave..."

"What's the status of the army?" Saliné looked at Vlaicu.

"From the eastern border, Devan will be here tomorrow. The Duke of Loxburg will arrive in three days. Vlad's scouts have seen nothing unusual."

"Don't you think that Maud and Drusila are acting strangely?" Verenius asked, suddenly. "For the last two weeks, I did not hear Maud speaking in the council. She likes to talk. And Drusila only pushes now and then to send an embassy to the Litvonian army."

Darkness and Shadow are always strange, Saline thought, remembering the name Codrin had given to Drusila and Maud. *Yet after the negotiations in Tolosa, they helped him take the throne and never opposed him. It was two days before he came for me in Laurden,* she could not stop her mind to wander in the past. *Yet the Wanderers and the Circle are not sworn to the Kingdom...* "The Litvonians would have not moved into Frankis without an agreement of some sort with the Circle and the Wanderers, and we thought it prudent to exclude them and their people from the most important talks of the council. I suppose that they've already realized that. We even fed them some wrong news, but to take a step further, we need proof." Saliné frowned, a glint of white teeth pressing into a lower lip gone dark red.

From his corner of the table, Cantemir shook his head before saying, "I am afraid that the proof will come too late, but your majesty is right about the need to wait. As a former Master Sage, I also have a sense of a plot involving the Circle. We are a bit ... cornered. In the sense that we don't have a clear direction, just feelings. We can't act based only on feelings."

"No, we can't. Vlad," Saliné turned toward him, "there may be people from Litvonia or from ... Frankis in Midia, helping my brother. Send scouts to block the roads. Anyone leaving Midia should be interrogated. Send any stranger here. You will no longer leave for Midia but let Maud and Drusila know that you will still leave tomorrow. Or the day after."

Out of the Council Room, the women were walking slowly in the long corridor. They were silent until they left the palace. "You moved a little too fast with the letter," Drusila said to Maud.

"We must increase the pressure. Soon, the news about the Duke of Loxburg will arrive in Arad."

"Wouldn't it have been better to have both betrayals coming at the same time?"

"This morning, I discussed everything with Calista's courier, and there was no way to warn you; I came back just a few minutes before the council. There is a second letter from Veres. A set of letters, with the same contents: brotherly advice for Saliné. You know well what kind of message," she laughed. "They will be sent at the right moment."

"No one will take Veres's advice seriously, but..." Drusila rubbed her brow for a while, "I think that it will have some influence."

"They all know that he is an idiot, but they also know that he is the Queen's brother. It's quite a weakness to have a family member betraying you, and people will see that it's the only way to avoid a war. That will make them forget about the sender's lack of wit, and once an idea roots in one's mind... There are fifty thousand Litvonians here, and the fear in the message will be in their minds too. Then, they will see hope. What better tools do we have to influence a flock of sheep other than fear and hope?"

"Did your Sages leave Midia?"

"One of them came with the letters, the other one is still there. And the renegade too."

"Ah, the renegade," Drusila smiled. "You spared and used him well. Send a message for them to leave Midia before Vlad arrives."

"My Sage will be advised."

"And the renegade?"

"He must face his fate. He will ... try to sell us out to save his skin, but what proof is there that he is working for us? Nothing. And who will believe him, after everything he has done? Nobody. The Sages I used are Hidden Sages from other places. No one knows about them. There will be some confusion about what we did or did not do. I will deny it, of course, and Saliné can't push too hard. She is clever enough not to talk too much about spreading treason. Meanwhile the negotiations with the Litvonians will be settled, and Saliné will accept to leave Arad."

"This new ... strategy, is not without risks for you."

"I know, but what's different now from other risks I took in the past? Did you have a Vision?"

"Saliné will realize soon that we are involved. I don't know when, but it will be before the news of Loxburg's betrayal arrives here. That may be days or hours, you know how our Visions work."

Her carriage and escort hidden on a secondary road, Calista was waiting. She was a patient woman. They have met some patrols on the road, but the soldiers couldn't see any danger in a sixty-two-year-old woman, who plainly stated that she was going to Arad for an audience with the Queen. She did not lie about that, at least. Her guards wore no colors. There were thirty soldiers in her escort. Ten of them were riding half a mile in front of her carriage, ten were riding with her, and another ten half a mile behind. Now they were all together, in a small forest, hidden from the riders going back and forth on the main road to Arad.

"Calista, Julien's couriers just passed toward Arad." Count Joachim woke her up from her reverie.

"Put on our colors, and let's move. We must arrive shortly after the couriers reach Arad. Count, I am relying on you to deliver me safely into the hands of the Queen."

"When did I ever fail you?" The Count grinned.

"No need to brag. Everybody fails from time to time. You've had your own share, but this is the most important thing I have done in my entire life. Or in your life," she laughed.

"Why then talk about small failures at a great time like this?"

"You always have something clever to say and lift my mood. That's the only reason I asked you to come with me. Now, raise Fate's banner for embassy, and take me to the Queen." She knocked his head with a bony finger and pushed him out of the carriage before he could answer, his lips still spread in a sort of grin. And hers too. The Count was thirty years younger, but they were good friends, and he helped her to stay in control.

That day started strangely for Saliné. She had strained a muscle during training, cut her finger at breakfast, and her son had splashed some mushy food in her hair. She had a bad feeling from early morning, but she just laughed, seeing her speckled hair in the mirror. And she was late to the council. There was nothing important in the briefing she had read carefully in the morning, yet she knew that something important would happen. She just knew; there was a surge of Light in her but no Vision. Seated, she looked through the large window; autumn was painting Arad in full splendor. From the corner of her eye, she focused on Drusila. "First Light," she said casually, using the Wanderer's official name for the first time in years. "Did you have any interesting Vision about the Litvonians?"

"Nothing important, your majesty." Drusila's voice carried no intonation. Under the table, she gripped the edge of the chair. She knew that at some point the strain would be reflected in her body, a small change that most people would not realize, and she relaxed her grip a little. *A few hours more... Or even less...*

She is nervous... Drusila is nervous... "And...?" Saliné gestured loosely, then glanced furtively at Maud, still pretending to look through the window. It was strange that Maud did not sit next to Drusila that morning. *Some years ago, Bucur poisoned Mother, at the Circle's request,* she thought suddenly. *Will they try something against me too?* She frowned at the window, without seeing it. *I don't think so. They would have done it already. And what for?*

"They may send an embassy here," Drusila said, the same flat voice.

"Ah, the embassy you wanted so much. Was that a Vision, or did the Master Sage learn something from her net of Sages?" Saliné looked at Maud. *I may embarrass myself, or I may learn something.*

"Whatever we learn from our Visions or informants, it is delivered to the Chancellery or to your majesty, the moment we think it's credible news," Drusila said, before Maud could answer.

Sitting on Saliné's left, Idonie was writing in her notebook, a habit that all of them knew. Gently, she moved her knee and touched Saliné's.

"Yes, of course," Saliné said, and rubbed her brow for a few moments. *Loxburg Duke – traitor*, she read on the notebook, and rubbed her brow harder, that little movement helping to keep her shock hidden. "I understood that the Secretary of Loxburg had joined the Duke's army." *We had already talked about this...*

"Yes, your majesty, we've informed you," Maud said, predictably. "We all know that the new Duke is not his father. There is a need for advisers."

"Unfortunately. Is that Agard's only reason to come here?"

"If there is another reason, he will for sure tell us."

"I am sure of that, but are you aware of another reason?"

At that moment, a secretary came in, and walked toward Saliné. He was an old and experienced man, yet she felt his uneasiness. The man looked at her, and she made the coded gesture for silence. He continued to walk slowly until he arrived behind her and whispered in her ear, "Two of Julien's men have returned. He was made prisoner by the Litvonians. Loxburg paid allegiance to Litvonia."

"Ah, yes," Saliné said casually, "we already know that. But..." she frowned for a moment, then whispered faintly: "take them away, and don't let anyone speak to them." She waited until the man left the room. "Where were we? Ah, yes. Are you aware of another reason, Maud?"

This is a delicate moment... Maud rubbed her fingers under the table. "The Litvonian army is camped close to the Tri Cross, so our army from Loxburg is delayed. It may be that Agard will try to learn more about their intentions."

"Have you some hints about what he may find there?"

Maud received the question with a catlike blink of her obsidian eyes. *I can't pretend anymore. I wonder if someone has betrayed us, or she is too clever a woman. Would that matter if I am executed? Perhaps it matters. It feels stupid to be executed by a stupid person.* "We all agreed that Litvonia has now an interest in Frankis." She moistened her lips, searching for words that did not come easily. "From what I understood a few minutes ago, their strategy is peaceful; they are not trying to conquer us."

"And that large army is here only to admire the beauty of Frankis," Saliné said, her eyes glittering with derision. "When not destroyed by war, it's a beautiful country indeed, but let's pass over this. What's their plan?"

"Today or tomorrow, their embassy will arrive here." Maud moistened her lips again.

She is trying to buy time, Saliné thought, but this time she no longer interjected.

"They will propose unifying the kingdoms." Maud looked at Saliné, searching for the slightest hint of understanding. She also hoped for another question that could advance things at a certain pace. Questions reveal things. It did not come. "They will propose your marriage with King Alfrid."

Saliné sucked a long breath of air through her slightly opened mouth. It felt like a hiss, and her blood was boiling. *How dare they?* "I am in mourning." Her voice was suddenly flat, hiding the tumult inside her, yet her lips moved into a snarl. She looked like a predator in search of prey. The kind of prey not needed to appease hunger, but for the sport of killing.

"I believe that this was taken into consideration. We will see in what way," Maud stated, carefully, feeling even more uncomfortable in her chair.

Drusila suddenly shook her head, as the Vision came to her, before saying, "They are coming. Calista, the Second Light of Litvonia and Count Joachim are leading the embassy."

A thick curtain of silence covered the room. Appalled, Saliné did not know what to ask. Maud did not want to speak; any word seemed to carry her closer to the rope. If Saliné did not speak, no one else tried either. She was not a violent woman, but under that calm appearance, they all guessed a fire that could burst and burn. It was not the right time for burning. The heavy silence lingered until the same old secretary entered the room again. Gripping the edge of her chair under the table, Saliné smiled coldly, nodding at the man, and with a visible relief in his voice, he announced the embassy from Litvonia.

"We will act as if we don't know," Saliné said and turned toward Maud again. "Did you know about Loxburg's betrayal?"

Yes, Maud nodded and, her eyes on fire, Saliné opened her mouth to ask more. Or to scream at the Master Sage, who seemed suddenly smaller and lost in her chair. Or to scream her anger at the whole world. The door opened, and Calista made her entrance. In a strange synchronization, both Saliné and Maud closed their eyes, breathed long and deeply, and opened them again. Suddenly cold and calm, their eyes locked, yet under Maud's coldness there was an inner storm, carrying a chill that made her shiver. *I may be dead by the end of the day*, Maud thought, and shifted her eyes from Saliné's hypnotic stare. *But what I have done is still right.*

When their small, war-like game ended, Saliné looked at the woman waiting in front of her. "Calista, the Second Light of Litvonia," she said casually, polishing a nail on the cloth covering the table. "Did you come to deliver the reason for your invasion? My husband died protecting Litvonia against the nomads. Perhaps you came to honor his memory."

Now that he is dead... "We will always honor his memory." *Wasn't that an interesting double speak?* Calista thought, amused by her wit. "And we are here for a courtesy visit, which is in the interest of both kingdoms."

"Your courtesy is fifty thousand soldiers stronger than needed."

"We are living in hard times, your majesty. The nomads are still a great threat for both kingdoms. Working together will help us survive."

"If the nomads are still such a great threat, I wonder why you left Muniker without defense."

"Muniker has strong walls, and enough soldiers to man them, your majesty, but let's not talk armies; the soldiers' presence was needed to a certain extent, but our embassy is about peace and collaboration, not war."

"Perhaps as much as a burglar's visit is about protecting a house, not stealing."

We are going nowhere, Calista thought, and stretched her mind into the Light. Nothing came, and that made her feel almost naked. *Why is she so eager to take revenge? What stirred her more, Loxburg's or her brother's betrayal? I was expecting her to be more tamed by the veiled threats.* Saliné felt her turmoil, and remained silent, letting it gnaw at the Wanderer. *It's perhaps too early, but I don't feel I have much choice. It must be done fast.* With calculated slowness, Calista took out a red tube which contained the letter written by Alfrid. "This is our statement that we are coming in peace. A letter from our King."

"A marriage contract," Saliné said, seeing the two martisor, red and white strings of cotton, rolled together in a single weave, which was both used to signal spring and marriage. She took the tube and kept it in her hands without opening it. "I wonder, which girl he wants from the court of Arad? I know none to match the interest of such a great King as Alfrid."

"There is one," Calista said, struggling to hide the effort she needed to speak even the most banal words. "Your majesty, the union between the Queen of Frankis and the King of Litvonia is needed for the Realm. The nomads will invade us again."

"Perhaps. What happened to Julien?"

"He is the guest of Prince Edric, in our camp."

"I didn't know that in Litvonia a prisoner is called a guest."

"Tomorrow, he will be here, together with Prince Edric. If your majesty would be kind enough to read the letter from our King, perhaps we can..."

"You look tired, Calista. Gislin," Saliné gestured toward the old secretary, "the Second Light of Litvonia is an honored guest in Arad. Make sure to attend to her needs."

Beginnings are sometimes difficult, but I have a good feeling about you. "Your majesty." Calista bowed, realizing that nothing more could be done for the moment.

Watching her leave, Saliné felt all the other eyes in the room pressing on her. They were all strong people, who could hide their feelings, but she already knew what was behind their masks, and the pressure became even stronger. *They are my enemies now,* she thought, *even my mother. They want the marriage. It's their hope of avoiding a long war.* Eyes closed, she tried to think of something else, something from the past, something to make her forget the present. She couldn't.

"Saliné," Jara said gently.

"Leave me. All of you. Come back in one hour. Cantemir, Pierre, Vlaicu, I need a strategy that leaves all options open."

"For negotiations?" Cantemir asked, tentatively.

"For sure there will be some negotiations. They may fail." *I want them to fail.* "Leave now." When they all left the room, Saliné leaned back against her chair. A few sobs shook her shoulders, and she started to cry silently.

"Saliné," Jara, who was standing unseen behind her, said gently, and embraced her.

"I miss him..." Saliné's voice drowned in her tears. "We are cursed. I lost my father when I was a child. My son lost his father too. He is even younger than I was. Each day, he is asking me when Codrin will return. When his father will return. He is too young to understand what death means."

"I know, he is asking me too."

"I don't want this marriage."

"It's a political option, like any other, and no one can force you."

"They think they can force me, and they may be right. This is an elaborate game to catch me, and we don't yet know all their traps. I hate the Circle. I hate the Wanderers. Perhaps I should jail Maud and Drusila."

"You will make enemies."

"Maud and..."

"They are not your friends, but they are not your enemies. And you will need a reason to arrest them. Maud was certainly involved with the Litvonians, but what proof do we have? You are not a ruler who jails people just because you can."

"Do you think that Manuc of Loxburg died naturally?"

"Perhaps not but, again, what proof do we have?"

"You already want this marriage."

"As I said, it's an option. We will talk in the council; the decision will be yours."

"What do you think will happen to my son, if I accept?"

"We will talk about that too. He is my grandson."

Maud and Drusila ambushed Verenius after the council. "So, Verenius, will you fight against the Circle again?" Maud asked.

"My dear Maud, you will never forgive me for helping a better man take the throne of Frankis."

"That I can agree with; Bucur was not half the man Codrin was. It doesn't mean that I forgive you for betraying the Circle."

"Maud, you are not the Circle. I am the Primus Itinerant, and what I did was for Frankis, and we had a good King. I am still not sure what you cared more for, to save Frankis, or to put your granddaughter on the throne."

"Both, perhaps, but wasn't I loyal to the King of Frankis?"

"Who knows if you were really loyal, or it was just fear? Some Sages ended with a placard hanging on their bodies. It had 'Sage and traitor' written on it."

"Look at me, Verenius. I never hid when I took a decision. Bad or good, it was mine. When I paid allegiance to Codrin, I meant it."

"So..."

"We need the marriage between Saliné and Alfrid. It would avoid a war and be a step forward in the plans to rebuild the Alban Empire. This is what the Circle was created for. Would you agree with that?"

"Yes," Verenius sighed. "I don't want another war. I don't want to see people die again. You were a daughter of a Seigneur; my father was a farmer. It's the commoners who suffer most in a war. We need to find an acceptable solution for Codrin's son."

"That's his mother's task, but we can help ... by suggesting to make him a Duke."

"I was thinking about something else. A title means nothing without the right protection."

"We will protect him, if Alfrid thinks ... otherwise."

"Yes, but how? How can you protect him from a powerful King? This is the weakness in your plan; Cosmin's fate, and a mother's love."

"The last soldiers arrived today, and we will be ready to march tomorrow, if needed," Pierre said. "Without the army from Loxburg, we have twenty thousand soldiers against fifty-five thousand." Pierre shrugged and moistened his lip. "With some luck, it will be manageable."

"What has luck to do with this?" Saliné asked, her voice cracked.

"You always need luck in a battle. If they come to besiege Arad, they will need more luck than we do. Fate helps you sometimes, but not that much. In one month, they will leave with their tails between their legs. Like I left Poenari. That, and an arrow in my chest. The arrow was bad luck, but it could have been worse. It's a matter of perspective after all."

"And if they don't besiege Arad?"

"They will go home, or ... they will go to take Peyris." Startled by Pierre's words, Saliné raised an eyebrow at him but said nothing. "There is a strange thing. Peyris was our capital for hundreds of years, but its walls are weaker than those of Arad. They are long and, in places, not very well maintained. We did not see an army large enough to siege Peyris for a long time."

"How long would they resist?"

"A month. Perhaps. We are back to luck again."

"Our army will keep the Litvonians busy."

"Yes, but they have enough soldiers to keep us busy and lay siege at the same time."

"Perhaps you should send some soldiers to Peyris."

"Peyris's army will return home tomorrow," Vlaicu said. "Three thousand men."

"How long should I negotiate, to give them enough time to reach Peyris?"

"Two days should be enough. The Litvonians are closer than us to Peyris, but a large army is slow."

Eyes half closed, Saliné pondered. "Let's suppose that we are lucky, and the Litvonians go home for whatever reason. They may come again next year. They already have Loxburg. Can we take it back in spring?"

"We can, but the price will be high. It's better to block the bridge over the Rhiun. They can still cross it, but it will take time. Once they cross it, they may try again to take Peyris."

"Are Count Joachim and Prince Edric good army commanders?"

"Yes, they are," Vlaicu said. "Edric is only nineteen years old. He may become a famous commander."

"I see." *I am trapped.* "Tomorrow, we will start the negotiations."

"Joachim and Edric want to join in," Cantemir said.

"Then let them join in," Saliné said, bitterly.

"Your majesty," Verenius interjected, "we need a direction during the negotiations. Did you decide where should we go?"

"I don't want this marriage, but I understand the political constraints too. Tomorrow is for probing their strategy. I want to learn how much they want the marriage. Are they ready for a long war? It's not that easy to move soldiers at distance, year after year. Does this decision for marriage and unification belong to Alfrid, to the Circle, or to the Wanderers? Can we split them?"

Verenius pinched the bridge of his nose between thumb and forefinger and thinned his eyes as if not looking at her. He was looking at her, and if his eyes had been wide open, a kind of love would have glittered there, a strange love, not necessarily a man loving a woman. *I am split*, he thought, *this woman deserves her choice, and yet I can't grant it. The Realm needs her, and in time, she may enjoy the decision we have made for her, the marriage and becoming an Empress. But now she will hate me.* "In my experience with the Circle, when a decision of such magnitude is taken, we and the Wanderers work together."

"Did you work together when Orban was chosen Candidate King?"

"No, but that's the only time I've heard about such divisions between the orders, and we all know the results. Before coming here, I talked with Maud, with Drusila, and with Calista. There are no divisions. They want what they want. I also used some other channels to learn more about Litvonia. Alfrid doesn't seem a bad man. He is intelligent. A bit of a coward in battle; perhaps Vlaicu can confirm that. He is the King of Litvonia, but Calista is the power behind the throne. She really rules there."

"So, my task in the marriage ... in the eventual marriage, is to provide an heir, raise him, weave tapestry and keep myself busy."

"I don't think..."

"Cantemir," Saliné said abruptly, "I want old treaties, old laws, old rules about sharing power, new rules about sharing power. The more, the better. I want protracted negotiations, to nail and claw each point on the list we give them. We will start from a basic point: I remain Queen of Frankis, and all the decrees for Frankis will be signed by me. Alfrid signs for Litvonia; I don't care. How long should I keep them busy until they are no longer able to take Peyris this year?"

"Three weeks... at least," Pierre said.

"That's a lot of time," Saliné grimaced. "Give me a hundred points for negotiations. Give me tough points. I want them to think twice before accepting the marriage. I want those three weeks of delay. I want them to renounce." She looked at Cantemir. There was such a fire in her eyes; it made the speechless Chancellor bow involuntarily.

Chapter 11 - Saliné

Edric arrived in Arad early in the morning, hoping for an audience. Saliné snubbed him. Cantemir lodged the prince with Calista and Joachim in a large suite having three separate chambers. The day passed slowly, and they finally received an invitation for the next day, in the afternoon.

"They are buying time," Calista said, playing with the invitation. She was alone in her room with Edric. "I wish we had come here earlier; the weather doesn't favor us. Did you decide where to send half of the army?"

"Peyris. I know, it sounds big and menacing, but from the information I have, it has strong defenses only on paper. Thirty thousand soldiers can take it in a month. Deva was also reachable, but threatening Peyris adds more pressure. My soldiers will make camp at a crossroads again, thirty miles away from Peyris. Soon, I will blockade most of northern Frankis."

"Be careful, easy steps, no pillage."

"Anyone caught pillaging will be hanged."

"When are they leaving?"

"They will ride in two days from now, at a slow pace, to be seen by many people, and will arrive close to Peyris while we are in the middle of the negotiations. I was expecting an invitation for lunch or dinner today. Isn't that a way to mollify the negotiators, with warm hosts, good food and wine? Some offer women." Edric took the invitation from Calista to read it again. He met her malicious eyes. "I did not ask for a woman; I can find one myself if I really need to. I was just trying to make a case."

"When women are involved, you become predictable. I forced you to take a defensive position with an amused look. We are playing games with them. They are playing games with us. Some of them we will understand, some we must pretend to understand, even if we don't. A cryptic answer can make the most innocent fool look knowledgeable. Let's focus on the important games. Not having lunch with them doesn't figure high on my list."

"Then let's focus on Saliné," Edric said, looking thoughtfully at Calista. "I need to find a way to prepare her for the *now* and the *later* at the same time."

"You need to make some informal bonds. Small things. They should be settled in her mind now and used later. In the negotiations, you will be always kind and courteous to her. That should pose no problems, you know how to enter under a woman's skin; it comes naturally to you. Just remember that she is not any woman. I've talked with Maud. Saliné had the best score in the Frankis Circle's test in the last two hundred years, and she grew up in a hostile environment. That and her Light sharpened her senses. It helped her learn how to read people and make herself unreadable. She is not fond of us. We are some sort of enemies. You should be firm in the negotiations, but take her part from time to time, when minor things are decided. She must have the feeling that you are naturally more open to her, and be angry at me, the Chancellor and Alfrid. She must come to trust you a little. I don't need to tell you how charming you should be when meeting her in private – we must be able to arrange such a thing too – but take your chance to become closer to her as a real man. In small steps. It will help with our long-term plot."

"How long do you think it will take until...?"

"Three years, even less. Saliné's first marriage was for love; now she will hate her husband for imposing this marriage on her. Things like this leave wounds, and we will act to keep them open for a while. You will build on those scars, and we will push her from behind. She is a strong woman, who likes strong men. Be her friend first, then her leman, then her lover, then her husband. I worked hard for this unification, and I can't let Alfrid ruin it. He almost destroyed us when he tried to run from the battle against the nomads. He is intelligent but weak, and he can't command an army. During the next fifteen years, we will have to deal with two or three more nomad invasions. You are the one I raised to defend the kingdom. An intelligent woman and a strong man on the throne may go far and build a new Empire. Make your first steps on the long road to conquering the woman you need. And Edric," she looked sternly at him, "don't disappoint me. It was hard to pass over Alfrid's cowardice on the battlefield." *And I had to change my plans. Dramatically. It had never happened before.*

The Council Room was carefully prepared for the negotiations. There were two parallel tables, one for each camp. For each table, the quickest route to the door was blocked. Saliné and her people were already seated when the Litvonians were brought inside. They had to walk between the tables while Saliné scrutinized them, hoping that her Assassin training, or Idonie's Light, would help reveal some things about them. She was expecting Edric to be the first one to enter, but it was Calista. Saliné gestured toward their reserved table, and the Wanderer frowned for a moment, then walked to her place, her face unreadable. Eyes half closed, Saliné looked at her, all her senses sharp and alert. She stretched her mind to feel the Light. To her surprise, she could not feel any danger. The Litvonian Chancellor and Count Joachim followed.

Edric was the last to enter. The Litvonians did not know about the peculiar arrangement of the tables in the Council Room, but Edric had his own game to play. He waited for a minute before going inside after Joachim. Eyes turned toward the door; Saliné was waiting too, and that short pause created a small surge of expectation. Edric entered with the feline movements of a well-trained soldier. He was tall and lean. Saliné blinked and, for a moment, Codrin appeared in front of her. If one looked at the face, there was not much resemblance between the blond, blue-eyed Edric and Codrin's light brown hair and eyes. But the bodies were similar in shape, and the way of walking even more so. In normal times, Saliné would have seen similarities, and that would have been all. But nothing was normal around her, and she forced herself to look away from Codrin's ghost. That did not escape Calista.

There were the necessary formalities and some small talk before Calista said, "Perhaps we should start with the letter from our King. It talks about family and future."

"Who knows what the future will bring to us?" Saliné shrugged and pointed at the paper in front of Calista. There were ten points to negotiate on the first day. Small things that would not engage Saliné in any meaningful way, if she could not get what she wanted. She fought for them tooth and nail, as if they were the most important things in her life. At the end of the day, she got eight of them, and partially lost the other two. *One day is gone*, she thought, when the Litvonians left the room. *It goes too fast.*

The next day, ten more points came into the negotiations but, this time, Calista accepted all of them before the morning session was over. Saliné invited them to lunch, and then she found some urgent things to do. There were no more negotiations that day.

Everything went much faster than Saliné wanted, and despite her tricks and lunches and dinners with the Litvonians, during the sixth day, she found that only the few most difficult points were left on her negotiation list.

She was with some of her people in the Council Room, preparing the day, when Vlad came like a storm. "Half of the Litvonian army is moving toward Peyris. They will arrive there in three days."

There was a sudden silence in the room until Saliné found the force to speak. "Vlaicu prepare the army to march toward Peyris.

You should leave in two days. How many soldiers should we keep here if they would try a simultaneous attack on Peyris and Arad?"

"Five thousand should be enough," Vlaicu said. "Valer will command them; he was the Black Dervil of Tolosa and a master of ambushes. He learned many things from Codrin too. Vlad should stay as his second-in-command. Pierre and Sava will make Arad ready for a siege. Perhaps we should send Boldur to Poenari to prepare..."

"Not yet," Saliné said, thoughtfully. "I will not run away. And during the negotiations ... we will pretend that we don't know about their move. There are only hard points left, and it will take a while."

Saliné hoped for some five or six more days of hard negotiations, but by the end of the second day, Calista accepted that she would remain Queen of Frankis and become Queen Consort of Litvonia. Alfrid would be the King Consort of Frankis. Calista accepted that, while the army would be under Alfrid's command, only Saliné could raise the Frankis army. And Calista accepted that no Litvonian soldier would enter Frankis without Saliné's written consent. Saliné got everything that she had asked for. She felt defeated. She felt even worse when news came that Peyris army could not reach home in time; it was blocked by the Litvonian second army; there was no way to reach Peyris before the Litvonians. The city was ill prepared against a siege.

In the evening, she gathered her enlarged council, without inviting Maud and Drusila. "The negotiations were shorter than I had hoped, and tomorrow I have to decide. It's this ... marriage or a kind of war that may take years before they renounce. I need to know who will be against the marriage." She fixed on a point far away, through the window, letting them decide.

Idonie, Vlad, Pintea and Mara, the Vice-Chancellor, were the first ones to raise their hands. Then Vlaicu, Boldur, Damian and Sava. Then Foy and Pierre. Valer too. Saliné looked at them, and at those not raising their hands. *All Codrin's captains are with me. And Mara.* There was a moment of disquiet when Pierre met the eyes of his son, Joffroy. After a while, the Duke of Tolosa looked down at his glass on the table, but he did not raise his hand. *Both Dukes are against me*, Saliné thought. *I wished Cleyre was here*. But Cleyre was at home, in Peyris, after a hard birth. She met Costa's eyes, and he looked away, red shame on his face. But he did not raise his hand. Neither did Cantemir and Verenius. *They are working for the Circle again, and against me.* Then came the hardest thing. She looked at her mother, who was sitting next to her. With one hand, Jara gripped Saliné's hand, but she did not raise her other one. Neither did Cernat. *Even my family is against me...*

"I will make my decision tonight," Saliné said, her flat voice hiding the storm in her mind.

When all had left, Saliné realized that Jara was still there, keeping a hand over hers. Her mother turned slowly and took both Saliné's hands in hers, before saying, "I know it's hard for you."

"Of course is hard, even my family is against me."

"No one is against you. They will follow you whatever decision you take. You asked for an opinion, and I gave it to you. They gave their opinion too. If there is a war, we may be able to defeat them, or we may lose. You may be forced to leave Arad and find refuge in Poenari. We already did this once when we were forced to leave Midia. We were attacked in our new house. I was attacked on the road. Think about that time. Then I was forced to leave Severin when Mohor was killed. In Arad, I was weak, and my daughter was killed. I don't want you or your son to have the life I lived. The Circle and the Wanderers will work against you. They want to unify Frankis and Litvonia. If we have a long war, they will turn people against you, or kill you. Their subterranean power is insidious. Think of what they did to the Dukes of Peyris and Loxburg. Codrin could subdue them, but there was no menace from Litvonia at that time. You must become the Queen of both Frankis and Litvonia. There is no other way. That's my opinion, but I will support you, whatever you choose."

Saliné did not feel better or worse after talking to Jara. There were flaws in both paths opening in front of her. She knew that.

For a while, she stayed alone in the Council Room, staring at a point on the opposite wall, then she sent for Vlad, Cantemir and Mara. Then Valer, Damian, Pintea and Vlaicu. Then Cantemir again, and they talked for more than two hours. No one knew what plans were made during those long hours.

In the morning, Calista led the Litvonian team into the Council Room again. Saliné's face was composed, even peaceful, but she could not fool the old Wanderer. Calista did not need much of her strong Light to know that Saliné had decided and what her decision was, and Saliné knew that the Wanderer knew. The game of negotiations was always played at the highest level between them.

"Negotiations of such importance are never easy, but things went smoothly between us, and I have to thank you for this," Calista said. "Perhaps we can start now to make plans for a bright future."

"In your plans," Saliné looked deceptively absently at Calista, "what is planned for my son?"

"Until a certain age, he will stay with his mother, of course. He will be a Duke of the kingdom, and even after his majority he will stay close to his mother."

"Do you have a specific Dukedom in mind?"

"The Duchy of Stettin. I think that your majesty understands the importance of settling him in Litvonia."

"My geographic knowledge of Litvonia is not so great. I did not take an army there, after all. Can you point out on the map where Stettin is?" Saliné gestured at one of the maps on the wall.

Edric stood up quickly and tapped on a point in the north-east of Litvonia. "It's one of the largest Duchies."

That's far from Muniker, and the city is in the way of the nomads' invasions. "Perhaps, but it doesn't look close to Muniker. It may be even farther than Arad."

"I think," Calista said carefully, "that Arad should become a royal city."

"Sittgart is a royal city too, and it's close to Muniker," Edric said, and tapped again on the map, over a point that was between Muniker and the border between Litvonia and Frankis. "It's the third largest city in Litvonia, and it can be the center of a great Duchy." He smiled, not very broadly, but with warmth and understanding, and his eyes locked with Saliné's. All she could do was nod at him. There was anger in her look, but there was a kind of relief too.

Almost on the point of tears, Saliné stuck her nails in her knees. She did not want to give them this satisfaction. Abruptly, she opened her eyes and met Calista's. "I will accept the marriage. There are two conditions related to the Chancellery and the Royal Guard in Muniker." She looked at Calista, who nodded, her face unreadable. "Cantemir will become Vice-Chancellor. You lost the Chief of the Royal Guard and a few captains during the nomad invasion. Vlad will become the Chief of the Guard. Damian, Pintea and Lisandru will become captains of the Guard."

"They are strong men," Calista said. "I see no reason to reject such a good proposal."

It took Cantemir and Klavis six hours to negotiate every word in the marriage contract, and it was signed by the end of the day. The wedding would be two weeks after the spring solstice; this was the only point Calista really insisted on; she was careful to let the nine months of Grey Respect for the dead end before the wedding.

"Just for your information." Saliné pushed the freshly signed marriage treaty away, and looked at Calista, then at Edric. "The Duke of Loxburg was stripped of his Duchy. Loxburg will go to his cousin."

"He was well intentioned," Edric said, casually. "And all these efforts helped us unify two great kingdoms, but I understand your choice. I would have done the same."

You would have done... What game are you playing, Edric? She knew that it was a game but did not know its rules or purpose. During the negotiations, Edric was the *good* negotiator, helping her from time to time, and she was expecting him to ask her a favor as it was usual. It did not happen, and there was nothing more to negotiate. "Perhaps. Such precedents are dangerous. Who knows what might happen during the next nomad invasion because of such weak men? And, Maud," Saliné turned toward the Master Sage, "my soldiers are preparing placards and ropes for Agard and Julius. Aron and the other Sage who were hiding in Midia are dead. My dear brother will stay in jail until his death." How could Aron work for Maud again?

She will eat Alfrid alive, Edric thought. *Then I will be on the menu, but I am a different course. I would like to be eaten by that mouth.*

Aron met his fate, but Elnard was a good Sage. There are always loses, even when things go peacefully, Maud pondered, avoiding to look at Saliné. "If there is guilt, then I am as guilty as they are, your majesty."

"Then write a confession that you helped them to poison Duke Manuc, and I will ask for a third placard and rope. Ah, you did not know that I learned about the poisoning. I think it was the same potion that killed Duke Stefan when the Circle needed Peyris." *Even when I leave Frankis, I am still its Queen. I need the Circle and the Wanderers, but this will weaken Drusila and Maud as all know that they have approved the killing of Manuc and what happened in Midia.* Not waiting for an answer, Saliné stood up. "I think we are done for today."

That night, Saliné took her son, Cosmin, to stay with her, and long after he fell asleep in her arms, she was still pondering about her past and future life. *Today, I lost your kingdom, my son. It may be that I was weak and afraid, or it may be that I was cautious and saved our lives. I will never know. When I was young, in my father's castle, I dreamed that my husband would be a Seigneur or a Grand Seigneur, and my first born too. I married a King, but you will be only a Duke. It's more than I dreamt for you when I was a child, but less than you deserve. I hope that one day you will forgive me.*

ꕥ

It was past midnight when Calista, Drusila and Maud met again. "That was a hard day," Maud said. "I came perilously close to being hanged."

"We are born to serve," Calista shrugged, "and danger is part of our life."

"Our role will diminish from now on," Drusila said, "but we will have a strong Queen and perhaps an Empress."

Calista rubbed her brow for a while. "Saliné is strong. But she is still young. And we still have our duty. She knows how to bargain and, in time, she will understand that we only pretended to negotiate with her. In time, she will learn that we agreed to give her those powers from the beginning. She will learn that Alfrid is not a strong man. He is intelligent but has no battle skills, and not much will. Edric inherited most of the will in their family, and he knows how to lead an army. By the marriage contract, Saliné will have almost the same power as Alfrid. The difference comes from Litvonia being larger, and the fact that Alfrid commands the army. Theoretically, as the soldiers answer to Edric and Count Joachim. After that attempt to run from the battle against the nomads, there is not much trust in him. I am sure that Saliné will be able to gain the upper hand in less than two years."

"I am sure too," Maud laughed. "She will lead both from the throne and from the imperial bed. Intelligent women know how to do that. Saliné is one of them."

There was a moment of silence, as Calista started to rub her brow again, harder, a habit that helped her concentrate. "I would advise her to make the imperial bed large enough for two men."

"Do you mean her to take Edric as her lover?" Drusila asked.

"Edric is our only hope of defeating the nomads during the next invasion, and Alfrid may prove himself a nuisance so, yes, she must take him as her lover. Unfortunately, the suggestion can't come from me."

"I will take care of that," Drusila said.

"You have to do it before we leave, to give Edric a chance of some innocent flirting. Small things may make a large imprint later. I will advise him about that. I will advise him to be innocent, though that's a hard thing when flirting with a woman of Saliné's beauty," Calista laughed.

It was a day later after the contract was signed, and there was no celebration for the new marriage. Drusila paused for a moment before entering Saliné's suite. She recalled her plan again and did not find any flaws in it. Frowning without knowing it, she handled the knob with a veined hand and entered the room. Saliné glanced at her and nodded toward a chair.

"If our plans go well, in a few years, your majesty will become Empress. You may still harbor some bad thoughts about our work, but it's your work too. And your Empire."

"If you have something to say, say it, but don't try to bolster my pride with useless words."

"You are strong woman and a builder. These are not vain words. Last night, I had a Vision. You already know that the nomads will invade Litvonia again in eight years. We have enough time to build a strong army, but there is only one commander who can bring us victory: Edric. He is the one who will defend you and your children."

"Did you see that in your Vision?" Saliné asked abruptly, stirred by the word 'children'. While the thought of unwanted intimacy made her curse Alfrid, children came with marriage. She knew that.

Drusila pondered for a while, and said, "You will have another son and a daughter. In that order. Things can change, though; sometimes a Vision may not come true. The bad thing is that Alfrid is not ... suited to lead an army. He tried to run from the battlefield during the last invasion. Your majesty knows what happened. That would have been a disaster for the whole Realm, and Edric was the one who stopped him. You must consider this; Edric should command the army. We need him, and Alfrid is a little jealous of his brother's military skills."

"Alfrid's jealousies are not something that I can control."

"Women may look weaker, but they have a strong lever of control on any man. Men have a weakness in ... bed. In my second Vision, there was a warm and close relationship between you and Edric."

"Are advising me to take a lover?"

"I am not advising anything. I am just explaining my Vision. Whatever decision your majesty takes ... it will change the future of your children."

"A lover," Saliné whispered with distaste.

"Yours is not a marriage for love, it's a political thing, a detailed contract that, for almost two weeks, was negotiated up to the last word. For a strong Queen, lovers are instruments of power, not a weakness. The Last Empress had three known lovers, and all were strong army commanders. She needed them, and replaced them, one by one, when a new need arrived. This is a sort of survival strategy when the husband is too weak to defend the house."

"I have to think about it."

"You have several years to think about it, but with each year, the decision will become harder. If your majesty accepts a suggestion from me, spend an hour with Edric before he leaves Arad, just the simple flirting that all women do from time to time. It will help you get to know each other." Drusila used the Light and fixed her old eyes on Saliné. They looked almost hypnotic.

"Was that a Vision too?" Unimpressed, Saliné returned a stare balanced on the edge of irony.

"No, that's from my own experience. My wrinkles are deep now, but this old woman was once young, and she had her share of flirting and loving before becoming a Wanderer, something that she missed in her new life inside the order. There are things that youth takes for granted and doesn't appreciate enough. Many learn that too late. I was no exception. You will lead two kingdoms, and perhaps an Empire, and it's your duty to make them survive for your children, whatever the costs. And there is no reason to have a boring life."

Saliné weighed the heavy Book of Muniker Manners, turned it this way, then that way; the cover was of elegant, burgundy leather, with embossed images. She let her fingers slid slowly to feel its softness. It was a gift from Edric, and her introduction to Muniker. A woman and a man were depicted on the cover, and Saliné grimaced. *I hope that I don't have to wear something like this.* The woman's left breast was exposed, and she recalled things from an old Alban history book; they used even more awful dresses at the end of the Empire. *Decadence*... She opened the book somewhere in the middle; it was describing 'lointain lovers', married people who had the agreement of their husband or wife to take a lover. *Lewd*... She went to another page. "Edric is allowed to embrace and kiss me on the mouth?" She finished the page, and closed the book, then threw it on the table; there was a long list of situations in which he, or other six relatives, could kiss her. "Only in Hispeyne, two brothers can marry the same woman, but they are poor and savage. I will be married to only one man. Forced to... Unfortunately, I dislike him. Perhaps even hate him." She shrugged.

The door opened, and the maid introduced Edric. Saliné had invited him for a cup of tea, just two hours before he was due to leave. Royal protocol mattered, and she wanted a short encounter. It was impolite to let her future brother-in-law leave like a stranger. Perhaps Drusila's words played a role too, in a corner of her mind. She should have invited Calista and the Litvonian Chancellor, she knew, but her bitterness about the marriage was too strong. Edric would represent the royal family in this brief farewell. She eyed him guardedly. For the first time, she tried to evaluate the man in a different way than an adversary in the negotiations, and she reached into the Light for help. *There is power in him.*

"I know," Eric raised his hands, before seating himself in front of her, across the table, "I am the evil stranger invading your lands." His voice was a warm baritone. His eyes were smiling as he looked at Saliné.

"Is that a sort of joke?" Saliné asked, coldly. During the negotiations, she had fought hard to ignore the resemblance between his and Codrin's voice.

"Needed something to break the ice. It seems that it was not my brightest idea. Our actions still feel unpleasant to you, but it was not a real invasion. There was no fighting. Only one man was killed. I executed him; he was caught trying to rape a woman." He raised his palms up, keeping his eyes on her. "In the long term, this little trick will help us to defeat the nomads. We no longer have a bright commander. Codrin was a great man. I apologize if my words..." Eyes wide, he looked at Saliné, who shrugged, looking away to hide her pain, and perhaps to escape from that blue stare, which felt strangely warm. "The Wanderers and the Circle have this responsibility of unifying the continent. You will become our Empress. If everything goes well. The nomads are dangerous." He shrugged too. "I am the King's brother, and the commander of the army. It was my duty to come for you."

This is true at least. Saliné moved a step further to reconsider him, and the feeling that he resembled Codrin came back to her. Not in the physical way, and not only that distracting voice; there was the same sort of royal coolness in Edric. *I know only two other people with such... character, tenderness at home and toughness on a battlefield. Pierre and Manuc were like Codrin. Is this man similar?*

"And my pleasure." Edric smiled with childish amusement. "You've started to learn about Muniker." Slowly, he pulled the Manners Book between them on the table. Tapped on it. A muffled sound. "I see some questions in your frown."

"This kind of dress," she tapped on the cover too, her finger only inches from his, "Do ... women wear something like this in Muniker?"

"It's just an allegory that life in Muniker is warm and full of colors. Something else?"

"It looks..." she said hesitantly, "that some people are allowed a sort of liberty when interacting with me."

"Litvonia is a foreign country to you, and we do things differently there, but as in Frankis, families are important to us. For me it's important to be close to you and Alfrid. Some things are too old and useless, but read everything, and let things come slowly to you. There is no hurry." He took her hand in his, as if making an incipient pact over the book, and she did not react; it was a closeness that she could accept. Their eyes met too, and this time it was not that sort of cold confrontation, which happened during the negotiations.

He has long elegant fingers. Like Codrin. "We talked enough politics during the negotiations. How is ... Alfrid?"

"Handsome." Edric flashed a bright smile at her. "Perhaps not as handsome as I am."

"Do you make this comparison often?" Saliné smiled, unwillingly, while his fingers played on her wrist.

"No, only now and then. I am trying to hone my courting skills. Any nineteen-year-old man is a beginner."

"Ah, it was courting." She gently pulled her hand while he delayed her as much as he could without being impolite – in Litvonia.

"Only as between relatives. Muniker is the Court of Love, but I will let you have the pleasure of discovering in what way. Alfrid is a nice, intelligent man, and I am sure that you will do well together. Muniker will like you; you are the kind of Queen who is loved by her subjects." The horologe struck the hour, and he stood up, ready to leave. Walked toward her. "In Litvonia, this is how we take our leave of relatives or friends." He opened his arms. Hesitantly, Saliné stood up too, and allowed him to embrace her. His arms were strong, and there was a certain warmth in his way of doing it. With a devilish smile, he leaned his head back. Their eyes met, then he looked at her lips.

"Don't..." *try to kiss me.* There was a surge of rage in Saliné, and a frozen smile on her lips, the result of many years of training to hide her feelings from Bucur. Her body was tense in a way that she had not felt for a long time, a spring coiled for extreme violence. Edric misjudged her smile, flashed a congenial grin, and pulled her tighter, his arms an iron cage around her. There was no pain, and no way for her to escape without an ugly scene; he was too strong. Before she realized, she stretched her right foot behind her, ready to spring it in his groin. She was able to control herself at the last moment. Her body was a little twisted, to allow the move, and they froze in a strange position, half embracing. There was a half-minute of embarrassment, as both understood what had happened, both unable to react. Slowly, she realigned her feet without looking at him. Edric did not move. Still trapped in his arms, Saliné decided in a split second that she had gone too far, and there was a political need for amelioration. Eyes closed, she raised her stiff mouth to let Edric have his farewell kiss.

There was another long moment of silence before Edric said, "I think that our rules are a little too strange for you now." By pure instinct, he stroked Saliné's hair with a gentle hand, then leaned forward and kissed her brow.

A little... Saliné relaxed suddenly on trembling feet, and even managed to smile. There was a strange silence in the room, as strange as she felt. All the tension and will that had kept her navigating through the negotiations melted during that moment of relief. It let her weak and lightheaded, and in need of comfort. Her mind half lost, she imagined herself in Codrin's arms and stopped shivering.

Unable to understand what had happened, Edric continued to stroke her hair. "I apologize if my manners have disturbed you," he said, when the pressure of the silence around became too strong and he lowered his head until his lips touched her ear, whispering in a conspiratorial tone, "There is one man in Muniker who already likes you. I am sure there will be many more, but I am glad to be the first one. Will you remember this?"

"Do I have a choice to forget?"

"No." He flashed that devilish grin again. "Next year, I will come to meet you at the border. It will be my duty. And my pleasure."

The border reminded Saliné of things she wanted to forget, but they felt far and remote. "I wish you a good journey, Edric." She realized that she was still nested in his arms and slowly disengaged from him.

"I wish to see you well, Saliné, and to kiss you welcome." He bowed and left the room. It took him only a few long strides.

Thoughtfully, Saliné watched him disappearing, and pondered about her life in Muniker. Because of the forced marriage, she disliked Alfrid, though she had never met him. Her marriage was political, and the political part of her mind considered the need for allies at court. If his character were true, this man could be such a thing in the long term. Through a quite different path, the unconscious part of her mind came to a similar conclusion, but only because of that resemblance to Codrin.

Chapter 12 - Codrin / Ildeko

The cart was filled with fifteen-foot-long logs, and Codrin leaned against it. He felt content. Tired, Pireska and Ildeko sat on a hard bench, carved in stone, to recover their strength. It was late in the morning, and they would have to hurry to catch the wood fair in Gyor, the large village ten miles away down the valley. The fair was open only for one day, tomorrow.

"I need change my clothes and pick my bow. We will leave now." Ildeko looked up into the clear sky and stood up.

"No, Ildeko, I will go with Codrin." Pireska caught her hand and pulled her back to the bench. "Listen to me. Fandras will be there; he is the Uber Captain of Baia and in charge of collecting the wood tax in the county. That bastard Count might be in the village too. If they see you... I am an old woman, and they prefer young ones. While we are away, take Ferent and sleep in the cave. If everything goes well, we will be back in three days. Go and prepare the food. I need to talk to Tudor. Fate knows how he will behave, seeing so many people."

On the road, Pireska gave Codrin a long introduction to the world around him. She told him stories, some of them happy, some of them sad. Most of them were just stories; others were real things that had happened to her family or friends in the past. She chose to make camp half a mile away from Gyor, and took a side road that she knew well, making camp after the first curve, where the cart was no longer visible from the main road. They lit no fire.

Weighing her words, Pireska took a long breath and said, "Tudor, you must listen to me carefully. As far as the people at the fair are concerned, you are Ildeko's husband." *You don't really know what that means but...* She would have liked to see his eyes, and gauge his reactions, but there were only a few stars in the sky, and the new moon was hidden behind a thin string of clouds. "She is known to be married to Tudor, my son who had died just before you came here, and your name is Tudor. There will be many people at the fair, and some men may speak a few words to you, make bad jokes, about you or about Ildeko, or both. Just ignore them. Most of them are stupid. Ignore the women too, they may be even worse." *Some of them will surely try to get under your skin. There are no young men like you in the village, and they know how to make a man talk too much. You don't have much experience...* "We will sell the wood quickly and go home. We will need to buy some things for the winter first; we'll get ten silvers, after all."

They entered Gyor early in the morning, the third cart to pass under the mobile barrier. Captain Fandras was already in place, counting carts and recording sales. Count Irvath of Baia always took more than the law allowed for every load sold. He fixed the prices too.

He will give us eight silvers instead of ten, Pireska thought, but they had no choice. She guided the horse to the check point.

Fandras scrutinized Pireska, then Codrin. "Where is the girl? She had fine teats. I still remember them in my hands."

"She stayed home with the child, Sir. He is sick," Pireska said, struggling to control her voice. This was the man who had killed her son and raped Ildeko. He and his Count. They had kept her daughter-in-law captive for one week. And the Countess was the worst. At home, Pireska called her the Madwoman; but the Countess was not mad, she was as intelligent and evil as she was beautiful.

"Next time bring her here. She will be honored to spend a few nights in the castle, and Sir Irvath and I will honor her bed. You get eight silvers for the wood."

"But it's worth ten silvers," Codrin protested.

"What?" Fandras turned abruptly toward him; his sword unsheathed in a blink, touching Codrin's neck. Fandras was an old hand.

"Please forgive him, Sir," Pireska pleaded. "Since he fell and hit his head, he hasn't been the same. He is like a small child now. We will sell the wood for six silvers."

For a while, Fandras played with the tip of his sword on Codrin's chest, measuring him. The young man seemed stupid indeed, but he was strong and healthy, and good for work; it would be a pity to maim or kill him; there was a shortage of workers in Count Irvath's villages. He pondered quickly and hit Codrin's face with the flat of his blade. It left behind a red band and a small line of blood. "Six silvers. Move and unload the cart; I don't have time to waste on scum like you. Next time, bring the girl here, or you will sell nothing."

Something strange started to boil in Codrin, a surge of tension that he could not understand or control. His fingers gripped the wood until his knuckles went white, then they clenched into tight fists; hit his knees. Once. The tension was now burning through his veins; his mouth became dry and bitter, and he tried to stand, without really knowing why.

"Sit," Pireska growled, and pulled him down. The force in her voice numbed him, and he sat abruptly, hitting the logs with his bottom. She led the cart to the discharge area. "We have to unload the cart." Her voice was calm now, and she squeezed his hand gently.

Pireska tired soon, and Codrin had to do most of the work, but he did not complain. He felt that he had done something wrong, though he did not understand what had happened. He knew that they had lost two silvers because of his reaction. At least, he did not feel tired. Codrin was well trained to fight; cutting wood for almost two months worked different groups of muscles on his body, and his strength was even greater than before. Seeing him handling a log as if it were a stick, Pireska shook her head. *What kind of man is he? Why did Fate send him to us? Is it for his sake, or for my family's sake?*

When the cart was emptied, she took her six silvers, and they left the fair. They were at least lucky that people ignored them. Captain Fandras's wrath took care of that; the villagers avoided their cart as if it carried some sort of pestilence. At the edge of the village, they met five riders storming along the road. Irvath looked at them but said nothing. His wife looked even longer, and she measured Codrin up and down, with a cold stare. She did not speak either, even when she turned her head to have another look at Codrin, and they were finally free to go.

The look of the Madwoman spells trouble, Pireska thought, glancing over her shoulder at the woman as she rode away.

"I am sorry," Codrin said to her after a while. "I thought..."

"Six silvers are good money. We will stop in the next village to make provisions for winter."

"But why did he...?"

"This is how our world functions. Forget about the fair; it's not worth remembering." *You were a man of power. Did you act like Fandras and the others? You seem to be a kind man, but what if you were just another rich bastard?* Pireska had seen many things in her past. Irvath was worse than many, and his wife was perhaps born from the devil, but Pireska knew that the small folks would always suffer from injustice. *Fate,* she shrugged, and pushed the horse to move faster. The cart was now empty, and she wanted to put some distance between them and that unpredictable, wicked Count.

They did not get the chance. A rider caught up with them and stopped his horse in front of the cart. "Old shrew, Sir Irvath will give a party in two weeks. The lady wants your girl and ... this," he pointed to Codrin, "to be there and serve. Make sure that both are clean. It seems the girl stank last time she visited the castle, and she has to entertain some fine people." He wrinkled his nose and rode back the way he had come.

"I've never seen a castle," Codrin said, split between a strange excitement and the memory of Fandras's behavior. Unconsciously, he touched the red spot on his face. It still stung. Pireska said nothing, just made the horse pull the cart faster. "Is it safe to go there?" he asked, unsettled by her silence.

"No."

They arrived home the next morning, and Pireska waited for the night to come before speaking to Ildeko. When the story ended, the young woman put her elbows on the low table, resting her chin on her clasped hands. "I will go alone," she said after a while. "There is no way to escape; the Madwoman will send riders after us. She is even worse than Irvath. You will hide with Tudor in the cave, and I will tell them that he got lost in the mountains. I think they will believe me. Then winter will come, and perhaps they will leave us alone. We must leave in spring, but where will we go?"

Pireska embraced her. "Perhaps Tudor will recover by spring."

By the time Ildeko saw the four riders coming up the road, it was already too late. *They are one week early*, she thought. *Why have they come now? And why is Irvath leading them?* "Take Ferent and hide in the cave," she said to Pireska, who tried to protest. "Don't argue; they are here for me, and I don't think it's about the party. Even if I hide, they will search, and Irvath is a stubborn man. Find Tudor and take him with you. They may provoke him and hurt him." She walked slowly toward the front of the house, struggling on shaky legs.

In a minute, the riders surrounded Ildeko. They dismounted, and Count Irvath stopped in front of her. "You know why we are here," he said, measuring her up and down.

"Yes, Sir."

One man groped her bottom and pushed her into Irvath's arms. He kissed her hard. "Let's go inside," the Count said after a while, and clasped her waist in one arm. "Fandras, take care that we are not disturbed. We will have a serious talk." He winked, and the men burst into laughter. "After me, you will have your talk with her too. Isn't it so, Ildeko? You are a generous woman."

"Yes, Sir," she said, her voice wobbling a little, she didn't want to give them reason to play on her weakness and humiliate her even more.

Codrin returned just as they were about to enter the house, and he stopped abruptly, staring at them; something seemed changed in the natural order of things on the small farm. He could not say if the change was good or bad. He was curious.

Irvath looked back at him, before asking Ildeko, "Is this your idiot?"

"He had an accident, Sir."

"Do you think I care?" He pulled out his dagger.

Ildeko clung to his arm, saying, "Please Sir, let him leave; he will not disturb us. Tudor, go and find Mother. There is some work for you to do while I talk with Sir Irvath inside the house. Do not disturb us. Go, now."

Codrin frowned, but he was accustomed to obeying, and moved away when they entered the house. Looking back at the vanishing pair, he crossed paths with Fandras and his men without seeing them. One of them hit him in the chest.

"He looks even more of an idiot than before," Fandras laughed. "Where are you going? We need some distraction until Sir Irvath finishes his job."

"I was told to find Pireska while Sir talks with Ildeko."

"Oh, yes, they are talking hard now. She is good in bed, your Ildeko. I will talk to her too. Then my men. A lot of talking and moaning."

"What do you mean?" Codrin asked, feeling that something was wrong. *Ildeko told me they would talk. There is nothing bad in talking.*

"He doesn't know," Fandras guffawed, followed by the soldiers. "We will spread her legs, you idiot. That's what women are good for."

Codrin frowned and moistened his lips. A brief memory of a young girl whose hands were glowing white came to him. Looking away, he breathed faster; there was something sad and bad in that memory, belonging to his forgotten twin sister, who was raped and killed by their cousins. He could not figure out what was bad, but he could feel it, and he started to rub his hands on the sides of his body. A trace of White Light spread from them. It lasted a mere moment and passed unobserved.

"You are too idiot even to make fun of you," Fandras snapped. He made to kick Codrin on the bottom.

In a split second, Codrin's arm sprang out, and the hardened lateral part of his palm crushed Fandras's windpipe. The captain lost his life even before he understood what was happening to him. Half turning, Codrin grabbed his limp body, and threw it against the closest soldier. They both went down behind one of the horses. Codrin kicked the animal hard. It pranced on its forelegs, and the head of the soldier exploded like a melon, bones, blood and brain spreading on the green grass. The second soldier drew his sword and went for Codrin's throat. He ducked aside, and the soldier pitched forward from his own inertia. He was not a tall man and Codrin's knee went hard into his ribs, cracking some of them. One splinter pierced his heart; there were three dead men in the grass now.

Without thinking, Codrin went toward the house and entered like a storm. Ildeko was already naked, lying on the table, Irvath's mouth pressed against her breast. The Count rose quickly, reaching for his sword, which lay on the table beside them.

"No!" she cried. "Run, Tudor!"

His sword raised, Irvath attacked with a high kick. Codrin caught his sword hand by the wrist, grunting in his fury. For the first time in his new life, anger mounted in Codrin like a storm, and he was not able to control it. Irvath was in rage at being challenged by a commoner and bit Codrin's hand, trying to force his sword down into his neck. Codrin could smell the stench of sweat and wine, though he did not know what wine was. His right hand found the Count's neck and gripped, his thumb pressing into the hollow of the throat.

By their own will, his strong fingers sank into the Count's neck muscles. Codrin wasn't conscious of what he was doing; his Assassin training, which was still alive in him, kicked in automatically. He pressed the Knight into the wall, hip against hip, keeping the man's spasms in check, slowly lifting him up until his legs were hanging, and he trembled in small contractions. Irvath's breath became harsh, in and out in spurts; then it became ragged and rattled, and finally silent. A last spasm of his feet, and he moved no more. Codrin was genuinely surprised when Irvath's right hand suddenly opened, and the sword fell from limp fingers. Leaning his head on the left side, he looked at the man: the protruding tongue, and the bloodshot eyes above it, bulging and sightless. Irvath was dead. Codrin shook him gently, not yet understanding what had happened.

Ildeko came and tried to pull his arm from the Count's neck. "Oh, no," she whispered, "he is dead." She pulled harder, but could not move Codrin's hand, which still gripped his adversary's throat like an iron trap. "Tudor," she said, her voice hoarse, "he is dead. Let him go."

Codrin turned his head toward her, as if seeing the young woman for the first time. "Dead?" he asked. "Why is he dead?"

"That's why," she said, pointing at the man's neck, but this time her voice was gentle, and she finally pulled his hand away.

Freed from his grip, Irvath's body hit the ground with a dull sound and, slowly, a touch of understanding came to Codrin. He shivered, and he fell to his knees, in front of Ildeko. Forgetting that she was naked, Ildeko pulled his head against her breast, embracing him tightly. Unable to speak, he embraced her waist. That was how Pireska found them, some minutes later. She had already seen the bodies in front of the house. She gasped, seeing the Count sprawled on the floor like a rag doll, his face swollen and hideous. Leaning against Ildeko, Codrin quivered, almost unconscious.

"He did this," Pireska whispered and pressed a hand to her mouth.

"We need to get him to bed," Ildeko said calmly. She was starting to think about the consequences of a Count's death in their house. She did not know about the dead outside, but that did not change the situation too much. "Oh, no," she said, and pressed a hand to her temple. "The men outside. We must run."

"They are dead too."

"What? How?"

"Fandras's windpipe was crushed, and he looks like a... He looks dead. One has no evident wound, and the last one's brains are spread in the grass. We must bury the bodies. Let's put Tudor in bed first. Be quick."

They carried Codrin, almost unconscious, into the bed, and left Ferent to watch him.

Leaving the house, the women froze, and they almost threw up. A bunch of carrion crows were feasting on the fragments of brain scattered on the grass. Ildeko turned abruptly, looking for a stone or a piece of wood.

"Don't," Pireska said, her voice trembling. "They are just helping us to clean the mess. We can't leave anything that offers a clue about their deaths. Irvath's men will come here tomorrow. If not today. I am curious if it's a sort of delicacy to them." She stared at the crows and shook her head in disgust.

Close to the house, there was an area of small limestone ravines and caves, where they would hide when robbers tried to attack the house. Panting from the effort, they placed the men on their bellies over their horses' saddles. The crows voiced some protest, but they continued to feast. The women tried their best not to look at them, and led the horses away, six hundred paces from the house. Pireska knew the area by heart, and by the time they arrived, she had already chosen which crevasse would offer the best place for the grave. It was a few feet deep, tight, and easy to cover.

"Wait," Pireska said, and searched the bodies. She found two purses; the one belonging to Irvath was heavy. "This will more than compensate for our losses at the fair. We may not need to cut and sell more wood for several years." One by one, the corpses were thrown in the crevasse, the last one only a foot underground. "We have to cover the grave. Roll those small boulders into the hole; I will go and bring a shovel. We need to put some dirt on top, to hide the rotting smell. It may drift up to the house and betray us."

When Pireska returned, there was already a layer of head-sized boulders almost filling the grave. There was not much soil around, and they had to carry it from some thirty feet away' then they piled on gravel and small stones until the dirt was no longer visible.

"I hope it rains," Ildeko said, looking up at the sky; there were some fringes of black clouds not far into the western mountains.

"I hope so too." Pireska threw her tired body onto the ground. "Give me a few minutes; then we have to take care of their horses.

They went back with the horses and walked down the small path going into the valley, parallel with the road. After ten minutes of walking, they slapped the horses on the rumps, driving them away. Tense, the women watched them running down the slope until they vanished from sight. Ildeko embraced the older woman, and they stayed like this for a while.

"It's not finished yet," Pireska whispered.

"I know, they will come tomorrow. Let's see to Tudor now."

It rained that night. Codrin was delirious again with fever and slept badly, but it was not as bad as after he had killed the stag. His mind was adapting, and the gap that this new shock started to fill with memories and knowledge was smaller. As before, Pireska watched him all night, placing cold poultices on his burning brow and chest. From time to time, images came to him, but they were not dreams, just disparate strings of memories from his past life. This time, he saw a few people that he knew well. His past mind knew them well. For his new one, they were still strangers, and he still thought that he was dreaming. He would forget them soon, though this time, his mind would be able to recall them when needed. He did not need them now; they were no longer part of his life.

When his fever had diminished, half awake, Codrin had a new set of Visions. For him, everything looked like a chain of strange dreams. He saw Saliné's wedding in Muniker. He saw her son being born. He saw the Wanderers and the Circle plotting against him. He saw many things in the future, but the people he saw in the Visions where still unknown to him.

Riding up the road, Horwath was dreaming of another, better place to be. He thought of leaving his position and running away. He wouldn't. Countess Elsebeth was too powerful, and her wrath would follow him everywhere. She was the King's cousin after all. *Perhaps I should leave Litvonia*, he thought. *To go where?* At twenty-one, he looked even younger, and no stranger would hire him as a captain, competent as he was. Two years ago, Lady Elsebeth had called him at midnight for an urgent problem. She was three years older than him, and her marriage one year old. Horwath left her bedroom in the morning, in love with that sweet woman who was so neglected by her cold husband. His services seemed to be satisfactory, as he was called again for another urgent issue. There was always an emergency in the lady's bedroom, which was solved by one young man or another, and sometimes by her husband. Horwath knew nothing about the other men. When he learned of them, he wanted to break their relationship. But there was no relationship. It was a call of duty. After a year, he was promoted to captain, and the experienced men in the guard laughed at his orders. The 'bedroom captain', they called him. The Countess was always discreet, but things could not be fully hidden. After a few duels, the guards decided it was better to obey Horwath's orders. Half a year later, the lady became bored by his services, and another young man took his place. Horwath felt relieved, but he had the presence of spirit to look sad when she told him. *Why did she choose to send me? There are more experienced captains in the castle.* Irvath had not come home last night, and he was charged to find out why. Lady Elsebeth knew where the Count had spent the day and sent him to Pireska's house. Horwath knew the old woman and that her son had been killed by the Count. The man's wife was taken to the castle and used as a tool for the Count's pleasure. Apart from Ildeko, no one knew that the Countess had used her too. There was no one in front of the house when Horwath arrived, and he dismounted, signaling the five soldiers following him to do the same.

"Was Sir Irvath here yesterday?" Horwath asked when Pireska came out of the house.

"Yes, he was. Have you come for her too? Was she not raped hard enough yesterday? Do you want your share?"

"I am not that kind of man," Horwath said, his voice suddenly lower, so he could not be heard by the soldiers. They were not his men after all. "Sir Irvath did not come home." He shoved Pireska, and she stepped back, almost falling.

"Perhaps they have found another woman to rape," Pireska answered in a low voice.

"Keep your filthy mouth shut," he shouted and pushed her again. She stepped back again. He glanced back at his soldiers and came close to her.

"Then how can I answer your questions?"

"It's better if you answer *my* questions. You know that." His voice was low again, but not so low as before; the soldiers could no longer hear him. Horwath was not an unkind man, and he had seen many things despite his youth. "Their horses came home in the morning."

"Ah," Pireska said, and pressed a hand to her mouth. "Perhaps Fate has answered our prayers."

"You won't live long with that tongue of yours. When did they leave your house?"

"When they finished... Late in the afternoon. They took their time."

"Where did they ride from here?"

"They took the western path down into the valley. I don't know why they did not leave by the main road."

"Did you see other people?"

"No, this is an isolated place, and if someone wanted to ... meet Sir Irvath, I doubt that they would have wanted to be seen."

"Where is your ... young man?"

"The stupid young man, you wanted to say. He is not stupid; he just had an accident. It didn't heal well. He had another seizure last night."

"Bring him here."

Pireska opened her mouth to protest, but the usually calm Horwath looked too irritated, and she changed her mind. She went inside the house and came out, pulling Codrin by his hand; he was pale, and had a catatonic look. "Please be gentle with him," she said to the captain.

"Are you wounded?" Horwath asked, assessing Codrin, who just stared back at him.

"Tudor," Pireska said, shaking his arm.

"Wounded," Codrin said.

"When?" Horwath's voice went suddenly cold, and his hand gripped the hilt of the sword.

"Some months ago."

"What happened yesterday?"

Pireska squeezed his palm twice, and Codrin said nothing, staring through Horwath as if he was not there. "He has no memories from yesterday. Because of the seizure. It's always like this." She shrugged, keeping her head half bowed, her eyes staring at a pebble on the road.

Horwath bit into his upper lip, looking thoughtfully at her. "I have the feeling that you are tricking me."

"Two women and two children. What could we do against four men? My son died last year. Ildeko gave Sir Irvath what he wanted. That's all."

"The lady may come and interrogate you."

"We have nothing to hide. I suppose that the ... party will be cancelled and there is no need for Ildeko to go there."

"You suppose wrong. There will be no party, but the Lady's maid has had an accident, and she needs a new one. The young man will come too and serve in the stables."

"What kind of accident?" Pireska asked, only to gain some time.

"She bit herself hard and lost her tongue. She can no longer perform her duties. After this ... situation with Sir Irvath is resolved, they will be called to the castle. A courier will come. If the Lady doesn't come here first."

"Yes, I understand," Pireska replied, and the captain turned to mount his horse.

"That was a bad accident, the maid can't speak without her tongue," Codrin said, looking at the riders going away. Something was mounting inside his mind, separate threads of memories about riding, and a sort of desire that he could not understand. It did not last long.

"No, she can't speak." *But the Madwoman did not need the poor woman's tongue for speaking.* "You did well with the captain." Earlier, in the house, she had told Codrin to stop speaking when she squeezed his hand twice. *How old is your mind now? Twelve, thirteen?*

In the next days, they stopped most of their work, Pireska and Ildeko watching the road by turns. When Elsebeth arrived, she found only Pireska in front of the house; the other three were already hiding in the cave.

"My lady." Pireska bowed.

"I need to talk to your daughter."

"I apologize, my lady, but she went to gather berries on the White Saddle." Pireska pointed to one of the peaks across the valley.

Elsebeth moved her horse abruptly and kicked the old women in the mouth with a heavy boot, throwing her to the ground. "Winter will be here in three weeks, there are no more berries at this time of the year. Tell me another lie, and you will regret it. Bring her and that young man here."

"I apologize, my lady," Pireska said without trying to stand. She just rolled a bit further away.

"You bitch," Elsebeth shouted and raised her whip. Horwath moved his horse closer and whispered in her ear. "Are you sure?" she asked, looking daggers at him.

She looks at me as if I am an enemy, not the man who pleased her for more than a year. "Yes, my lady."

"Then I have to apologize," Elsebeth said, and dismounted with a speed that few were capable of. She was well trained as a fighter, including with the sword. She used a handkerchief to wipe the blood from Pireska's lips and helped her to stand. "Could you please tell me what happened here five days ago?" Her voice became low and seductive, hypnotic.

Fate, she has the Light, Pireska moaned inside and fought to gather all her strength for a mental battle that was hard to win. "Sir Irvath came to visit us. He wanted to ... talk to Ildeko."

"When did he come, and where did they talk?"

"He came at noon, and they talked in the house, my lady."

"Was there any other talking?"

"Yes, my lady. The captain talked to her too, then the soldiers."

"Ildeko is a kind woman, always ready to please. What happened next?"

"Sir Irvath left. They took the small path that goes parallel to the road."

"Do you know why?" Elsebeth placed her hands on Pireska's shoulders. Their eyes locked, and there was a sudden surge of Light at a level Pireska had never encountered before. "Tell me the truth." Her right hand went to the back of Pireska's neck, massaging it gently.

The old woman shivered. Moistened her lips. Breathed as if the world was void of air. The words came slowly from her mouth. "No, my lady."

"Did he leave?" Elsebeth's head leaned forward until there was only a palm's width between their eyes. "Did my husband really leave this place?"

"Yes, my lady, in the afternoon. They stayed around an hour and half."

Elsebeth straightened abruptly and stepped back. "When did your daughter leave the house to pick berries?"

"They left yesterday, before noon."

"What berries are they after?"

"Fate's berries and geese blueberries."

"When will they return?"

"In three days, my lady."

"Tudor, the young man. When did he arrive here?"

"At the end of spring, my lady. He was a scout in the Silvanian army, and he was wounded by the nomads. He barely escaped, and I treated his wounds. There were two arrows in him." She touched her right shoulder. "He chose to remain here, but then he had the accident. He fell in the stream and hit a rock with his head." Pireska touched the back of her head. "He is no longer himself. He acts like a twelve-year-old child."

"That's a pity. I suppose Ildeko enjoyed him. He seems to be well clad."

"Yes, my lady, but after the accident, he is a child in every aspect, even in his pants."

That's even more the pity. I feel a strange link with this man. Perhaps he will recover. My stupid husband has vanished, and now this. Never mind, I wanted to get rid of Irvath next year. "I need a new maid. In a week, send Ildeko to the castle. Last time I met her, she seemed competent enough."

"Yes, my lady."

Elsebeth turned to leave, took a step, then turned again like a storm, and hit Pireska in the face with her fist, throwing the old woman to the ground again. In a second, Elsebeth mounted her, hit her a few more times, until Pireska's face was bloody, then pressed a knife at her neck. "When did my husband come here?"

"At noon."

"What berries are they picking on the mountains?" Elsebeth slapped her twice, turning her head left and right. The stone of her ring left another thin line of blood on Pireska's face.

"Fate's berries and geese blueberries."

"Who was the third man to spread your daughter's legs?" She slapped the old woman again.

"A soldier."

"When is Ildeko returning?" Another slap.

"In three days."

"When did my husband leave?" This time she punched Pireska in the stomach, and she was left without air. "When?"

"An hour and a half later," Pireska gasped.

"Why did they take the path? Tell me or I will kill you." Elsebeth pressed her knife and a small line of blood appeared on Pireska's neck.

"I don't know."

As abruptly as she went down on Pireska, Elsebeth stood up and mounted her horse. "Don't forget to send Ildeko. Tell her to bring her son too. I can't separate a mother from her child," she said as if nothing had happened. She rode away, followed by Horwath and her soldiers. *It seems that the old bitch did not lie. She gave me the same answers, even under duress, and under the pressure from my Light. Then who killed my idiot husband? I will try again with Ildeko. She won't be able to lie in front of her son.*

Slowly, Pireska got up to her knees. Her face was swollen, and blood still flowed from the cut on her neck. She touched it gently. *It's not a bad cut. The blow in the stomach was the worst. It went into my liver. The Madwoman knows where to hit. And her Light... So strong... I never heard of someone being able to use the Light like this woman. A few moments more, and I would have told her the truth.* Too weak to stand, she remained crouched, her head on her hands. *We must hide in six days. But they will burn the house, and there will be no place to return to.* She looked north-west; there was a thin line of black-white clouds, but the rest of the sky was clear, and the sun was still strong. Then she sniffed the wind. *Fate, you never listen much to my pleas, and I have lost almost everything. Take me if you like but let them live. Give them enough snow to block the road in two days.* After a while, she let her mind go into the Light. *I think that it will snow*, she thought and fell to the ground, unconscious.

Pireska woke in her bed, her hand between Ildeko's. "I am hurt, but it is nothing that won't heal in a week. We need to talk. It will not be easy. When you were kept in the castle, did you feel something strange when the Madwoman was with you?"

"Yes," Ildeko breathed and closed her eyes for a few moments. "It shames me even now, but I... I enjoyed being with her, even though she made me do bad things." She bit her lip.

"Don't," Pireska said gently. "She has a sort of Light and used it on you; something that I have not felt before. I must talk with Thais when she returns. This woman is an abomination. The Wanderers must deal with her."

The sky was clear, and it was cold that evening. Ildeko sensed that the first freeze of the year would come that night. The land was covered by a foot-thick blanket of snow, and the road was no longer visible. She was safe for a while from the Madwoman; the road would be blocked for several months. Through the window, the full moon played light into the room. It was not late, but Ferent and Pireska were already in bed, the old woman still not fully recovered from the beating. People go to sleep early during the winter. Ildeko was waiting for Codrin to end his work. He was stubborn in his will to help them, and that evening he wanted to finish splitting the logs; they had enough wood to burn for the whole winter and spring now. When he came in, for the first time she sensed he was tired, and helped him take off his heavy boots. Alone at the table, he ate slowly, caught in his thoughts. She wondered what was in his mind. At times, he acted like a mature man, but that was still rare, though she would have laughed now, knowing what he was thinking about.

Codrin liked the venison, yet there was a feeling that something was missing, something that he had enjoyed in the past. Raising a piece of meat in the fork, a spark of curiosity in his eyes, he turned it this way, then that way.

"Is it too cold?" Ildeko asked.

"No, it's good. But..." He stopped, unwilling to upset her. *Yes*, she nodded at him. "I ... remember something about a sort of red liquid I drank when I ate a steak. Perhaps I was dreaming," he added swiftly.

"Wine. We don't have it in the mountains." *We are too poor.*

"Wine," he repeated and continued to eat. *What's wine?* But he did not ask, sensing her uneasiness. When he finished, he took his chair and sat in front of the fire, rubbing his hands close to the flames. It was warm in the room, but he stayed there mostly for pleasure. Sometimes, he waited until everybody fell asleep, and he sat in the front of the large fireplace until the fire was dead, the same way it happened in a forgotten past with Saliné. He turned his head toward Ildeko, wanting to ask about... She was wiping the freshly washed plates, and her breasts were moving up and down. She caught his stare, and he turned his head abruptly, a touch of red on his face.

"That's fine," she said, and a small grin flashed on her lips. "Men look at women like that."

"Am I a man?"

"For sure you are not a woman," she laughed. "Ferent is small, he is a child. You are a man."

"Those men who..." he said, hesitantly. "They were men too."

"There are men and men. Don't worry about them, they were bad apples. Scum. You are not like them."

"They wanted to talk, but talk is not evil. And why were you naked when you were talking to him?"

"It happens sometimes that men and women talk like that."

"It's bad," Codrin grunted.

"It's not bad when both want to talk."

"But you wanted to talk. You told me that..."

"No, I didn't." For the first time Ildeko's voice was angry, and Codrin became unhappy.

"Sorry if I upset you," he said, not understanding why.

"You did not upset me, and you saved me from that man." *Though you did not understand from what.*

"I did not want to kill them." He stared at his hands, which trembled slightly.

"I know." Ildeko came and took his hands in hers. "You just wanted to protect me, Ferent and Pireska. That's what real men do, protecting women and children." She felt Codrin trembling harder, and hugged him, pulling his head toward her chest. Codrin embraced Ildeko and pressed his face even more against her. It comforted him, and a strange warmth rose in him. His body reacted physically, in a way that he would recall later, perhaps from her fingers stroking his skin, or from her firm breasts pressed against his face, yet he did not embrace her like a man.

Before the spring equinox, Elsebeth was invited to the royal wedding, in Muniker; Alfrid was her cousin. She spent her spring, summer and autumn there, hunting for another husband. She was a patient hunter, and everybody recalled the beautiful and reserved Countess, still grieving for her beloved husband, who was killed while trying to save a poor woman from a band of mercenaries. "The woman was able to escape," Elsebeth told everybody in a trembling voice, "but my poor Irvath was killed, and his body was burned by those evil men. We have an empty grave in our castle." She even managed to make a good impression on Saliné. And she managed to keep the title and riches, though she had no heir from Irvath. Her beloved husband had signed a paper that everything would go to her at his death. It was countersigned by three more nobles as witnesses. Irvath's younger brother went mad, but there was nothing anyone could do; the paper was officially stamped, and Elsebeth was the King's cousin. During her stay, despite her appetites, she kept her bed empty of lovers, and left Muniker and four suitors unhappy by her departure. At home, she thought again about Ildeko and Codrin, and wondered if the young man had recovered his mind and manhood. It was autumn again. *Strange how much I am attracted by him... It has not happened to me for a long time. Horwath... I had to break with him... In a castle full of servants, one is never careful enough. I must see that young man. I have the feeling that it's important. Why would that be? A woodcutter. No, he was a Silvanian soldier.* She let her mind into the Light, and the feeling grew stronger in her. *It makes no sense.* Captain Horwath was dispatched and came back with the news that the young man seemed to be in good shape. There was a kind of effervescence in Elsebeth's body that had not been touched by a man or woman for several long months, but she knew that from now on there would be many spies around her, at the request of the men who courted her in Muniker. Until her next marriage, Elsebeth would be an exemplary woman. Or at least very discreet. *I was a Knight's daughter, yet I married a rich Count. He never knew why. A Duke should follow. It will take time, but I made that two-year-long vow of chastity in front of the court; it will keep the men waiting for a while until I can pick the right one.* "Waiting strengthens a man's desire," she laughed. "Desire strengthens my control over them."

The sun was above the peaks, its pale red disc shining now and then through a thin stretch of clouds moved by the eastern wind. Alone, Elsebeth dismounted in front of Codrin, at the edge of the forest. Two hundred paces away, Horwath was tense on his horse, sword in hand. "Do you know who I am?" she asked and slid a finger over the scar on Codrin's jaw.

"Yes."

"Yes, my lady."

"Yes, my lady." Codrin shrugged, looking down at her for a few moments, Elsebeth was not a tall woman; she was not short either. Not knowing how to react further, he fixed a peak in the far away.

She walked around, measuring his body, then stopped again in front of him. "Do I know you? The one before the accident?"

"I don't know." *Perhaps.* Slowly, Codrin stretched an arm and placed his hand around the nape of her neck. His gesture surprised both. *I can kill her now. But I can't. I feel weak. Why?*

Horwath cursed, and pushed his horse forward, rising his sword. A few steps, and he reevaluated the charade in front of him. Swiftly, he pulled the halter, stopping the horse.

Elsebeth's long neck arched backward, and her eyes met Codrin's. In the slanting sunlight their expression was unreadable, save for the frown of concentration as both were unable to understand what was happening to them. Elsebeth placed a palm on his chest and let her Light pass through him. Codrin's skin was tingling, the hairs on his neck standing up. Both shivered, and he pulled Elsebeth closer, almost to embrace her. She did not oppose.

I can't feel him, and I can't see his future. The Light returns to me like an echo. I feel weak. "Who are you?" she asked and received no answer. Abruptly, Elsebeth went away from Codrin, mounted her horse, and rode away. *I will come again when he recovers his memories. There is a strange power in him, and I am sure that I've met him in the past.* She still felt weak, not in the body; her will was faltering, and that strong will had made Elsebeth a powerful Countess. She had felt like this only once in her life, a long time ago. It was a disaster.

Chapter 13 - Saliné

First came the tune, then the words:

"Codrin is gone to war,
Mironton, mironton, mirontaine,
But when will he ever come home?"

It was just a stupid war song, Saliné knew that. She had sung it with other children when her father went to war. Just the name in the first verse was different: 'Orban is gone to war.' It was always the name of the enemy in the song, implying that he might never come home. *But it was Father who did not return. Why did it come to me now? And why Codrin?* She had not sung it since her father's death in a war he was supposed to win. The song was old, much older than she or most people knew. It came from the Talant Empire, and the words had changed over millennia, as the old language that had been spoken in Frankis was long gone, but the sense of the verses remained, moving slowly from one language to another, in several waves of translation. Any translator is a traitor, goes the saying, but that did not match the evolution of this song. The melody was almost the same too; it was an easy song, even the most stupid child or soldier could learn the words, or at least follow the simple melody. Strangely, what did not change was the refrain: 'mironton, mironton, mirontaine'. It meant nothing in the old language. It meant nothing in the new language. Perhaps that was the reason for the continuity. Without knowing why, she sang it again. For a few months now, she no longer burst into tears when she spoke or heard Codrin's name. Memories related to him now felt like a dream, or like a nightmare, depending on factors that she could never understand or control.

At the border, Saliné was separated from her people, a matter of Litvonian protocol that even Cantemir could not solve. The Litvonian rules were strict and many. Saliné had to be alone the next days and nights; not even her son was allowed to join her. For five days, she traveled alone in her carriage, she ate alone and, during the nights, she could not sleep, her mood going from bad to worse without Jara or her son to keep company. The nights without sleep recalled the bad time spent with Bucur, and she started to attach his hated memory to Alfrid. The first day was relatively easy to bear, the next one was bad, the next ones worse. All the time, she was surrounded by fifty Litvonian guards, who never spoke to her, even when she was fluent in their language. Last day at noon, Edric would pick her up in another carriage. Everything was a symbol; Saliné had to leave her previous life behind and start a new one in Litvonia. There was a sort of calculated pressure on the bride to make her feel happy and thriving when meeting the King, as an old secretary had whispered to her. Some things were the same everywhere, some were different. *They are idiots to think that this will make me feel happy to meet Alfrid. I may feel the need to slap him.* During the long periods in the carriage, she felt miserable and cursed Alfrid, imagining that he was lame or hunchbacked, and she could refuse him and return home. Or perhaps she would marry Edric – he had left a good impression on her in Arad. Alfrid would wait for her at Swestgate, Muniker's western gate, with the royal phaeton. *Swestgate...* she thought. *Ten years ago, Codrin left Muniker through Swestgate, running from Baraki's men. He was coming to Frankis. To me. Last year, he went back to Litvonia. To a grave. There is no grave. I hate this country.* She shook her head, trying to think of nothing.

"But when will he ever come home?" She repeated the last verse, and tears that did not fall filled her eyes. *I won't cry,* she shook her head*, but why did I choose this song?*

"Sister Saliné." Edric sneaked his head through the window of the carriage, pulling her out of her reverie. "I am here to welcome you."

"Thank you, Edric." Eyes still closed, Saliné grimaced; she was getting closer to Muniker. Stepping out, she stretched her stiff body. The sky was clear and bright; it was the second week after the spring equinox. Her mind was far from being clear.

"Welcome to Litvonia." With his impetuous move that she recalled from Arad, Edric embraced her. After four nights without sleep and those awful hours alone in the carriage, Saliné found some comfort. Feeling her tension, he gently massaged the back of her neck. "I apologize for our magnificent rules regarding traveling brides. It was a long road, perhaps you want to walk a few steps."

"Yes." She wanted to say more but clamped her mouth shut afraid that her voice would betray her weakness.

Edric leaned his head back to look at her and flashed a large, warm smile. "You look beautiful." *But tired*... "Let's go." He placed an arm around her shoulders and made her walk along the road. With his other arm, he signaled the soldiers to follow them at a distance.

He is allowed to do this, Saliné thought, feeling his hand gripping her shoulder gently, recalling that terrible Book of Muniker Manners, which Edric had left to her in Arad. There were rules even for such things. He was even allowed to kiss her on the mouth. There was a list of seven relatives who could be so close to her. *Alfrid will do more than kiss me, and I must accept that too. There is another rule*... She had to reciprocate to Edric, and she placed her arm around his waist. They walked in silence for a few minutes, and Saliné felt better.

Edric helped her into the new carriage and joined her inside. "We will arrive in about three hours. I will try to make them feel shorter. This carriage is comfortable." He made Saliné half turn, lifted her feet on the bench, in parallel with the backrest. There was a large pillow, and she leaned against it.

Feeling better, Saliné thought again of that book full of strange rules. There were things that she would accept because she had to adapt, like being so close to her brother-in-law. At least this did not feel bad. There were things that she would never accept, like taking lovers, a common thing in Muniker, although perhaps Alfrid deserved that.

Minute by minute, Edric introduced Muniker to Saliné. He knew many picaresque stories, all of them of good quality, but his last one was different, an old romantic tale, made even more attractive by his soft, baritone voice that reminded her of Codrin. It resembled Saliné's own story a little and, eyes closed, she lost track of it, her tired mind wandering in the past, in Severin and Arad. "I think now we can have our welcome kiss," Edric whispered.

Her mouth was open, as she was trying to speak, and Edric parted her lips fully. His strong arms embraced her firmly, stirring sensations from a time long gone, her mind traveling in a past when Codrin was still with her. There were three or four kisses, or five, she could not remember, but she had to pretend that it was only one; this was the rule. Edric began to tell another story and, under his seductive voice, Saliné fell slowly asleep in his arms.

Confused, she woke up in the arms of an unknown man, looking into a pair of blue eyes, which were watching her with a sort of amusement. Then she remembered. And she smiled, wryly, moving away from him.

"We will arrive in a minute. If you have problems falling asleep again, I am ready to offer my services."

"They seem to be of good quality, but I don't know if I can afford your fees."

"We can negotiate." For a few moments, Edric looked at her, a trace of smile in his eyes. And a trace of expectation; she had the choice to give her own welcome kiss. She chose not to. The carriage slowed down, and Edric looked outside, then nodded at the large gate, visible through the window. "Muniker. I hope that our journey did not feel long and unpleasant."

There was disappointment in his voice, and Saliné touched his face briefly, before saying with calculated indifference, "It didn't." Composed, she stepped down from the carriage, and found herself face to face with Alfrid.

"My Queen," Alfrid said, bowing, "Muniker is eager to meet you."

Looking at him, Saliné found a man who was as tall as her, dressed in two vests, yellow, green and blue. He wore a gold chain, a long earring, three large rings, and an even larger medallion. There was something resembling a blue hat on his head, a long peacock feather attached to it. "My King," she bowed too. *I was once married to a man, now I will marry a peacock.* Dressed in a dark red, refined costume, Edric stood next to his brother, a discreet smile on his lips, and he looked so different, so much like Codrin. She measured the other men around, all dressed as colorfully as their King. *Peacocks*, she shrugged. *A court of peacocks. Why is Edric not the King?*

I always make a good impression on women. Alfrid pondered at her reaction, stifling the start of a smile. In Muniker, he was considered a handsome and elegant man. It was a strange city. Or perhaps just different. He helped Saliné to climb in an open phaeton. Took her in his arms, so everyone around could see them. Kissed her long. The memory of another pair of lips still fresh in her mind; it was not unpleasant for Saliné in the beginning. It became when Alfrid made it a sort of sport void of feelings, using some tricks she disliked. That sort of tricks done with the tongue, associated in Frankis with the whores. It ended at some point, and they went into the city together.

Discreetly, Saliné wiped her mouth. She wanted to spit. She forced herself to swallow. *This will not happen again; I am not his whore.* Passing through the gate, Saliné could not stop living in the past. *Codrin left Muniker through this gate...* She shook her head under Alfrid's scrutiny. *I must rein into my memories.* She tried, but they continued to storm her mind like a wild animal, and she pressed her nails hard into her skin, the pain in her flesh seeming to overcome the pain in her mind.

The phaeton rumbled slowly through the streets, and thousands of people expressed their joy, throwing flowers at Saliné. Their enthusiasm felt strange to her, and she did not know if it was genuine, or there was some theater at play, to make her feel better. It did feel better, but not enough to make her forget. She would learn later that the people's enthusiasm was genuine; they now had a beautiful Queen, who was marked by the Seer, the man who had saved them from the nomads. The Munikers liked the dead hero more than they liked Alfrid. Many legends about Codrin circled in the city, and most of them were told in the Caravans Inn, which was a kind of pilgrimage place, where good wine and good stories could be found.

Two days later, at noon, the wedding commenced. *All I have to do is to smile*, Saliné thought. This was a grandiose ceremony, but her thoughts went to her first wedding in Valeni. *It was small, but our feelings made it wonderful. Now it's only politics, a large ceremony, where I am paraded for the kingdom...* She felt as if she were being displayed to an audience, half naked with that overcomplicated Litvonian dress on her body, in a high position where all could ogle her. *Some people will like me, some will dislike me, and some will hate me, though they don't know me*. She lost her composure for a few moments, and then restored the smile on her lips. *A smiling Queen looks more acceptable. And more stupid*. She was accustomed to hiding her feelings under a mask of calm enjoyment; a long time ago, Bucur had schooled her more than well enough. *Isn't that strange? I killed Bucur, my first husband. Codrin was killed by the nomads. Everything has ended in death. If I am cursed by Fate, what will happen to Alfrid? I won't kill him, but I won't cry if it happens either. I cried enough, for almost a year. Then what? I will be pressured to marry Edric. At least he seems to be a real man.*

“I declare you husband and wife, queen and king,” the priest sang, in a warm voice, and Saliné almost started; she had passed through the whole ceremony almost absently.

Did I say the right words?

Alfrid leaned in to kiss her, and she forced herself to answer. She felt no joy or desire, she felt sadness but, at least, she did not feel much hate.

The morning after the wedding, Calista took Saliné to the royal park. They walked in silence for a while, and the old woman’s quiet presence brought to her memories, both old and fresh. She could not stop to compare again her weddings, and even worse her wedding nights. Her mood was bad, she had passed through the ceremony almost absently; the night was different. Saliné felt almost as bad as when the Circle forced her to marry Bucur. *At least I killed Bucur...* She disliked the old woman, who was the source of her misery, but she could be composed when she wanted it. During her way through the park and through the contrasts of her life, somewhere inside, her own voice was saying: *The world can change, so can you. The world has changed. And Alfrid is not Bucur. But I still feel like an object to be used in bed...* At least the park was a wonder, and at the back of the palace, just under the terrace of her suite, there was a maze made of yew hedges, almost as large as her whole garden in Arad. That was where Calista led her. After a few minutes, Saliné’s eyes widened, and she forced herself to look away from one of the benches. It was half hidden inside the hedge, shaped like a broken circle, almost surrounding two people who were kissing without care for spectators.

“Isn’t she the Countess...? Saliné asked. “I’ve forgotten her name.”

“Yes,” Calista said, a glimmer in her eyes. “You want to say that she is married, and that the young man in her arms is not her husband.”

"Something like that."

"Muniker is different to Arad. You will see. Courting is not only acceptable but also expected. It's part of the local culture, you might say. This is the Court of Love. The people on the bench are called lemans, and both have the consent of their husband and wife for this sort of pleasant activity. A woman or man without a leman is considered a kind of an outcast. A savage."

"Are they actually lovers?"

"That's a completely different thing. If they are, they will keep it secret; it doesn't happen often. To lose your head for a leman is a sign of weakness. Weakness is dangerous. The openly accepted lovers are the political ones, the lointain lovers, and love is a rare thing in this sort of affair; it's about power and survival."

"And it's ... an open thing." As they continued to walk, Saliné looked at the next pair of lemans, and at the next one. The half-hidden places were set at thirty paces from one another, and the garden was full of them, and full of people. On one bench, there was a woman sharing her charms with two men. The next woman was half naked, with one breast out of her chemise, half covered by a man's hand.

"Yes, my dear. They are enjoying it ... openly." Calista laughed, pointing at the half naked woman. "There was something that we could not discuss in Arad, and Alfrid is too proud to admit. Litvonia is unstable. The end of the civil war is more an armistice than an end, with three strong parties still vying for power, and that's why you are here, to bring stability. This is your kingdom now, and your family. Children will come, and you will use all the tools you have to protect them. Including your charm."

This is a depraved city, and Alfrid must be like his subjects. "Are you suggesting...?"

"I am not suggesting anything; you will learn everything yourself. You will decide how many men are allowed to court you, and when to take a lointain lover. There are rules too; the Queen can't accept men of lesser status than a Count."

"Courting," Saliné shrugged with studied indifference, "that I can accept. Without the kissing stuff. But I am married, I will not accept lovers." *Edric already kissed me. It was allowed...*

"Kissing will come naturally, you will see, and you will have lovers if necessity begs. A Queen is a political thing. A real Queen, and you are one of them, will not waste time on painting or embroidery. She will rule. It may be unpleasant; it can be made pleasant... Everybody makes a decision."

Saliné's green eyes glittered with derision as she said, "And you will guide me as to whom I should spend my charms on. Or it will be Alfrid?"

"Neither. Your children will demand it, and they can be very demanding. To help you, I had a Vision of one of your future lovers."

Like Drusila, and no doubt it is Edric. Saliné said nothing, looked at Calista.

"I won't tell you his name," Calista laughed. "It will spoil your learning curve and expectations. You have to think about the next nomad invasion too."

Back in her suite, Saliné found Edric waiting for her with a huge bouquet of lavender flowers. "Thank you, Edric, they are wonderful." She pressed her face against the flowers, her mind going back to Frankis, the land of lavender, and remembered the rules and the price attached to the gift only when Edric placed his arms around her waist. Silent, she kept herself busy with the flowers.

"Do you accept my gift?"

If I say yes, Edric is allowed to kiss me, Saliné thought. *If I refuse, it's a lack of manners. I fell in his trap. Did I want to...?* "Yes." Saliné placed the bouquet on the table and turned toward him. There was a surge of warmth in her; there were things to ponder. *It is allowed. It is pleasant. I can't avoid it now. It must not happen again. Or at least not so often.* "The rules are always playing in your favor."

She stayed hidden when Edric came with his next gift and the next one, avoiding to refuse him, and from that day, they never remained alone again. He was an inventive man, always trying, but she learned the game fast and used Alfrid, her child, mother, and maids as her shield. It was a tight game, but it was not unpleasant; Saliné found that she was adapting fast to this strange, rotten city and its even stranger rules.

Postponed because of the wedding, the Royal Ball was waited with great anticipation. The hall was bustling of people eager to dance and to flirt; Munikers liked to dance as much as they liked courting. In the morning, Saliné had learned the rules from Calista. They were not many; she had to open the ball and the last suite with Alfrid, then both were on their own; the etiquette would demand to dance with different partners. It suited Saliné. It worried her too; she did not know many people there, and she had the feeling that, in Muniker, the dancers were too intimate with their partners. A Queen was a political thing; she had to take care to allow a place on her dancing list for this Duke or that Count, whose names she had memorized in the afternoon. No one was allowed two dances during the same suite or more than two dances during the evening, not even the royal pair. She felt a little lost, sitting alone with Edric in the royal lodge while Alfrid was still caught in some political talk down on the floor.

"Would you grant me the last dance of the second suite?" Edric asked, and Saliné felt a hidden tension under his calm demeanor. It was for the first time in three weeks when they were alone, but the lodge was an open space.

This will allow you to invite me for a walk in the garden. Involuntarily, Saliné glanced at his lips, and arched her brows to the edge of irony, though no one could say if she was mocking him or herself. *A gift must be already prepared for me. This evening I will accept it.* With a guarded look, she studied Edric, trying to learn his reactions. There were not many, his face was immobile, hiding behind a trace of a smile; his body relaxed, only the little finger of his right hand was twitching a little. "What would you think about the last dance of the first and the second suite?"

His finger stopped twitching. "It seems that Fate answered my call."

"To ask Fate's guidance for a dance... You must be a devoted person." Saliné laughed quietly.

"I am your most devoted person, but I must leave now; there is a long queue of men waiting for their chance to dance with you. They want to kill me." He grinned and pointed at the more than fifty men aligned behind Saliné – there were only eleven places still free on her list, and five were not really free, if those important Dukes and Counts would come to invite her.

She glanced back then said to Edric, her lips moving without sound, "Fate take you all."

Edric burst into laughter and left her alone with the waiting men. Saliné filled her list. Danced her dances. Let herself being caught in the cheerful mood around. She was right about men being too intimate during the dances. Alfrid was intimate too, but at least he was her husband. Unfortunately. The other three men never missed an occasion to take her measures. She found that it was a common thing for all the pairs in the hall and forced herself to take it naturally. Some women were even dancing with the back at the men, their hands inside the generous cleavages. At least she was spared this. Edric was a perfect dancer. At the end of the suite, they walked into a small balcony – there were fifty around the ballroom, discreetly built for privacy. They were alone, and a dark red rose was waiting on the balustrade, its delicate contours enhanced by the twilight. Saliné picked it and leaned back against Edric.

"I have a surprise for you," Edric said at the end of the second suite. "There is a bush that opens its flowers only at night. They look like the magnolias in Frankis and have a sweet perfume – the wonder of our park."

During their walk, Edric was silent and, placing an arm around her shoulders, guided her to a side alley that got darker as the lights of the castle remained far behind them.

"Is it far?" Saliné broke the silence. "My next dance is with Alfrid, so we must be back in time."

"This break is one hour long. There is enough time."

Plenty of time, for plenty of things. Saliné shrugged, a sense of pleasant anticipation mounting inside her.

It was a bit cold outside, and she shivered when they stopped. There was a delicate scent in the air, but the praised flowers were not yet open. Passing through a thirty-foot-wide gap between two giant trees, the strong moonlight was painting a band of light on the ground. Somewhere above, a nightingale was singing his love. They were in the middle of an enchanting place.

"I understand that springs are warmer in Arad," Edric said and embraced her from behind.

"Yes, they are." She leaned against him; Edric felt so much like Codrin. He was the same height, and had the same strong hands, with long, elegant fingers that could be also gentle. Edric's lips were gentle too, and skilled, she had learned that well. The flow of memories warmed her and came with Drusila's Vision: You will be close to Edric, and he will save your kingdom and children.

"These three weeks... Did I bother you?"

"No." *I like to be bothered by you, but you are not my husband. That was the point in avoiding you.*

Edric opened a flower and plucked a large petal, the size of a child's palm, rubbed it between his fingers until it became a thin paste, then made her lean against the large tree that towered over the bush. "This is a wish tree, and we have a ritual when one sees it for the first time, the Whish Flower Ritual. It's ancient. Pagan." The pleasant scent became stronger as he traced the contour of her mouth with a finger, leaving behind a sort of lipstick.

It warmed her lips, and Saliné moistened them with her tongue. The taste was bittersweet. "Dangerous?"

"Of course." He picked nectar from the same flower and made a thin line down her neck. Then another one. "The warmth will spread and linger in your body. The ritual is long and usually carried out by someone who is ... close to the victim. The rules allow me to go as far as you feel comfortable. Should I continue? You can stop me at any time."

Saliné compared the way Edric was making her feel against her unpleasant nights with Alfrid, and for the first time she thought that, perhaps, Muniker rules were not all bad. "Yes."

Their embrace was tender, and they shared the sweet-biter taste of the wish flower lipstick. It was a long and slow kiss, their lips moving gently, exploring, prolonging the pleasant tension running through their bodies. The bird above was still singing, and they listened for a while. When they recovered their breath, Edric opened another flower and moistened his fingers in its nectar. His hands moved down from the base of her neck, one unbuttoning her chemise, the other sliding two moistened fingers until they reached her navel. He pressed his wet thumbs on her navel, sliding up until they reached her breastbone. They went down, then up again, a few times, spreading warmth and pleasure on her skin, then cupped her breasts, his thumbs rubbing them gently. His touch and the nectar felt like fire in her chest.

Saliné leaned her head back against the tree, and let her body drown in a pleasure that she had not felt for a long time. *My start with Alfrid was bad, and I think that I need this. The evening will follow its course, wherever it will take me, but this will not happen again.*

Taking more nectar, Edric touched her fingers. Saliné painted the contours of his lips, then his neck, then opened his shirt to paint his chest. This time, Edric pulled her tighter, and his lips went hard on hers. Hers became fierce. His fingers stirred her body, and he touched and kissed her everywhere. She answered in kind. Her skirts rose and fell, stormed by his hands; her breasts were touched, kissed, and bitten. Saliné kissed and bit him too.

Gently, Edric pressed his body against hers. She gasped, tightening her arms around his neck while he moved slowly until they found their rhythm. When Saliné reached her highest moment, she whispered, "Oh, Codrin," and arched abruptly against Edric's strong body, pressing her nails deep into his skin. Caught in his own moment of pleasure, Edric did not hear her. Their moves slowed down; their breaths slowed down.

Leaning her head on Edric's shoulder, Saliné did not move, but her mind started to spin. *I am fooling myself. Codrin will never come back. Yet this ... was so...* She bit her lip, and forced herself to stop thinking, and let the pleasant memories sweep back through her. She wanted them. *Is Edric who I really want, or is this only because he reminds me of Codrin? Both, perhaps?* She opened her eyes on the myriad stars above and started to count, trying to stop her thoughts. It did not help. *This night, I am living again.*

Edric sensed her uneasiness and lifted her head, pressing his mouth on hers. After the storm before, it was like a breeze, gentle and calming. "The ritual goes on for one night," he whispered in her ear. "Should it continue?"

"Yes." *This will be my wedding night.*

"You can make a wish now. Once, I wished to see the south of Frankis. There were stories about good wine, good food, orange orchards, and beautiful women. I started to dream of them."

I wish Codrin to come back, she thought, caught in his game. *I am becoming childish.* "And what did you dream more of? Beautiful women?" Saliné laughed.

"What's life without beautiful women?" He laughed too. "And what's a beautiful woman without intelligence?"

"Most men prefer only beauty."

"Are they really men?"

"You tell me," she said and disengaged from him. "We need to go back."

There was a delicate and romantic moonlight, and they returned through a park filled with subtle shadows, walking hand in hand, Edric telling her stories. In the ballroom, they went to the royal lodge, where Alfred was waiting. Saliné pointed at Edric.

"Your brother wanted to show me the bush which opens its perfumed flowers at night."

"He likes to impress beautiful women with the ritual of the wish flowers." Alfrid's voice was half amused, but nothing could be read on his face. *Did they have a ritual? How far did they go?* He knew that it was allowed, and there was nothing to do about it, but he felt annoyed. Everything he had tried with Saliné did not work well, despite his great fame as a lover. Trying too much to impress Saliné with his skills during their nights together, Alfrid was a clever man unable to realize that he was making her feel like an object.

"Unfortunately, the bush was not impressed by Edric's wish. There were no open flowers, but I believe you," Saliné laughed. "He told me something about the beautiful women from the south of Frankis. Perhaps Edric wants to find a wife."

"I am too young to marry." Edric laughed too, his voice a little higher than usual.

"Ah, the orchestra is ready," Saliné said, nodding to Alfrid, who stood up. She placed her hand in his, and they went down together.

"Did he bother you?" Alfrid asked after a while.

No, he didn't. "Edric is charming, and he schooled me on Muniker's hidden life. I need to know that part too, it may prove useful later. And I agree with him that he is too young to marry. One needs more experience to have a wife." She smiled, and Alfrid burst into laughter.

Alone in her bedroom, Saliné opened the Book of Manners to read about rituals. Everything was there, and everything that happened with Edric was allowed. "This is a strange place." She closed the book and laughed quietly. "Why should I care *now* about some stupid rules after everything that happened in the garden?"

At midnight, Edric came to her suite through a secret passage. There were two of them, one going into the Queen's suite, another one to the King's, built for the lointain lovers. That night, they went again into the same frenzied ritual, a feeling that Saliné had not experienced for a long time, since the first months after her marriage with Codrin. They woke up in the morning, after a night without much sleep, and Edric pulled her above him, his hands moving gently over her lower back.

"I will come in the evening to take you for a walk in the garden," Edric said.

"No, Edric. We will not be alone again, at least for a while."

"Do you regret this night?"

"No. It was my best night in Muniker, and I have not felt like this for a long time. But this was a ritual, and it must remain unique. I think that we still have one hour left." Saliné's lips covered his, and Edric pulled her to him. And everything counted as a Wish Flower Ritual and one thank you kiss for a gift, because of the rules. This was Muniker.

Saliné's life had forked like a branch the year before, her new path going east, far from her home in Frankis, but now she started to consider Muniker as home too. One must take from life what it offers. At least her path was better than she had thought in the beginning. One month and a half ago, she had come here against her will, knowing that she was embarking on something new and strange without being sure of her way. She shook her head and opened the door to the terrace, then stayed in the doorway naked, waiting for the wind to cool her skin and calm her mind. Something was bothering her, a feeling that had followed her from the first moment she woke. Eyes closed, she listened to the night. *Five weeks since our ... first night together.* She opened her eyes abruptly. *I am pregnant.* Looking back at the man still sleeping in her bed, the moment came when she fully knew her way. *More children will come, my family is growing... I will wait one more month to be sure before announcing that I am pregnant.* She did not love Alfrid, but no longer felt repulsion at seeing him, or perhaps just a little. They were some sort of comrades now, ruling two kingdoms and sharing the same bed once a week. There was no need to make a fuss about it, her marriage was just a fact of existence; the same thing happened to most women, and few of them were queens.

Walking slowly, she went to the margin of the terrace and placed her hands against the parapet. Wind-blown leaves fell into her hair; there was a large tree just in front and above her. Sometimes, it reminded her of the cherry tree in their hunting house in Severin. Those moments always brought her memories involving Codrin, a dream from another life. Many times she'd been in this park, by daylight or under torches at night, and she was still conscious of its beauty. The park was made for Alfrid's grandmother, by his grandfather. Under the strong moonlight, she became aware of the effect this garden could have on someone seeing it for the first time, someone who was not affected by the same contradictions that stormed her mind when she had arrived here. It was her garden now, and her life, but there might be a day when she would regret decisions made and the ones not made, on the paths that had led her to Muniker.

Chapter 14 - Saliné / Edric

Even Saliné's private life was different in Muniker. In Arad, Codrin's and her lives mingled. They shared the same bedroom; they ate together; they planned everything together. Life at the court of Muniker was constrained by a long list of rigid rules. She had her own large suite, an army of servants and secretaries. Each time Alfrid wanted to eat, or to spend the night together, a secretary came with a letter of request. She had to write an answer back to him. She did not complain about this; it would have been hard to share every evening or night with Alfrid. They did not have the chemistry she had tasted in her previous life, and once a week was enough. Love doesn't come easily for people half-living in the past.

It was almost evening, Saliné realized, and there were many issues still unsolved. She thought for a while and sent a secretary to invite Edric to walk with her. *He is still upset*, she shrugged, *but I need him*. After the Wish Flower Ritual, Saliné had not stayed alone with him again.

Outside, Saliné took Edric by the arm. "I need to know more about the situation in the north of Litvonia. Alfrid is avoiding the subject."

"The peace treaty is more an armistice. Maltia, the Duchess of Kolugn, and the Duke of Hamborg, are buying time. Our military victory was a bit of luck; the nomads have helped to keep the peace, ironically. The Duchess's husband died in battle against

Duke Hamborg, and she preferred some kind of neutrality until we dealt with him. She hates the Duke more than she hates Alfrid. She loved her husband."

"So Alfrid is courting her."

"Not yet. They are still in negotiations for the preliminaries to becoming lemans, which can be quite long. There are a lot of rules. Sometimes they make everything too boring. Soon, you must find one or two men to court you, and one of them may be the Duke of Hamborg."

"Why should they court me?"

"You are loved in Muniker, but the mood changes quickly here; some people may think that you are hardnosed, and don't like Litvonians. This will weaken us politically. Courting is part of Muniker culture, and it is not dangerous for a woman of your strength. It can even be pleasant." A little grin flashed on Edric's lips, as he studied her face.

"Perhaps. I wonder," Saliné said, struggling to ignore his grin and the memories behind it, "what if we are able to keep Maltia closer, and deal harder with Duke Hamborg."

"You mean if Alfrid became her lointain lover? He may like the idea." Edric laughed, and Saliné slapped the back of his head gently.

"No, he is not allowed to like it." She laughed too.

"Hmm, I thought that we brought Alfrid a mare to ride two kingdoms. Now I think he received a saddle for his back." She slapped him again, and he passed an arm around her waist, turning her until they were face to face. "Do you really want Alfrid to become Maltia's lover?"

I won't be bothered... "No. I want *you* to become her leman, then her lointain lover, and move to Kolugn for a while, to control her better."

"Ah, so you want to be a saddle for me too. Why should I accept?"

"For the same reason I agreed to come here. You told me about the great political need and so on. Do the same rules not apply to you too?"

"This is Muniker, the Court of Love. They will think badly of you if you don't take a leman or two, and while it's good for a Queen to be feared, it's also good to be loved. Alfrid will tell you the same thing."

He avoided answering about the Duchess, but he will accept. "Edric, I need you to find me someone I can trust, and with whom I can make an agreement for being my first leman. Walking together, talking, things like this, but no close relation, no touching, no kissing." *Later, we can talk about my second leman, the real one.*

"First, because of your rank, you need at least a Count. A Duke is preferably. No one will accept such courting rules; for them it will mean humiliation, and you will only make enemies by proposing that. Enemies are not good for your health. Second, no one will believe that you have a leman until they see you kissing in public."

"Why did I agree to come here?" Saliné whispered and moved away from him.

"There were reasons." He placed an arm around her shoulders, and they walked in silence for a while, through a path that was long and deserted, through some dense patches of bushes and artificial ruins.

"Would you feel humiliated if we set some rules about you courting me?" Saliné raised her head to catch his eyes.

"Yes," he said curtly, then turned her until they came face to face again. "But if we can show the necessary display in public, so I can save face, I can survive it."

"Thank you, Edric. How long it will take you to solve the thing with Maltia?"

"Two weeks to negotiate the preliminaries and three more weeks to become her leman; she has her pride too. The political part... I don't know. It may take a year."

A year is too long. "Would you mind if I talk to her?"

"You can talk as much as you like to her, but I prefer to deal with a woman by myself." Edric's lips twitched, and the lines between his brows deepened.

"I was just thinking to make her more receptive to our plan. We need to maintain the calm during the summer and autumn. Winter keeps soldiers home, and by spring many things may happen."

"You are a hard woman."

"I am a hard woman with myself too. But," Saliné smiled, a little wryly, "I will let you deal at your own pace with the *courting* of the other ... woman in discussion and have a face-saving solution in two months." *For them, everything is a courting game. For me it's not. I need to find my way... It will take time. In two months, everybody will know that I am pregnant. A few weeks of courting, and they will leave me alone. Is everything only a game for Edric? I am becoming too attached to him.*

"Usually, the preliminaries take two weeks, and they would consider me an idiot if it took more than one month." Edric looked at Saliné, and she nodded. They walked again, and he started another story, to break the silence. "So," Edric said, ready to finish, "the Countess suddenly found herself with her two lointain lovers in her bed. By mistake, she had written the same date and hour on both invitations, and told the servants to let them enter alone while she waited, naked. Intrigued, they came together, and none of them wanted to leave; it was a matter of honor. And from that night she was called Two-legged Countess, because she had to give each of them a leg and half of her body until a certain arrangement could be negotiated regarding her ... in-between. There are rumors that she enjoyed the night. There are also rumors that she made the *mistake* with the invitations again."

Saliné burst into laughter, moved away from him, and placed her hand on a large oak. "Two-legged Countess; only in Muniker could such things happen."

"What a wonderful place," Edric said, and put his arm around her waist, pulling her gently against him while he leaned against the tree. "Why are you making everything so hard?"

"Perhaps because it's not easy. You need to be patient." *Things are going too fast.*

"Saliné, I never thought that I could be so patient, our preliminaries started in the carriage bringing you to Muniker."

"That's not fair," she protested, just before his mouth covered hers.

"After the Wish Flower Ritual, you kept me away from you. *That* was not fair," Edric complained, some minutes later.

"There were reasons, but so much for my one-month preliminaries." Saliné leaned her head back, to reach his eyes. "I still want that month, no kissing, and no touching. As you've said, it's a matter of pride. A Queen can't afford to look weak."

"You will have it. In public." Edric grinned, and she could not stop a smile either.

In the palace, Alfrid listened patiently. "This is a good solution, but Saliné doesn't know all the rules of courting, and what it means to be a leman. It may take months to learn everything, and I can't teach her that," he laughed, "so I trust that you will teach her. We should now have the agreement regarding the allotted days for your time together."

"What do you mean by allotted?" Saliné asked. "This is not planning for a military campaign. We will meet once a month, somewhere in the garden." *Public and private... No rituals.*

"Twice a week?" Alfrid looked at Edric, who nodded.

Fate, she moaned inside, *this can't be true. My husband is negotiating with my lover. With my leman*, she corrected herself fast, *how many hours and day I will spend with him. What else will they negotiate? How many times we will...?* "Fate blast your rules," Saliné said, and her lips twitched in dry humor. "Well," she shrugged, "Let's get to the most important point. Maltia."

"You told her." Abruptly, Alfrid turned toward his brother.

"No, it was not him," Saliné said. "And it's better that you don't keep important things from me. I want to hear them from you, not from other people. They may not know them well enough, or they may try to mislead me."

"We are still talking, Maltia and I. Once we have decided to start the preliminaries for becoming lemans, the same agreement for the allotted days will be negotiated between you and Maltia."

Maltia and I? Saliné thought, frowning at him. She did not know if she should laugh or shout. *Blast. Your. Rules*, she said, her lips moving without sound, and the men laughed.

When all was settled, Saliné went to her bed with a flurry of cavalcading thoughts, which kept her awake. At midnight, she left her bed and filled a glass of wine. *It went well*, she thought, *but in the morning, I need to convince the Duchess.* Three days ago, Saliné had sent an invitation to her. There were strict rules in Muniker, even a Queen had to respect them; she found many of them pointless and called the city Stiffmuni. *The leman agreement with Edric has a kind of potential that I can't predict. It may be important. It may be dangerous. It went too fast. At least it will not be unpleasant.* She shrugged. When Saliné fell asleep, as many times in the past, Codrin filled her dreams but, once, he was replaced by Edric. It was already morning, and she woke up abruptly, his warm touch still lingering in her mind.

Duchess Maltia was one of the few people who had not welcomed Saliné's arrival in Muniker. There was a cold smile on her lips, and she threw an arrogant look at Saliné, when she entered the Queen's office. Maltia was there only because she had received an official invitation.

"Duchess," Saliné said in a warm tone, "I am glad that you came. Litvonia is still a stranger to me, and I am trying to fix my lack of knowledge. You have not been in Muniker for a while." The Duchess had chosen to snub their wedding and stayed in her castle, not that Saliné cared about that. "I wanted to meet you and to learn more about your place. Let's have tea first." She spoke almost alone for some ten minutes; there was not much reaction from Maltia, and her little answers were cold and sarcastic. "Now let me show you why I needed to meet you," Saliné finally said and stood up. There was a map of Litvonia on the wall, and she pointed to it. "I understand that your lands are in the north-west, on both sides of the Rhiun River." She looked at Maltia, who nodded. "They are good lands, and you govern them well. But an interesting old thing stirred my curiosity. I remembered that this part," she tapped on the map over the western lands of the Duchess, "belonged once to Frankis. It doesn't matter now with our union, it's just a historical curiosity."

"That was a hundred and fifty years ago, after the second civil war in Frankis. Your kingdom was too weak to take it back. Weakness is, well ... weakness." The Duchess's voice was calculated and sardonic.

"You are right; weakness always plays an important role. This is Loxburg, and here is Peyris." Saliné slid her finger over the map. "They border your land and can gather seven thousand riders in a week. The best cavalry in Frankis. One thousand can block the only remaining bridge over the Rhiun, and the other six thousand can overwhelm your western lands in a few days. You can gather only three thousand soldiers there, and once the bridge is blocked, the only way to get soldiers over the river is by boat. Infantry may be relatively easy to transport, but riders," Saliné shook her head, "riders are not easy. As I said, it doesn't matter anymore; it was only a historical curiosity. I want to see if there are some books in the library which can explain what happened. Now, tell me more about your lands and castle. I've heard that you have a great collection of paintings and books."

Pretending to still look at the map, Saliné studied the other woman, seeing her face going white, but when she turned the Duchess's face was already composed, and Maltia suddenly found that she could speak with warmth and deference to the Queen, and she became more than willing to answer her questions. They separated on apparent good terms, and the next day the Duchess agreed that Edric would become her leman in two weeks.

Chapter 15 - Saliné / Edric

Saliné hated the horde of ogling people following her and Edric through the park. Some of them were only twenty paces away from her, ready to catch the smallest gesture she made, letting her think that perhaps her hair was wrong, or her dress, or that she was wrong. Their eyes made her skin crawl. She understood that they were there more for her than for Edric; the previous King was not married, and the last Leman Queen was some forty years ago. It did not make her feel better. She felt like there was not enough air in the large garden.

They met Calista, and there was an aura of mystery around her; Saliné could feel it, but she could not tell if it was good or bad.

"Edric, find another girl to pester, I need to talk to Saliné without being bothered by your big mouth."

"Calista, I don't want to eat or kiss you, there is no need to fear my mouth," he said and produced an even wider grin.

"See what I mean." Calista turned toward Saliné, pointing at her nephew, then took her by the arm, looking around. "Let's have a walk. Those bloody benches are always far away when you need them." After a brief walk, they found one that was free. "It's a leman's bench, but we can survive that." Seated, Calista closed her eyes for a moment, then pointed at Saliné's belly. "His name will be Arnis."

"A son," Saliné whispered, struggling to hide her surprise, she had kept her pregnancy hidden until she was fully sure.

"Yes, the one who will inherit the Empire from you. It's a long road, though. It seems that we have some disturbances in the Light." *It will be your daughter who inherits it, but that's another story, for another time.*

"What kind of disturbances?"

"The kind which blurs the future. You have the Light too. We think now that the new nomad invasion will be earlier than it was first predicted. We can't agree on the date. Most probably in six years from now, instead of seven. One year may not be much, but what if we are wrong, and they come earlier? Anyway, I heard that you are becoming a Muniker woman."

"Ah, the news about my preliminaries with Edric has arrived in your Hive."

"Of course not. They don't look for such things there. I do. Didn't I tell you that Edric has a big mouth? No, it was not him who told me," Calista chuckled. "In three years from now, you will have a daughter. Other children may come later. Perhaps four or five years later; it's hard to see so far in the future. I told you once that you will have a lover. Now I can tell you that you've made the right choice." Saliné tried to speak, but the Wanderer caught her hand. "I tell you only what I need to tell you. Then you make your decision. This is how it works with me. Or with other Wanderers." Calista shrugged, keeping her eyes on Saliné.

"I will think about it."

"Good. Now, I will introduce you to someone important." Calista gripped Saliné's hand tightly with her bony fingers and waved with her other hand.

There was a surge of Light, and a translucent woman appeared in front of Saliné; Calista was gone. She recognized the strange woman from Codrin's description, but waited patiently, her look cold and severe; this was the woman who took the Seer power from Codrin and let him die.

"Saliné," the Empress spoke first, and nodded to her.

"Empress." Saliné nodded too.

"Calista told you about some disturbances in the Light. It happens from time to time. We think that you can help."

"I don't have a strong Light."

"It's not about you; it's about Codrin."

"You let Codrin die. Don't speak to me about him."

"The decision to take his Seer powers was not mine. I am just a sort of middle-spirit between there," she pointed up, "and here," she pointed down. "Just think a little of him while I watch you."

"Why?"

I have a feeling that he is alive, and I need to find him before it's too late, but I can't tell you that. He may ruin everything we have built here with you. "It is necessary for the Realm."

This woman cheated Codrin, she will cheat me too, Saliné thought. "You and your Wanderers sold me out. I wonder if you did not take Codrin's power to let him die and send me here."

The Empress was shocked beyond words; she was not accustomed to being treated like this, and Saliné's words about Codrin's death frightened her. Nothing of her anger was visible on her translucent face. "Nobody sold you. There were negotiations for a marriage, as it happens everywhere. Not every woman has the chance to marry for love. You and Alfrid were chosen to build an empire. That's what counts in the end. You should stop acting like a child." *I can't ask her more about Codrin. If he is alive, she may learn that too. It will ruin everything. At least not until I find more about what she knows, or she thinks she knows*. "I understand that you are still not at ease when speaking about Codrin. You must get over this; it will clear your mind. No empire can be built without a good mind. We will speak again in the future. You still need my Wanderers and me, and your children need us even more." Her voice was flat and cold. She vanished, pointing at Saliné's belly.

I think that I've made an enemy, Saliné thought, her eyes still closed outside and open in that inner world. *But there was something strange in her request about Codrin. I must be more careful next time and learn more.*

"Will you let me look at your son?" Calista woke her up, after having her own talk with the Empress and, feeling a hint of curiosity, Saliné nodded. "You know how the Light works, and I have a strong one. You may feel warmth, but there is no danger for the child or for you."

Calista did not wait for an answer and placed a hand on Saliné's belly, rubbing it gently. There was warmth; there were some strange sensations of desire, and Saliné felt like a woman who had not seen her lover for a long time.

"I know that it felt a bit strange to you. Your son is healthy, and you will have an easy birth. You should restart your fighting training for two or three months. It helps to keep your body in good shape, and his body too. Now I have to leave."

Eyes half closed, Saliné looked at the old Wanderer walking away. She breathed long and slow, the Assassin Cool, until she was able to control the warm desire storming her body. *This is Calista's work. She used the Light to push me into Edric's bed. If we get to that, it will be on my own timing, and for my own reasons. I did not know they can use the Light like this. It should be forbidden.* Saliné was aware of Calista's influence on her body, but the decision to take a lointain lover would be hers, and she still had a few years to think about it. Edric came and pulled her up, and they walked together, hand in hand, toward the middle of the garden. *Yesterday, he walked like this with Maltia... Why should I care?*

Saliné did not sleep well that night; she had walked into the unknown, and many dreams came to her. There was a meaning in them – she could feel that through her Light – but no understanding. At least neither Codrin nor Edric came into her dreams. Strangely, that relieved her. She woke up a little late in the morning and ate quickly, reading the briefing for the Royal Council. It was brief, indeed; there was only one point on the agenda: The Invasion of Silvania. She almost spilled the tea in her mouth when she read it. *They were preparing a war, and I knew nothing.* Her hand trembled a little, and she placed the cup on the table. *I lost my appetite.* Abruptly, she stood up and left her suite.

The Council Room was already full when she arrived. Her face was composed, and she walked without hurrying toward her seat, next to Alfrid on the head of the long table.

Her studied calm could not fool Calista. "Saliné, this action was conceived before your arrival here, and put to one side, waiting for favorable conditions. Yesterday, we received a letter from the Dukes of Silvania. They agreed with our plan." It was a smaller kingdom with only two Duchies.

"And what is our plan? The briefing was ... brief."

It was Alfrid who answered. "We plan to gather our army in one week and leave for Silvania. The Dukes' armies will join us at the border."

"And what are *we* hoping to achieve from the invasion?"

"Silvania." Alfrid smiled, and placed his hand on hers, over the table. "The Silvanian King will remain King, but the kingdom will come to us at his death. The man was unfortunate; he lost his son and two of his daughters. He has no more male heirs, and in Silvania women can't inherit the throne. His cousin is the one who will inherit. The King hates him. Fortunately."

Eyes half closed, Saliné considered this. "What about Duchess Maltia and Duke Hamborg? Will they send soldiers too?"

"We hope that Maltia will send a thousand riders. There will be no infantry in this war. We must be swift. Duke Hamborg will oppose the move and stay home."

"He may stay home until you reach Silvania, then come here with his army. If I remember well, he can gather eight thousand soldiers. Half of them infantry, half of them Teutons. Heavy cavalry." *The Teutons and the Hussaris forced me to accept this marriage*. Saliné's mind went back to Frankis, recalling how the heavy cavalry made the fight against the Litvonian army too hard. *Perhaps if Manuc would have not been poisoned by the Circle... I must not live in the past.*

"Two thousand infantry men will stay outside Muniker. They will enter the city and join the guard if Hamborg comes, and Vlad, the Chief of the Guard, is an experienced man. I think you know him." Alfrid smiled.

That will be enough to defend Muniker for more than three months, and Vlad was trained by Codrin, Saliné thought. *If Maltia does not join Hamborg... It's better to avoid a siege. Too many soldiers would die, and we will need them later.* "I will ask Vlaicu to gather three thousand riders from Peyris and Loxburg and station them at the border of Maltia's Duchy. That will keep her quiet. I will write to him today, so his army will arrive at the border when you enter Silvania." Vlaicu was now the governor of Arad, and still the Spatar of Frankis.

"A good move," Alfrid said, with a newfound appreciation in his eyes. "Edric, Joachim, send the orders for the army."

Things advanced slowly; soldiers from all the parts of the kingdom started to gather in Muniker, and Saliné found that her life was moving in a strange rhythm that seemed familiar.

It was the day before the army was due to leave Muniker, toward Silvania. On her horse, flanked by Alfrid and Edric, Saliné stared at the thirty thousand soldiers swarming the place. *They are not well organized*, she thought, making comparison with the way Codrin trained his army. It was the wrong thing to think about; she recalled the day Codrin had left Arad to fight the nomads.

Codrin is gone to war,
Mironton, mironton, mirontaine,
But when will he ever come home?

She sang in her mind, and something hard pressed inside her chest. *It can be Edric now or Alfrid*. Struggling to contain her tears, she turned her horse abruptly, riding back into the city.

The men looked at each other, and nodded in understanding, then followed her. That day was a peculiar thing, not only because of the upcoming war, but because Edric would have his courting evening. Saliné was so distracted that she did not realize it until Edric came to take her out, and she understood why Alfrid had not sent her a request for the night; even the King had to respect the leman day. It was almost dark, and Edric guided her to a secluded place at edge of the park through a gap in an artificial ruin.

"We will have more privacy there." Edric pointed to a tree, and a thick blanket that was already laid under it. He sat, leaning against the tree and took her in his arms, feeling that she was uneasy and tense. "You are worrying."

"Yes," Saliné said curtly, her voice hoarse.

"We are soldiers, and this is not a hard war."

"Talk to me. Whatever you want, but not about war."

Edric knew how to talk, and his stories brought to her many things about Litvonia. There was nothing like his piquant stories before; these ones were enchanting old tales about long dead knights or princesses.

Half of his face was hidden in the shadow, but Saliné could see the full moon, large and red, an angry eye hovering over the world. *Edric will lead our army in battle. I may not see him again,* she thought. *Fate, you've ruined my family once. Let both return home from Silvania.* Gently, she pressed her fingers on Edric's lips until he stopped talking. "Love me." Her faint voice carried a strange tenderness and clarity in the quiet night. *And Fate take the rules.*

Running, the maid came into Saliné's bedroom, and closed the door behind her. She was breathing hard and leaned against the door. "Your majesty, a guard from the palace gate just came. There is a courier from our army in Silvania. He came with ten men in a hurry. It must be important."

Saliné coughed to gather her voice, and the words came out slow. "Who is the courier?" It was late, she had just had her bath, and her hair was still a little wet. Unconsciously, her fingers played with a rebel strand. *Why did he come so late? Why in a hurry? Why?*

"The guard did not know. They've just arrived in the palace, and the captain sent him here to warn your majesty. The courier will be here shortly. Should I ask him to give me the message?" She looked at Saliné's silk bathrobe, which barely covered her knees; the soft silk did not hide much of her curves.

"No, I want to hear him."

Once the maid left, Saliné went to the window, and leaned against it, wringing her hands. *Something bad has happened.* Her hands were trembling, and she grabbed a book from the table. It helped with the hands, but she was still trembling inside. She let her mind reach the Light. *I don't feel anything bad... Then why am I trembling?* The maid opened the door again, and before she could speak, Edric entered the room. Saliné nodded to the maid to leave them alone.

"What happened?" Saliné asked, playing with the book in her hands as he walked toward her.

"We won. That's a way of saying it; there was no fight. Their army surrendered, and the old King agreed with most of our stipulations. I will marry his daughter when she comes of age, but the Kingdom will come to you and Alfrid."

"You came like a storm, close to midnight, to tell me that...? You... You scared me." She sighed and hit his head – not very gently – with the book. "I like the sound it makes." She hit him again.

"I thought it was important for you to know that everything went well." He smiled, and she hit him again with the book. Three times. Gently. "Alfrid will stay there for three weeks and visit the Dukedoms. I returned because of Duke Hamborg."

"He has assembled an army of ten thousand, and I have already requested two thousand more soldiers to gather in Muniker. Some are already here; some will come soon. In a few days, Vlaicu will cross the bridge over the Rhiun with five thousand cavalry and come here. Three thousand soldiers are still at Maltia's border. I want to avoid a siege."

"You moved fast," Edric said, his eyes on hers; their bodies were now almost touching. He took the book from her hands, and let it fall, before taking her in his arms. There was a kind of hunger in his lips and fingers that she had not felt before. He stopped kissing her, and slowly untied her girdle. She felt her bathrobe slipping down, and Edric followed its fall until no part of her body remained hidden. He undressed too, and Saliné saw a map of past battles written on his skin. It resembled Codrin's so much. There was a large scar on his left, between his ribs.

"A spear," she whispered, touching it.

"How did you know that?"

Codrin had one too, in the same place. "It was just a guess. This is new." She touched a two-inch-long cut on his upper arm. You said that there was no fight."

"There wasn't. I had a duel on the way back, five hours ago, and it's just a scratch. That's why I arrived so late."

"Over what?" *Duels are for childish men.*

"Over a woman." A mischievous grin flashed on Edric's lips, and there was a long moment of silence. "They tried to kidnap her." He lifted Saliné in his arms, walked fast and laid her gently in bed. For the next three weeks, they spent all their nights together.

During the third morning after Edric's arrival, Saliné went to her office, and placed a piece of paper on the desk. She put her elbows over the paper, resting her chin on her clasped hands, recalling her night with Edric. After a while, she sighed and started to write to Cleyre Peyris. When she finished, she sealed the letter, and kept it for some minutes in her hand. *This is the most important letter I have ever written*, she thought, but instead of placing it in the tray for outgoing letters, she hid it in her cabinet. The next morning, she weighed the letter in her hand again, and let it go to the couriers. *I should receive an answer in less than three weeks.*

Back in Muniker, Alfrid sent Saliné the usual written request for a visit during the night. Reading it, she rubbed her brow. *I can't... After these nights with Edric, I just can't*... She wrote back with the excuse that her pregnancy was giving her a hard time.

The next days were difficult for her, but at least Edric said nothing about their allotted days for courting, and found some duties to attend to, outside the city.

Ten days after Alfrid's arrival, Duchess Maltia came to Muniker in a hurry. Her face was white, and her hands were trembling a little when she entered the Queen's office. When she left, she was still white, but at least her hands were no longer trembling, and she went to see the King. That evening, her and Edric's official status as lointain lovers was settled and, in a week, he would go to Maltia's home in Kolugn, to help her govern her lands.

Before leaving with Maltia, Edric embraced her, and for a moment, Saliné was afraid that he would kiss her in front of Alfrid. "I will always love you," he whispered into her ear, and then said loudly, "You will need a new leman." An enigmatic smile wrinkled his lips. She could not see it.

Still in his arms, Saliné said, "Muniker got what it wanted; they should be content. Soon, my pregnancy will show, and I will have a year of ... respite." She moved away from him and took Alfrid by the arm, her eyes locked with Edric's. "You are the only leman I will ever accept. There is no one else I can trust to be so close to me. Your two-year stay with Duchess Maltia is important, but if things here ... require it, we will ask you to come back for a few weeks, once or twice a year. I have already agreed this with Alfrid, and I am sure that the Duchess will not object either. You are her lointain lover now, but you are still allowed to have two lemans."

That strange smile still playing about his lips, Edric bowed to her, then he embraced Alfrid. With his large stride, he was out of the room in a few moments.

"The Chancellor told me that you had a hand in Duchess Maltia's sudden acceptance of Edric as her lointain lover. She is a hard woman..." Alfrid looked thoughtfully at Saliné, his eyes narrowed.

"I had a full arm, not just a hand," Saliné laughed. "The Chancellor doesn't know much, and I imagine he just played you to learn more about what happened. What I tell you, stays between us." She looked at Alfrid, and after a few moments of thought, he nodded. "I wrote to Cleyre Peyris, advising her to claim back the land that her Duchy had lost a hundred fifty years ago, the land which now belongs to Maltia. She sent three thousand riders to check the status of the land. The claim was sent to me and to Maltia, who came to me, because the army in her lands was from Frankis. We agreed together that the claim was too old still to be valid, and that she needed Edric's help to govern her lands. We also agreed that she would tell no one about what happened. It was in her interest too."

"But, with those soldiers still on Maltia's land, would Cleyre accept your ... judgment?" Alfrid frowned, thinking of the consequences.

"Yes, Cleyre had already written that to me. The letter in which she accepted my judgment that the claim was too old to be valid came together with the claim. The acceptance letter was date three weeks later, and her soldiers must be home by now." Saliné smiled and looked innocently at him.

"Ah, that was clever," Alfrid said. "Would you join me for lunch today?"

"It's a beautiful day; perhaps we can eat on the terrace. Just send me a written request. See? I have started to be a real Muniker wife." She laughed and pulled him toward the terrace.

The old horologe of Muniker struck midnight. Saliné was alone in her bedroom, leaning on her elbow on the heavy tiger fur in front of the fireplace. It was a rare ornament, from far away, which gave her a strange sensation of comfort, strength and smoothness, all at the same time. There was a small fire, its flickering shapes painting shadows on the wall. Thoughtfully, she sipped some wine. Behind her, a few candles in the chandelier enhanced the shades of dark green and gold of the carpet on the opposite wall. A hunting scene. She felt at peace, in a way that she had not felt for a long time. *A few days ago, I rolled with Edric on this fur, our last night together. It* was *Edric; I did not think of Codrin when we made love*. Surprised, she let her thoughts sneak further into the past. *It has happened for some nights already, making love with him without thinking of Codrin. Perhaps my mourning has finally ended. Perhaps Edric was the cure I needed.* She sipped some more wine. *I will always love Codrin, but now I can start to live again. A new family... I am no longer afraid of that. Alfrid is not Codrin, but he is not as bad as I thought in the beginning. Perhaps I rejected him because I was upset about them forcing this marriage on me. I would have preferred Edric as my husband; there are ... feelings between us, but... It was a hard decision to send him away with Maltia.* She put her glass down, and lay on her back, leaning her head on her entwined fingers. Her bathrobe opened and the flames painted playful lights on her breasts. Warmth spread into her body, from the fire, and she felt content. *Yes, I think that I now have enough courage to start a real family with Alfrid. I am only twenty-four years old.*

Chapter 16 – Saliné

Time passed slowly during the autumn. The bad weather forced Saliné and Alfrid to spend more time together; there were no more lemans to bother them, as he had also released his. They found more things in common that they had realized in the beginning, like the pleasure of reading. At the end of the year, they were almost lovers, though her pregnancy separated them physically. Strangely, the physically separation helped to bring them closer; Saliné no longer felt like an object brought to Muniker for Alfrid's pleasure.

Before the Solstice Party, Calista came to Muniker; she would stay there until spring, as usual. Speaking to her for the first time after summer, Saliné found the old Wanderer even more worried.

"The disturbance in the Light is growing," Calista said, playing with her wineglass.

"The Empress told me that it had happened before."

"Not in our lifetime, not in the lifetime of our teachers. Such rarity is disturbing."

Why can't I feel any disturbance if it's so strong? Saliné thought, knowing that the disturbance was real. Soon after Calista's first warning, Saliné had written to Idonie, who had confirmed the old Wanderer's worries. "You are still afraid that the nomads will attack us earlier than it was foreseen."

"We are not able to see much about them. And they still have a Seer." Calista shrugged, thinking that it was not the best thing to tell Saliné. "Your idea to send Edric to Kolugn with Maltia was a good political move; it has established your authority on the north-east, but you must call him back after dealing with Hamborg."

"Edric will be my only leman, and he will come here for a few weeks, each summer."

"Saliné," Calista gripped her hand, "you know what I mean. Alfrid is a nice man, and you are doing well together, but Edric will defend the kingdom – and Arnis." She pointed at Saliné's round belly. "You must make Edric your lointain lover. Alfrid will understand."

"I will think about it."

Calista nodded, then pointed again at Saliné's belly. "Would you allow me to see his future again? There will be no ... desire in you this time." She smiled a little, apologetically, knowing that Saliné understood what had happened to her body after the Wanderer had used the Light on her some months ago. Saliné surprised her, and smiled back, nodding her approval. Calista did not know that her trick had helped Saliné understand the White Light better. She could make more use of it; she could defend herself better. "There will be no problems at birth, and he will be a healthy child," Calista said after ending her probing.

"This disturbance with the Light," Saliné said, hesitantly. "Could it be related to Codrin losing his Seer power and to his death?"

"What?" For all her experience, Calista dropped the wineglass. It produced a crystalline sound in the sudden silent room. "What makes you say that?" She leaned forward to pick the glass, which was not broken. Her training took over, and it was a swift move, but she just needed to hide herself. To gain time.

"I don't know. It's just a feeling. What the Empress did to him felt wrong to me."

Calista stayed silent for a while, fighting the storm inside her mind. *She can't know, but how did she come to that question?* "It's not the Empress. The powers of the Seer come from Fate before a Fracture. They are taken by Fate when the Fracture is no longer a menace. Closing the Sanctuary in Nerval weakened the Serpent."

"But the nomads still have a Seer."

"That Seer belongs to the Serpent. Their god, their rules. Because of Baraki, the nomads will still come for fifteen or more years, and you have to deal with their invasions."

Yes, Saliné nodded and asked nothing more.

Midwinter, Saliné gave birth to a healthy son, and Alfrid called him Arnis, the name of his father. They had agreed that he would name the first child if he was a boy. The name of their next child would be Saliné's choice. Exhausted in her bed, Saliné caressed the face of her newborn, and let her mind wander into the past. Most of her recalled memories were from Muniker, but from time to time, Codrin came to her too. Arnis made a sort of snorting noise, and she moved his body a little, a faint smile on her lisps; Muniker started to feel like home. Perhaps the arrival of Jara and Cernat, three weeks before Arnis came into this world, had helped her too.

A month later, in their house at the edge of the forest, Ildeko gave birth to a boy. Without understanding why, Codrin called him Ioan. Deep in his mind, there was a blurred memory of his twin sister, Ioana.

Unseen, Alfrid sneaked in the room and watched his wife keeping their son at her breast. "You are so beautiful, my love," he said and, startled, Saliné turned her head, frowning jokingly at him.

Five months old, little Arnis stopped feeding and fell asleep instantly. Smiling, Saliné arranged him in bed and turned toward Alfrid, sensing that he was just behind her. Her bathrobe was half open, revealing her breasts, and he cupped one of them, squeezing it gently. Then he sighed.

"I think that it's still too early for..."

Surprised by the sudden warmth spreading through her body, Saliné blinked, and a wicked smile played on her lips. "You think wrong, Alfrid; at your age you should know more about women."

Entangled, they moved toward the bed, she stepping back, Alfrid pushing her, then pinning her on the mattress. There was a frenzy in their bodies that neither of them had felt before, and they were by turns gently and raw, kind and demanding. When they had finished, they remained silent and embraced, an intimacy they did not try to spoil with words. Like little Arnis before, Alfrid fell soon asleep.

After a while, Saliné stood up and went out on the terrace, letting the gentle wind cool her skin. *I never thought that I would love a man other than Codrin. It's not the same, though, with neither Alfrid nor Edric. There was more ... depth before. There is no one like Codrin, and there will never be; we were more than lovers, we were twin souls. I should not live in the past,* she sighed, and her thoughts went back in the room, but it was little Arnis who occupied her mind this time. She leaned back against a marble column, feeling refreshed by its coldness. Eyes closed, she focused, and a surge of Light went through her. The revelation it carried came to her like a shock. *It's true that we will build an Empire.* And the more she thought, more things came to her, including the fact that Frankis and Litvonia were unified without a bloody war. *Arnis will revive the Alban Empire. That was Codrin's dream and mine. Codrin...* The message from the Light was strong and unclear at the same time. Deep inside her, she felt that something was wrong, and that the future would be different to her interpretation of the Vision, but who was she to change the order of things?

"Codrin is gone to war,
Mironton, mironton, mirontaine,
But when will he ever come home?"

A tear ran down her face, and she traced it gently with her finger. *Oh, Codrin, this is not fair to you or to our son, as he will never inherit a kingdom, but I will carry our dream further. I will make Cosmin a powerful Duke, and my next son will take your name. That's the only thing I can do for you, my love. And please, don't be upset that I love Alfrid too, it's not the same thing; it will never be the same thing.*

In midsummer, riders started to gather in Muniker, and the large field south of the city was swarming with soldiers. It was the King's personal army; there were ten thousand riders from Frankis, led by Vlaicu, considered the Queen's personal army. There were four thousand soldiers from Duchess Maltia, led by Edric, and all the Dukes and Counts in Litvonia sent their men. There was one exception though; there were no soldiers from the Duchy of Hamborg. It was decided that Edric would lead the army against the restless Duke.

There were many people in Saliné's antechamber when Edric entered, and there was a moment of silence. She felt the pressure in their eyes; Jara was in the room too.

I must tell Mother about Muniker and that Manners Book. "Ah, my leman has returned," she said and stood up so Edric could embrace her. Then kiss her. "We have five days to refresh their memories," she whispered into his ear.

"So, everything is about this need for refreshing?" he asked, his voice a bit edgy.

"You already know the answer." Saliné laughed, and this time she kissed him. The women in the room nodded to each other, smiles on their lips; the Queen was a true Litvonian now; she was one of them.

"Can we dine together this evening?"

"I will wait for you here."

Before leaving, Edric walked a few steps toward a corner of the room. "So, you are Arnis," he said to the little boy sleeping in his bed. "You resemble your father. Alfrid used to sleep a lot."

"I am sure that you were well informed at that time, little brother," Saliné laughed.

"Of course." Edric laughed too. "And Cosmin is growing." Edric gestured toward Saliné's first born, who was playing with two other children of his age.

Saliné struggled to tell Jara about lemans and lointain lovers. The Frankis part of her had become stronger with her mother's return. "I know that my behavior looks strange to you; it was not easy for me either, in the beginning, but this is Muniker. You will find everything you need to know here." She gave Jara the Manners Book and smiled wryly.

In the evening, Saliné and Edric dinned together, then spent the rest of their time together on the tiger fur in front of the fireplace. That was a place Saliné had never used with Alfrid. It was already dark outside, and only the fire and a small chandelier brought a playful light into the room. Edric kept her entertained with his seductive voice, telling stories from Kolugn, with his lips, with his fingers. After a while, his hand moved under her skirt, reaching her knees. Gently, Saliné pulled his head away by the hair, and shook her head, stopping him.

The Duke of Hamborg sued for peace before the Litvonian army was ready to move north, and he came in person to pay homage to the Queen and King. His two strongest southern fortresses were the price paid for peace.

"I will give the fortresses to her majesty the Queen," he said at the end of the negotiations, a breach of protocol, as Saliné was only Consort Queen of Litvonia.

"I accept them," Saliné said calmly, touching Alfrid's knee under the table while the Duke smiled. There was a little murmur in the room, but Saliné stopped all the talk with a firm gesture of her hand, and the treaty was signed as she had decided.

Two hours later, she donated the fortresses to Alfrid. "Hamborg hoped to create a split between us, buying me with his fortresses. Let him think that he achieved something. His next moves will be predictable. Sometimes, you must give them some space and allow their little games; they make the defeat easier to swallow," she said, signing the document, and pushing it toward the secretary. "Litvonia is a safer place now."

"Perhaps we should call Edric back from Kolugn," Alfrid said, still worried by Calista's warning about the nomads.

Saliné thought about that. *It's too early. For Maltia. For me too*. "Maltia is a proud woman. It will harm our interests, if we break the political link between her and Edric so soon after the peace treaty with Hamborg. It will look too obvious. We should wait until spring. Autumn is coming; there will be no military threat this year."

"Her majesty is right," Klavis, the Chancellor said, and bowed slightly toward her.

Chapter 17 - Aliana / Dochia / Kasia

Spring came late in Nerval. Long winters were something normal for the locals, and even Dochia and her guards had become accustomed to them after several years there, but it was Aliana's first hard winter, and she craved sun and warmth. They did not know, but the first day without freeze came one month after Saliné's wedding in Muniker. News from the west of the continent was scarce, and they did not know about Codrin's *death*, either. It was a curious thing; they could not have any Visions of Codrin or Saliné, or even about Frankis. It seemed that their Visions were blocked at the eastern Litvonian border. That bothered Dochia, but she agreed with her team that the long distance was the cause. She did not fully believe it, but there was no other valid explanation. As far as they were concerned, after the nomads' defeat, things should have been fine in Frankis, with such a good ruling couple, and the continent was now safe. The gates of Nerval were still watched by Baraki's men, so they could not leave easily, and they still wanted to kill him. He knew that Dochia was alive. He wanted her. Afraid of another arrow, he never left the palace. There was a three hundred galbeni reward for her head, and one hundred for Aliana and Kasia. Baraki knew Dochia well and had given her description to the best artists in Nerval, and after a few sketches, he picked the closest one, which was copied by all the other artists, and her portrait now graced all the intersections inside the city. There were drawings of Aliana and

Kasia too, but they were nowhere near as accurate as Dochia's, and depicted women in their early thirties. Such evil and strong women could not be some feeble teenagers. Kasia's scar, going down from her right breast was described too; the priests who had *purified* her knew well about it. There were no drawings of Mira and Irina, Dochia's guards.

People came back to life with the spring. They saw the drawings. They saw the price. Compared with other capitals, Nerval was a poor, hard place, and most of them did not make three hundred galbeni in twenty years of hard work. Some of them shook their heads seeing the prize and went away. The cowards, the wise and the compassionate. There were rumors about those women; they had killed Meriaduk, the Great Priest; they had killed his seven main priests, the Vicarius. Men of power, priests of the powerful Serpent that no one could imagine dying a violent death. In hiding, some people started to worship Fate again. The cowards feared the three women; the wise were just cautious; the compassionate loved them for releasing the city from Meriaduk's grip, but they were not compassionate enough to try and save them. The cowards forced themselves to forget. The wise started to gather information. The compassionate hid themselves. The bold and the strong combed the city, searching for the women who were weighed in gold.

The house did not attract much attention, it was relatively small, and the inhabitants were well known by the neighbors living in the few scattered houses dispersed in a two hundred feet radius, at the edge of the city, close to the wall. The house belonged to a family of merchants and was well maintained. The men were most of the time on the road. Sometimes, the neighbors had issues remembering when the two men have been last seen in the house. The women did not wear ostentatious clothes or jewelry. They were all blonde or had light brown hair, as all the rosin women had. Walking on the empty path, five strong men arrived in front of the house at noon. They were already a little drunk, and they saw three women walking in and out, young and desirable. They returned after a while, looking for men who would guard the house. What responsible families would let such women alone at home? Two hundred feet from the house, there was a row of thick bushes, and they hid behind them to observe better.

"They are alone," one of them said two hours later, and took a long sip from his bottle. The strong vadka warmed his blood, stirring his mind. He seemed to be in charge. Perhaps because of the ugly scar cutting the right side of his face diagonally.

"Scar, are you thinking what I am thinking?"

"Perhaps. We have a duty to interrogate all suspicious women. There is a good reward for some of them. I think that we shall take our duty seriously and interrogate them for a few nights. One of them vaguely resembles the ones in the drawings, though they are much younger. We are covered, but we still need to be careful. There may be men hidden inside the house. Let's come back tomorrow." *I don't fear the guards; they don't care if the low-born are killed or raped, but if my father learns about this...* Quietly, they left the place as darkness fell.

For two days, they came and went, scouting with care, one of them always watching the house. The next day, they came again, in plain view, all dressed in fake uniforms of the Guard; Scar was dressed in his real, former uniform. He had been a captain once. Two years earlier, he had been thrown out of the Guard by his own father, who was a powerful Count. This time, they walked without trying to hide, like any other patrol on a mission in the city. On the path, there was an old woman sitting on a bench.

"Do you know who owns that house?" Scar asked, pointing at it with his forefinger.

"Kaspar, the wool merchant. What business do you have with him?"

"Official business. What kind of man is he?"

"One who swallowed his tongue. He speaks little more often than a mute. And he is even less often in his house. It's quite a pity to leave such young and beautiful wife alone at home."

"I suppose that she finds some consolation."

"There is a young man. He always come when Kaspar is away. I don't think that he visits the woman to help her in the kitchen," the old woman chuckled.

"In the bedroom, perhaps?" Scar laughed.

"Perhaps. In my time, my bedroom was more interesting than my kitchen. Now it's the other way round."

"Well, I have to go and talk with the merchant. Or with his wife, if he is not at home."

"He isn't. I know everything that moves. Don't look at me like that. I am an old woman. I have nothing else to do."

"I understand. I may come later and ask you some more questions; you seem to be well informed." He threw a small coin in her lap.

"Did they do something wrong? Kaspar has three girls."

"I hope not." Scar nodded at the old woman and went away. *The women are alone.*

In front of the house, the men laughed to encourage themselves, and one of them opened the gate, letting Scar enter first.

"Girl," he said to the one sitting on the bench close to the door. "We are guards in charge of this part of the city; we need to interrogate you about those evil women... You know what women. It's a serious investigation." He stopped in front of her and took a sip of vadka. "It will go better if you cooperate." He offered the bottle to the girl and sat next to her. It was late in the afternoon, and the strong sun warmed them.

"Of course. We all want to help the Guard," the girl said, ignoring the bottle. "They were evil women. To kill priests..." She shook her head and made the sign of the Serpent with two fingers. "I am not sure how these things are done... Inside the house, I suppose? How do you want to proceed?"

"You are a clever girl. Each of us will interrogate one of you. Do you have enough rooms? It's always better to be alone for such talks. Some questions can be embarrassing. You understand..."

"Yes. The house doesn't look too large, but there are four rooms and the kitchen. Will a kitchen work for you?"

"Yes, of course. I can interrogate you on the table."

"On the table?" The girl frowned and looked at the man, then at the other four, but they were all guards.

"There must be a table and chairs. I will write the report on the table. Where is your father?"

"He is a merchant and left the city a week ago with my uncle. They will return in one month."

The girl is stupid to reveal such a weakness to a stranger. One month... We will spend some pleasant nights in their house. "How old are you?"

"I am fifteen."

A maiden... She looks older with that good body. I will pick her for myself. "Who else is in the house?"

"Mother, Aunt Zaria and my two sisters." She raised a finger for each person. "My sisters are older; Ava is sixteen and Lenia is seventeen. We are *string sisters*, born one year after another." The girl grinned at her own joke.

Wonderful. We can swap them between us later. "You seem to be a kind girl, so I will interrogate you." Scar raised the bottle to her mouth. "You have to drink; it's our away of starting a friendly conversation."

The girl drank this time. She grimaced and tried to push the bottle away but had to gulp again. Then again. "It's too strong," she whispered, and wiped her mouth.

"You will like it. Everybody likes vadka, and this is good quality. There is a pear inside. See?" He raised the bottle so she could look at the fruit. "It warms our minds. Makes talking easier." He made her drink again. "What kind of merchant is your father?"

"He is in the wool trade, but we are not rich."

"It's a nice house." Scar pointed at the house behind him. "And the garden is well maintained."

"My uncle likes gardening, and I help him. When he is away, I take care of it." The girl smiled warmly, and that enhanced her beautiful face.

Beautiful girl but stupid. "You have wonderful flowers." Scar pressed the bottle to her mouth again, and she grimaced again when he let her free. "Call your mother; we should speak to her first."

"Mother!" the girl shouted, and a woman appeared in the doorway, looking at the men with wide eyes. "They are some officials here and they want to ask us about those evil women."

"What kind of officials are you?" Tense, the woman evaluated them, a touch of fear in her eyes.

"City Guard. Can't you see our uniforms? I am a captain." Scar pointed at the insignia on his chest. Keeping his eyes on the woman, he walked in front of her. "We are looking for some evil women. You know what those women did. You know that it's an important matter. Each of my men will interrogate one of you."

"You should wait until my husband and brother-in-law come home. They will be here in a few days."

"That is a lie. Your daughter already told us that they will return in a month. We can't wait that long. Woman," he gripped her chin between his fingers, "you lied to a high-ranking official charged with important matters. This is a grave offense. I could send you and your daughter to jail. You always know when you enter; you never know when you might leave. If you leave. I am a kind man; let's forget about that little blunder. My men are competent, and we will finish faster this way. We need a room for each of us. A kitchen will work too; there is not much need for space. Your daughter here resembles this Kasia." He showed the drawing to the mother, kept it open for a few seconds, then folded it again, before the woman could really see it.

"But it's not her. My daughter is much younger, and her name is Lidia."

"Perhaps. I hope that you won't interfere with an official investigation. I can jail you for a year. Think of your daughters. The wardens in Nerval's jail are not kind. Things may happen to them there. You won't want that." Scar's voice became harsh, and he measured her with a cold look, then took a set of handcuffs from his pocket.

"No. No. Please," the woman said, her voice trembling, wringing her hands nervously. "You can interrogate me, and I will do everything you want. Just let my girls alone."

"It doesn't work that way. Your daughter is a suspect now. Your family is suspect. You lied to us. We must interrogate all of you. Here, or in jail. It's your choice."

"Here," the woman whispered and bit her lip, struggling to contain her tears. "We are just cleaning the house for spring. Only one room is ready right now. You can start there while we ready the other three rooms and the kitchen. It will only take half an hour."

"We don't want to disturb you too much, but you must obey and answer all our questions." Scar smiled and his hideous face became even uglier. "Volod," he whispered to one of his men, "take the mother; be harsh with her; scare her; make noise, but without... You understand. For the pleasant things, wait until all of us come inside. They seem quite frightened and stupid."

"What's your name?" Volod asked, forcing his voice to be harsh; he was a plump man with a thin voice, only his small, round eyes had something of an animal, a boar. In general, he was making people laugh at him when trying to be tough, but this time he got what he wanted; the woman was scared, and he puffed his chest, which was much smaller than his belly. Without waiting for an answer, he took the woman by the arm, and pushed her inside. She stumbled, but he kept her walking with an iron hand. "Where is the room?"

"There." Barely able to speak, the woman pointed to one of the two open doors inside the hall; two girls were cleaning the other room.

"When a room is ready for interrogation, a girl should go out and tell the captain. A soldier will interrogate her. Tell them from here. The youngest one will go first."

"Please," she whispered, "they are too young. I can…" She stopped abruptly as the man squeezed her arm, glaring at her with a ferocious look. The woman took a long breath, and he felt intoxicated with power like never before. "Girls, there are guards outside. They want to interrogate all of us. They may not be kind to you, but you have to obey … do whatever they ask you to do." She breathed long again. "Ava, when you finish this room, go out and a guard will come with you. Lenia, clean the other room, then tell Zaria to leave the cellar and prepare the fourth room and the kitchen." She fell silent and let herself be led into the room. "Please let me close the door."

In the doorway, Volod pressed her against the wall. "Listen carefully to me. We caught you misleading an important official. It's a serious offence. I will give you a chance to save your daughters from jail. One chance." His hand moved down her neck, inside her cleavage, finding her breast. Then he kissed her. The woman was too lost inside her fear to resist. Looking at Scar, who was still in front of the main door, Volod started to undress her. Reacting to Scar's angry gesture, he grinned and pushed the woman inside. Threw her onto the bed. The door closed.

Outside, Scar sat next to Lidia again, pressed the bottle to her mouth, and kept it there even longer this time. She grimaced again and swallowed, then swallowed again. "This girl looks like you." He placed the drawing on her knees and half covered it with his hand. "I want to believe that you are not her, but you must cooperate. It was not helpful that your mother lied to me. You will do whatever I ask you. Understand?" He looked at Lidia, who nodded, unable to speak. "This criminal has a scar under her right breast. We will start from there."

"But … I have a scar. I am not her," Lidia cried and tried to stand, stumbling a little. "I fell from a tree when I was young. A broken branch cut my skin."

"You will not move until I tell you." Scar gripped her arm and pulled the girl down on the bench. "That scar complicates everything. I must see it." *That's why the mother was so scared. This is my lucky day. We are covered, and they will be very pliant from now on. We will come to check them twice a week until the husband returns.*

"But you are a man..."

"In jail, there will be many men allowed to look at you, touch you, do whatever they want to you. Don't move." He frowned at her, then opened her chemise. "Hmm. The scar is the same length and is in the same position."

"But I am not her," Lidia cried and started to sob.

"I want to believe you." Scar made her drink from his bottle again. Then again. "We have a serious situation. This scar," he started to fondle her breast, "looks bad for you, and I must check your whole body, but I will be gentle. There is no need to cry. Come here." He pulled Lidia onto his lap and stroked her hair; she was sobbing quietly. "I am a kind man." He pulled her head against his shoulder while she still sobbed.

"What are you doing to my sister?" Ava asked; she had just come to the doorway. "Why did you open her chemise?"

"Your sister has a scar, which she shouldn't have. She is a suspect now, but I have the feeling that she is not the woman we are looking for. As you see, I am being gentle with her."

"You should not touch my sister."

Scar took out his handcuffs and gave them to the closest man. "This bad-mouthed girl with a weak mind resembles one of those evil women who killed so many priests. She is not cooperative. Take her to jail. We will interrogate her there."

"But I am not that girl," Ava cried and pressed a hand to her mouth.

The man grabbed her hand and prepared to handcuff her.

"Please," she whispered, "I am not one of those women."

"This is something that we need to verify. We will go inside," the man said and returned the handcuffs to Scar. He took the girl by the arm. "Let's go."

"I... I can't move."

"You are scared. I understand that. Let me carry you." The man lifted the stunned girl in his arms and went inside.

"See?" Scar asked Lidia when they were alone. "Your sister was not sensible, and she almost ended up in jail. You are sensible. I think. Are you?"

"Yes," Lidia breathed and closed her eyes.

The third girl went inside with another man without commenting too much; she was older and knew that things like this were common in Nerval.

When the second woman came out, Scar's eyes widened. "Are you finished already?"

"I suppose that you are talking about my twin sister. I understand that you are carrying out an ... investigation."

"You seem a rational woman. Lidia has a strange scar. Your sister lied to me, and there are consequences for that. I think that you understand. My man will interrogate you."

"Yes, I understand. Perhaps I can replace Lidia during the interrogation. She is too young to know about such things," the woman said, strangely calm.

"I am afraid that it's not possible. She has that incriminating scar, and we need to check everything."

"I understand," she repeated. "Follow me." She looked at the standing man and went inside.

Ten minutes later, Scar had to carry Lidia; she was no longer able to walk. The door of the kitchen was fully open, on his right. Unable to restrain himself, he walked quickly toward the table and laid the girl on her back, then buried his head between her breasts, his hands busy pulling at her skirts.

"Close the door...," the girl whispered.

Scar turned and found himself in front of a closed door and the most wanted woman in Nerval. He did not have much time to wonder; Dochia's hammer smashed the side of his head. The strike was clean; there was not even a drop of blood on the floor when his body slumped on it.

"Kasia, go on the bench outside again until we bury the bodies in the cellar. There may be people around," Dochia said, checking the pulse of the fallen man. There was none.

At sunset, everything was done, and Kasia returned to the house. "Mira," she laughed, "you really resemble your *twin sister*. Scar's eyes bulged out of his head when he saw you for the second time. I wished I could have cut his hands off before we killed him. But," she shrugged, "he no longer needs them. I have the feeling that I have seen him before... I don't think that he is a guard. Was."

"He was. Two years ago, Count Sevreski threw him out of the Guard after catching him stealing a silver statue from the palace. The Count is his father. A fair man; it's a pity that he works for Baraki. He has no choice." Dochia shrugged. "Sevreski disliked his son, even disinherited him, but he was still his son. We will have problems."

"When the men came, they talked with old Babusa; she was on the bench in front of her house. As always." Umbra, Dochia's peregrine raven, laughed, perched on the top of the chair next to her. "She told them about Mira's secret lover." For the people in the neighborhood, Mira was known as Mashia, Kaspar's wife.

"I did not know that I had a lover," Mira chuckled, "but if the old woman *knows* it, then half of the city knows it. I hope that he is good looking."

"It must be Iger, Gresha's courier. Eighteen years old. Good looking. And a *husband* like Scorta. You are a lucky woman." Kasia laughed. Scorta, the Assassin Master, played the role of Kaspar, and he came to Nerval only now and then. A wool merchant was always on the road, and the Assassins Triangles were lodged in a village, twenty miles from the city.

"Yes, I am. Did the men say anything important?" Mira looked at Umbra, then at Fortitude, Aliana's raven.

"Nothing that we did not know from the previous days when we spied on them," Umbra answered. "We also know that, for the past three days, the other four men visited Scar's house. One of them is married. Soon, questions will be asked, and old Babusa will tell everyone that a patrol of the Guard visited us, and that the captain had a scar. The guards will come here."

"We must leave the house tonight. Count Sevreski is both intelligent and efficient." Dochia stood up and went toward the window; it was almost dark outside. "We will move into the hall that hides the little entrance to the Sanctuary, which only Aliana and I could open when the magic was still active. I took all the keys of the outer door, so no one can get in. Baraki did not let his people break the door. He still hopes to reopen the Sanctuary. Take your backpacks and everything you need for a long journey. And food for a week. We must leave Nerval." She looked at Kasia.

"Tomorrow night, I will visit Gresha."

"He must act fast; we can't stay more than a few days in the Sanctuary." Dochia frowned; there were not many choices. "I don't think that he will come to Nerval for a while, but we need to leave a sign at the end of the street for Scorta to tell him to avoid the house. And he must find another name; he can't use Kaspar anymore. I am sorry, Mira, but you just lost your husband." Dochia smiled and there was laughter in the room, though a little tense.

The long scratch on the door sounded strong in the silent room. Iron on wood. The darkness accentuated the hearing of the women inside. The reverberation accentuated the noise. Another long scratch sounded, then three more. Shorter.

"It's Gresha," Kasia said, and stood up. The small hall had no furniture. No windows. No light. She placed a hand on the wall and walked toward the door. It was dark outside too. Imitating a rat, she scratched the old wood with her knife. Three times.

"Open the door," Gresha said, his voice muffled by the thick wood.

In five minutes, they were all in the wagon. Mira and Irina sat on the bench behind Gresha. Dochia, Kasia and Aliana were hidden inside. It was an old but sturdy two horse tilt van. There was now a faint line of pink in the east. When they arrived at the southern gate, the light was already strong. Their cart was the sixth in line, and Gresha climbed down to wait for the guards.

"If I hadn't heard your voice..." Mira said, seeing him for the first time in good light. Gresha's blond hair was now black, spotted with red and yellow dirt, and seemingly unwashed for at least a year. Two of his front teeth were missing.

"Pioter, the mason, could not look like Gresha, the merchant." He smiled, and the missing teeth made his face look grotesque. "I have family, Mira, and my wife is pregnant. I hope that my painted teeth don't scare you too much." He smiled again, this time without revealing his gums.

"But..." Mira said hesitantly, "do you have a mason's permit?"

"Of course. Two days ago, I poured a lot of vadka in the Mester Mason, and sold him some merchandise at a good price. Good for him. He signed every paper I put on the table, including my permit. Pioter is a proud member of the Mason's Guild. A small one. Insignificant. Invisible. No mason in the Guild knows anything about poor Pioter. Not even the Mester." He grinned again, then turned as Mira pointed guardedly with her forefinger.

"Where are you going?" the captain asked. He looked briefly at Gresha and longer at Mira, who smiled shyly at him. *I know her. Mashia...* Six months ago, Mira had been harassed by two drunkards on the street. She could manage them, but the captain dealt with them harshly, leaving the men unconscious. He even escorted her home, making some plans, but then he learned from Mira that she was married.

"Voltava," Gresha said. "We have a contract to repair a house. My brothers are already there. My wife," he pointed at Mira, "and my sister-in-law," he pointed at Irina and smiled broadly at the captain.

What a fine wife this monkey has. "Show me your mason's permit, then go to the back and open the wagon for inspection." The captain waited for Gresha to leave, followed by two other guards. "You have to leave the wagon," he said to the women. "Let's go inside to check the permit." He stretched his hand toward Mira and helped her down, then walked her inside the room, which was empty. *Mason*... he looked at the permit. *Wasn't she married to a wool merchant? Obviously not, the monkey husband is a mason. I am getting old.* "A woman like you should not be forced to work. Or married to someone like..."

"That was my luck," Mira said with a wry smile. "My parents..." She shrugged.

"I can be your luck. Do you have children?" The captain looked her up and down, and their eyes met.

He recognized me. "No." This time Mira smiled warmly. In his early thirties, the man was good looking and powerful, and he knew that. To become a captain of the Guard's mistress was a stroke of luck for any poor woman in Nerval. It meant protection for a single woman, or for her family; even the husbands agreed on that and looked the other way. Nerval was the most dangerous city on the continent. A day never passed without murders or rapes.

"When are you coming back?" He sat on a bench and patted it, making her sit too.

"In a week. I will cook some food and leave them to work in Voltava. My husband will return in two months."

"That's fortunate. Perhaps we will get to know each other better." He touched her chin and turned Mira's face toward him.

"You are a good man, and I remember that day..." She smiled shyly again.

"I am not known to be an unkind man. When...?"

The door opened abruptly, and a guard came in. "The wagon is ready for inspection." His eyes fixed a point on the opposite wall.

"Bring the man and the other woman in and check the permit. I will check the wagon. She will help me." The captain made Mira stand and walked her out.

In the wagon, the captain did not hurry her. One by one, Mira opened and closed the six barrels while he watched her closely. *Only lime and oil. There is a strange grace and fluidity in her movement*, he thought. *She is no ordinary woman. How could her parents marry her to that man? He is not even rich.* When the last barrel was inspected and closed, he caught Mira in his arms and kissed her. Gently, and he took his time. *I never did this on duty... She responded. Now, I am being stupid; what else could she do? But we already agreed about a common future...* "When you return, ask for captain Kozlaw." *She already knows my name.* "Are you literate?" He pondered for a while when Mira nodded, then said, "If everything goes well between us, I will divorce you from that ... man." There was a genuine interest in his voice. "We should leave now. I think that I have searched this wagon too carefully. There are more people waiting to leave Nerval." He tried to say more, a kind of apology, but just shook his head and jumped down, then helped Mira.

The wagon passed through the gate at a slow pace; Gresha was a cautious man. He kept to that speed for a while, whistling a merry song. He looked back at Mira and smiled, this time without realizing the effect of his missing teeth. "The captain seemed to have been smitten by you."

"What did you expect? That he would be smitten by you?" She laughed. Thinking back, Mira did not feel repulsion for what had happened in the wagon. It surprised her. She and Dochia had killed five men in their house for something similar. The captain did not feel like them. *I have not spent a night with a man since I left Frankis. But we call that a stolen night; it's only for pleasure, feelings are not involved.* Mira became silent. Misunderstanding her reaction, Gresha no longer bothered her. *I am not a Light; at thirty, I can request a dispensation from the First Light and start a family. I will become a Helper for the Wanderers. If I find the right man. Kozlaw felt like the right kind of man.* She shook her head.

"Move faster!" Aliana shouted from her barrel, her voice muffled by the hard wood. Mira and Irina jumped from their places and raised one of the barrels, which had no bottom. Aliana sneaked out from the lower compartment and grabbed a package hanging on the wall of the wagon. "Baraki is coming after us." She opened the package and brought out her bow and quiver. In a minute, Dochia and Kasia were out too, and armed.

"Prepare the fuel barrel," Gresha said and pushed the horses into a slight canter. The road was good. The horses were strong. In a minute, he passed the first cart. There were four more in front of them; the guards had let each of them out after a ten-minute search. The check of their wagon took longer. Gresha could only guess why.

Mira and Aliana were the strongest, and they moved the oil barrel close to the tail of the cart. From a box, Kasia took out a small oil lamp, and lighted it.

"Did you have a Vision?" Dochia asked, just to break the tension.

"Yes. He will come out of the gate in a few minutes. We will still be on the straight part of the road before the curve that leads into the forest." Aliana looked at the gate; another cart was leaving the city. There was nothing more she could say, and the tension rose again in the wagon. It felt strange, unlike the feeling they usually had before a battle. She closed her eyes, forcing her Light into the future. This time nothing came to her, but they were already lucky that she had had a Vision of her own future. It was a rare thing for a Wanderer, but Aliana was of a kind that Dochia always felt was different. The young woman was and was not a Wanderer. Her powers were different; she could even use the Light to heal people. No other Wanderer could do that. Perhaps Fate did not want them to become too powerful.

Tense, the women waited, bows gripped in their hands. "Strange," Aliana whispered after a while. She looked at the road through the gap in front of the wagon. "Soon, we will reach the curve. Baraki should have been out of the city by now."

"I can't see well, but it looks like something happened at the gate," Dochia said. "A sort of ... gathering. Sometimes, a Vision can be overturned or mitigated by unexpected events." *But what could that unexpected event be?*

A new Vision surprised Aliana, and they became silent again, staring at the gate as it receded into the distance behind them.

She moved like a trained fighter, Kozlaw realized suddenly. He was in the postern looking at their wagon, which was moving slowly away, some five hundred feet from the gate. *A trained fighter...* The captain was trained by the Assassins of the Serpent. His eyes and memory were taught to register minor details. He let his mind return to the past. *If I hadn't ogled so much at Mashia's curves, I would have observed that the man's teeth were painted. And perhaps his hair too. The second woman... She moved like a trained fighter too. In Nerval, women are not trained to fight. The women who did what they did to Meriaduk were Wanderers. Trained fighters of Fate.* He looked again at the wagon, then at the soldiers behind him. *The barrels were filled with lime and oil, but I should have knocked on their lower part. I bet a bottle of good vadka that people were hidden there. Women. Three women.* Eyes closed, he let his mind wander again. He opened his mouth to sound the alarm. Closed it. *Grandfather was a priest of Fate. They burned him alive. The Serpentists. He was a priest. Meriaduk was a scourge.* He looked back through the gate, and a strange feeling came to him. A sort of flow. Later, he tried to understand that feeling. He never managed to.

"Guards!" Kozlaw shouted. "Stop this cart." He pointed at the one trying to leave the gate.

"But we were searched," the man protested.

Kozlaw threw a cold stare at him, and the man hurried to unload the twenty barrels from his cart. At least they were empty. In five minutes, the gate was fully blocked by the cart and the barrels spread around it. The captain stifled a smile at the scene, then looked again at the wagon on the road, which was now even farther away. *I will never see her again.*

"Clear the gate!" Baraki shouted and stopped his horse abruptly a few paces from a bunch of barrels spread in disorder. "Incompetents. What happened here?"

"Your majesty." Kozlaw bowed. "I asked to search the barrels again; they could be hiding people trying to sneak out of the city."

"That has happened already, but it's not this cart. There was a wagon before."

"The barrels were filled with lime," the captain said, hesitantly.

"And women. Clear the gate; we need to catch up with them." Unable to calm himself, Baraki turned his horse on the spot. It neighed. The sound reverberated in the narrow tunnel, stunning the soldiers for a few moments.

It took the captain three minutes to clear the gate so the riders could pass. Baraki threw a cold stare at Kozlaw, opened his mouth to bark an order. *I have no time now. I will deal with him later*. "Ride!" he shouted and pushed his horse into a gallop.

I am a dead man, Kozlaw thought, looking at the soldiers riding as if they were touched by madness.

"Baraki is out." Aliana pointed at the thirty riders pouring out of the city. They were arranged in two rows at the back of the wagon; three of them knelt on one knee in front, Dochia and Mira standing behind them. Their bows were nocked.

The riders were coming fast, and soon their figures could be seen. "Slow the horses," Aliana said.

"Are you sure?" Gresha asked without turning.

"Yes." She waited for a minute. Tensed her bow. Waited. She aimed long, her bow moving slowly. She stopped breathing. Released her arrow. "Speed!" she shouted and nocked again.

Her arrow found Baraki. He felt it coming and turned, a repetition of the last encounter with Aliana's arrow. It pierced his upper arm and reached his chest, on the right. Again. He slowed the horse and dismounted, on weak legs. Ten guards stopped with him; the other twenty continued their ride.

"Baraki escaped again; the wound is not lethal. His bloody Seer's powers," Aliana murmured, and fell silent.

"It's fine. They split as you planned it." Dochia patted her shoulder and tried a tentative smile, not realizing that Aliana could not see it.

Following the wagon, the riders spread along the road in an uneven formation. The first two fell, then three more. "Wait," Dochia said. "Let them come closer. Let them hope that they can capture us. I don't want them to send a courier for reinforcements. Shoot only the ones within fifty feet." She looked around: they were already in the forest, and half of Nerval was now hidden behind the trees. A minute more, and Nerval vanished. There were only twelve soldiers still riding, gathered in one compact group; they had waited for the slower riders. "Release the oil."

Mira and Aliana handled the barrel, tipped it, and the oil started to flow. It slowed the riders. When the barrel was half empty, they let it fall. Kasia threw the lamp. The fire started slowly, then it spread fast; there was alcohol too, most of it at the bottom of the barrel. The riders stopped abruptly, then fled into the forest to avoid the wild fire. The place was rocky under the tall grass, and they lost precious time. When they reached the road again, the wagon was three hundred feet away.

"In two minutes, we will reach the crossroads," Gresha said. "After the curve."

"Fire at will," Dochia ordered and released her first arrow.

The last soldier died just before they reached the crossroads. Each of the five riders who had passed the curve and was able to see the crossroads had three arrows in his body. The fugitives needed no witness to tell what road their wagon would follow. It was a small road used by the shepherds and woodcutters. For a while, it went back toward Nerval, then it entered the mountains. The road left the valley of the small river, went up for a while and followed the river on the edge high above. The place where Gresha stopped the wagon was narrow, the road squeezed between a tall rock and the edge of the two-hundred-foot-deep precipice. "We will make some sport on foot from now on." He smiled broadly, then pretended a frown. "You should not look at me like that."

"Gresha, you are a wonderful sight," Kasia laughed and embraced him.

"Women, they only care about handsome men." He laughed too and unharnessed the horses. "Take whatever you need from the wagon." He looked over the edge of the precipice and sighed.

"It's a good wagon, but I have no choice." He took two long poles out of the wagon and placed them under it. "You need to work, until now you only killed innocent people."

The noise of the wagon crashing onto the rocks below thundered between the ridges. Birds scattered above the forest. The sound echoed back and forth. It diminished slowly until the place became silent again. Gresha wiped his brow, listening to the silence. The women were silent too. "Well." He shrugged. "I don't hear horses on the road. What are you doing?" he asked Aliana, who was lying on the ground, her ear on the rocks.

"The land is silent," she said and stood up. "Codrin taught me this."

"That friend of yours, King and Seer. He seems to be a wise man. Send him greetings from Gresha, the great merchant of Nerval." He laughed and started to walk. "Let's go now; on foot, the road is longer."

They slept in a small cave that night and passed on the other side of the small mountains the next day at noon. When the road going toward the village was close to the edge of the forest, Dochia made them leave it through a small path.

"You Wanderers are so predictable," a man said from the top of a tall rock, then he climbed down using both feet and hands.

"Scorta." Dochia laughed and embraced him.

"This is an amazing thing, a Wanderer and an Assassin in a tight embrace. I am enjoying it." He laughed and embraced the other women too. "Is this scarecrow Gresha?"

"At your service," Gresha bowed mockingly. "Am I so scary?"

"I think your smile could scare a mighty bear. What happened? A column of riders passed through our village, asking about some evil women who killed some important bastards."

"Only this village?" Dochia asked.

"Every village on the southern road. I bet that the same happened on all the roads going out of Nerval."

"There was a sort of attack on our house. A bunch of idiots wanted to have fun with some undefended women."

"Undefended?" Scorta interjected and burst into laughter.

"Sort of. One of them was Sevrenski's son. We had to leave. Can we go into the village?"

"No, they left a few guards in it. We are watching all the roads. Our horses are already in the forest. We will leave tomorrow. Gresha," he looked at the merchant, "wash your teeth and hair. Two of my men will escort you back into Nerval; the road may be dangerous."

Five days later, the Assassins who went with Gresha joined the main group again at the place they had established, the entry into a long gorge, going south. It was a secondary and less frequented road. "You are being followed," one of them said.

"I know." Scorta touched his spyglass. "A lone rider. He is skilled. There may be more behind him. Did he see you?"

"We left the road and went through the forest." The man halted, lost in his thoughts. "I think that he was aware of us, but he did not let us know. There are twenty guards from Nerval on the road too. The man will be here in fifteen minutes, the guards in one hour. They seem cautious. I suppose they have a reason for that. There are rumors that three evil women wounded Baraki and killed more than a hundred guards. Or two hundred, it depends on who you ask. Impressive." He glanced at Dochia, who smiled briefly.

Thoughtfully, Scorta looked up at the edges of the gorge, at the road. "We will wait for him here. It's a good place for an ambush. We need bait. I don't want to kill a man only because he follows the same road."

"What better bait than a woman." Mira laughed without looking at Scorta. "I will do it."

The gorge was narrow at that point, and Mira stayed in the middle of the road, at the end of a tight curve. Her bow was in its usual place on her back. She waited. The man appeared after a few minutes, riding at leisure. He did not slow his horse until he was in front of her.

"It's dangerous for a woman to be alone in this place, but I wager that you are not alone," he said, a touch of humor in his voice. "Perhaps you will tell your friends that I mean no harm."

"Why should I do that?"

"They will come anyway." The man dismounted, sat on a long, red rock, well-polished by wind and water, and looked around. "This is a nice place. For whatever..."

Mira dismounted too and sat next to him. She said nothing. The man did not speak either. One by one, most of her people came down. Two of them remained hidden to watch the road from above.

"Quite a lot of Assassins and Wanderers for such an isolated place," the man said.

"Are you an Assassin?" Scorta scrutinized him, assessing the man's skills. He was and was not an Assassin.

"No, but I was trained by two of your kind."

"The ones who followed Baraki to Nerval. In our order, we consider them traitors."

"I figured that, but I did not follow Baraki. I was born in Nerval."

"Why are you following us?"

"I am going south, like many other people." The man turned his palms out. "There are some riders behind me, guards of Nerval. They may or may not be following you. The captain leading them is a skilled man. Trained by an Assassin." Looking at Scorta, he allowed himself a brief smile.

"Why did you delay Baraki at the gate?" It was Aliana.

"What makes you say that?"

She stepped forward and crouched in front of him. "I have a good memory, and I saw you there."

"From the barrel?" The man laughed.

"From the barrel."

The man stopped laughing and shrugged. "Decisions are made sometimes. They can change lives, in one way or another. This one changed mine; I am no longer a captain of Nerval's Guard. I am a fugitive. Traitor."

"Why?" Aliana insisted.

"You don't think much when making a hasty decision of this sort." The man shrugged again. "It's difficult to explain it, even to myself. It happened after your wagon had left the city. She," he gestured loosely at Mira, "did a good job distracting me."

"Kozlaw, I did not know that the captains of the guards were so dedicated in searching the women who want to pass through the gate." *I should be harsher with him,* Mira thought.

"I did not know it either, but I suppose that it happens from time to time. It depends on both man and woman." He looked at Mira. "You were already far away when I recalled the way you climbed into the wagon. You moved like a trained fighter. She," he gestured at Irina, "was moving the same way. That's when I realized that I should have paid less attention to the woman and more to the barrels. It was a little too late."

"You did not answer my question," Aliana said.

"Are you sure that I delayed Baraki?"

"Yes."

"Then you know that I am a traitor. I need more time to answer your question."

"What makes you think that you have more time?"

"Whatever decision you make, make it fast. The guards will be here soon." Kozlaw pointed back to the road, toward Nerval.

"This is a good place for an ambush," Scorta said.

"They are guards of Nerval. They serve the Khad in Nerval because of that. Some of them are good men, some aren't. Most of them have families. Wives. Children. It's hard to live in a city like Nerval without a father or husband. I think that you know that." He looked at Mira, then at Scorta.

"Do you have a suggestion to make?" It was Dochia.

"No."

"And if I insist?"

"They want to return home, so they will not hurry to find danger. Is this good enough for you?"

Scorta looked at him, then met Dochia's eyes, who nodded. With his left hand, which could not be seen by Kozlaw, he made a discreet gesture telling his men behind the rock to come down.

"Did you follow us?" Mira asked.

"No." *I followed you, not them. I may pay a price for that. I could have run north, or east, or west. I ran south.*

After three hours at a fast canter, they arrived at a peak from where the road back was visible for many miles. Scorta went up and looked with his spyglass. There were only two carts on the road, no riders. In the evening, they even made a fire, hidden in a small valley, far from the road; the nights were still cold.

"You will sleep close to the fire," Scorta said to Kozlaw. "Don't leave the fire without asking one of us. There will be two people on watch all the time."

"Why should I leave the fire on a night like this?"

"Do you always have something *clever* to say?" Mira asked.

"Always? No." Kozlaw shook his head. "Only when I can be heard by beautiful women." Kozlaw laughed, and it became contagious.

It was late, and most of them were almost asleep when Mira asked, "Where do you want to go?"

Kozlaw thought for a while. "Arenia. Perhaps. Or any other place where a soldier like me can find a new life. Or a man like me." *With a woman like you*. He looked at her in the low light of the flames.

Mira said nothing, only felt the need to stir the fire. The evening became quiet; the burning logs made the only noise in the camp.

In the morning, they left in haste and arrived at a small crossroads. "Which road is safer?" Scorta asked, looking at Kozlaw.

"None. Until now, there were only guards on the roads. The Toltars will come from both south and north, sweeping the land. Thousands of them. No road is safe." He looked at Scorta and frowned. "You knew that."

"Yes, but I was hoping that you knew some hidden paths."

"My village is behind that hill." Kozlaw pointed east. "Baraki's men must be there already, but my parents are dead. My older brother died young, killed by the Serpentists when they burned my grandfather. He was a priest of Fate. There are many shepherds' paths around here. Some of them follow the hills, close to their crests." He looked at Scorta, who nodded, and the former captain led them through the forest.

It happened that Kozlaw's journey was much longer than he had imagined. It was a strange journey for everybody. In Silvania, they learned that Codrin had been killed by the nomads, and Saliné was now the Queen of Frankis and Litvonia. Dochia learned that Aliana had been kidnapped by the Wanderers. Mira learned things of her own, and Kozlaw even more; he was far from home. It took them a while to adjust to the new reality, and even when they arrived in Muniker, many things were not yet settled in their minds.

❧

"I am Vio, the Queen's sister," Aliana said to the guards of the Muniker Palace. "And this is Dochia, the Third Light of the Frankis Wanderers.

I had no idea that the Queen had a sister, the Captain of the Palace Gate thought, but he was a cautious man and sent a courier into the palace. "Wait here until word from the palace reaches us. I have sent a courier," he told Vio.

The courier found Alfrid, who was in a hurry to leave. "The Queen's sister died a long time ago. Throw this imposter out of the city, and don't let her come back again," the King ordered, and the soldier did not dare to mention Dochia.

"I am sorry, lady," the captain said when the courier returned, "but the King said to... To escort you out of the city. These two men will go with you. Please don't try anything funny."

Aliana frowned at him, glanced around, and decided that there was not much chance of getting in with so many guards around.

"This is wrong," Dochia said, "she is the Queen's sister, and I am Dochia, the Third Light of Frankis."

"These are my orders; I can't do anything," the captain said, tentatively.

Aliana shrugged and continued her walk away from the palace.

"No, Aliana, stay here. Someone who knows us may come. There must be a misunderstanding." Dochia walked briskly until she reached her and grabbed her arm.

That was when Vlad came by, riding toward the gate. At a slow canter, he passed the two women. Abruptly, he turned his horse and came to them. "Dochia." His voice was warm, and he dismounted to greet her. "Well come back. Sorry that I can't stay, but I don't have much time. The King needs me. I will return in a few days. I hope you will not leave so soon. Do I know you?" He addressed Aliana this time.

"Yes, Vlad."

"This is not possible..." Vlad whispered, his eyes suddenly wide. He stepped back to see her better, then forward. The last time they had met was in Arad when they had tried to free her from Orban. She was only fourteen then, and he saw her only briefly. "But you were..." He shook his head and embraced her like a bear. "In my mind, you are still that little girl, faster than the wind. A beautiful woman I see now." Keeping her in his arms, he leaned back to look at her. "Vio..." he moistened his lips, "there is something that you should know." Unable to find words, Vlad stopped.

"Maybe you can tell the guards. They were escorting us out of Muniker," Dochia said before he could continue.

"What?" Vlad frowned. "Yes... This is what I wanted to say. Vio... We all know that you ... were killed by Orban."

"What?" both women asked at the same time, and both came closer to him.

"Do you mean to say that the Wanderers never told Mother I am alive?" Aliana gripped Vlad's arm and shook it vehemently.

"Sorry," she said, realizing what she was doing and released his arm.

"No, they never told us. Neither did Orban. I don't know how this could have happened. You must go inside. Captain, escort them back to the palace. If anyone asks, I gave the order. Vio, Dochia, I am sorry that I can't stay longer now, but I will return soon."

"Thank you, Vlad. What kind of commander are you?" Aliana asked.

"I am the Chief of the Muniker Guard."

"Are others from Frankis here too?"

"Plenty," Vlad laughed, yet he felt a hidden uneasiness growing in her. "Damian, Lisandru, Cantemir. Frankis moved here with Saliné." *And Pintea...* "I am now married and have a daughter."

"I see," Aliana said, her voice cold, and after Vlad excused himself again, they separated. "I did not expect them to be here."

"They are good people and I suppose they followed Saliné. She needed them."

"I did not expect her to be here either. It looks like they all forgot about Codrin."

"Aliana," Dochia said gently, and placed a hand on her arm. "It seems that things have changed. We should not make our minds up until we learn what happened. There is a new future we need to understand. Decisions were taken. We need to know why. But first, we need to understand your ... *death*. That was awful. Let me go first; it will be quite a shock."

"I don't know what future this is, but we are nothing without the past," Aliana said, morose.

They entered the hall of the palace as Alfrid was leaving through the door opening into the park, where his horse and his men were waiting.

"I will return soon, my love," he said and embraced Saliné, who held their son in her arms. "This attack is just a minor disturbance."

"Come back in one piece," she said, and pulled him toward her, with one arm, into a long kiss. "This was to make you return faster."

Saliné has already forgotten Codrin, Aliana thought, bitterly.

Silent, Aliana and Dochia stopped just behind Jara and Cernat, waiting for Saliné to turn toward them, which she did once Alfrid was out of the hall. Saliné had a fleeting glimpse of Aliana, then she saw Dochia, and she smiled warmly. Of all of them, Saliné was the one who had not seen her sister for the longest time, since Severin, before Aron sent her and Jara to Arad. In her mind, there was the image of a little girl with long hair, a girl she had mourned a long time ago. In front of her now was a tall woman, her hair cut short, almost like a man, the Wanderer's style. There was not much in common between this beautiful, yet tough woman, and the exuberant girl from the past.

"Dochia," she said, making both Jara and Cernat turn.

"Oh, no." Jara's voice was a rough whisper, and she looked at her daughter as if seeing a ghost. "Who are you?" She stumbled, and Aliana ran toward her.

"I am Vio," Aliana said, and embraced her; Jara was ready to collapse. "We have just learned that everybody thought me dead." They embraced for a long time, Jara sobbing quietly, and shuddering.

"My beautiful daughter," Jara finally found her voice, and she stroked Aliana's hair, then her face, absorbing her. "You have grown a lot." She leaned her head back, tears running down her face. "I made a grave for you. I cried. I mourned you. I will kill both Orban and Drusila. But now I am happy." Jara leaned her head on Aliana's shoulder, crying again, and it took some long minutes until she was able to release her daughter from her arms, to meet the rest of the family.

Saliné held Arnis in her arms and, unconsciously, Aliana avoided her and embraced Cernat. For the first time, they saw a tear running down the tough's man face. Then Aliana finally faced her sister. Their embrace was warm too; yet Saliné felt her uneasiness but could not know what was causing it.

"Arnis, my second son," Saliné said, presenting the sleeping toddler.

Aliana touched him briefly, forcing herself to smile. "And your other son?"

"Cosmin is eating right now. You must meet him too."

Aliana's encounter with Codrin's son was much warmer, and that did not escape to all the others around. "You don't know me, Cosmin," she said gently, "but I am your aunt."

"Mother told me about you. You left us a long time ago. You were..."

"True, but it was a misunderstanding. You see... I was very far away from here. Ten times farther than from here to Frankis, and news travels slowly over such a distance, but now I am back, and I am glad to see you." Aliana embraced him again, feeling as if she was embracing Codrin.

"I hope that my father will return too. Perhaps his death was a misunderstanding too."

Aliana had no words for him, and she just held him tight. Coming from nowhere, a wave of Light passed through her, and stirred her mind in a way that had not happened before. It was so strong that Aliana felt it like a breeze. *Codrin is alive*, she suddenly realized. *How could they do this to him?* She opened her mouth to warn Saliné when the Empress materialized in front of her. The ancient woman was silent, and shook her head with a stern look, enhanced by a heavy frown. Aliana wanted to ask and to protest, but the Empress vanished, and she did not dare disobey until knowing more.

Dochia sensed the presence too, and she guessed that it was the Empress, but she did not ask, yet from Aliana's thoughtful face, she knew that something important had happened.

Aliana was in shock, both from Cosmin's words and from learning that Codrin was alive and, with all her inner strength, she could not keep her composure. It took her a while to use the Assassin Cool breathing to calm herself. She stood up, and glanced around, her eyes wide. "My Wanderer name is Aliana," she said, only to say something and calm her mind.

"Aliana," Saliné said gently, feeling the storm in her sister's mind, though she could only partially guess what troubled her. "You must be tired and hungry. Please come and eat with us. I will have a suite and a bath prepared for you."

I will leave Muniker, it's not my world, Aliana thought. *It will never be my world, but I must stay for a while. They are my family.*

They gathered at the table with the feeling that the family was whole again, and everyone avoided, for different reasons, mentioning Codrin. There was happiness. There were some clouds too; Aliana could not pass over Saliné's marriage with Alfrid. It was her sister's decision to make, she knew, but deep inside she thought that everything was wrong. She felt that something terrible had happened, but she could not know that Alfrid and the Wanderers were the ones who planned to kill Codrin. Close to the end of the evening, she became silent and lost in her own thoughts. The more she thought about what had happened, the more she felt that things were going in the wrong direction. And the interdiction of the Empress was burning her, yet she was still a Wanderer and sworn to obey her; the Empress had founded the order and was still considered its head.

"Vio," Jara said gently when the silence went too long.

"I am sorry. It takes time to adjust. We met Vlad at the gate. He let us enter. Is Pintea here too?"

"Ah," Jara mused, a touch of amusement in her voice. "You still remember your 'guardian' in Severin. He is in Silvania right now. Our best shadow for secret jobs. He will return in a month."

I will no longer be here, but he may have already forgot about me; I was just a little girl in Severin.

A week later, Aliana finally made her decision; they were after dinner. "Tomorrow, I have to leave." *Alfrid will return, and I don't want to meet him.*

"Don't," Jara said. "We have not seen you for so long. I mourned you once. You can't leave like this." She stood up and went to her daughter to embrace her again; Aliana did not resist but did not answer either.

"I have to," Aliana said, her voice sad.

"Please stay, Aliana," Saliné said. "I understand that you need more time to adjust to what has happened."

"That's exactly what I don't want."

"Then it's me you are upset at. I had to decide, under the threat of a full-scale war between Frankis and Litvonia; I chose the best for my child, the people who would die in a useless war and me. It was mine to make, I wear its burden, and I want to be respected. I will stay away from you as long as you think it necessary, but don't leave your family. They love you, and I love you too."

"I am sure Mother had a hand in your decision too. She always made the wrong decisions where Codrin was involved, only now it touches his son too."

"The decision was mine, and Cosmin is *my* son. My marriage protects him, and he is now Duke of Sittgart. It's the most powerful Duchy in both Frankis and Litvonia."

"How will you protect Cosmin when he grows up and asks to inherit Frankis from his father? Which son will you protect in such a dynastic dispute?"

"I will protect both. Cosmin will be a Duke, it's what I had to accept for his protection, and he will have good men around him."

"Good men to keep him down, and Alfrid to watch him. It might work, but you never know. I am glad to see you again, but now I have to leave." She turned abruptly and made for the door.

"Aliana." Cernat used his tough voice, a thing he did rarely. "As Saliné said, we are family."

"Grandfather." Aliana turned slowly. "I hope that Cosmin is family too. I can take care of myself; take care of him. He needs it. My dear sister is living in a different world. And Alfrid will never be family to me. One day, you will wish that all this had not happened, but it will be too late. You have no idea what a storm is gathering over your ... new family." She gestured with her forefinger at the palace around them, and left the room, followed by Dochia.

"For sure what happened was unfair to Codrin, but I can't say about other things. Decisions were made. The world has changed in our absence. We can't change the past. We can't live in the past. We need to lead the future." Dochia was surprised too, but she was more detached by age and experience.

"Alfrid is the future," Aliana snapped.

"Thanks to this situation that no one foresaw, we have now two unified kingdoms, and the third one may come too. The Wanderers' goal is to revive the Alban Empire. Alfrid is not Codrin, but he is not worthless. It's unfortunate for Codrin but as it looks – she turned her palms out – his death opened the path to unify Frankis and Litvonia in a peaceful way. Let's talk about this later. We need to learn more about what happened."

ಌ

The Empress materialized inside Aliana's mind and measured her for a while. "I can tell you that Codrin, in his corner of the world, is happy. He has a new family and a new son, Ioan, who, by an interesting chance, was born in the same month as Arnis. He is no longer a king; he is a commoner, but he is happy. There is no need to be a king to be happy."

"What happened to him?

"He was wounded, but he survived, that's all that you need to know. And we are the only two who know about this." *And perhaps Thais... How that I did not think about this before?*

"Codrin would have never left Saliné and his child."

"You will know more about that in less than five years."

"Five years..." *You want to keep Codrin away from his son. And kingdom...?* "Alfrid will kill Cosmin."

"It may happen; as you said, we could have a dynastic dispute, and usually they are bloody."

"And you will let him do it."

"I said that it may happen, not that it will happen. And there is no need for me to interfere."

"You did not interfere for Codrin either. You will not interfere for his son. He was the Seer of the Realm, and you let Alfrid take his place. A nobody."

"He is not a nobody; he is the King of Frankis and Litvonia. You must get this into your mind. The world has changed around you. It will change even more. A new Empire will be built from the ashes of the old one."

"That's why you harmed Codrin, for Alfrid." *I have the feeling that you were involved in Codrin's disappearance. You and the Wanderers.*

"I don't harm people. Alfrid managed a peaceful unification of Frankis and Litvonia. Codrin wanted the same thing through war. My allegiance is to the Realm, not to a person, however capable. Your allegiance is to the Realm too. Don't try to meet Codrin. I will not be able to stop you; I will not even try, but I will advise you to let this course of events reach its maturity. The Realm needs him. Five years from now, he will reveal himself again, and he will lead the army against the next nomad invasion. He will become the Pillar of the Realm. That's the path of any Seer; you know it."

"Alfrid's empire," Aliana snorted. "Why would Codrin accept this?"

"Because it's his duty. We all have duties to the Realm; he more than others. Seers and Pillars are not ordinary men; they don't look for titles; they are born to serve, and the Empire will belong mostly to Saliné, not to Alfrid."

"But it will be passed to Alfrid's son."

"It will be their daughter who inherits it if that matters to you. Keep this to yourself."

"From now on, I am no longer a Wanderer."

"Don't let today's anger blind tomorrow. You are a powerful Wanderer, and the Realm needs you."

"The Realm doesn't mean only the Wanderers. In Frankis they did only bad things for decades. They kidnapped me and told my family that I was dead. I thought that the Wanderers have some honor."

"I can't follow everybody's fate, and each Wanderer has a choice to make and answer for it," the Empress said and vanished. Under her studied calm, she was nervous; for almost two years she had lived in incertitude, feeling that Codrin was alive, and found him only three weeks ago. Codrin was the Seer once, the man who defeated the nomads, but now he was a danger for the new empire; her work for more than six hundred years. She did not know what had happened; Thais had kept her work hidden. The Empress needed to find a path to integrate Codrin in the new political construct. This time, she will forbid the Wanderers to kill him; there must have been a meaning in his survival. At times, she doubted the Wanderers' plan, but she had never opposed a project, which had a chance to succeed. And this one started well, even when Codrin was sacrificed, two kingdoms were unified without wars, and the third one would follow soon. There was a brief Vision, telling her that Codrin will recover in five years, before the next nomad invasion. She did not know what caused his loss of memories. With all her power, that was the only Vision she had about Codrin. No other Vision came to her. It was like his future was hidden. She felt blind.

"You don't look happy," Dochia said, when Aliana returned from her inner talk.

"No," Aliana shook his head. "The Empress was involved in Codrin's disappearance and Saliné's marriage. I no longer trust her."

"There must be a reason for that," Dochia said gently. "We may learn more in time. I suppose that she set some restrictions on you. Do you plan to fight them?"

"I can't act without knowing the full picture, and I have only small fragments, yet I can't be member of an order in which I no longer believe. I will still help people which come my way, but that's all."

"Sometimes, I was as upset as you for what happened in Frankis, but I still continued. The Realm needs us, and you are still one of us."

"I am still your friend, if you want me be, but I am no longer a Wanderer. I can't be. The Wanderers are now against most things I believe in. In five years from now, you will learn more about what happened. It's a sad and ignoble thing, driven by the Wanderers and the Empress. Even the Circle is better than us now. I agreed to keep quiet and not to look further until that period expires, because I really don't know what to do. I may change my mind later."

"Aliana," Dochia said gently, passing an arm around her shoulders, "you are more than a friend to me, you are my Wanderer daughter. I trained you in Nerval, and you were like my daughter even before."

"Thank you, Dochia," Aliana said, embracing her.

"Why will you not ... react?"

"I can't oppose the Empress, and wrecking things here or there may be even worse than doing nothing. As you said, I need to learn more."

"I am sorry, Aliana."

"I will survive. Let's go, now."

"Where do you want to settle?"

"Poenari, if they accept me."

"They will. Jara told me that there are many good people there. I think... I think that, like you, they preferred to retire to their own corner of the world and hide from the rest of it."

"Then they are my people." Aliana's eyes narrowed, then widened, and her face looked calm again. *Poenari*, she thought. *There is something there... Something more than the people I want to meet. A sort of destiny. Is Codrin in Poenari?* She forced her mind into the Light but could not find him. It came only the feeling that Codrin was not in Poenari. She felt disappointed.

It was past midnight when Pintea arrived in Muniker and found Vlad waiting for him. There was a bottle of old wine on the table. "You will need this," Vlad said and filled two glasses.

"Well," Pintea shrugged and took the glass. "I suppose that I have to leave early in the morning again. Things went well in Silvania. I will write my report this night. Where do I have to go?"

"Nowhere." Vlad moistened his lips in the wine without drinking, then watched his brother through the ruby color.

"Trouble at home." Pintea shrugged again and drank some wine. "A good one. It smells of south Frankis. With all our efforts, it will take years to make Litvonia a safe kingdom. Alfrid is not Codrin. Without Saliné..."

"Vio is alive."

"It can't be." Pintea drank his glass, filled it again, and emptied it again. He looked at the empty glass, then at Vlad. "Frankis wine, lots of memories from my second life..." he muttered. "Tell me again." His voice became low and demanding.

"Pintea," Vlad said gently. "Yes, she is alive. Yes, she has left. I don't know why. But she is a Wanderer now."

"I was always unlucky," Pintea sighed.

"You will find another girl one day."

I am chasing a ghost. Vio doesn't know that I have loved her from the first day we met in Severin. I was a nobody then, she was a Signora's daughter, now she is a Queen's sister. And a Wanderer. Perhaps it is better that way. Better than a refuse. "I will take leave for a few months. I want to talk to Orban. Or to kill him. I am not sure which will come first."

"This is not your task. Jara already wants his head, through I can say that everybody is ... happy now. Orban may have a good story to save his head. And Drusila too. There is a sort of mystery. I am sure that we will learn it. In time. You should sleep now."

Aliana settled in Poenari. Immersing in her new life calmed her mind a little, but she tried each day to find Codrin. She would keep her word to stay away from him, but it was always useful to know his place. Something might happen to him. For the hundredth time, she let her mind stretch into the Light, and let it wander free. Nothing happened. She tried again, and she failed again. After a few weeks, she realized that the Light was blind to

Codrin; it was impossible to have a Vision about him. *Is the disturbance we are feeling in the Light due to what happened to Codrin?* She needed Dochia to talk about that, but her friend had chosen to return to Muniker and help Saliné. Aliana could not do that. She hated the city, which she had seen only for a few days, and she hated Alfrid even more; there was something wicked in him. She felt it with her Light, even when they never met, and wondered how that Dochia and Saliné were not able to feel his true character. Drusila came to Poenari to see her, but they parted on bad terms.

"For what you did to my mother," Aliana pointed an angry finger at Drusila, "lying to her that I died, I should hang you with a 'traitor' placard on your chest."

"Sages are hanged in Frankis, so why not Wanderers too? Sometimes we are not proud of the choices we make. Keeping you hidden is one of them."

"Perhaps you even cried."

"I have not cried since I was a fourteen-year-old girl, when I was bitten by a snake." Drusila raised her sleeves and revealed two small marks on her old skin. "The Serpent's mark. I was related to the Prophecy, knowing nothing. So are you. Old decisions have a way of visiting you during the night and gnawing at you. Wait and see; your time will come. There were spies of the Serpent looking for you in Arad. One day, when your anger subsides, I will be able to tell you more. Your *death* is related to the Prophecy, and it's too early to talk about it. Whatever you think of me, I am sad that you are leaving the Wanderers; you are stronger than me, perhaps even stronger than Dochia. It's your choice, and I always keep my word. Your Oath will be annulled at our next Conclave."

Chapter 18 - Codrin

The headache came abruptly. It felt like a stroke. Codrin moaned and bent over in pain. The ax fell from his hand. His eyes blurred, and he gasped for air. In slow motion, he rolled on the ground. He tried to crawl away to a place easier to defend. There was a mother bear and her cub somewhere around. He knew it. Almost blind, he leaned against a tree, and tried to unsheathe his dagger. He couldn't. Behind his closed eyes, he saw the bears coming toward him. They were now only some thirty paces away, standing on their back legs. The mother was grunting and shaking her large head. She seemed in a rage. He did not realize that it was a Vision. He did not know what a Vision was. He did not know that the effect of the potion that Thais had fed him was going away. He did not know about the potion at all. It had chosen to vanish from his brain at the wrong time, but a potion had no sense of time. It was a problem of quantity, because of the accident that happened in the third day after Thais fed him the potion. That event purged some potion from his blood. There would be a long path to recovering his mind and memories, perhaps months, or even more. Only if he could escape from the bears.

Pireska felt the Light; it surged inside her mind like fire, and she ran out of the house. Hot Light means trouble. Always. "Ildeko, bring your bow!" she shouted and picked up a hayfork that was leaning against the wall. Across the meadow in front of the house, she ran even faster. When she arrived at the slope, she was already panting, and out of breath. From there on, she could do no more than walk. It was painfully slow.

Running with the vigor of a young woman, Ildeko caught up with her, and asked, "Where should I go?"

"That tree there," Pireska pointed at a large yew, at the edge of the forest. "Tudor is lying against it. Don't go too close; there are two bears. Just make a lot of noise and be ready to shoot."

The cub was young and full of life. It liked to run and roll in the grass. With each sprint, it came closer to Codrin. When close was too close, the mother bear stood on her back legs and grunted. The cub did not listen. She grunted again, and went on all fours, then started to walk briskly toward her cub and Codrin.

Still running, Ildeko realized that she would arrive too late; the bear cub was now only thirty paces away from Codrin; she was two hundred paces behind the adult bear. The cub seemed interested in the prone man; he had not seen such a strange thing before. The mother seemed angry. She had seen humans before. She did not have fond memories of them. After a few more steps, Ildeko stopped abruptly and nocked her bow. She aimed long. With a hint of caution, the cub stood on his back legs, to look and sniff at Codrin. Ten paces behind, the mother imitated him. Ildeko walked a bit further and aimed again. She would have liked to have a different view of the mother bear, to see her eyes or her chest. She could see her back. The bears were no longer moving. Ildeko pulled the bowstring tighter, aiming at the mother bear's left front leg. A serious wound on a front leg might make a bear run. A wound on the back leg would make it attack, just because it could not run. *If she chooses to attack me, I won't be able to stop her with another shot*. Ready to release the arrow, she held her breath. Then she held it longer. After a while, her hand seemed to tremble a little, but the bears were still not moving, and she was a patient woman.

Still sniffing into the wind, the cub shook his head; the scent was new, attractive, and dangerous at the same time. He walked three steps more, and snarled, showing small sharp teeth; the scent became stronger. Suddenly, the cub fell onto all fours and ran back to his mother. She pushed him with her muzzle, rolling the small body in the grass, then hit him hard with her paw, rolling him again. The cub squealed and ran. The mother followed him, looking back from time to time.

Followed by Iantha, Thais came out of the forest, and looked at the departing bears, then at Codrin, who was still unconscious. "It seems that we've came just in time. My Vision was right. I wonder what happened; he doesn't seem wounded." She looked around and saw Ildeko and Pireska coming closer. "Perhaps he would have escaped anyway."

They put Codrin on a horse's back and carried him to the house. Once he was in bed, Thais had a closer look at him. "Does this happen often, that he loses consciousness?"

"This is the fifth time. It happens when he is in danger. Sometimes," Pireska said cautiously; she did not trust these two Wanderers.

"The bears." *Is Codrin so weak now?*

"Yes, I think so."

"Has he recovered some of his memories?" Thais lifted one of Codrin's eyelids and looked at his eye. It was glassy and immobile.

"I don't think he would stay here if he recovered his memories. And you said that he will need seven years."

"Isn't that child his son?" Thais pointed at Ioan, who was sleeping.

"Yes, he is," Ildeko said, and sat on the bed, taking Codrin's hand in hers.

Four more years, and Codrin will have lived a full life here. A second child will follow. Saliné is happy with her new husband and son. She will have another child too, the daughter who will inherit the Empire. This will make it easier to keep them apart when Codrin returns. He must become the Pillar of the Realm and stand behind Saliné and Alfrid. Thais moved closer to little Ioan and stretched her mind to feel the Light. She did not see much, only a glimpse of a toddler walking in the grass in some indefinite future. He was still here; Thais recognized the meadow behind the house, but she also felt a silver line into the future. *There is something in this child, a sort of strength. He may be important... I need to watch him growing.* She returned to Codrin. "Is he able to defend himself or his family?"

"Yes," Ildeko said, and hesitated. "He is good at fist fighting and has learned how to use a bow. He has never touched his swords, though." *He killed four armed men to defend us, but there is no need for you to know this, or that he fights like no one I saw before. Or that he trained me.*

"Well," Thais shrugged, "it seems that Marcus feels at home here, and you are doing well together."

Ildeko wasn't sure if it was wise to correct the Wanderer, but they will find out anyway. "He had chosen the name Tudor."

"Do you know why?" Thais asked, and her brows furrowed into a deep frown. *That was the name of his mentor, the Assassin Grandmaster from the Prophecy.*

"No. He has no memories from the past."

Thais did not insist but realized that she should have come here earlier. *There is no way to know how that name will influence the future.* Eyes closed, she tried again to call the Light. There was nothing to see, just the feeling that some good and bad things would come, but that happened in everybody's life. *I will come here every six months from now on.* She gestured at Iantha, and in a few minutes, they were gone.

Codrin stayed unconscious for seven days while the vanishing potion worked on him, and seven more in a sort of dreaming, half awake, while its effects disappeared from his mind. Things came to him during the nights, long fragments of a life that felt like a strange dream. They came in a disconcerting way, not following a chronologic path. On moment he was in Frankis with a woman and two girls, all of them still unknown to him. The next he was in the Caravan's Inn in Muniker. He learned that his parents were dead. He still did not know who they were. He found himself kneeling by the graves of his brother and mentor, but his mind knew no brother and no mentor. He saw a young woman with green eyes and auburn hair at the end of it. She was unknown to him, and she called him Codrin. "I am Tudor," he mumbled, half conscious. He woke up late in the morning. His head was still throbbing with sickening waves of pain. He felt weak and hungry. But his memories were finally available to him, if he could find them in that mess which was his mind. It would take a while to access and sort everything, and even longer to merge his two lives.

"What happened?" Pireska asked.

"I don't know." He tried to stand, but the effort was too much, and he moaned, unable to move; Ildeko took his hand in hers. He clung to Ildeko's hands, and she grimaced from the pain that his strong fingers inflicted but said nothing. His own pain did not lessen, but her touch calmed him. "There is something strange in my head. Things... I don't know where they came from. They look like dreams, but... I don't think they are dreams. But what can they be?" He lessened his grip and caressed her hand. It calmed him even more. Ildeko felt his need, freed one of her hands, and stroked his hair. Fighting his pain, Codrin moved closer, and Ildeko raised his head from the pillow, settling it on her knees.

"You are getting your memories back. You lost them after the accident. We've talked about this," Pireska said again.

"Am I? They look strange to me, as if they are not mine."

"They are from your other life, the life from before ... coming here. What do you remember?"

"Are they? There is someone from Arenia. I suppose that's me. I can't see myself." He pondered for a while. "I am young."

"Yes, you are a young man," Pireska said.

"No, no. In those memories ... I am really young."

"How do you know that?"

"I see my hands. A child's hands. Fourteen? Fifteen years old? I don't know."

"What were you doing?"

"Running away. Ah," he gasped, "I am at a grave. Alone. My family is dead. All of them."

"Can you see ... your family?"

"No, only the grave. There is nothing from before that moment. They were killed. I don't know by whom."

"What happens next?"

"I am in Litvonia, in Baia."

"Yes, we are in Baia."

"No, no. That young me, he is in Baia. At a farm. No, it was an inn. Or both. I can't remember."

"Are you alone?"

"There is a woman. Gran. And two boys, her grandchildren. Vlad. Pintea. They call me... Why did you call me Tudor?"

"It's the name of my son. You are ... my new son. But I don't really know why I did it. Perhaps because I missed him. Is it your name?" Pireska asked, her eyes wide.

"No, but I used it for a while. I don't know why. Perhaps because I was running. Some royal guards were searching for me. I don't know why."

"Do you know your name?"

"No, they don't know it, so I don't know either. It's like am living through their memories. No, they are not their memories, they are mine, but I remember only what happens when I am interacting with them."

"Does the name Marcus mean anything to you?"

"No." Codrin shook his head and moaned.

"Can you stand?" Ildeko asked when he seemed to feel better.

Codrin nodded hesitantly. It seemed that he was slowly healing; it involved a lot of pain. Grinding his teeth, he pushed himself up until he was able to sit on the edge of the bed, his feet trembling a little. There was a carafe of water on the table by the bed. Ildeko lifted it to his dry lips and helped him to drink.

"I don't know why I was so thirsty," he whispered.

"Healing needs water."

His memories are recovering faster that Thais had told me, Pireska thought. She helped Codrin stand, Ildeko at his other side, and forced him to walk and leave the house, none of them trying to speak. *And he will leave us. The sooner he will recover, the faster he will leave. I am a healer. I am bound to help him. He deserves that, and perhaps he will...*

They walked toward the bench at the back of the house. An eagle was circling above the meadow, high in the sky, almost a dot, gliding with the warm wind from the south. It looked deceptively peaceful. The morning sun broke through the high clouds, and the short green grass grew bright, wet with rain in the branching light. It was warmer than usual for the third week after the Spring Equinox and, leaning his head back to catch more sunshine, Codrin felt better.

"What else do you remember from Baia?" Pireska asked. "The more you try, the faster you will recall."

"And what if I won't like what I recall?" Codrin asked, his voice edgy; they did not know that one of the first things that came into his mind was Shadow, his long sword. And the man he had killed with it.

"There is only one way to know." Pireska touched his forehead. *You were a strong man, not a bad man. You killed, but you did not kill like Irvath. There is something strange in your long sword, sometimes I had the feeling that it was trying to speak to me. I never heard of enchanted swords, but never heard doesn't mean never happened.* She let her Light into Codrin. *You protected other women before; I feel it.* "Baia," she whispered, and forced even more Light into him.

Eyes closed, Codrin let his mind wander. "Weapons, I had weapons with me."

"Do you still have them?"

"Yes, those two swords that hang in the house, and two more. One belonged to my dead brother."

"Do you remember his name?"

Codrin opened his mouth, closed it. "No," he breathed. "The curved swords belonged to Tudor. My mentor. I took his name. He is dead too. Everyone is dead. Everyone. Mother. Father. Even my twin sister." He shook his head in pain, then gripped it between his palms. "Ioana, my twin sister," he repeated, barely audible, and a few tears ran down his face.

"Shh." Ildeko embraced him, pressing his head against her chest. She frowned and shook her head at Pireska.

"We. Have. To," Pireska said without sounds. "Baia," she said again, using her Light on Codrin. "Leave the grave behind and tell me about Baia."

"I have ring-mail. Why is everything about death and weapons?"

"You were running. Weapons keep a man alive."

"That winter... My ring-mail became too small. I modified it by taking off some rings. And some things."

"What things?"

"I don't know. They were a danger, but I don't know why. A sort of insignia, two ravens and a crown."

The House of Arenia... Who is this man? "Leave Baia." Pireska's voice was precise and commanding.

Codrin's breath was ragged, and his words barely intelligible. Both women had to lean toward him to hear better. "I am in

Muniker. It's an inn. I don't know its name. Movil... That must be a man's name. Perhaps the innkeeper. He gave me a bottle of wine and asked me to keep the peace at the inn. Ah," he gasped. "I hit a man."

"Did you kill him?"

"No, I hit him the same way I hit Fandras, but gently." Codrin briefly touched his windpipe. "He fell but recovered later." Eyes closed, he stayed silent for a while, forcing his mind to focus on the inn. It seemed important. "They came after me."

"Who?"

"The Royal Guards."

"Litvonian?"

"No Arenian. And some nomads from the east. They wanted me; I don't know what for." Codrin moaned and clenched his mouth. Gently, Ildeko laid him on the bench and took his head in her lap. In a few moments, he fell asleep.

For days, Codrin refused to talk again about his memories. Refused to even remember, running from his past. Now and then, there were flashes in his mind, figments of his life. Most of them were violent, and that frightened him. He knew now that his past belonged to a man of power, and the only man of power in his new life was Count Irvath. He did not want to be like the Count. He would hate to be like the Count and, each time new memories came to him, he shook his head vigorously to chase them away. Sometimes it worked; sometimes it didn't. Most of the day, he ran from Pireska, coming late into the house. The old woman waited patiently until his guard was down. It was midnight, and he was almost asleep at the table when she placed Shadow in his hand.

Unconsciously, Codrin gripped the hilt and opened his eyes abruptly.

"Shadow," the sword whispered in his mind.

Mesmerized, he gripped the hilt tighter, and images came to him. He was alone in a forest, watching six men trying to rape a woman, the first time he had used Shadow in a fight. Everything moved forward at a strange speed. It took only a few seconds to end, and he gasped, letting the sword fall on the floor. "I killed five men," he whispered.

"There must be a reason for that." Pireska took his hand between hers.

"They tried to rape a woman." Codrin felt that the woman was important to him but could not remember why, or her name. "She killed the sixth one. A strong woman, trained to fight."

"That is a good reason to ... punish them." *But to kill them?* "Do you know the woman?"

"Yes ... and no."

Pireska picked the sword up from the floor and pushed it into his hand again. Another fragment of his life came to him. A battle. That night, Codrin slept badly, in a sort of trance filled with strange memories. He turned in his bed, and two times kicked Ildeko away until she chose to sleep on the floor.

Late in the morning, Ildeko woke up in bed. Codrin was gone, and she saw him through the window, sitting on the bench, head in hands. She hurried out, then with a stroke of intuition returned to pick a small object from a decrepit cabinet. Reaching Codrin, she raised his head, playing with his hair. He avoided looking in her eyes and lowered his head again. "Tell me," she said, gently.

"I am married," Codrin whispered, without raising his head. "I am sorry. I did not know."

"I knew. This is your wedding ring." She took his hand and placed the ring on his finger. "You are my lover."

"It's not fair to you." For the first time, Codrin dared to look in her eyes. "I have a son with her. I can't remember his name."

"Then you have two sons. I am sure that you will take care of our child too."

"It's strange. I don't remember my wife, only her name, Saliné. I think that it's a Frankis name." *I am talking too much.* He pulled Ildeko onto his lap and embraced her. "After three years ... perhaps she has divorced me." A surge of bitterness came over him. Deep in his mind, there was a Vision, Saliné's wedding, one Vision among many. Codrin was not yet able to access the Visions he had had while he was still unconscious; another shock was needed to open his mind. It would come when he expected it the least. *I loved that woman. My wife.* He searched deeper inside; there were feelings and memories, waiting to resurface. A woman playing the lyre; he could see only her delicate fingers. A woman laughing. He liked that laughter. *Saliné... I still love her.* He struggled to remember her face, but all he could get was a vision of rebellious auburn hair. It belonged to the woman playing the lyre, her face still hidden.

"How long were you...?" Ildeko tried to ask, but he pressed a finger to her lips, feeling that her voice was trembling a little. *Married?*

I need time, Codrin thought. *Time to reconcile myself with my past, without hurting Ildeko.* Codrin's simple life had become suddenly complicated, and his mind was not yet able to handle such complications. He felt that unconsciously and embraced her tighter. He did not speak, trying to sort his life. The woman playing the lyre seemed rich. Her room, which was the Music Room in Arad, was larger than Pireska's house. There were fragments of conversations too, from people who he still did not know. Sometimes, they used the word castle; Codrin could not understand what a castle really meant, but he could recognize the signs of things that were out of reach in his new life. *I no longer fit there. This is my life. Ildeko and Ioan need me more than my previous family.* Another room came to him, then another, then the walls of Arad, and he started to understand what a castle meant. He felt small and insignificant to live in such immensity, filled with many more people than the only village he had seen in his new life. *I no longer fit there,* he repeated.

He did not sleep much that night, or the following one. During the day, he preferred to work without respite, cutting more wood than was needed. The hard effort calmed his mind. He needed it. Memories were coming to him, sometimes slow and understandable, sometimes swifter than a mountain river, filled with too many things, some of them making no sense at all. There was a strange effervescence in him, as his mind tried to recover the face of his wife. It did not happen.

Slowly, Codrin unsheathed Shadow. The sword attracted him. The sword frightened him.

"Shadow," it whispered into his mind, and old memories came to him. Battle after battle. Poenari. Eagle Nest. The Battle of Mist. He dropped the sword, trying to run from his bloody past. It remained on the floor for several days, and this time Pireska did not try to push him. Each day, Codrin walked out of the house, glancing at the sword still lying on the floor.

"You must train."

Codrin recognized the whispering voice inside his mind. Tried to ignore it. Went toward the door.

"You are the King of Frankis. You must train." The sword was insistent, and its voice was pressuring his mind. The bond between them was still intact, only the sword could break it. If it chose too. It didn't; they were meant to each other by a prophecy made when Codrin was still a toddler.

Abruptly, he turned, picked Shadow up from the floor, and left the house. In the middle of the meadow, he balanced the sword in his hand. He frowned, trying to remember. It took him a few minutes to visualize the Assassin Dance. The low, initial position of the body. The first move. The second. Pirouette. He felt joy in the sword, and strange feelings mounting in him. His movements were clumsy in the beginning and, sometimes, he looked like a madman. Pireska and Ildeko watched him, trying to understand. The old woman was trained once to use a sword, but what she was seeing now did not make much sense to her; it was too different from her own knowledge, but at least she understood how Codrin was able to kill four armed men with his bare hands. After two long hours, exhausted, Codrin sat in the grass, legs crossed, the Assassin Meditation posture. He looked at his hands. *I am not King. I am a woodcutter. This small house is my home.* He felt suddenly at peace and let his breath calm down. His mind started to wander. It brought him the name of his son, Cosmin, then he learned about Mara and their son, Radu, fragmented strings of memories that told him almost nothing about his past life. *What kind of man am I? A child here, another one there? How many children have I? I must leave that kind of life behind and take care of my family here. No more women, and no more children. I am no longer that irresponsible man.* He stood up and went to find Ildeko. Silent, he took her in his arms.

Day after day, Codrin's technique improved and, after a while, he started to train Ildeko, letting her use Flame, his short sword. Pireska watched them closely; there were things to learn, and their future depended on them and on this strange man, who was still a big child in some respects. Her Wanderer Light and experience with people revealed to her an evolution that even Codrin was not able to understand.

A week later, the face of the woman with auburn hair came to Codrin with the first light of the dawn. It felt like a revelation, and he found a new meaning for love and life; Saliné was too much part of him to forget her. Her absence felt like pain, yet it took him more than a month to decide, each passing day more painful than the previous one.

"I understand that you have to leave," Pireska said, forcing the words out. "Here are seven galbeni and some silvers. They will help you get home. I took them from Irvath after you killed him. I have kept twenty silvers. I am an old woman, and I have lived my life. Please take Ildeko and ... her children with you. Make her your servant, or whatever you like, but take her from here. They will not survive another year."

"Pireska," Codrin said gently, and took the old woman's hand in his. "Ildeko will never be a servant, and you will all come with me. I have a large home." He had not told them yet that he was the King of Frankis. They would become scared of him, perhaps not even willing to join him. They knew that he was a powerful Seigneur in Frankis. He did not say anything about the Seer either. There will be enough time on the long road toward his home.

"Thank you," she whispered, and tears filled her eyes. "But we have only two horses, so I will stay here. Don't worry about this old woman; she has lived her life."

Codrin took her in his arms, and the old woman began to cry silently. "There are fifty galbeni hidden in Zor's saddle. Tomorrow, I will go to buy a horse. Then we will leave."

Codrin was eager to leave and meet his old life again, his wife, his children. He did not realize that it was too early. He could not know how much of his memories and personality was not yet recovered. He knew nothing about the three-year-old Visions still hiding inside his mind. Some of them came to him as a future that was now past. And as for Saliné, there might be a day when he would regret decisions made and the ones not made, on the path that would lead him to Muniker.

Chapter 19 - Codrin / Saliné

Soon after the Summer Solstice, Codrin arrived in Muniker. His new family was lodged at the Broken Bridge Inn, ten miles away from the city, and he went alone to meet Alfrid.

Slamming the door onto the wall, the guard burst into the gate-room. It took him a long moment to find his voice; he was still stunned by what he had seen. "The Seer has returned!" he finally cried, his voice strangled; it felt like a child's who found himself in front of bear.

Frinz, the captain of the day, turned his large head toward the soldier. There was a chicken leg in his hand; he was just taking his lunch. His teeth were deep in the meat, and he stayed that way, unable to free his jaws. He blinked at the guard.

"The Seer has returned," the soldier repeated, elation and fear filling his voice.

The captain threw the meat on the plate, wiped his mouth, and jumped to his feet. He ran. Outside, the soldiers at the gate were already aligned to give the honors, facing Codrin, looking at him in awe, even when he was alone.

"Seer," Frinz said, bowing deeply. "We thought that... We are glad that you... Are the nomads coming?" He finally voiced everybody's fear; there had to be a reason for the Seer to return.

"They will come again, Frinz," Codrin said, "but not this year. I have come to see Alfrid."

"Yes, of course. Please allow me to escort you." Frinz puffed out his chest, proud that the Seer remembered his name, and that so many soldiers witnessed that fact. Many evenings he would tell that story to anyone willing to listen, and to anyone not willing. "You," he gestured to a group of six soldiers, "come with us." And for the first time in many years of serving in the Muniker Guard, Frinz broke the rules, and left the gate without a captain.

They walked in silence toward the palace, Codrin lost in his own thoughts. Frinz had many questions to ask, but he did not dare to disturb the Seer. At the gate of the palace, the captain knocked at the hard wood.

"Frinz, you came to the wrong gate," a soldier mocked him. "You should drink less."

"Open the gate," Frinz whispered, "the Seer has returned from death."

"What? The nomads?"

"They are coming again. Next year. The Seer told us. Open the gate, you fool."

Walking the long corridor toward the Royal Suite, Codrin tried to remember his previous visit, more than three years ago, before he went to fight the nomads. He got something else instead, a flash of the cowardly attack from behind that had left five arrows in him. "Oh, no," he whispered, "they were Alfrid's soldiers, led by Captain Roderick. The bastard tried to kill me, and I came here..." He glanced behind and saw the same seven guards still following him. *There is no way I can leave.* He was just in front of the massive door of the Royal Suite. Not knowing him, the two guards looked at Codrin, then at the soldiers behind.

"The Seer has returned," Frinz said, gesturing at Codrin, and the soldiers hurried to open the large, sculpted door for him.

Taking a deep breath, Codrin entered the room.

"You have to catch me, if you want to kiss me." Saliné laughed, moving away from her husband. There was a serene atmosphere, a party, with five people gathered around the small bed of Arnis, their son, a child of almost eighteen months. Jara,

Dochia and Cernat were watching, amused, at the two adults playing like two children.

Alfrid sprang and, knowing that she was faster, Saliné let him catch her. "I've got you," he said and kissed her; her arms went around his neck. "I will always love you, wife."

"Always," Saliné said, mussing his curly hair with her hands.

Dochia noticed Codrin, standing stunned in front of the door the soldiers had just closed behind him, and her heart missed several beats. She tried to speak, but no sound left her mouth. She coughed discreetly. Jara and Cernat heard her; the other two were too caught up in their game. Codrin's hand went for the hilt of Flame, his short sword; Dochia and Cernat moved to stand between him and Alfrid. Jara's face went white, and she leaned against the table; her legs were betraying her.

"Saliné," Codrin snapped, his voice echoing in the large room. For two or three moments, there was a strange stillness. Then they moved at once, slowly, each at its own pace.

Saliné turned toward him, eyes wide, breathing hard. *He is alive... What have I done? Fate, what have I done?* Unable to speak, she stared at him, as he stared at her. *I still love him. I will always love him.*

"Well," Alfrid was the first one to recover, and he coughed several times to control his voice. "Welcome to Muniker, Codrin. We thought you were dead, but we are glad that you proved us wrong. You are a revenant," he laughed, edgily. "More than three years have passed since you disappeared, and you have returned to a different world. As I said, we thought you were dead, and Saliné is now my love, my wife, my queen, and the mother of my son, Arnis. You can see him there in that small bed, our pride. We are celebrating because our good friend Dochia has just arrived, though she can't stay long; the real party will be in the evening."

There was almost no visible reaction in Codrin, and only Dochia, with her Wanderer senses, perceived them all; the grip of his fingers on the hilt contracted and released slightly at each word like 'love' and 'wife' and even at 'Dochia the good friend'. Alfrid's description was a complete demolition of Codrin's life.

“Indeed, many things seems to have changed while I was away,” Codrin said, still staring at Saliné.

“Alfrid, let me speak to Codrin.” Saliné finally found her voice.

“You are right my love, it’s better to let you explain everything to him. I will leave you alone.” *Saliné will keep him busy until I bring ten soldiers. How did he escape from my trap?*

“I am so happy that you are alive, Codrin,” Saliné said, searching her words with care, there were many words to say, and even more to avoid. Fighting to calm the storm in her mind, she walked slowly until they were face to face. Their eyes locked, absorbing each other. She stopped carefully, four paces away from him, and breathed deeply. Once. “I missed you so much.” The smile on her lips was both happy and sad. She wanted to embrace him, to feel him in her arms, and slowly, she stepped forward. He moved forward too, and their fingers almost touched. Abruptly, she clasped her hands behind her.

Codrin stopped too, even more disappointed than a few moments ago. His anger was now matched by sadness, and the corners of his mouths slumped down. “When did you miss me? When you kissed Alfrid?”

“Codrin, we thought you dead, and I wish now that I had not married Alfrid. I still love you, but I had to marry him. There was no other way. I am sorry.”

“Ah, yes, as always. I thought that it meant something, you and me. Only you and me. I was wrong.”

“It meant something, and it always will. Please Codrin, I did not know...”

“From the age of your son, you did not lose much time in finding a replacement husband and love.”

“We married one year after ... one year after we were told you were dead. We...” She paused, feeling like crossing river ice, and hearing a first faint cracking sound coming from under her feet.

“You married earlier than one year after, and that means that the negotiations for the marriage contract started soon after I went missing. As it looks, nobody missed me. I am just an unwanted ghost, disturbing this big happy family." He gestured to include the other three people in the room.

"We had no choice, Codrin. We were in a bad position."

"Why? You had a good army, good people, and nobody could take Poenari. Nobody." A new flash of memories came to him, and he moaned, as they came with pain. It was one of the Visions he had had almost three years ago, one that he did not understand at that time – all the people he saw there were unknown to him at that time, and he had forgotten it fast.

"Codrin?"

"You pushed for this." Codrin half turned and gestured menacingly at Jara. "'This is your best choice, Saliné, and you will be Queen of both Frankis and Litvonia.' This is what you said, Jara. You sold me and my son, to make your daughter Queen in both kingdoms. This had nothing to do with a bad position. You have always sold me, Jara. You asked for loyalty, but you never gave loyalty. None of you gave me your loyalty. A curse on you, woman. I wish I have never met you."

"Codrin, we thought you were dead, and we had no choice," Saliné said, and tears ran down her face.

"There was no body, and you did not find Zor either. I could have been wounded and in hiding, I could have been taken prisoner by the nomads. And you had a choice, but you wanted to be Queen of Frankis and Litvonia."

"Our scouts searched more than two months for you, and all the soldiers from your guard were dead. The Litvonian scouts helped us. We thought that the nomads had killed you too."

"It was not the nomads. The Litvonian troops attacked us by surprise, from behind. I escaped only because Zor was fast. I had five Litvonian arrows in me. Five. And now I find my wife married to the man who tried to kill me. She loves an assassin. She is happy with him."

"What?" Cernat asked, moving forward jerkily, trembling, his face going paler and paler, like a man seeing a ghost. Nobody could have recognized the composed Grand Seigneur in the troubled man speaking now. "The Litvonians?"

"This was in my body," Codrin said bitterly, and threw an arrowhead onto the table. "Along with four more."

"Litvonian," Cernat whispered, playing it between his fingers. "This thing should stay hidden." Hesitantly, he put the arrowhead into his pocket. "And everything we have just heard should remain between us. Understand?" One by one, he looked at the women in the room, and they all nodded. *Is Alfrid so bad? But he is always gentle; he always listens. He is not wicked. I have not seen him punishing people in a bad way. Have I become senile and unable to read people?*

"I did not know," Saliné repeated, as Codrin stared at her. *I need to protect Codrin.*

"Now, you know. Will you come home with me? There will be enough trusted men there to take back what was ours."

I wish I could, Codrin. How I wish I could. "There is no more home, Codrin, and most of our best men moved here with me. Vlad is the Chief of the Guard and a Seigneur; Damian is a Seigneur too. Cantemir is our Vice-Chancellor, although he is presently in Frankis. Almost all of us are here." *Please understand, Codrin, I am Alfrid's wife, and I have a child with him. This is my family now, and this is not the world you left three years ago. Even if I wanted to leave, Alfrid would simply kill you. He has the power to do it. And I can't run with two small children. They will be in danger.*

"You took everything from me. You left me nothing. For the second time on my life, I have lost everything," Codrin said bitterly, his stare lost in confusion.

"I am sorry." Jara came to him, took his hand in hers and burst into tears. "I am sorry, Codrin."

"That was always the way with your family. 'I am sorry, but don't worry, Codrin, after you help us, we will betray you again.'" He pushed her away, and Jara did not try to come close again. Trembling and unable to move, she was rescued by Cernat, who seated her in a chair.

I have seen Jara crying only when her mother was killed and Vio returned; she is such a strong woman, Dochia thought.

"Codrin, we should discuss more pressing things." Her voice was warm, and she came to embrace him, trying to buy some respite for everybody.

"Embrace your good friend Alfrid," he snapped and pushed Dochia away too; she had watched the game between Saliné and Alfrid approvingly when he entered. He remembered that. And Alfrid called her a friend. "I have to leave. Some people here want me dead. I am a threat for the Queen and the King of Frankis and Litvonia."

"But if you knew that Alfrid tried to kill you... Why did you come here? And why did you not come earlier? Three years... Why?" Dochia shook her head.

"Because of the wounds, I lost my memories. I did not know who I was. For three years, I worked as a woodcutter and hunter in a forest. Two months ago, some memories returned to me. Only some, and there is no way of knowing what I've lost. It would have been better if I had forgotten about my lovely wife. And the thing with the Litvonian troop attacking us came to me only when I came here. If I had known this earlier, I would have avoided Muniker like the plague, and I would have been spared seeing my wife kissing and proclaiming her love for my assassin. Always," he growled, and Saliné flinched at their secret word, but she said nothing. "And the Vision of Jara betraying me came just now."

"Jara did not betray you, she loves you like her son, but yes, she helped Saliné make a hard decision. There was too much pressure on Saliné. You will learn what happened." Dochia glanced at Jara, who was still sobbing silently.

"Empty words," Codrin shrugged. "So, your majesty, Queen of Frankis and Litvonia, can we agree that I leave your city, and go I don't know where?"

"Yes, Codrin. If your report about the attack on you is true..."

"If? I am not a scoundrel like your beloved husband, to lie about such things. I may be nobody now, but at least I have my honor. I don't kill men who saved my life to steal their wives."

"I believe you, and you are not nobody."

"I am nothing to you. Where is my son?"

"He is with his governess."

"Of course; he can't be part of this happy royal family. There is now only one son that counts for you." *There is not enough time to see my son; I must leave as fast as I can.*

"He is my son, too."

"I hear soldiers coming," Cernat said.

"I should have guessed. The scoundrel. No wonder he is called the Pig King." Codrin moved as far away from the door as he could, and set himself in a narrow space, between an armoire and the outer wall, where he could not be attacked by more than two soldiers at once. *At least I will kill him. But the Pig will not come close; he will send his soldiers. They may have crossbows. Why didn't I get that memory back earlier? What game is being played on me? And by whom?*

"You are in my house, Codrin. Nothing will happen to you," Saliné said, her voice strong again, but before she could finish, the door opened, and Alfrid entered, followed by ten soldiers. She moved fast to intercept him. "What is the meaning of this?" she asked in a harsh whisper.

"Just a precaution," Alfrid said, his voice low, and pulled her into a corner of the room.

"Alfrid, Codrin understood the situation much better than I thought, and he will leave now."

"I am afraid that he must stay as our guest for a while longer."

"I have already agreed this with him. He is an intelligent man, and he realizes that I am now your wife, we love each other, and we have a child together. Time can't turn back."

"The situation is still fluid in Frankis. We can't let him go there. He is too strong, and some are alert for the smallest sign of our weakness. They will gather around him, and our dream will shatter. I can't let that happen." Alfrid shook his head vehemently. "We have such a strong dream, Saliné, to unify the continent again, to stop all the wars. Next year, we will take Silvania without a fight. Everything is prepared. You know that. We can't take a false step now."

"He is alone. I brought his best men here. They will not leave their families and positions for this. We need to be respectful with him. If we treat him badly..."

"I will not treat him badly. He saved my kingdom and my life, and I am forever in his debt. Let's keep him for a while as our guest. Here, in the palace." *Until I find a way to...*

"It will be too hard for him to see us. He was going home to his wife. He found us."

"Then the house in the park. It's in a nice place, and it's a good house."

"Well," Saliné said, tentatively, understanding that there was no way to convince Alfrid. "Let me tell him our decision." *I promised Codrin to let him go. Let's hope that he will not erupt; he must stay calm.* "Codrin," she turned toward him, speaking gently, "my husband and I want to have you as our guest in Muniker. You saved Litvonia and his life, and we are in your debt. And you have nowhere to go right now. It's our way to thank you for everything you have done for us."

She has betrayed me once more. Codrin gripped the hilt of the sword as if trying to break it. The corner of his left mouth raised, giving him that look, which always scared people away. "How long do you want to keep me here?" His flat voice contrasted with the turmoil in his mind, which showed only in his white knuckles.

Unable to react, Saliné pressed a hand to her mouth. *He used that voice on me. He is more troubled than I thought. Of course he is.*

"Why talk about the end of your visit now?" Alfrid asked. "We are glad to have you as a guest of honor. Soon, the Summer Royal Balls will start, and Muniker is an interesting city. Much more pleasant than Arad or Peyris, I assure you. You will have your own house here, set in the park behind the castle. I stayed there for three years when I was an unruly child. You will enjoy it too."

"Yes, it's a nice house," Cernat said, trying in vain to capture Codrin's attention; his bitter eyes were still on Saliné. "When we moved to Muniker, I was thinking to stay there. It reminded me of the hunting house in Severin. It is not so large, but you don't need much space anyway." He went toward Codrin and, placing an arm around his shoulders, pushed him to walk. "I will come with you to visit the house. Who knows? Maybe one day I will move there. Come, Codrin. There is no way to avoid this." His last words were a faint whisper, which only Codrin could hear.

"Would you mind if I come too?" Dochia asked and, without waiting for an answer, she followed them. "Stay here," she whispered to Saliné, and Jara stayed behind too, knowing that Codrin would not want her to come, and anyway she could not walk.

It took almost half an hour before the key was found, the old door was opened, and some minutes more until Alfrid left them alone. They sat around the table. Silent. For a while, no one could speak.

"I know it's hard for you, but you have come through worse things," Dochia finally said, and Codrin glanced sullenly at her, saying nothing.

"There was no way to go against Alfrid," Cernat said. "So long as he is unaware that you know who tried to kill you, he may think you useful; he knows the nomads will attack us again."

"Do you really believe what you say?" Codrin asked gruffly; pain throbbed in his voice.

"You must believe something and be prepared for everything."

"Tell him what the Queen and the King really said about me." Codrin looked at Dochia this time.

"Alfrid said that you will raise Frankis against him, which, by the way, is true, but Saliné disagreed. Formally. She knows you better than Alfrid."

"How do you know that?" Cernat asked her.

"I can lip-read, and so can Codrin."

"I will never leave Muniker, and it's not this house that Saliné and her husband will finally give me, but a grave."

"Saliné will never..."

"She will. For them, I am an enemy. The woman I love is my worst enemy. The sooner I am dispatched, the better. They only need to find a way to make it resemble an accident. It looks bad to kill a former husband and the man who saved your life and kingdom. That's why they put me in this nice house. They need to buy time."

"She has not changed that much."

"She is in love with the Pig King, and he is not called that without a reason. When you stay with the pigs, you become like them. When you stay with their King it is even more so."

"I know, it's hard for you to believe, but that name was spread by his enemies, when he and his cousins fought for the throne of Litvonia, at the death of the last King, who was their uncle. He is surprisingly charming and intelligent."

"Like Bucur was too, except that your *good* friend Alfrid is more intelligent. More powerful. More evil. They share the same lack of character and other bad traits. This man tried to assassinate me after I saved his life and kingdom, and you babble about his charm. Saliné is like him now. He tried to kill me. You do not care."

"We care, but you should let a few days pass and try to understand the new world around you," Dochia said.

"What part of what I said doesn't match the new world around me?"

"The part about Saliné."

"You want to say that she has shared his bed for three years without realizing what a scoundrel he is? She knows. Two scoundrels faking kindness, waiting to kill me."

"He conceals himself well. I also did not think he is able to kill you just like that."

Codrin tried to speak, but he bent in pain, and a new Vision from the past came to him. It involved a Wanderer and Alfrid. He breathed hard until the pain was almost gone. *Why are they coming back to me when they are not useful anymore?* "I recalled another Vision, and I don't know why they always come with pain. You did not *want* to know about the assassination attempt, Dochia; your order was involved in the plot to kill me too. A Wanderer named Calista came with the idea to assassinate me after I defeated the nomads. I want you to hear how she and Alfrid laughed about my fate. The 'Arenian tool', they called me. That worthless man who was made Seer for no reason."

"She is the Second Light of Litvonia. Are you suggesting that I knew of this?" Dochia asked.

"The Frankis Wanderers were involved in my assassination too. Your Wanderers made way for Alfrid, on my throne and in my bed. I escaped, but you ruined my life. You sold everything I had, even my wife and child. But you sold your honor too. The Wanderers are a plague now, even worse than the Circle. They are like Baraki now; you should and join the Serpent."

"I was still in Nerval when this happened, and no one informed me when I took my place in the Council of Three," Dochia said, edgily.

"The Wanderers have no honor," Codrin repeated. "Your *friend* Alfrid was your choice to replace me. Dirty game, dirty King, dirty Wanderers. Don't tell me that Saliné doesn't know his game. You can't hide such things from your wife, at least not from a wife like Saliné. Intelligent, but, yes, the loving wife of her pig husband."

"Let's talk again in two days," Dochia said, and the fine lines of her face deepened with her frown.

"I don't need to talk; I need to leave. The charming family wants my head, and it will not take long until they convince Jara and Cernat too."

"You don't put much trust in us," Cernat said, his voice sad.

"Why should I?" Codrin snapped and nodded toward the door. He needed to be alone.

When they had left, Codrin made a tour of his new house. All the windows had bars, even the ones on the second floor. *This is a prison*, he thought. *I can leave the house only through the front door. There will be guards...*

Walking through the park on the way back to the palace, Dochia made Cernat change their paths a few times.

"The new sentries?" Cernat asked.

"I was counting them. They were only three when we left the palace; there are ten now. At least."

"Usually there are four sentries during the day around the park and ten during the night. Codrin may be right; things are moving fast in the wrong direction."

"Did you not feel anything wrong in Alfrid?"

"No. I did not see this coming. Involuntarily, I always compared him to Codrin. Alfrid lacks his fighting skills and war experience. Their political skills and capacity for organization are similar, and Alfrid is more sociable and more able to convince people to see things his way. He loves Saliné, and that can't be faked. He is always polite and... I really don't know what to say."

"Do you believe Codrin about the attack?"

"Yes, he would not lie just to garner sympathy or influence Saliné. He has too much character. It appears he doesn't find such character in me anymore."

"Put yourself in his position. He has lost everything. And that Vision about Jara advising Saliné to take the Litvonian throne. It's true."

"Dochia, who knew that Codrin was still alive? We can't change anything. She is Queen, the wife of the King of Frankis and Litvonia, and they have a child together. She belongs here. Alfrid will never let her go. He will kill Codrin whatever the costs. You know that. I really don't know what to do."

"Keep Codrin alive. I will stay three more days. We should keep an eye on him all the time. Just you and I, unfortunately; we can't use Jara or Saliné. I wish Cantemir were here. Do you think that we can fully trust Vlad, Damian, and their brothers? You know them better."

"They will not want to see Codrin dead."

"Bring them in, then. They will make Codrin feel better. Even with those new sentries," she gestured around, "Alfrid will not try anything soon. He needs time to calculate his next steps, and maybe he will decide that some sort of accommodation can be made. You are right that the new nomad invasion may influence his decisions in a good way. So long as Codrin doesn't give Alfrid an ideal occasion to kill him which, seeing his erratic behavior, he might. I am afraid that Codrin will misinterpret a situation and, feeling that he is in danger, he will try to kill Alfrid."

"I am afraid of that too." Lost in a flurry of strange thoughts, Cernat walked in silence for a while. "I feel Codrin is somehow diminished. He acts more like the young man I knew in Severin, not like the established King of Frankis. Even with the shock of seeing his wife married to another man, the King would have reacted coldly, trying to find the best solution to escape, keeping his composure and pretending that he was not affected at all by what he found here after more than three years. He wasted time complaining like an angry youngster. That young man in him will take more risks and will be prone to more temper than I would like. In Severin, he was free to play his game; here, he is in a large prison with a warden who is not his friend. Fear, hate and bitterness are bad advisors. And there are plenty of those feelings in him right now."

"For a good reason."

"Good reasons can kill you as well as bad reasons. This ... behavior may be related to the loss of his memories. I hope that he will recover them soon. He needs them, and I also need to put some order in my thoughts. He needs us too."

"Was Saliné's marriage with Codrin annulled?"

"Yes, as there was no body, the Church of Fate and the Chancellor of Frankis annulled it. Everything is clear. For Fate and people, she is Alfrid's wife."

Dochia and Cernat could not reach Jara – when she was able to walk again, she went to her room, and locked herself inside, unwilling to talk to anyone. In the evening, they found Saliné alone, in the small office of her suite. Head in hands, she was sitting at her desk, traces of dried tears visible on her face.

"It was a hard day," Cernat said calmly, letting his warm baritone voice fill the room. He knew the effect of that tone.

"One of the hardest I have ever had, and the bad in my life is a never-ending story. Eight years ago, when I married Codrin, I thought that my bad days were gone. I thought the same after my new marriage went much better than I had expected. Isn't that ironic? It was a hard day when I lost Codrin. It may be even harder now that he is back. But at least he is alive. That's the only thing keeping me sane right now."

"What do you think about his story?" Cernat asked, tentatively.

"I suppose you ask about the assassination attempt. It's true. Codrin would not lie about it, and Alfrid is certainly capable of putting such a plan into practice."

"Won't be a problem that he tried to kill Codrin, in general, and the man who saved his life in particular?" Dochia asked.

"Before the nomad invasion, we planned to take Litvonia from Alfrid. How were we different from him? Once, Alfrid intimated that he knew about our plans, from a spy or from a Wanderer's Vision; I don't know, and we both chose to avoid the subject. Yes, Codrin saved his life in battle, because he had to, if not the army would have collapsed, and yes, we still planned to take Litvonia after the nomad invasion. Alfrid planned his move before he met Codrin. In the end, the one who planned better won, and the kingdoms were unified without the war Codrin and I had planned. I love both Codrin and Alfrid, and I need to find a way to keep them safe. Add to this that I have a child from both." Saliné raised her head, and looked by turns at Dochia and Cernat, her eyes tired and sad. "As it is, we all have a dilemma right now, though we differ on the issue. That's normal; our interactions with the main subjects are different."

"Where is Alfrid?" Cernat looked through the window, but it was already dark, and anyway Codrin's house was not visible from there.

"I suppose he is strengthening the guard around Codrin. He is ... confused."

"Yes, the man Alfrid tried to assassinate is still alive. But he will try to make things right. That's his point of view." Cernat shrugged.

"It depends on how things evolve. If I were allowed to ask Fate for a wish, I would need two wishes. Alfrid to stop considering Codrin a threat and see him as an ally against the nomads. Codrin to give up his desire for revenge and recover what was his in the past and become part of ... our world. I think that may be four wishes rather than two."

"No wish for yourself?" Dochia asked.

"I should have refused Alfrid's marriage proposal, but I didn't, and I can't turn time back or my back on him. He is my husband, and I love him too. We have a good marriage. I could even be cynical and say that he represents the most stable future."

"It's good that you are less ... emotional." Cernat looked distracted and worried.

"You are wrong, Grandfather. You have no idea what turmoil is in my mind, but I am in a better position than Codrin, and perhaps more rational right now. On the other hand, he has fewer problems than me. His cause is simple. Mine..."

"Whatever the differences, we need to find a ... peaceful solution. As Codrin is in a more dangerous position right now, he should be our main interest," Dochia said.

"You are thinking of helping him to escape." There was unexpected sadness and a dose of rejection in Saliné's voice.

"That would be the safest way."

"A few hours ago, I would have thought the same," Saliné said, passing a hand through her hair. "I even promised Codrin that he could leave Muniker. Now, I don't think it is the best solution. I had to take back my word."

Dochia lifted an eyebrow, but said nothing, waiting for Saliné to clarify her position.

It was Cernat who spoke in the end. "You are afraid that Codrin will raise Frankis against Litvonia."

"Yes, Grandfather; if Codrin leaves now, we will have a war before the end of the summer, and who knows when and how it will end? I want him safe, but he can leave only when he understands the new world around him. And when he ... becomes part of it. Duke of Sittgart, a new family, Chancellor, whatever he wants, without destroying everything around him and us. I will find him a good wife that he can love. He deserves to be happy again." *Codrin's wife*... There was a sudden heaviness in her chest, and tears threatened to well. She bit her lip and went to the window. There was nothing to see.

"That won't be easy. You want him to renounce all his dreams while you and Alfrid keep them."

"No, it won't be easy. And it won't be easy to convince Alfrid either, but I think that doing so is less difficult than changing Codrin. He understands that Codrin can be a powerful ally against the nomads. He also understands the danger Codrin can be." Saliné tried to add something more, but in the end chose not to comment about Codrin's dreams. *I need to postpone things, to keep everybody safe. We can talk about dreams later.*

"You know," Dochia said, thoughtfully, "if Codrin has his way, leaves and starts a war, things can go one way or the other, but some negotiations are still possible to find an acceptable solution. Like one king here, and another in Frankis. But if Alfrid has his way, there will be no negotiations. There is nothing you can do for the dead."

"That's why we need to keep Codrin safe. But we must keep him safe here until a solution can be found. Dochia, if a war starts, it will not be Codrin against Alfrid; it will be Codrin against my family. For both Fate and people, I am Alfrid's wife, and this is my family now. And my family is growing; I am pregnant. There is no way to avoid my responsibilities."

"And if no acceptable solution can be found?"

"I think that I would prefer the peaceful solution, not war. There is no need for so many people to die because of our political games. But I don't want to think about this now." Saliné shook her head vehemently, then bit her lip to stifle away a sudden urge to sob.

"Let's not go that far," Cernat said gently. "Perhaps the Duchy, a new marriage and a strong position at the court for Codrin will be enough to make a workable arrangement."

Perhaps..., Dochia thought, before saying, "You should wait for a while."

"No, we have to move fast," Saliné said, struggling to control her voice. "I will tell Codrin soon, and wait a few weeks for him to understand, and then, well ... some persuasion and some pressure. I hope that it will work."

Saliné did not sleep much that night. There were dreams. There were nightmares. In one of them, she found herself watching Codrin, Alfrid and Edric. They argued at first, then they started to fight. She could see their wounds, and the blood flowing out. "Nooo!" she shouted, waking up abruptly, almost falling from her bed. Shaking, she embraced her knees, unable to stop her tears. *Fate, I thank you for keeping Codrin alive when we all thought him dead. And I curse you for returning him to me when I am no longer able to have him. My pregnancy...* She shook her head. *I will name this child after Codrin, or after his twin sister; the only thing I can do for the man I will always love. That and keeping him alive.*

Just before dawn she went into another dream with the three men who had marked her life. There was no fight this time, and they came to her having that look a man has when he wants a woman. She felt their hands and their lips. Saliné tried to fight or to wake herself. She could not, and everything mixed into shadow of dream and nightmare, and making love with all three at the same time. It was a long dream. She woke tired, and with pleasure lingering in her body, as if everything had been real. Afraid to sleep again, she got up and dressed in a bathrobe.

"That's perhaps the best future," said the translucent woman who materialized in front of Saliné. "To take Codrin and Edric as your lointain lovers. Six hundred years ago, I did the same to build the Litvonian Kingdom from the ashes of the Empire. Your charge is higher, to rebuild the Alban Empire and stop the wars."

"You are sneaking into our dreams, into our minds..." Saliné snapped.

"I can't sneak into anyone's mind. My presence must be acknowledged if not, I am rejected after a few moments. Even in your dream, you acknowledged me, involuntarily, because you also considered the same solution. You wanted my opinion." The Empress smiled.

"And you really think that..."

"I think that, and you think that too. Don't try to hide from yourself. They love you, and you love them. That dream came from your unconscious mind, and I felt it using the Light. It's a sort of ... Vision. A way into the future. Edric and Codrin, the powers behind the throne. Two strong men are easier to control than one; there is a balance in your hands. And it's mostly your throne; in the long game, Alfrid doesn't count much. It will not happen tomorrow, but you must start to plan today. It's the safest way for you and for your children. And the most pleasant." The Empress smiled knowingly and vanished.

I hate that woman, Saliné thought. *She is always scheming. I can think of Edric as my lointain lover while I'm married to Alfrid. But not Codrin. There can't be another man in my life while I am with him. I can't be with him. It's not possible. That would mean war and death. Even Codrin and Alfrid could die, and my children will suffer. I can't allow another war. I hate wars; they only bring misery.* She went to the table and filled a glass of wine, then took her time to make a list of marriageable Duchesses and Countesses worthy of becoming Codrin's wife. *Maltia's daughter is only fifteen years old; we can't wait that long; it would be too hard for Codrin. If we can have the smallest agreement, he may leave Muniker at the end of autumn.* Litvonia was a large kingdom with many Duchies but, in the end, she could find only two women she deemed worth of Codrin: the daughter of the Duke of Drasdin, and the widowed Countess of Baia, who was Alfrid's cousin. Saliné had met the woman at the royal wedding, and she had left a good impression on everybody. A lot of men had tried to court her, but the widow rejected them with dignity. *She has made a kind of vow...* Saliné forced herself to remember. *She will not marry for two years after the Grey Respect ends. That would be this summer. I will invite her and the Duke of Drasdin to come here.* She pondered for a while. *Drasdin's daughter will give a better position to Codrin. And he will receive the Duchy of Sittgart too and pass it to our son.*

She sipped some wine. Walked across the room, gesticulating with her free hand. *I hope to convince Codrin, but I need to be prepared for...* She gestured with the hand holding the glass, and wine spilled on her and on the floor. *I am careless... Or perhaps cornered.* It felt suddenly hot in the room, and she let her wine-stained bathrobe fall, then walked naked toward the window. Opened it with a brusque movement and looked up at the nascent dawn. *If things fail, all will push for war: Alfrid, Calista, Edric... And Codrin. I can convince Alfrid, but I can't control Calista. I have to make Edric my lointain lover. With Alfrid and Edric on my side, I will be able to start some sort of negotiations. That will be later, if my plan fails; now I must focus on finding a wife for Codrin.* The cold breeze stirred her skin, and her mind seemed to calm. *I must find a wife for...,* she repeated, and a lone tear ran down her face. Then she started to sob.

Captain Frinz took his usual dinner at the Caravans Inn. From the door, he coughed to gather everybody's attention. He was a known person, and people turned their heads toward him, perhaps the King had to make some announcement. Frinz coughed again. "The Seer has returned from death." His voice was proud and loud. "Next year, the nomads will attack us." His voice became lower. "The Seer will help us again." She stayed silent, his eyes straying in the room. There were no questions, only fear, and he went to his reserved table.

Movil listened to everything with his keen ears and mind. *I never heard of someone who returned from death. The Seer is a great man, the greatest I ever saw, but even he could not resurrect. There must be an explanation for this, and I may live long enough to learn it. He is a great man,* he repeated, *but he is not in a great position right now. King Alfrid is in a great position, but he is not a great man. He just happened to be in the right place at the right time to take somebody else's wife and kingdom. And he cares nothing about people like me. The Seer cares. He stopped in my inn when he was the King of Frankis. We met years before, and only for a few days, yet he stopped here and made my inn famous. However strong he is, he needs help. So that's it: The Seer has returned from death to save us. The part about saving us again may even be true. The nomads are stubborn and greedy. And Alfrid is weak. Frinz is a clever man, fond of the Seer; he will help me. He knows how to speak.*

Late in the evening, Frinz had to tell his story again, and his words spread both fear and hope in the city. "Next year, the nomads will invade our land again. The Seer told me that himself." Standing up in front of the people, he tapped with a finger on his chest while Movil filled his glass. "And he will defend us again." The inn was now full, and Frinz was never short of the best wine Muniker had to offer. Drinking for free made it taste even better. He went home feeling like a hero, the man who had opened the gate for the Seer to save Muniker. It was late when Movil and three more men came to see him. Then two more men. They left his house long after midnight.

Two days later, Movil wrote in huge dark blue letters on a white plank: Free drinks for the Seer's resurrection. It was a known thing that the Seer always dressed in dark blue. And Frinz had to tell his story again, this time in front of a small crowd gathered in front of the inn, ready to drink Movil's wine and hear the story. Frinz's mouth was never dry, and after a few glasses, his story became epic.

It took Saliné two days to gather enough courage to meet Codrin. She spoke a lot with Alfrid, and a compromise was found. It was her task to convince Codrin to accept her plan too.

"I know it's hard for us both, but we need to speak," she said to Codrin. Dochia and Cernat were there too, in what was now considered to be his house.

"You came to tell me that I can leave. It should not be that hard." Codrin mustered a fine touch of cold irony in his voice.

"I think you know already that this is not possible, not until we agree on some terms."

"What exactly is hard for you? The Queen of Frankis and Litvonia gave her word that I can leave. The Queen reneged her word. She came now to impose her terms and will call it negotiations."

"Let's try to find a solution acceptable for everyone. Codrin, in my heart, I am the same Saliné who still loves you. True, I love another man too, but only because I thought you were dead. It's just... It's just that the world has changed around us."

"You changed it, Saliné. You, Alfrid and my *death*. Nobody wants to talk about the assassination attempt. You only talk about the *changes,* the bright future. It sounds better, isn't it? You got the husband you wanted, the child you wanted, on top of the kingdom you wanted. I got death. I hope it was worth it, to become such a powerful Queen over my dead body."

"Please Codrin, it was a hard price, and I tried to postpone my decision about marriage as long as I could."

"Perhaps for better negotiations. If you solve the issue I represent for your new world, what will you do when your son requests his inheritance?"

It was not for better negotiations, Codrin. I did not want the marriage. Now everything is different. It makes no sense to argue. "Our son will receive the Duchy of Sittgart."

"His inheritance is Frankis," Codrin snapped. "The kingdom I built. Sittgart is just a piece of paper signed by a Pig. And if my son claims Frankis, you will destroy him for the benefit of the only son who counts for you. Arnis. Your pride. I don't remember you calling Cosmin your pride."

Saliné swallowed at the Pig word but chose to ignore it. "Both are my pride, but we are talking about you now. You must understand that Alfrid is the King. There is no way to change that. We must find a solution together."

Codrin wanted to snap an angry answer, but Dochia said, before he could find his words, "Let's keep calm."

"There is no solution; I am someone that no one wanted to come back. The great Queen and King, who tried to kill me, their family, the Wanderers and the Circle that planned my death to make this happy family. You are working together against me. Your negotiations are the first step to killing me." Codrin pointed at Saliné.

"I will never..." Saliné said, her voice bitter.

"Yes, you will. You will do it for your crown, husband and son. Your family will support you as well, as they supported your marriage over my body. The Wanderers want me dead too. There is nothing more to say. Leave me alone." Codrin turned with his back at them, making them leave, only Dochia stayed behind. Seeing her, he grimaced angrily and said, "Some of you are merely upset that the plot to kill me failed."

"I don't think they fully realized what happened. Give them some more time," Dochia said gently. "And give me your hand." She stretched her arm toward Codrin. He obeyed, and she cut him slightly, her thumb rubbing the blood on his palm. Eyes closed, she started to hum, and her palm started to glow white. Then she hummed more, the White Light seeping from her body, growing stronger, while Codrin's worried eyes settled on her frowning face. She opened her eyes abruptly and pushed his hand away.

"They will kill me. I was expecting it." Codrin shrugged.

"It's not that," Dochia rasped. "I could not see your future. Nothing. It has never happened to me, and I am the strongest Wanderer." She calmed her breath, her eyes searching Codrin's face. "Are you still a Seer?" she asked, though she knew that he had lost his powers, thinking that maybe there were some new developments of which she was not aware.

"No, the Empress demoted me just before the battle with the nomads, when I needed my power the most. She knew that her Wanderers had condemned me to death, to make the Great Pig of Frankis and Litvonia. If you still pretend that this was wrong, fight to make it right. I need to escape."

"That's difficult now."

"Of course, you will come with a good plan soon, but only after they kill me. You are a Wanderer after all." Codrin stormed out of his own house and slammed the door.

Chapter 20 - Codrin / Saliné

Cosmin did not recognize his father; he was too young to remember the tall man who left Arad to save the Realm. He knew the stories, as Saliné and Jara had told him many, but he did not really know his father. He was a shy child, a little introverted, and his first gesture was to hide behind his mother's skirt.

Codrin crouched and stretched out his arm. "We should have a handshake, like two men who did not meet for a long time."

Cosmin smiled for the first time since the tall, frightening man had come in, and stretched out his hand too, clasping the large palm with his little hand. Then he looked at Saliné. "Mother, now that Father returned, we will go home together, won't we?"

Saliné hoped that Codrin would intervene, but he did not. "Unfortunately, my love, that is no longer possible."

"But this is what you told me. You married that man only because Father did not come back, and we were in danger. There is no danger anymore. This is not our home."

"Yes, this is what I told you, but too much time has passed, and things can't be changed anymore. There is a different kind of danger now." *I can't tell him that Alfrid may still want to kill Codrin. He is too young to understand and keep everything to himself. Is he old enough to understand that it's not possible to break the marriage?*

"Two years are not so much."

"It depends on who you ask," Codrin said, bitterly.

"Please Codrin, don't try to set my son against me," Saliné pleaded. "I wish I had not married Alfrid, but nothing can be changed, and Cosmin depends on me."

"No one has harmed my son's future more than you, Saliné. Like me, he has lost everything in the favor of your real child, Arnis," Codrin said, icily.

"Being a king is not everything in life, Codrin. I am still his mother."

"Tell that to him when he asks you why he lost his inheritance. He will ask you, as he asked you today why you don't want to return his life to him, and you had no answer. You can't justify your decision, Saliné; there was no danger, only your family's desire for more power, and my son has no future here."

She took a deep breath, trying to stop a talk that was going nowhere. *Codrin suffered much more. He still suffers, and it will not stop today, but I have at least to make him understand.* "I was alone, Codrin. It was not your fault, but I was alone, and made the decision I thought would be best for my son and me. I don't need to justify my decision to anyone, not even to you or to my son. There is nothing that we can do about the past, but I hope that we can try to be a little more ... constructive about the future," she said, fighting hard to control her voice, and she left him alone, taking their son with her.

Can I trust them? Alfrid thought as they walked away from his office. *With Vlaicu, Sava, Valer and Boldur, they were his main captains. And Cantemir was his Chancellor, now my Vice-Chancellor. Four of them refused to come here.*

Vlad, Damian, Pintea and Lisandru came to see Codrin the next day. Though they knew that Codrin had returned, there were a few moments of astonishment for the five men, and they searched for words and gestures. Then the spell was broken, and the past became a sort of present. They were all on the same side, but they still needed to acknowledge it and find their way.

"I was your Chief of the Scouts," Vlad said, "and it's my failure that I couldn't find you. The nomads who attacked you somehow tricked us. I am sorry, Codrin."

"They were not nomads, they were Litvonian soldiers," Codrin said.

There was a sudden silence in the room, and Vlad closed his eyes, trying to remember the smallest detail of that dark day. "When I arrived at the place where twenty of our best guards were lying dead," he said reluctantly, "I did not have much time to check, as it was clear that you had escaped, and eight to ten riders went after you. We followed the trail, yet I remember now that the arrows which killed our men were longer than the ones that the nomads used. Three days later, when I returned, they were gone."

There was another moment of silence, before Vlad found his words again. "When we came here, I convinced them," he gestured at the other three, "that we need to find a negotiated solution. You have lost everything, but I thought that the best thing was to help you integrate into this new system of power. Taking back your kingdom would be hard and being the Duke of Sittgart could be a solution. At least for a while. Don't curse me; that was what I thought. This ... story changes everything. I am your man, and I will do whatever is necessary to protect you and help you."

"The same for me," the other three said like instant echoes.

"Thank you." Codrin's voice was suddenly hoarse, as emotion stirred in him. That, and sudden memories of a better past.

"Damian and I are married and have children, and my wife is ... Alfrid's niece, so we must move in stages."

"Who is now in Poenari?"

"Sava, Boldur, Mara, Varia and Calin. Vlaicu and Valer are in Arad and Severin. They refused to come here, so..."

"If I take Poenari, my life will simplify, but first I have to escape from here."

"We will find a way and, as Chief of the Guard, I will be able to send Pintea or Lisandru with you to Frankis, for whatever official reason I can find. In fact, I must send them away before you leave, just to maintain the appearances that they still work for Alfrid. We must plan carefully, as I have no control over the Palace Guard, and there are no men from Frankis there. You will not have a second chance."

"I need a way to leave the house; there are bars everywhere, even on the terrace."

"We will find a way," Vlad said thoughtfully, "but it may take a while."

"Vlad, there is something else. At the Broken Bridge Inn, there are two women and two children. They saved my life when Alfrid's men almost killed me, and they may be in danger. Find them another place until I can leave."

"In a week, I will go home and take them with me. They will stay in my castle and be treated..." Vlad looked at Codrin.

"As if they are family. I need to send them a letter. They are waiting for me."

"I can deliver it tomorrow," Pintea said. "Perhaps I should go incognito, no uniform." He looked at Codrin, who nodded.

The day he received the invitation to the Royal Ball, Codrin cursed both the Litvonian King and his Queen. They only wanted to parade him before the court. They wanted to display their non-existent gratitude. Only so they could kill him later. At least his curses were voiced after the Chamberlain had left his house. The old man was terrified by Codrin's stare when he gave him the invitation. There was a frightening coldness in that stare. Perhaps it could even kill. He left the house as fast as he could without losing his dignity. Then came the tailor. The Chamberlain had pleaded with the Queen to give some protection to the poor man, perhaps ten soldiers. Or even more. For the first time since Codrin had returned she smiled, and Vlad was sent with the tailor. And it was Vlad who convinced Codrin to accept the clothes and to go to the ball. It was a political game, and he had to play.

Codrin went to the ball as late as he could, yet something was wrong, many people were still outside. *They may have different rules*, he thought, and tried to move away.

"Codrin, please wait," Saliné said, and he had no choice but to stay, meeting both her and Jara. "I am glad that you have come. It will be a great affair, and I hope that you enjoy it."

"I am enjoying it as much as you enjoyed Aron's and Bucur's hospitality in Severin. In fact, I am enjoying it even less."

"Why?" Saliné asked involuntarily, her voice suddenly cold.

"You had at least the pleasure of knowing a secret tunnel from where you could kill Aron's guards, and put an arrow in Bucur's buttocks. I don't have that. Now please excuse me, your majesty, I will be back when the great affair starts. Don't worry; I won't bring my bow."

"If you don't let Codrin go, he will become more and more nervous, and a disaster will happen," Jara said, watching him walk away.

"I can't, Mother," Saliné said despondently. "I have a strong influence on Alfrid and at the court, but there is no way to convince him on this, especially as he is right; Codrin will go to Frankis to stir a revolt. We can't afford this, too many people would die."

"He will kill Codrin, and all this is my fault." Jara's voice wobbled. "I will not be able to live with the shame that he was killed because of my weakness."

"It was my decision, Mother. One that I regret, but I can't change."

"But it was me who..."

"Walk with me, Mother. I don't want them seeing you crying." *I saw her crying only once, when Vio returned. Now she cries every night, and even during the day.*

"Help me," Jara whispered, unable to move.

Saliné took her by the arm, and they walked until they were hidden by the hedge labyrinth. "There is a bench around the next corner." It took Jara half an hour to fully recover.

Codrin returned just when the ball was about to start, the Queen and the King ready to open the first suite of dances. His eyes met Saliné's and, without knowing, he grimaced savagely and turned back toward the door, left the hall, and hid behind one of the large outdoor columns; there was no one else outside. Her smile vanished, and she stumbled for a moment.

"Emotions?" Alfrid asked, unaware of her encounter with Codrin.

"Just a headache. I will survive." *I hope Codrin will survive too. There is too much pain in him, and all because of me. Mother is in a bad state, crying every night. I have lost any appetite for dancing. And I am lost too. I don't know what to do.*

Hidden behind the column, Codrin heard voices, and for a while he thought that another Vision or memory was coming back to him; the man's voice seemed vaguely familiar, and he braced for the pain that came with the recovery of his memories.

"You don't need to meet him," the man said, "so there is no danger. You go outside and do what I told you. Dishevel your dress and come into the hall crying that he tried to rape you."

Count Joachim, Codrin thought, still listening. *I saved his life during the first charge against the nomads. I saved Alfrid's life too. It brought only misery to me.* When the two had finished talking, Codrin waited a little longer, then entered the hall too. He forced himself to dance twice, and there was no issue in finding partners, many women were trying to capture his attention. *I need to give Alfrid the impression that I feel secure and a ... guest.* At the end of the first suite of dances, he stood around for a while, then left the hall, followed by Saliné's worried eyes.

"Good luck, Ana," Count Joachim said, "and don't forget that your brother's fate depends on this. Come back in fifteen minutes." Silent, Joachim watched the young woman leaving the hall, half vanishing in the garden under the torches' light. He did not look happy. Nervous and caught in his inner worries, he did not see Codrin entering the hall, walking hesitantly.

"You are drunk," Codrin said, with a hiccup, and pushed Count Joachim with the joviality of a drunken man. Taken aback, Joachim looked at Ana walking away into the night, and tried to sneak out after her. Codrin pushed him again, harder this time, and Joachim almost fell. "You are drunk," Codrin repeated and pushed him again, before the stunned man could react. Joachim stepped back, lost his equilibrium, and touched the floor briefly with his left hand. He had no idea what was happening or what to say, so he concentrated on keeping himself away from Codrin's long arms.

Amused, people came toward them, until they surrounded the entertaining pair, staying at a safe distance, and they were now close to the middle of the large hall.

"You are blocking my way," Codrin complained, gesturing like a drunk. "And you are drunk."

"You are drunk, not me," Joachim snapped, and tried to step around Codrin and leave the hall.

From her lodge, Saliné saw them and shook her head in despair, unable to understand how Codrin could get so drunk; he never indulged much in wine. *He is in pain*, she sighed. *And I can't help him.* She stood up abruptly, and left the royal lodge, going downstairs, forcing herself not to run.

From his place in another lodge, Alfrid followed her, carrying a thin smile. *It's good that he is drunk*, the King thought. *It will help Ana play him better. Step by step, I will drive him insane until...*

Below, on the floor of the hall, the people were enjoying the show, Joachim still trying to leave, and Codrin still able to catch and push him back for all clumsy drunken moves. Some even made bets if the Count would be able to leave. At times, Codrin's funny speech made them laugh. It was a warm reaction; Codrin was loved in Muniker for saving the city, and his sudden resurrection had been greeted with joy.

"The Queen," someone whispered, and people split, letting Saliné get closer.

"Codrin," she said gently, trying to grab his arm, but he slipped away with a shift that was suddenly swift.

"Oh, my queen," Codrin said, grinning. "There is no need for royal intervention. This stubborn man is so drunk that he got in my way. Don't worry; I am sober and able to manage the situation without help."

Joachim thought he could finally escape and tried to slip away between two people. Codrin grabbed him again and pushed him so hard that the smaller man almost bumped into the people on the other side of the circle around them. He struggled to stay on his feet, his arms akimbo, moving in jerks and staggers, which stirred another round of laughter.

"Your majesty," Joachim said, resigned, "it seems that indeed I am too drunk to walk."

"Ha," Codrin exclaimed with the gaiety of a child who had just found a large cake, "finally you admit it."

"Codrin," Saliné said, sadly, "now that Joachim is out of your way, you can go home. He will not bother you there." *Please Codrin, I don't want them to laugh at you.* Overwhelmed by her own worries about him, she did not notice that the crowd was on Codrin's side, even when Joachim was the Spatar of Litvonia.

"Are you sure?" Codrin asked, frowning hard and pouting like a girl. "He is still here."

"Yes, he is still here, but you will go into the other direction." She pointed toward the large door leading into the garden, and the people around them parted to give him space to walk.

"That direction," Codrin said, hesitantly; the door was now almost fully visible.

"Yes, Codrin, that direction. Please."

Codrin took his time, looking again at the door, took one step toward it, and then turned. "Just be sure that he doesn't come my way again." He eyed Joachim again, took another step, and stopped again, hesitantly. Nobody tried to help him, nobody spoke and, except for Saliné, people were enjoying the show. In Muniker, this light level of drunkenness was accepted.

"Help me!" Ana burst into the hall, her dress and hair disheveled. "Please help me, he tried to rape me," she cried.

Joachim ran, trying to reach her in time.

"Guards!" Alfrid shouted.

"Stop!" Codrin cried, extending his arms aside. His right palm hit Joachim's chest, and the unfortunate man suddenly writhed on the ground. "I will deal with this. Come closer, fair lady," he said, and Ana pushed herself into him, trembling while he gently embraced her with one arm.

"Please sir," she breathed, "that man tried to rape me."

"Who tried to rape you?" Codrin leaned his head aside, and his eyes locked with Ana's. "Let her speak." He sprang his right arm, and Joachim fell on the floor again.

He is strong as a bull. Joachim massaged his chest, thinking that maybe he should give up. *And what rape? She was not supposed to say that.*

Saliné took the arm of the fallen man and stopped him trying to reach Ana again. She wanted to go toward the distressed girl, but she worried that a shove from Codrin would cause her more damage than Joachim, who was a sturdy and agile man, and hitting the Queen would push both Alfrid and the guards to react.

"That man who was the King of Frankis," Ana cried, her voice loud enough to be heard throughout the hall. "He stopped me in the garden and said that he wants me, and that he will take me with him and make me rich."

Several people gasped and, behind Saliné, Joachim slapped his forefront and walked away. He bumped into the King, who frowned nervously at him.

"Sorry, your majesty, it went wrong," Joachim whispered and went toward the other door of the hall as fast as he could without attracting attention. *And Fate take the King; Codrin saved my life once, and now I had to play this miserable trick on him. It's the last time I agree to do such a thing.* Joachim shook his head, and his mouth set in a grim line.

"That is so un-kingly," Codrin said. "Don't worry my lady, I will punish him. Lashes, I will give him twenty lashes. Will that satisfy you?"

"Yes, sir, thank you. That will be a good punishment. I am recently married, and it was such a rude affront. Look at my dress."

There was a heavy silence in the hall now, eyes glued to the drama before them.

"I will do it," Codrin said, "but..."

"But?" Ana asked, frowning at him. "You promised."

"Yes, I promised, the thing is I don't know how to lash myself," he said, and a swift grin flashed on his lips.

"What do you mean?"

"I am that former King of Frankis, and while I am in quite a good shape and can walk really fast, I could not get to the garden and back in such a short time. My friend Joachim here can be witness, if he is not too drunk to speak."

"What?" *Stupid Joachim. He told me that the man is in the garden. I destroyed my dress for nothing, but I did what he wanted. He must free my brother.* "Then who was that man?"

"That's quite an interesting question, my lady. Who was that man, and why did he impersonate me while attacking you? Your majesty," he turned toward Saliné, who forced herself to stay calm, "the girl is afraid and shaking. You will offer her better comfort than me." Codrin's eyes were now as icy and sharp as his voice. Mechanically, Saliné took the poor girl by her arm; he was already walking toward the door, apparently unable to keep to a straight line, but not looking very drunk either.

"I did not know that you liked Litvonian wine so much," Cernat joked.

"Their wine is poor, and yesterday I drank only water." Codrin's voice was cold, and he did not even look at Cernat, or at Saliné who was in his room too. His eyes were set on a small spot on the wall.

"So, they have bad wine and strong water. What really happened yesterday?"

"Just luck. The gracious King planned to put me in jail for attempted rape. Joachim sent the girl after me, in the garden. I happened to be hiding behind a column listening as they planned everything. I returned to the hall soon after she left it and stopped Joachim from warning her."

"You fooled everybody." With all her worries and lack of information to fully understand what happened, Saliné could not stop her laughter.

Codrin looked at her: that stance he knew so well from his previous life, her body leaning forward a little, her large green eyes smiling at him, and when the laugh subsided, a warm smile teased her lips. That smile always made him want to kiss her, and he leaned forward too, his arm stretching to go around her shoulders. He regained control in a moment, his face altered by the deep bitterness mounting inside him, and he stood up abruptly, walked toward the window and leaned against the sill. Everyone in the room realized what had happened, and no one knew how to react, not wanting to hurt him even more.

"I may have fooled you, but that doesn't change that the Pig on the throne played that game on me. He tried to ruin my reputation, put me in jail and kill me." His voice was emotionless and distant, the shadow on his face was still bitter, unable to recover from that desired and hated proximity with Saliné.

"It was a shameful trick indeed, but we don't know who played it," Saliné said, equally cold. "And don't speak about my husband in that tone and those words, at least not in front of me. I understand your bitterness, but we must keep some civility."

"As you wish, your majesty. What the great King of Litvonia did was indeed civil. Perhaps Muniker has different standards for civility, and games like this are a common thing. Is there anything else you want from me?"

"No, but I am glad that you escaped unharmed." She stood up and left the room without a word.

"Was that necessary?" Cernat asked.

"That helped me overcome a moment of weakness I can't afford right now, and from how it looks, I won't get much help from you. There is a happy family on one side, and me the unwanted thorn, alone, on the other side."

"Fate was not kind to you in the last three years, and I understand that, but we are still your only friends here."

"Fate has nothing to do with this," Codrin snapped. "It's you, Jara and Saliné who were not kind to me, or to my son. You see a great achievement and a great queen where I see betrayal. You see the great man on the throne. I see a Pig."

"Yes, Alfrid was ruthless; he tried to kill you and take your wife. Does my acknowledging that change your situation? No. He is the King. He is too strong..."

"You made him strong. My dear wife loves him because he is such a strong and kind man, and I am his prisoner because you did nothing to help me, even after we agreed that I can leave. Your great Queen has no word. Even after what happened last night…" Codrin shrugged.

"Is this what you want? To create a rift between Saliné and her husband?"

"I was naive enough to believe that once I showed the real man behind the mask..."

"There are two men in Alfrid. A loving man, who cares for his family, and one that is ruthless with his enemies. You are the same. I am the same. You are his enemy. Saliné is his queen, and the mother of his son."

"And by association, I am your enemy too, and you try hard to avoid that without the dose of good luck I had yesterday, I would now be in jail for attempting to rape a woman. Perhaps you are even upset that it did not happen. Jail and a ruined reputation would have smoothed the path to my execution and eliminated an enemy of your happy family. At least we have an understanding right now. I am alone."

"You are not alone, but you are fighting hard to become so. I am sorry that we could not help you yesterday. Maybe we can do more in the future. For the moment, we will spread the news that someone tried to frame you. It will bring you more sympathy. The people in Muniker are fond of you; you saved the kingdom from the nomads. That should keep you safe for a while. And there is a strange thing," Cernat added. "Rumors are spreading that you are still the Seer of the Realm and have returned from death to save the kingdom once more. I don't know where they come from, but they play to your advantage."

"Safe from direct assassination, but not safe from ... accidents."

"Yes, you must be careful to avoid ... accidents. I am confident that you will be able to do it," Cernat said and left him.

Codrin went out of the small house, trying to calm his nerves. From the door, he saw Saliné walking with her grandfather, and he returned inside, slamming the door behind him. To his surprise, she came back half an hour later and, in silence, she sat at the table while he went again to lean against the wall, far from any temptation, looking away. Unable to find the right words, she was wringing her hands on the table, and he did not try to speak.

"I have to remind myself that you are in a much worse position than I am. Father told me that you think we are your enemies because... The truth is that you are our enemy. It's not because you want to be, but because you are an opponent of what we are now. I am the Queen of Frankis and Litvonia. You are the former King of Frankis who wants his kingdom back."

"And my wife back."

"And your former wife back."

"Unfortunately, she doesn't share my desire."

"I still love you, Codrin. I love my husband too, though we will never have the same spark that was between you and me, and we have lived very different lives in the last three years. Good or bad, I took a decision that can't be changed. I have a new family, a child who will be the next King of Frankis and Litvonia. I also have our child, who will become the Duke of Sittgart. There is a certain configuration of power around us. It doesn't work in your favor, and I am not sure that I want it to work in your favor. That future would be bloody. I prefer a peaceful solution in which you become the Duke of Sittgart and pass the title to our son. I prefer that both my children still have a father." *Should I tell him that I am pregnant?* She chose not to. “I prefer you to become part of what I represent now, the Queen of this unified kingdom. It’s the safest path for all of us. I know that it will be hard for you because you still dream that the past will return but, in time, you will find your way, find a wife, and make a new family. You can be happy again, and safe, together with our son. My husband knows from the Wanderers that the nomads will attack us again in five years. He is not a great army commander, and while his brother may be, Edric is young and still untested. Alfrid is not fully convinced, but he is willing to consider you as an ally, and, in time, you can be even more than an army commander. I know no better Chancellor than you.”

“Would you change this situation if you could do so peacefully?”

There is no peaceful solution on that path, Codrin, only war and death. “I wish now that I did not take the decision to marry Alfrid, but I took it. I took the sacred marriage wows, knowing that you were dead, and if I made them, I have to respect my decision, and I have to protect my children.”

“Despite knowing what he did to me.”

“Alfrid had people killed for his own interests; you did the same, and so did I. In any position of power, one uses violence at a certain point. He did not use it against me or against my family. I know that it sounds awful to you, but, if you remember,” she smiled tentatively, “once long ago, you took me just before I was to wed another man, Eduin, a man who loved me too, and even saved my life. And you would have killed Eduin if he had not agreed to free me. Now, you know what I wish from you. Please think of the consequences a new war would bring. Think how many would die.” For a few moments, she stared at his ashen, unconvinced face, and a tear ran down her face. “I am sorry, Codrin,” Saliné whispered and left him alone.

For a while, she walked alone in the park; then she went to meet Alfrid. “I am still thinking about what happened yesterday at the ball,” she said.

"That young girl who tried to frame Codrin," Alfrid said, evasively.

"That young girl and Joachim."

"It was me, not Joachim, but the girl overreacted. She was supposed to cry against a forced kiss and slap Codrin. It seems that she wanted to please us and free her brother."

"Why?" Saliné asked abruptly, her voice cold; her eyes locked with Alfrid's.

"We have issues because of his arrival. There is only one topic of talk in Muniker: The Seer has returned from death to save Litvonia, and the next nomad invasion will happen next year. Everybody hails the Seer right now. You have seen the same reports as me. Everything started when Codrin entered in Muniker. He told our people two lies. Why? He is no longer the Seer of the Ream, and the Wanderers know that the next invasion is in five years. There is a hidden plan behind his lies, and he is a dangerous man. What does he want? He did not expect to find you here, so everything was planned against me. He came to take Muniker from me. But now Muniker belongs to us, not only to me. This derailed his plans. We need to change people's perceptions about him. Don't you think that he will stir problems in Muniker?"

"I don't know. He wants to leave."

"And to return with an army. Who will fight for us, if everybody thinks him the Seer, and the only one who can save Litvonia from the nomads? Saliné, we must be more cautious. We could lose everything because of Codrin, all our dreams for peaceful unification. I agreed to let you convince him to accept the Duchy of Sittgart and take a new wife. Let me put a stop this reverence that people have for him now. It's dangerous."

"I wish I had known what you were doing."

"It was difficult to talk to you about my plan, but I agree that it was a mistake. Saliné," he said gently, and passed an arm around her shoulders, "some measures are necessary. I will be more cautious next time, and I will talk to you before I plan something else, but we must act."

~

Dochia rode hard, arriving in the Alba Hive of the Alpas Mountains in just two days. She passed the shore of Lake Costanze, and that stirred some memories related to the nomads and their Maletera. *They are buried at the edge of that forest,* she recalled, and looked at her guards. Irina remembered too, but her other guard was new; Mira had left the Wanderers and married Kozlaw, the captain from Nerval. They entered the Hive at noon, and a few minutes later, Dochia was face to face with Elagia, the First Light of Litvonia.

"A few months ago, I met a young Wanderer who had a strange Vision," Dochia said carefully. She was alone with Elagia. "The King of Litvonia and one of your Wanderers were in her Vision. They talked about Codrin. In fact, they talked about killing Codrin."

"Killing him after he defeated the nomads."

"You knew," Dochia breathed.

"Yes, I knew, and it was a hard decision. There was a chance to unify both kingdoms peacefully, no blood spilled. I took it in good faith."

"Codrin was the Seer of the Realm."

"I had a Vision that he would lose his position before the fight against the nomads. I am sorry for what we did to him, but unifying the kingdoms was more important. The Wanderers have long-term plans. I know that he was your friend," Elagia said gently and gripped Dochia's hand. "That's why things were kept hidden from you."

"Yes, he was my friend, and he saved the Realm."

"The Hive in Frankis was informed, and they approved our plans. I understand if you want to gather a Conclave of all the Hives and judge me. Tomorrow, I will give you a document explaining everything that happened, so you will have proof. I agree to step down as the First Light of the Litvonian Wanderers. I have lived long enough."

"I don't want to judge you. Your death would change nothing, in fact it will make things worse; Calista is too ... strange. What I am telling you now, should stay between us. Codrin is alive."

"Oh, Dochia," Elagia said, and grabbed her hand. "You don't know what joy you have brought me. Even when our plan worked so well, Codrin did not deserve what we did to him."

"I can't say that I don't understand your reasons, but I still think that we should abide by our code of honor. And the main issue is that Alfrid is not a man we can trust."

"That's why we gave Saliné to him, to control him. Oh, no," Elagia covered her face with her palms. "Codrin is alive and..." She stood up abruptly and walked around the room. "What have I done? Why did I not see it in my Visions?"

"Elagia," Dochia said gently.

"Does he know?"

"Yes, he is now a prisoner in Muniker. Not in jail, but..."

"I am too frail to leave the Hive, but I can give you a letter for Alfrid. I don't know how effective that will be."

It will solve nothing. "It's better than nothing. Elagia, would you try to have a Vision of Codrin? Something strange happened when I tried. It did not work, even when I did the blood link. All I could see was darkness. It has never happened to me."

"Dochia, you are the strongest Wanderer, even stronger than Ada. You preempted the Fracture almost alone. What can I do that you cannot? Fine, I will try it."

Elagia tried with all her power and long experience. And failed. Tried again. Failed again. "I think Codrin's future is blocked from us. It happens rarely, and only the Empress or Fate herself can do it. I am not sure about the Empress, though," Elagia said, thoughtfully.

"What would that mean?"

"I don't know. Maybe they are preparing him for something new, and they want to keep everything hidden because of my betrayal. Or..." Elagia sighed and turned her palms up. "They don't think he is useful anymore and want him out of the game."

"I am not expecting the Empress to think that way."

"She has had her share of tough decisions, and her allegiance is to the Realm, not one person, however valuable that person might be, but ... I don't think that she can block our Visions."

Elagia considered. “Last time we met, the Empress did not know that Codrin was alive. The more I think on it, the more it seems that only Fate could block our Visions. There must be a plan.”

Dochia closed her eyes. *Perhaps Vio was right, and we are no longer able to make the right decision. What did she see when we returned to Muniker? Codrin...? I wish she were here now*. Another thought passed through her mind, and she opened her eyes abruptly, meeting the older Wanderer’s worry.

“I am sorry, Dochia. I did what I thought best for the Realm. We may have an even bigger issue right now, if Codrin escapes and raises Frankis against Litvonia. We need to find a solution. One which doesn’t kill him again. One that will not bring a disastrous war between the kingdoms and weaken us for the nomads. It may not be easy...” The old First Light stood abruptly and paced around the room, rubbing her chin.

“Perhaps. Do you remember the disturbance we had in the Light?” Dochia asked and the First Light nodded. “It arrived three years ago, and it vanished a month ago.”

Elagia frowned. “Are you trying to link it to Codrin?”

“I am not sure, but both Codrin and the disturbance vanished and appeared in a strange synchronicity. We need to investigate that too.”

Chapter 21 - Calista / Codrin

Calista was in a hurry to reach Muniker, but she had to wait for dusk to come, her plan was to sneak inside unseen. The Broken Bridge Inn was almost empty, and she stayed alone at her table. She had to think. Since she had learned that Codrin had reappeared, her nights became long and without sleep. Something had gone utterly wrong, and the Realm was in danger. Or at least her plans for the Realm were in danger. She nodded absently to the innkeeper, who hurried toward her. "I don't like this wine; it tastes too strong. Give me something lighter. Give this one to my guards. They are younger." *Alfrid is becoming a nuisance. First the attempt to run away from the battle. Now this botched attempt to kill Codrin. And I don't understand Saliné. How could she fall in love with such a weak man? I was expecting her to fall for Edric. He is so like Codrin.* She drummed the table with her fingers, recalling everything she could about Saliné, Alfrid and Edric, and a Wanderer's memory is powerful. *I am wrong. Edric was her lover without being lointain, but she chose to send him to Kolugn with Maltia. It was masked as a political decision, which it was, but it was more than that. Saliné loves Edric but wanted to give Alfrid a chance. She is a fair woman. Sometimes, a small step like this can sink a kingdom. And now Codrin... Is his escape just luck and poor organization, or there is something else?*

The innkeeper came with a new bottle and filled her glass, then waited dutifully. "Much better," Calista said, tasting the wine. She nodded at the man, who vanished from her sight. There was a surge of Light, and she ducked her head, her eyes gleaming from under her thick brows. She felt a stare like a hand on her back. She turned her head to see two women and two children coming to eat. "Pireska, come and join my table. Come, all of you." Calista underlined her words by flexing her forefinger, then pointed to the chairs.

"Calista," Pireska bowed slightly, "I don't know what rank you have..."

"I am the Second Light," Calista said curtly. "Take a seat. Do you still have the house at the edge of the forest? I was there three times with your aunt." Pireska nodded. "You must be Ildeko." She assessed the young woman. "You were just fifteen and wounded when I saw you. And these must be your children. And your son?" She looked again at Pireska, who shook her head. "I am sorry. Where are you going?" *And why this surge of Light when I saw you?*

"My son died last winter, and our place is dangerous for single women. A friend of my husband called for us. He has a son and a granddaughter. Her mother died at the birth of the second child. We think that his son and..." She pointed at Ildeko.

"That was good thinking. Why are you staying at this inn?"

"We couldn't afford it, but on the road, there was a wounded Knight and his family. I took care of his wounds."

"Ah, yes, you are a good healer." There was another surge of Light, and Calista stopped. *It's rare to have two of them so fast. What is the importance of these women?* Hungry, Codrin's son started to cry, and his mother put him to her breast. Unwillingly, Calista touched his hand, and a Vision came to her, the boy some seven years old. *Training with a sword?* "Is the Knight ... married?"

"Knight Theodrick. As far as I know, he is not married," Pireska said.

That may explain the sword in the child's hand. Ildeko is still young and beautiful. She may switch from a poor man's wife to a Knight's mistress. Perhaps she is already his mistress, and this is his son. I must learn more about the boy; there is strength in him, and there must be a reason for those surges of Light around him. I will ask Edric to bring them to Muniker for a while. And the Knight too.

It was dark when Calista reached Muniker; she entered the city through the southern gate and went directly to the royal stable to leave her carriage. Both her escort and the Muniker guards were surprised, as usually she went directly to the main door of the castle and let them take her carriage from there. From the stable, she went to the left wing of the castle. She did not use the main entrance; instead, she knocked at a window from which some light chased the night.

"Vorlos," she whispered when the window opened, "I need to enter without being seen."

"Yes, my lady," the man said, and fifteen minutes later, she was in Alfrid's suite, entering through a secret door.

"Calista," he said, surprised, and stood up to embrace her. "What was the need for such secrecy?"

"Your wife must not know that I am here. Not yet. I've learned that Codrin has returned."

"Yes, we have a ... small complication right now."

"Small?" Calista snapped. "This is a complication as large as a kingdom. Codrin was supposed to be dead. All my plans for the Realm are falling because you failed to kill one man. I did not ask you to defeat the nomads. I did not ask you to conquer Frankis. All I asked you to do was to kill one man. One man." She raised the forefinger of her right hand, as if to poke him in the eye. She calmed herself as fast as she had become angry.

"It was Edric who..." Alfrid used the break in her speech to protest.

"I. Asked. You." With each word, Calista tapped with her bent finger on his chest. "Not Edric. You should have been there with two hundred men, blocked all the paths and had Codrin killed. You guaranteed that..." *He is unnerving me more than he deserves. And Edric has disappointed me too, but they were not his men there. They were chosen by Alfrid, including that captain...*

Roderick? I will have his skin. "I hope that you have kept Codrin here. We need time to plan."

"He is our *guest* for a while. I have him in the house in the park."

"Did you have any reason to choose that house?"

"I don't really enjoy seeing him around. The place is isolated, well suited for action when the right time arrives."

"That right moment is important. And the men you choose. The last ones were a bunch of incompetents." *As were you.* "How did Codrin survive?"

"I don't know. He said nothing," Alfrid shrugged. "Luck, perhaps."

He is becoming useless. The crown and the lovely breasts of his wife have settled into his head, replacing his mind. Unable to reign in her thoughts, Calista drummed her fingers on the table, then pointed at a bottle of wine, and waited patiently until he filled and brought a glass to her. *I must ask Saliné. That will be a hard task. And a test.* "How do the Munikers see Codrin?"

"The Seer has come back from the dead," Alfrid growled and hit the table with his fist. "That's what he said at the gate, and everybody hailed him like a hero. I am the King of Litvonia." Alfrid's voice became higher in pitch.

"That thing with the resurrection is nonsense; he was alive and well, but he *is* the hero. He saved Muniker from the nomads. What would you expect from them, to hail you? There is no one out there," Calista pointed toward the window and the city, "who considers you a hero. And everyone knows that you tried to run from the battle. Codrin is no longer the Seer; he is now the Pillar of the Realm." She sipped some wine. "I doubt that will matter much to the people on the streets. We will see what we can do to influence their opinion. What else?"

"He claims that next year, the nomads will invade us again. It's a lie, he just wants to..."

"Codrin would not lie about such things, but this is something that I need to look at." *The disturbance in the Light vanished almost a month ago. We will be better able to investigate the future again. Supposing that his Vision is right, how did he...?* She turned her glass of wine, seeing the room become red. *Saliné... She told me something important once about the issue with the Light. I must remember. I am getting old.* She drummed the table with her fingers again, and when Alfrid tried to talk, she snapped at him, "Keep your mouth shut. I need to think." *Saliné thought there was a link between Codrin's disappearance and the trouble with the Light. He vanished, and the Light got weaker. He reappeared, and the Light... No.* She shook her head. *It must be just a coincidence. Yet I will raise the issue with Elagia. Or perhaps with Dochia. But now that Codrin has returned, I can't fully trust Dochia.* "You said something about a plan." Calista realized that she was drumming the table again, and sipped some wine, to keep her hands busy.

"Yes, but I must be careful; my subjects seem to like Codrin; they still see him as the Seer who saved Muniker, and my wife still loves him. I must be careful," Alfrid repeated like a mantra, then moistened his lips.

"Do you think Saliné will betray you?"

"No, we are a happy family, and she knows her interest too; it's just that he arrived and took everybody by surprise. I knew well, even before, that she still has feelings for him, but she loves me too. We have a son, and she is pregnant again; she told me three days ago. There is a bit of chaos in her mind right now, it's normal, but nothing that I can't manage."

She told you about her pregnancy to calm you. "We need to use that chaos. The longer Codrin stays, the more issues for us, but he can't be allowed to leave, dead or alive, until we have a plan."

"The first thing he will do is to stir Frankis, and things are still fluid there."

"Every child knows that. Have you a plan?"

"I had one, but it failed from bad luck."

"Plans fail from bad execution, not from bad luck." *Like the one to kill Codrin.*

"Perhaps it could have been done better, but no one thought that Codrin would be drunk at the ball. In fact, no one thought he liked to drink so much."

"Maybe we should encourage him to drink more."

"He has not been drunk since, but I will consider your advice."

"Any other plans?" Calista used that voice women use for small children, then looked into his eyes, her lips drawn like a recurved bow. The mockery was too subtle for Alfrid.

"Yes." He relaxed a little. "A different one, a more dangerous one. The best way to get rid of Codrin is to make him attack me. Or to attack Saliné. I consider that less probable, but... Perhaps we should use Cosmin to upset him."

"Cosmin..." Calista said thoughtfully, as if unable to make up her mind. "We must be careful; many of Codrin's men are here. I will sleep in the left wing, in my secret room. No one in the palace, apart from Vorlos and Edric, should know that I am in Muniker."

"So, you think my plan could work."

"Perhaps. We need some sort of incident to provoke a harsh and unexpected reaction from Codrin. That will set Saliné and her family completely on your side, and he will find himself without allies."

"That won't be easy."

"If you look only for easy things, then I might not be your best adviser."

"Calista, you always were my best adviser; without you I wouldn't be King of both Frankis and Litvonia. And I can say that I really enjoy the wife you brought me," he laughed, his voice a little edgy.

"She is beautiful and intelligent but try not to lose your head between her breasts."

"There is another thing. Saliné wants to make Codrin Duke of Sittgart."

"Excellent idea. That will show your goodwill, and no one will blame you if accidents happen."

"Are you sure? If he goes there..."

"I am sure that you can find good reasons to keep him here until spring. Give him a wife too."

"Saliné said the same, but another wife and another son will only endanger my son. I can't risk that."

"Don't be silly, Alfrid. Saliné is right. Let her find him a beautiful and intelligent girl and plan the wedding for next year. She may be a widow before the wedding. I am tired now. Tomorrow, tell me how the plans for Codrin's Dukedom and marriage are advancing." *Marriage... If Codrin accepts to be the Pillar of the Realm... It may be a solution, but we must keep him in a tight leash until he adapts.*

ꕥ

"Come with me, Saliné, I have a surprise for you." Alfrid grinned, raising his eyebrows. "But I request a kiss in advance." He pulled her closer and pressed his lips to hers.

"I hope that your surprise merits my attention and the ruin of my hair," Saliné said when they left the room.

"I am sure it will." He laughed, walking her toward a side door leading into the park. "Look." He opened the door and pushed her out. "Cosmin looks wonderful on the horse. I suppose he inherited the skills from his father." In front of them, a guard led a pony by the halter; Cosmin was enjoying himself riding it. "I would say my surprise deserved some messing of your hair, which looks perfect disturbed or not." Alfrid embraced her from behind, amused by her mute reaction. "We created a secret order, the Brotherhood of the Horse, to keep everything hidden, and your son trained for half an hour for two days to impress you."

"Look, Mother," Cosmin cried with delight. "I am riding. Alfrid said that I will be as good a rider as Father. And I am part of the Brotherhood of the Horse. I am almost a Knight. In two days, I *will* be a Knight."

"What is it?" Alfrid asked, sensing some tension in Saliné's body.

I was expecting that Alfrid would talk with me before giving the horse to Cosmin and let me speak with Codrin first. Two days and I knew nothing. "I just think that he may be too young to ride," she said, cautiously.

"Nonsense, his training is overdue, and it's my fault. I should have started his instruction earlier. I learned to ride when I was a year younger than him. And the mare is very tame, a bit old and slow, so she will not create problems. Cosmin doesn't need to gallop from the beginning, just to learn some basic things. Come on, Saliné," he said, gripping her fingers. "Don't spoil his surprise, he was so delighted. Just look at him. I arranged everything myself. I signed a decree to name Cosmin a Knight in the Brotherhood of the Horse, because he can't be a real knight until he reaches fifteen; you know the rules. He will be *knighted* in two days, in your presence. Codrin will be invited too. I even gave Cosmin two pages. He can't wait to pass the ceremony."

"I am thinking," Saliné said, cautiously, "that maybe it would be a good thing to allow Codrin to train his son."

"Of course. That was what I was thinking too. It will give Codrin something to do and bring him closer to us. This will be a first step, then the marriage... We need him against those bloody nomads. In time, he may agree to fight for us. We have no better commander than him."

"Thank you, Alfrid," she said. "Cosmin is indeed delighted by his new friend, and I like your idea about Codrin leading our army."

"It was your idea, and it took me a while to get accustomed to it. You must understand that it was not easy for me. I think I deserve another kiss," he said and turned her slowly. "Ah, we have guests."

Saliné turned and found Calista watching her. The Wanderer came, took her by the arm and walked her away. "My dear Saliné, this morning you look ... pregnant. How is your daughter?" She pointed with her chin toward Saliné's belly. *Does she know that the girl is Edric's daughter? I wonder why Saliné allowed him that night? It was his first night here after ending the lointain lover contract with Maltia, and it did not happen again. Premonition? Does she know that her daughter will inherit the Empire and make it stronger?*

A daughter... "I can't hide anything from you. Do you know her name too?"

"We both know it," Calista laughed. "It's an unusual name."

"Arenian."

"Ah, I understand your choice, and that brings me to an important subject that may be not as pleasant as speaking about your daughter."

"Codrin is alive."

"Yes, that's the pleasant part. The unpleasant part is what may happen next. Alfrid told me about a marriage plan."

"He is ... cautious in this regard."

"Alfrid is stupid. Marriage is the best outcome. It will tie Codrin's hands and give him a rank at the same time. Not completely, though. Go ahead with it. Do you have someone in mind already?"

"The daughter of Duke Drasdin. And, perhaps, Elsebeth, the Countess of Baia."

Elsebeth fooled everybody in Muniker, but I know her past. It's ugly. She is an ambitious young woman, and one of the most intelligent persons I know. Perhaps too ambitious, but her past offers a great level of control for those who know it. "Drasdin's daughter... She is intelligent and beautiful. A bit young tough. Codrin is a mature man; an experienced woman would suit him better, but you know him better. Elsebeth is cultivated; she speaks four languages, including Arenian, has read a full library, and visited Arenia in the past. She is a mature woman too, who can offer more to a man like Codrin. And a marriage in the royal family will serve us well. It's just an opinion. What is this thing with the riding?"

"Alfrid surprised Cosmin and me with a horse."

"He did not tell you? Don't think wrong of me, but isn't Cosmin a little too weak to ride? Alfrid was too eager to please you and did not think much about the child. You should knock his head from time to time. Who will train Cosmin?"

"Codrin."

"That's good. It will give him something to do, instead of having bad thoughts about us, and he is a good trainer. Now," she sighed, "I have a tough conversation ahead."

"Codrin?" Saliné asked, hesitantly.

"Of course, my dear. I wish to bring him the Wanderers' greetings. And to learn... I think you understand what I need to learn from him."

Calista found Codrin shaving himself; he had refused the palace barber. He stopped abruptly when the Wanderer entered his living room, holding the razor blade a half inch from his skin. Their eyes locked for a few long moments, and a flurry of feelings passed between them. There was a surge of Light too, and both tried to learn from it.

"Calista," he said and pointed to a chair. *I would prefer to have gallows there, not a chair.*

We've never met before, but he knew me, and that knowledge came from a Vision. Fate knows what was in it. Or in them. And that predator look... He may know that I am linked to the assassination attempt. He will deny it, of course. This makes everything more difficult. Instead of sitting, she walked toward him. "May I?" She pointed at his razor when they were face to face. "I will get it done it faster."

"I wonder what you want to get done," Codrin said and gave her the sharp blade. He felt a cringe of fear but did not move until she had finished. "Where did you learn to shave? I don't imagine there is much need for such skills in a Hive."

He feared I might cut his throat for a moment, Calista chuckled inside. *Even the strongest men have their moments of fear. It's normal*. Cleaning the blade, she waited patiently until he washed his face, then gave him a towel. Their fingers touched for a moment, and there was a spark of Light, as both tried to use it on the other one. "I am a healer, and I have shaved many wounded men. So are you. Would you let me use a blood bond to see your future?" She stretched her hand toward him, and Codrin hesitated for a moment, then placed his hand in hers. Swiftly, Calista made a small cut on his thumb with the razor, then started to rub the blood gently on his skin, humming a song that was slightly different to the one he had heard from Dochia. Her hands glowed white. She stopped after a while and breathed slow and long, then started again. After one more minute, she let his hand fall from hers, and stared into his eyes. "I can't see anything of your future. You knew that." *There are strange lines forming at this moment. Who knows where they will take us? Should I consider Codrin as a replacement for Alfrid? I thought about this more than once. It went nowhere. Cosmin is frail and not healthy. He will die in his early thirties, without inheritors, and we will have a bloody succession. That will ruin everything. Great men and women bring lesser children to life. It's almost a rule.*

"When it happens once, it may be a fluke. Twice..."

"Who was the other Wanderer who tried the blood bond?"

"Dochia."

"She is no fluke; she is the most powerful Wanderer right now."

"I never said she was a fluke." *Yet I can't say that she is still a friend.* "It was worth checking."

"I can't see your future. Would you agree to talk about it?" *Will you accept my plan for the Realm? Arnis is weak too, like his father. Saliné's daughter will carry the burden further. Will you accept her? Your son, Cosmin, would be the kind of King who stays in the library and makes laws, a lawmaker. He would be the perfect choice in two or three generations from now, when the Empire is established, and needs to create its legacy. We are not there yet... If Cosmin had been a daughter, he might have replaced Saliné's daughter in our plans. And Codrin would have replaced Edric. Perhaps.*

"People talk about future," Codrin shrugged.

"I know it's hard for you. The world is quite different from the one you left three years ago." *Three years ago, I learned about Saliné's unborn daughter, and I am still trying to understand who her husband will be, the Emperor Consort. I have found nothing. I looked at the children of many men of power. I found no one able to take the burden. Isn't that strange?* She frowned. *That toddler I met at the Broken Bridge Inn had the highest potential I've found until now. Ildeko is a strong woman, but the difference is too great. It must be his father... I must see the boy again. And his father.*

"A lot of changes in such a short time."

Things change faster when there is a plan. Is that what you are trying to say? "Change happens all the time. Who wounded you?"

The Pig on the throne. His men. Your idea. "I don't know. They shot me in the back. I had five arrows in me."

Thais told me the same. She thought you were dead. She had to run because riders were coming. Whose riders were they? "What happened next?"

"I woke in an unfamiliar place, far from here."

Calista looked at him, puzzled. He was a man who could hide his thoughts and feelings, but a Wanderer could always find something to read even in the most guarded face and eyes. *He is not lying, but he will say nothing more. Did the nomads take him? Was he a slave? That would make his resentment even greater.* "What kind of life did you have there?" *I don't feel many shadows in the life you had.*

"I was not a King."

You are no longer a King. "Do you know what a Seer becomes after losing his powers?"

"He is no longer a Seer."

"He becomes the Pillar of the Realm, the power behind the throne. Are you strong enough to fulfill that destiny?"

That's why you tried to kill me? Because I was the Pillar...? "Is the throne strong enough to stand on only one pillar?" *She tries to buy me with empty words.* Then he searched deeper inside and found that indeed the Seer becomes the Pillar after losing some of his powers. *Perhaps I could accept that if Alfrid had not tried to kill me. Could I?*

"The throne is stronger than you think, and there is another pillar behind it. In a year, Silvania will come to us too." *I need to push Saliné to accept Edric as her lointain lover, and soon.*

"The Silvanian King is not so old."

"What has age to do with this?" Calista shrugged. "There are two ways to move in life. Running with the waves or running against them. Like it or not, the burden of the Seer will always be yours. It has been like this since the Prophecy was made. You were only six years old at that time. Think on it. Think on my words. Think on the Realm. Think on your destiny." Calista turned her body, but not her head, her eyes still locked with Codrin's. Then she left. *I hope you will agree to be the Pillar of the Realm. That's the destiny of the Seer. You have two months to convince me, Codrin.*

Oblivious of the beauty of the garden, Calista walked slowly, bothered by a feeling that she felt was linked to Codrin.

Something was eluding her, and she knew it. *This is not about Codrin, yet it is about him.* Like an unrestrained girl, Calista kicked a pebble on the path, and burst into laughter. That brought to her the laughter of the child in the Broken Bridge Inn and, seeing Edric, she gestured at him to come.

"When was your last time with Saliné, as her leman?" she asked abruptly, then continued before he could answer. "You have not met her since Codrin returned. I don't care about his hurt feelings. In three days, I want to see you together."

"Give me a few weeks," Edric said. "It's about her feelings. She needs to calm down."

Calista frowned, and seemed to hold a curse just behind her lips. "Two weeks. Tomorrow, you will go to the Broken Bridge Inn and bring me two women who are staying there, Pireska and Ildeko, and their children. Be careful that no one sees them entering the palace and keep them in your quarters. Go now, before I start to think that you are too soft."

The next day, close to noon, four people gathered around the table in Codrin's house; for the first time, Saliné brought Jara with her. Cernat was there too. Codrin said nothing, not about Jara's first visit, nothing at all. He already knew that Cosmin had received a horse; he had heard two women speaking about it in the park, just an hour ago. They took care to let Codrin know, pretending not to see him. At the end, Codrin bowed slightly to them, and they smiled.

"We were thinking," Saliné said cautiously, "that you should spend more time with Cosmin; it would help both of you. We gave him a horse, and you can take over his training, three days a week. There will be plenty of time to spend together."

"That's why you allowed me to see him only once until now, because you were worried that we did not spend enough time together?"

"We have a difficult situation. Cosmin's training would make things easier for everybody."

"Cosmin is not fit yet for riding. His body is weak for his age, and his coordination is not good enough to ride a horse. What possessed you to give him one? Can't you see his body, or the way he is moving? Or do you have eyes only for your pride, Arnis?"

Saliné swallowed hard. "Our son likes the horse. He has been riding it for three days, and everything has gone well. If you train him, there will be no problems."

"I want this to stop. He should not ride a horse for another two years."

"It would be too difficult to take the horse from him now, he is happy with it."

"He would be happy to get a sword too. Would you give him one?"

"Codrin, it will not be possible to stop this; we already took the decision to train him, and we hope that you will agree to it."

"What do you mean, we?"

"Alfrid and I took the decision."

"Since when does Alfrid take decisions regarding my son?"

"Officially, he is Cosmin's father. Please understand that this is a normal thing. With ... my new marriage, and what we thought about you, a Royal Decree made Alfrid his father, not his stepfather. Alfrid was kind to accept this. We can talk later about rescinding the decree. About the training... Let's make it once a week. You will let him ride the horse for a brief time, and everything will be fine."

You want to blackmail me with the decree. "What happens if someone else trains him?"

"No one else will be allowed to train him. I will not allow it."

"Then how is it that you did not know for two days that he was training?"

Saliné looked through the window, trying to hide her tension and impatience. "Alfrid wanted to surprise me, and it was a bit of a ploy, but we've already agreed that only you will be allowed to train Cosmin. And Alfrid has started to change his thoughts about you. He sees you as the best commander against the nomads. He made this gesture with Cosmin to please you too. He created a Brotherhood of the Horse, to make Cosmin a kind of Knight, because he can't be a real Knight until he is old enough. There is a ceremony tomorrow, and you will make our son a Knight. Cosmin asks me constantly about the ceremony. Alfrid has made a half-step toward you. You should go halfway too."

It may help to take Cosmin with me, Codrin thought. *We should arrange my escape during a training day. We may...* He did not like how this started, everything being driven by Alfrid, but he was ready to accept, yet it felt wrong. He avoided Saliné's stare and let his mind wander. A faint memory came to him, old and fragmented. His mind tried to catch it, to anchor it to known things. *Idonie... It was something about Idonie. A Vision... An accident? Yes, it was an accident. Whose accident? Why did it come to me now?* Eyes closed, he tried harder, yet he could not get more. He opened his eyes, seeing all other staring at him. "Alfrid is planning an accident."

"Codrin, don't be ridiculous." Saliné forced herself to speak calmly.

"Alfrid *is* planning an accident. I had a Vision in Arad, years ago, and I can't remember it well." Codrin stood up abruptly and started to pace around the room.

"Was Cosmin or Alfrid in your Vision?" Cernat asked.

"I can't remember, but it came to me now. There must be a link."

"Alfrid will never try to kill my son. He doesn't kill children." Saliné enunciated each word slowly as she was speaking to a child.

"Alfrid will kill anyone for his interest. You still prefer to forget that he tried to kill me."

"Let's not walk that path again. I have a long list of people I've killed with my own hands. Yours is even longer. They were our enemies. You planned to take Alfrid's throne. He did what you would have done in his place. He has changed his mind, because you are the best army commander, and the nomads will come again. I will say it to you once more: Alfrid made a half-step toward you. You should go halfway too."

"He still wants to kill me, and he is using Cosmin to get me," Codrin snapped.

"We will stop here. Tomorrow, Cosmin will wait for you at the ceremony. A courier will come to take you in time. I hope that you will come." Saliné stood up too, ready to leave.

"You don't really care about Cosmin. In your mind there is only Alfrid and Arnis."

"You should not say such words to a mother. I care about my son, and I care about you. That's why I am in this room. See you tomorrow." She turned and walked toward the door.

"If something happens to my son, it will be on you." Codrin stepped swiftly toward her, but Saliné just slammed the door in his face. He walked back to his chair and sat abruptly. "What do you want?" he said gruffly, looking at Jara and Cernat.

"Perhaps a better question is what *you* want," Cernat said.

"To stop Cosmin's training."

"This is no longer possible, and you know that. I will consider your warning, and we can work together to..."

"You just imposed your will, without asking my opinion. That's not working together."

"Even regarding your son, the decisions will be made in the palace, because the power is there. Perhaps it's time for you to understand this. Cosmin will be unhappy if you will not come tomorrow. It will not serve you well. And Saliné is right, Alfrid made a step toward you."

During Cosmin's ceremony, Codrin was positioned at the edge of the large room, twenty-five feet from his son, and he had to fake joy when Cosmin was declared a knight by Alfrid, though Cosmin mostly ignored him. Happy, he had eyes only for his mother and Alfrid. At the end, when Saliné tried to speak to him, Codrin snapped before she could say a word. "You did everything to humiliate me today." He turned his back on her and walked away, only to be stopped by the guards at the door, who pointed to the Queen.

Saliné walked toward him; an unreadable face hiding a deep bitterness. *I am sorry, Codrin, but you must understand this new world*. "At the ceremony, the King arranged people based on their rank. It's a normal thing at any court; you have done the same in Arad. And as in Arad, no one leaves the room until the Queen and the King are gone. I hope that soon you will receive a title: Duke of Sittgart. In the next days, I will introduce you to a charming young woman." Their eyes were locked, and Codrin's face looked as if it was carved in stone, showing nothing, but she knew better.

Her voice lost its harshness, and she smiled tentatively. “Thank you for coming today. Cosmin’s training will start tomorrow, once a week. I am counting on you to keep him safe and teach him things that a man needs to know. Later, we will talk about rescinding the Royal Decree that makes Alfrid his father.” Saliné turned her back on him and walked toward Alfrid, who was struggling to stay serious. “Don’t act like a child,” she snapped at Alfrid and left the room.

Chapter 22 - Codrin / Elsebeth / Calista

Codrin weighed the paper in his hand: Saliné's writing, and a touch of suave perfume. Her writing had not changed, but her perfume was different. *What should I care?* They did not speak to each other since Cosmin's ceremony. He shrugged, and shuffled the paper between his fingers, then read it again. *...to meet us in the pavilion. It's about that stupid marriage. Well,* he shrugged again; *it will buy me more time to plan my escape. Those two women who always talk, pretending of not seeing me, said something about the daughter of Duke Drasdin.* He had a glimpse of the girl at the Royal Ball, but they did not dance together. *A beautiful young woman. I have to play the game to gain time, but I must be careful. The girl does not deserve this. And her father led the Hedgehog against the nomads. A fine man.* Codrin's mind wandered in the past. The battle against the nomads. The thrill of the fight. Alfrid's cowardice. Drasdin, Joachim and Homburg were the Litvonian commanders he relied on to defeat the nomads. *And Edric...* He shook his head and threw the paper away.

Each day, Codrin searched his house, trying to find a way out, so he could leave unseen; Vlad had assured him that everything would be ready in a month. He tried in vain; every window, the ones on the second floor, even the terrace, had a lattice of bars as thick as a thumb, made of forged iron. The house was richly decorated and impressive, but it looked more like a prison. It looked old too, more than five hundred years old, the only remaining part of the previous Royal Court. Perhaps it was once a prison for some high nobility. It was again now. He thought about cutting the bars with sandstone, but the soldiers regularly checked them. They were discreet, but they did it every three or four days. He would need almost a week to make a single cut, and he needed six cuts to squeeze out.

Codrin was the first one to arrive at the pavilion, and Saliné appeared from behind a yew hedge some fifty paces away from him. Seeing the other woman, Codrin found himself gasping for breath; he clamped his mouth shut and went into the Assassin Cool to calm his mind, then waited patiently in front of the open pavilion until they arrived. Saliné was charming and all smiles, and he forced himself to ignore her. He also forced himself to ignore the other woman.

"Codrin," Saliné said in a warm voice, "it's a wonderful day, and we can spend the afternoon in the pavilion; it will keep the sun away. Countess Elsebeth came to Muniker a week ago, and she agreed to join us." She gestured with a hand between him and the other woman. "Countess Elsebeth. Codrin, the Seer of the Realm. Except it's the Pillar now. I was always confused by those titles."

"Countess," Codrin bowed.

"Seer," Elsebeth curtsied.

"There is no need to be so formal," Saliné laughed, feeling that they were a little stiff; perhaps the first encounter regarding a possible future marriage was always like this. She did not notice her own stiffness. The other two were too preoccupied with hiding their feelings to sense anything else. Still laughing, Saliné went inside and seated herself at the table. The maid had already sliced the cozonac cake, and the air was filled with the scent of baked nuts and raisins coming from it. There was an open bottle of Porto Wine too. She nodded at the maid, who curtsied and left, to sit on a bench outside. "We have a nice view from here." Saliné pointed at the garden; the pavilion had only four poles and a roof. The other two joined her at the table, and Codrin filled the glasses. His hand was steady, and he forced himself to look anywhere but at Elsebeth.

"Countess of...?" Codrin asked, filling his own glass.

Elsebeth swallowed. "Baia." As in Frankis, the name of the main city and the region were the same in most places.

"I once stayed in the region during winter." Codrin looked at Elsebeth, and their eyes locked. Neither of them flinched, and after a while, he took a slice of cozonac. "Fourteen, or perhaps fifteen years ago. I can't remember the name of the inn, but it was on a secondary road from Silvania. I was going to Frankis." He gestured toward Saliné, who struggled to hide a sudden surge of memories behind a stiff smile. Looking away, he bit into the cake and chewed. The taste was good, and the slow movement of his jaws helped to release his tension.

Is that man in Ildeko's house his twin brother? Elsebeth thought and took a piece of cozonac too. She picked up a raisin and rubbed it unconsciously. She wanted to ask the Light for a clue, any clue, but she was afraid to use it front of the Seer. That was her deepest secret; even the Wanderers did not know that she had the Light. "There are many inns in Baia, it's on the main route from Silvania to Muniker." *His name was Tudor... He was... He was strange, and there was power in him. I feel Codrin the same way I felt Tudor, the same power. They must be twins, separated by Fate a long time ago. The Seer has no known siblings. Are they aware of Tudor in Muniker?*

There was a moment of silence, and Saliné played role of the host between two people struggling to find their way. She misunderstood their reasons, though. "I heard that your castle is built on the Dunaris River. It must be a nice place to live."

"It's built between mountain and water. From my room, I can see both the peaks and the sun's reflection in the low waves. Sometimes the mist comes in long tendrils that resemble a giant's fingers, and the land looks magical," Elsebeth said, seeming absent, transported to her lands. Her eyes crossed Codrin's for a moment, and the hint of a smile creased her lips.

She is as beautiful as she is evil, Codrin thought. *Without knowing her, I would praise her in poetry now. I still have to do it. Courting this shrew will be a nightmare, but I need to buy time.* He unleashed his Light to read her. Codrin felt almost nothing, and he recalled the moment when they had met at the edge of the forest. Her power. The mystery around her. *Who is this woman?* "It's like you described Alba, the capital of Arenia. I was still a child when I left my home. Your words feel like a long-gone dream. They sent me back in time when I still had a family. Now..." He locked eyes with Saliné, who dug her nails in her palm, and struggled to pull her eyes from his.

"I know Alba." Elsebeth's smile was a little more than a hint now. *How did I not realize until now who he really is?*

"Then you have an advantage on me, I have not seen your city. When did you visit Arenia?"

"A long time ago. For the wedding of Mesarosh, the son of Duke Anghel. I was one of the bride's maids in the church. She was my mother's cousin." This time, Elsebeth's lips went into a full smile, and her eyes opened wide in amusement. It felt warm and attractive.

"Ah," Codrin said, and closed his eyes for a few moments. Anghel was his second uncle. His memory went into the past, running from Baraki's men through the Cursed Forest, when Captain Ioan had told him that Anghel could still be trusted. Unwillingly, he moved further into the past, to his cousin's wedding, and his Silvanian bride. Those were joyful memories from the time when he still had a family. He had lost his first family. He had lost his second family. *How much do I still have to lose to please the Prophecy?* Codrin opened his eyes abruptly into Elsebeth's green stare. *She has Saliné's eyes.* He forced himself not to turn toward the woman he still loved. "A fourteen-year-old girl, dressed in pale green." *I was fifteen... Two months before my parents were killed.* These were memories that Codrin had suppressed for a long time. They returned with a kind of vengeance, which weakened him.

I was twelve, but everybody thought me older. "Yes," Elsebeth laughed, "that was me."

It's going well, I can leave now, Saliné thought, and nodded discreetly at the maid waiting outside. In a minute, a courier came with a message for her. “Unfortunately, I have to leave. There is an embassy from Silvania,” she said, taking her time to read the paper, which was only a pretext. “The maid is at your service.” Twenty paces outside the pavilion, she turned her head briefly. Elsebeth and Codrin seemed to suit each other. She could not see the grimace on her own lips; she could feel the sudden heaviness in her chest. Saliné shook her head and walked faster.

“I was one of the two cavaliers of the groom. From the door of the church to the Sacred Place we walked hand in hand. It was the custom.” Codrin shrugged.

“And on the way out. During the wedding party, you invited me to see the garden of the palace.”

They had the Light, and could recall old memories, and for a while both stayed silent, looking into the past. Codrin stretched his arm to take another slice of cozonac.

Unconsciously, Elsebeth was ready to do the same, and her hand moved naturally towards the large plate. It was a good moment to touch him involuntarily and let her Light into him. She coughed abruptly to mask the fast retreat of her hand. *Stupid woman, you can’t use the Light on the Seer. It’s too dangerous. Use your charm and mind.*

Codrin looked a bit embarrassed. “In the garden ... I think that I was a little too gallant with you. I even tried to...”

“You did not try, you kissed me. Four times. Don’t worry, I told no one. Perhaps because it was pleasant.” This time, Elsebeth’s laugh was long and full of delight, and she turned a little to her right, swelling her chest. It offered a perfect view of her perfect body. Her dress was tight, but not that tight, and everything that was hidden was also revealed.

Without realizing it, Codrin drank her in. “Well,” he said, caught in the net of memories, “young men are relieved when their gestures were not considered ... inappropriate.” Involuntarily, he looked at her lips, still set in a pleasant smile. *Yes, I kissed her. But four times...?*

“Are you trying to recall that moment?” Elsebeth asked, and her voice became demanding and mysterious. “I understood that people with the Light are able to remember many things. If I remember my first kiss so well ... How does it feel for you now?" *Your lips were warm and inquisitive. It was not bad for a fifteen-year-old boy.*

She is trying to force the memory on me. Sometimes, pleasant memories can be a weakness. Her lips were shy. I remember... Weakness... And I remember my family... Weakness... "Warm, and a little timid. I did not have much experience." *I am talking too much.*

"Inexperienced?" she laughed. "I did not think so."

She was the first girl I kissed. I won't tell her. "You are not from Baia."

"I was born in Muniker. My father was a Silvanian Knight. Then I married the Count of Baia. He was killed a few years ago." Elsebeth looked at him. *Why do I feel a link between Codrin and my idiot husband?* "Did you meet my husband during your travels in Baia?"

"What? No. Perhaps. I find Muniker a little strange."

"Because of your current situation?" she asked, deliberately.

"That is strange too. It's the atmosphere around. People are different."

"Ah," she laughed, "the lemans kissing in the park. Foreigners have some problems at first, but they get accustomed to it soon enough, and some always find a reason to return to the Court of Love." She moistened her lips, and the red on them became stronger. Seeing Codrin staring at her mouth, she split her lips a little, and her tongue became visible against the white of her teeth. *He remembers... Look at my lips Codrin.* Oblivious to it, she let a little Light into him, a feeling of desire.

"Even with the lemans, I still enjoy the park. Would you like to walk?" Codrin asked suddenly, and his invitation shortened her visit, but he had to walk with Elsebeth hanging on his arm, through the park, and then toward the gate. It took longer than he had in mind, and it was not unpleasant; Elsebeth knew her game.

Sitting on his terrace, Codrin looked away into the garden, but his eyes were more attracted by the bars spoiling the view. And his escape. His fingers played with a slice of cozonac; the plate from the pavilion lay in front of him. The cake was of Arenian origin, and the recipe was slightly different in Frankis. This one tasted more like home. It sent him back home. So it did the talk with Elsebeth. He did not try to eat, just crushed it a little from time to time, to release the sweet fragrance of nuts and raisins. *Elsebeth... Intelligent. Beautiful. Evil. There is something in her...* Absently, he tasted the cake. *A sort of power. A sort of dark past. Something evil happened to her and changed her. It's not that her memory is influencing my thoughts, or only a little. Isn't it strange that I can feel someone's past? It's not possible to have a Vision of the past; perhaps this is something different, just a feeling. And it's even stranger that I could see nothing in her future. My future can't be seen either. Is she a sort of ... me? No, I can't be like her.* He took another slice of cozonac and decided to spend the rest of the evening without thinking about Elsebeth.

From the Palace Gate, Elsebeth walked home as fast she could without raising much attention, and Horwath was the first man she found in her house. "Horwath, take two men and go to Baia. You will leave now. I need Pireska and her family here. And that man, Tudor. I needed them *unharmed*. Ask my dressmaker to find them something to wear, good enough for Muniker. Tell her to make them elegant. The sort of elegance that belongs to a rich merchant. Go now." *Ildeko was a merchant's daughter. She had some sort of education. Will this work?*

Horwath hesitated for a while as if needing to say something more, but not really wanting to. Suddenly, Elsebeth gripped his hand, and her Light went through him. "I think they are already here, my lady," he said against his will. *How is she doing this to me?* "Three days ago, I saw Ildeko in a carriage that came to Muniker. I was at the southern gate."

And you are telling me only now... This can wait. "Is that relative of yours ... Frinz, still a Gate Captain?" Her deep green eyes locked with his, and Horwath nodded. "Where did they take Ildeko?"

"I don't know, but the guards escorting the carriage belonged to Prince Edric. That young man, Tudor, was not with them." Their eyes were still locked; Horwath did not even think to try to escape from her stare. There was a moment of silence, then those eyes pressured him into speaking again. "There is something strange, my lady. The man you met today ... the Seer. Frinz told me that the Seer has returned from death to save Litvonia again from the nomads. Next year, it seems that they will invade us again. And..." Horwath moistened his lips. "The Seer vanished three years ago, and ... *resurrected* a month ago."

"How credible is this Frinz? This resurrection..." Elsebeth frowned and released Horwath from her stare. Close to her temple, she drew a few circles in the air with her forefinger, the sign for madness. *Three years ago, Tudor appeared in Ildeko's house. She lied to me that he came only two years ago. Even Horwath is having second thoughts about that. Why did she lie?*

"Frinz became a captain fifteen years ago and is now an Uber Captain. There are only a few Ubers in Muniker."

"Find out where Ildeko is lodged. And, Horwath..." Elsebeth looked at him again, "did you see the Seer?"

"Yes," he whispered. "Yesterday, I joined Frinz in the Royal Park. He wanted to show me the Seer."

"Then you understand why I need to find Ildeko and Tudor. And you also understand that I should have known this three days ago. Leave now."

Alone in her room, Elsebeth sat on the floor, leaning against the wall, her knees to her chest. *A twin brother could explain everything that happened in Ildeko's house. But how could one explain the fact that both men have a two-inch scar on their jaw. On the same side. In the same position. The same color. The same curvature. How? There was no twin brother in Arenia, only an older brother, who looked different. And a twin sister. I liked her. Her fate was even worse than mine.*

ᏊᏉ

With ten men, Vlad and Pintea arrived at the Broken Bridge Inn late in the morning. They wore no royal uniforms or colors; Vlad was now a Seigneur. Already knowing the women from when he came with a letter from Codrin, Pintea went inside to find them. The inn was empty; the locals would come later for a drink, and travelers had already eaten and left.

"I came to find two women, Pireska and Ildeko," Pintea said.

"There are no women with those names here," the innkeeper said, busy cleaning glasses. He had not been in the inn during Pintea's first two visits.

"Did they leave?"

"They never stayed here."

In a split second, Pintea's long arm stretched out and grabbed the innkeeper by his hair, pulling him over the counter, and pressing his neck on the edge of it. A knife brushed the man's ear. "I wonder if an innkeeper can take orders from his customers without an ear. Or with no ears. Where are the women?"

"Three days ago, they took them." The innkeeper's voice came out strangled; the edge of the counter was pressing hard on his throat. The fear was pressing even more.

"Who?"

"Royal Guards. They wanted the Knight too, but he did not come back. They told me to keep quiet."

They were not Royal Guards; Vlad would have known... Perhaps Palace Guards. "Did they ask anything particular about the Knight?" *Like about his curved swords?*

"No."

Then they may not know about Codrin. "I have very bad ears," Pintea said, releasing the innkeeper. "I've heard nothing from you. And you've heard nothing about me." He threw a heavy purse on the counter and left.

"Edric's men?" Codrin asked when Vlad and Pintea returned, one hour after Elsebeth had left him alone. He stood up abruptly and went to the window. It did not help, and he started to pace around the room, his hands clasped at his back. "Edric's men took them three days ago, and I knew nothing of it. I am failing everyone." He stopped abruptly and, eyes closed, he leaned against the wall. *I felt nothing about them, but I never had much control of the Light; it comes and goes at its own will.* "They were Edric's men, but this must be Calista's work." *Why? She saw the future of my son... Did she guess that he is my son? She can't see my future, but she saw something.* "Calista is waiting for me to make a move. But..." he frowned, "she did not make the slightest allusion to them. I have to see Calista". *She now has a good advantage over me.* "Vlad, can you find where they are kept?"

"They must be in Edric's quarters. Calista is there too, but it will take a while to find where, or even ... if they are there. Edric's place is somehow isolated, and he has his own men. Do you think they are in danger?"

"Danger comes when you expect it least. This is a game. They are safe as long as the game goes on, but I don't really know what sort of game we are playing right now. If Calista knows that Ioan is my son, she will expect me to agree to marriage. Then she will make her next step and let them return to the Broken Bridge under guard. Then I have to make the next step. But if she doesn't know... If she is only guessing, which I think is more probable..."

"Let's switch places," Pintea said. "They don't know Knight Theodrick. I will take his identity and claim Ildeko as my lover. I will claim the child too. Two years ago, I was wounded, and stayed away from Muniker for several months. It will fit the story. Vlad will come and back me against Calista, as the Chief of the Royal Guard. If it's not working, we will appeal to Saliné."

"Saliné will pressure me even harder into the marriage," Codrin said, bitterly. "Let's find where they are lodged first. You can't go to Calista until we know where they are."

✤

The future was weighing hard on Calista. That morning, she checked the future of little Ioan, Ildeko's son, three times, each time keeping his hand in hers. There was something, yet there was nothing. She could not use the blood bond; he was too small. At noon, she ordered Edric to keep Ildeko and her family in his quarters; they were isolated from the main part of the palace.

"It's done," Edric said and sat in a chair not far from Calista. "I put them in one of my best unused rooms. You look thoughtful. Why is that child so important that I had to kidnap the family from the Broken Bridge? A Knight's son."

"Don't be stupid, Edric. What do we *really* know about the man? He could be a Count or a Duke. The more I think on it, the more he seems other than a Knight. The only Vision I see of him is his hand when he is training the child, who is some seven years old in my Visions. The man is married; there is a simple wedding ring on his finger. His hand is that of a man in his mid-thirties."

"A Duke with a simple wedding ring." Edric shrugged.

"Not all men are peacocks." Calista shrugged too and looked at his clothes.

"I am not a peacock," Edric smiled.

"You used to be one until I taught you how to dress like Codrin and impress Saliné. Now be quiet, I have to think." There was something important in what she could see. Or perhaps in what she could not see. *Seeing a hand, it's not like seeing one's future. I see the boy's future; the man's is hidden. Codrin... I can't see his future either, and he vanished in Baia, close to Ildeko's house. Well, not close, but not far either. The boy has an Arenian name...* "Edric, I want you to seduce Ildeko and learn more about her and her Knight."

"Wouldn't be easier to lean on them?"

"They are tougher women than you think; in that isolated place, the weak die fast. And since when are you unwilling to seduce a woman? She has a certain beauty. A little bit raw, perhaps, but she is more a woman than most Duchesses and Countesses in the kingdom." Calista looked at him, and her voice became harsh. "The second thing you should have thought about, before proposing duress, is that we need that child to grow and stay well, with his parents. And we must keep an eye on them."

In the evening, Ildeko found herself dressed in a Countess' dress, dinning with the Prince of Litvonia. She was dressed, yet she felt half naked. Her shoulders *were* naked, and each time she looked down at her deep V-like neckline, she had the impression that her breasts were fully exposed. Moving, she was able to see her nipples. She was too confused to realize that someone in front of her could not see that much, because of a different perspective; Litvonian dresses were made to allow lovely games between a man and a woman. Ildeko knew that her dinner was only a preamble for going to bed with the man across the table. Her dress was made to be easily taken off; she had seen that when the maid was dressing her. Open the belt and the dress would simply slide down her body. *There is nothing I can do*, she thought. *I must let him take what he wants to protect my family. The same way Irvath took what he wanted. Or his wife.*

The musicians began to play, and Edric nodded at the page, who left them alone at the table, and went into a corner of the room, which was sixty feet long, then he filled two glasses of wine. "It just came from Tolosa. A little red spark of their warm sun, land and women."

Ildeko frowned at the glass and sniffed without realizing it.

"Have you tasted wine before?" Edric asked, and she shook her head. *I hope you will not get drunk; I won't like that. And poetry about wine is not helping my cause too much*. "Why not try it? You may like it." *A little sip of wine will help.*

Carefully, she sipped, more tasting than drinking. "It's cold, but it tastes of wild berries and brings warmth," she said, letting the taste take over.

Not a bad answer, Edric thought. *Perhaps she will offer some enjoyment, not just a little wrestling in bed.*

Ildeko took care to drink only half a glass, but it was already coursing through her veins, and she started to feel less miserable. Edric stirred her to talk and, slowly, memories from when she was a rich merchant's daughter came to her, and she told her own stories. An hour later, Calista came to look again into her future, and used her powerful Light to stir Ildeko's body, the same way she had used it once on Saliné. But Ildeko was not Saliné, and she thought that the warmth and desire in her belly came from the wine.

Then they danced, and to the surprise of both, Ildeko soon remembered that she had danced once at balls, when her father was still alive. The dances went through her, joining the wine and Calista's Light, and with each turn, more old memories came, even the one related to the young Knight who was supposed to be her husband once. She became a lady, dancing at a ball, and that Knight became the man now dancing with her. At the end, Edric walked her to the terrace, and took her in his arms from behind, talking to her. In a corner of her mind, Ildeko realized that Edric was not Irvath; there would be no violence. The last traces of her fear vanished, and there was only desire left. She felt his lips on her naked shoulders, moving up toward her neck, and unconsciously, she leaned against his body. When he turned her, searching for her mouth, Ildeko found herself answering him. His hand went inside that deep neckline, which she had hated and did not care about anymore; his hand was gentle and pleasant on her breast. She raised her arms around his neck at the same time as her dress slid down her body. There was a bed prepared for them in a corner of the terrace; a violin was still playing in the room, and their naked bodies moved together in that slow rhythm. That night resembled no night she had spent with a man before.

Ildeko returned late in the morning to her room, after a long night without much sleep, and sat at the table, leaning her head on her elbow. "Last evening, I lost my head. Perhaps because of the wine, yet I am not sure. Edric was nothing like that brute Irvath, and I am his lover now," she said, when Pireska stroked her hair, and she told her everything that happened. Almost everything. Edric had stirred her body in ways she did not know before. With her husband, they had learned together how to make love, and for Codrin, she was the teacher. Edric needed no lessons, he had had the best teachers in Litvonia, and she was feeling the touch of his lips and fingers even now. "I don't know how long he will keep me here. I've endangered everybody with my weakness."

"It was good that you lost your head; the night was not hard for you. And it's good that you've recovered it now. Edric is not, and will never be, your lover. You are just one of his many mistresses. He expected this from you, and there is no way to refuse a Prince, as there was no way to refuse Irvath, who was much worse. Perhaps Edric expected a little resistance from you. You offered none and being easy may make him bored soon. And who says that an unmarried woman can't have an agreeable night?" She lifted Ildeko's chin with a finger until they were eye to eye. "Codrin is not your husband. He will never be your husband."

"I loved my husband. I like Codrin. It's not the same, but I like him. Or perhaps I am fooling myself, and I love him too. I don't know, and I feel bad now, like a..." *Whore? What kind of woman am I?*

"And Codrin likes you. You know that. But right now, he can't do anything for us. I learned last evening that his wife is now the wife of the Litvonian King, and Codrin is no longer a King; he is a prisoner here. Prisoner of his own wife. That hurts. Codrin should have waited and learned more before leaving our house and going back to her. You are Edric's mistress now. It is not your fault. Make him feel good. It seems that he likes to make you feel good too. Your children need his protection, and you may be able to help Codrin a little. He deserves to be helped. Now drink this." She pushed a cup of tea in front of Ildeko. "Bloody Moon. It's not wise to fall pregnant to a prince. Accidents can happen in such situations."

The third morning, when they woke, Edric played his fingers on Ildeko's body. "Now that you are my lover, I need to know more about you. Calista told me about a Knight that you rescued on the road, Theodrick."

Eyes half closed, her attention was split between his fingers fondling her breast so gently and his question. "We did not rescue him now, but before."

"Is he the father of your younger son?"

"Yes."

"When did you meet him?" His fingers moved down her belly, and she arched a little.

"Two years ago; he was wounded and stayed in our house for a while." *I hate his fingers. I like his fingers.* Unconsciously, she turned toward him, to offer more of herself.

"Two years, not three or four?"

"My son is only one year old." Ildeko smiled and placed her hand behind his neck, sliding her fingers gently on his skin. She waited for another question, which did not come, but Edric's eyes were still questioning her. His fingers were searching her too, distracting her. "Theodrick was wounded, an arrow in his right shoulder, and his servants were killed by a band of mercenaries. He left a few months later, and one of his servants came three months ago, returning home from Silvania."

"Where is Theodrick's home?"

"Close to the Rhiun River, but he never told me exactly where. He wanted it to be a surprise. He waited for us at the Broken Bridge Inn, then he had to leave. He should return in a few days."

"Would that matter to you?"

"I don't know. You should tell me if it should matter or not. I am not a Duchess, and he is only a Knight."

She doesn't lack wit, Edric mused. *And she is right; my decision will drive her future. Perhaps she will get me a bastard, and I will take care of her.* "We will talk more when he returns, but even then, you are my lover. And if you get pregnant, you will always be in my charge." *I am changing Calista's Vision, and I will train that boy. He will become my tool.*

"Well," Ildeko laughed, "men like to have more than one lover. "Women don't." She pulled his head closer and kissed him, then something stirred in them, and they made love again.

"Can I walk in the park? I have heard that it is wonderful," she asked just before leaving his bedroom.

"You can go with the two maids I gave you. You are not known, and the guards may ask questions. Some parts of the park are not open to you. The maids know all this. If anyone asks, you are one of Calista's new maids. Your family can use only the eastern garden."

"Thank you, Edric." *I have maids*, she thought, closing the door behind her. *Who could have thought that even a few days ago? But I will never consider them servants.*

Ildeko enjoyed the park, and her days were split between her family and walking between flowers that she did not know they existed. Most of her nights belonged to Edric. On one of her walks, she saw Codrin. It was the fourth day after he had learned about her abduction.

"Isn't that man the Seer?" Ildeko asked Agathe, her older maid, who nodded. "Can we see him from a bit closer?"

"We are already at the boundary for the main servants," Agathe said.

"Please, Agathe, who knows when we can see him again? We can hide behind the bushes there." Ildeko pointed to a thick row of mock oranges which were full of flowers, their sweet scent spreading, and pulled her by the arm. The older maid walked with her, followed by the second, both struggling to hide their own eagerness to see the Seer. Hidden behind the bush, Ildeko watched Codrin walking until he arrived sixty paces away from them, then he turned a little, ready to move away on his path. "He is good looking," Ildeko chuckled. "I thought him older."

"He is thirty," Agathe whispered, craning her neck.

"Ah!" Ildeko cried and jumped out of the bush, shaking the lower part of her dress frantically. The maids followed her, and Codrin turned and hurried toward them.

"Seer." The women curtsied, elated.

"What happened?" Codrin locked eyes with Ildeko.

"It was... It was just a mouse, it attacked me," Ildeko breathed. "I am sorry for disturbing you."

"Mice can be vicious sometimes," Codrin laughed. "Has it gone?" He walked around Ildeko, forcing the other two women to move away.

"I think so, but I am not really sure."

"Are you new here?"

"I am one of the new maids of Lady Calista."

Codrin looked at her clothes, and they were nothing like a maid's. He also saw the slight redness on Ildeko's face and asked nothing about them. "I suppose that you are lodged in that area." He pointed somewhere behind the women.

"No, Sir, we are lodged in Prince's Edric quarters. If you look there," Ildeko pointed, "there are three large magnolias. The room where I stay with my family is on the second floor, just in front of the magnolia in the middle. Ah!" With a brusque gesture, she shook her dress again.

"Let me see," Codrin said and walked in a larger circle around her, forcing the other two women to move further away. He stepped abruptly forward, miming taking something from her dress. "Pintea will come and present himself as Theodrick," Codrin whispered, and stepped back, opening his palm, showing a milk thistle flowerhead with large thorns that he had picked earlier from the grass. "I think," he said, struggling to stop his laughter, "that this is the vicious mouse that attacked you." He looked at a silent Ildeko, then at the other two women, who were behind her again, covering their mouths to hide their smiles.

"Thank you," Ildeko breathed in embarrassment, and lowered her head.

On their way back, Agathe said, "I have to tell Sir Edric about this."

"Of course, you must tell him, and everything is on me, but please don't mention the milk thistle. I was attacked by a vicious mouse, not by a flower." *Pintea will come... Oh, no.* She turned abruptly, only to see Codrin walking away. *Pintea should not come. Edric will not let me leave, and everything can go badly. What can I do now?*

"That I can do." Agathe smiled; she liked Ildeko.

At noon, Agathe reported everything to Edric and Calista, and when she left, Edric waited for his aunt to speak first. *Why do I have the feeling that Calista is not surprised?* he thought. *But what link can there be between Ildeko and Codrin?*

Lost in her thoughts, Calista ignored him. She drummed her fingers on the table, then looked at Edric. "You stare like a girl who wants to hear the latest gossip."

"And what gossip should I hear?"

"Who cares about gossip? Did you find some inconsistencies in Ildeko's story about her Knight?"

"I asked her two times, under a certain type of sweet pressure, and each time, she gave me the same answer. Theodrick appeared two years ago, gave her a child, and left. Three months ago, he sent a letter with a servant. The only thing which raised my interest is that he has *interests* in Silvania. That's unusual for a minor Knight whose lands are so far from the Silvanian border."

"Two years, not three years ago," Calista whispered. "Yesterday, someone remarked that Ildeko is too well dressed for a simple maid. I had to pretend that she is the niece of a good friend of mine, and she is a special servant."

"But she is a special one," Edric laughed.

Calista leaned toward him and slapped the back of his head. "The bad thing is that news about the *special maid* has spread too quickly. The good thing is that, perhaps, Theodrick will learn it too. There may be a sort of reaction. If..." she looked at Edric, "he is not too scared that Ildeko is now your mistress." *And I will never know for sure if her talk with Codrin was a spontaneous thing.*

It was late morning when Pintea and Vlad entered Calista's office, the fifth day after Ildeko had met Codrin. She gestured at them to take a seat until she finished reading the paper in her hand, then she nodded at them to speak.

"We are looking for some friends, two women and their children," Vlad said. "They vanished two weeks ago from the Broken Bridge Inn."

"You are talking about my friend, Pireska," Calista said. "But why are you saying that she vanished from the Broken Bridge Inn? She did not disappear."

"Perhaps because she is no longer there," Pintea said. "And Ildeko left no message for me."

"Perhaps she did not think it necessary. I suppose you want to talk to her." Calista called her secretary and whispered something to him.

Ildeko entered a few minutes later, followed by Edric. "Theodrick," she said and tried to walk toward Pintea, but Edric placed an arm around her shoulders, pulling her toward him. It was a gentle reminder that she was not allowed to interact much, and that she would remain his lover even though *Theodrick* had returned. Edric had made that clear to her.

Calista watched silently. Pintea and Vlad were men who could hide their feelings, but her Wanderer senses felt the quiet tension mounting in them. Edric led Ildeko around the room and seated her on a sofa, then placed an arm around her shoulders again.

This time, Calista frowned slightly. *Edric should have let her go.* "So," she looked at Pintea, "are you Pintea or Theodrick?"

"Both. I am a captain and scout lead. Sometimes, I must use different names when working for the kingdom. I have come to take Ildeko and my son."

"Perhaps you should ask her if she wants to leave," Edric said and gripped Ildeko's shoulder tight, to keep her silent, but she grimaced, looking at Pintea. Edric could not see it.

Calista could see it. *Edric wants Pintea to escalate this to Saliné*, she thought. *He will accept her judgment, which will be in Pintea's favor. His acceptance will be a goodwill gesture toward Saliné. Edric is thinking two steps ahead, but he never thinks of the third. These two will be his men in the future we are planning for him. They are men of value. There is no need to antagonize them.* "Can you tell us more about this story?" She looked at Pintea and gestured between him and Ildeko.

"I want to see my son, too," Pintea said, his voice slightly menacing.

He knows how to put pressure on. Calista let her mind search for the Light. *I don't feel any link between Pintea and Ildeko. Is he really Theodrick? She said the word, but it did not feel true to me. And if he is not Theodrick, then what is going on? Then it is even more probable that Codrin is, and he sent Pintea here. I need some more time. A few days at least.* "Is Ioan Pintea's son?" Calista asked, her voice suddenly sharp, and her eyes bored into Ildeko. *Ioan is an Arenian name.*

"Yes," Ildeko said, a slight hesitation in her voice.

"Since when are Pintea's children your concern?" Vlad asked quickly, his voice as sharp as Calista's.

Calista raised her forefinger, silencing Edric, who was ready to snap an angry answer. *Vlad wants to escalate this too.* Calista turned toward him. "I am always concerned about children." Her voice was now soft, but the tension in the room did not disappear, and she struggled to find a way out that would not escalate things too much. "I always liked the view from Pireska's house. That mountain with a strange name..."

"The White Saddle. I spent my childhood at the foot of the White Saddle, the other side of Pireska's house. I knew their home even before Ildeko arrived there," Pintea said.

Ah, that I did not know, but I still feel that there nothing between them. Ioan is not his child. "It's a nice area indeed."

"We don't want to bother you," Pintea said, his voice calm, even a little bored. "We just came to take my son, Ildeko and her family."

"You've made your request. In a few days, you will receive an answer," Edric said.

"I did not make a request. I made a statement." Pintea crossed eyes with Edric, and a long moment of silence covered the room like a blanket.

They are in cold mood, not fighting mood, there is still some hope. "I am..." Calista tried to say, but the door opened, and Countess Elsebeth entered the room. Ildeko became livid, but no one looked at her. In a second, everybody's head turned toward the newcomer in a synchronization that looked hilarious, revealing the tension in the room. Elsebeth *did* look at Ildeko, and a little grin flashed across her lips.

"I had no idea that so many people would be here. I hope I did not interrupt anything important," Elsebeth said, her voice careless.

Her presence will keep them silent. I must keep Elsebeth here longer, Calista thought. "Some talk about families. I think you know most of the people in the room."

"I know them all." Elsebeth took a chair and sat a little away from everybody, her eyes in direct contact with Calista, Ildeko and Edric, across Calista's large desk.

"I've just learned that Vlad and Pintea are from Baia. Isn't it strange how some links appear from nowhere?" Calista looked at Elsebeth.

Calista wants something from me... She is using her Light on me. "Yes, there are some old links." Elsebeth gestured loosely toward Vlad, Pintea and Ildeko, and it happened that Pintea was between her and Vlad. *Everybody will understand what they want from my words. Let see what I can learn from this. There is a lot of tension in the room.*

Pintea may be the father after all, Calista pondered before saying, "I was lost in my thoughts and did not ask why you are here."

"I came for Ildeko, of course. I need a Secretary Maid, and she is the only qualified one that I know of in Muniker. In fact, we already agreed on this before she got pregnant."

This would be a good temporary solution. "Yes, I understand the importance of having a good secretary, and it seems to me that Ildeko is qualified. And if you have already agreed..." Calista gestured loosely between the two women.

"Yes, we agreed, didn't we, Ildeko?" Elsebeth said, looking at the frightened woman, who could only nod, there was no way to avoid it; she would go from Edric's bed into another bed that was not empty. At least she had enjoyed being with Edric.

Elsebeth's house is outside the castle, a less guarded area, Ildeko thought. *Perhaps in a few weeks...*

Calista said, tentatively, "There was a little problem related to Pintea's ... son. He just wanted to visit him."

"Pintea will be allowed to see his son once a week." Elsebeth shrugged, looking at Calista. "Do you think that she can move to my house today? I am behind with my letters."

In one hour, they were in Elsebeth's house. It was large and close to the Royal Palace. On the road everyone kept silent, Elsebeth had requested it, and they walked behind her, asking themselves questions that had no answer.

In the hall of the house, Elsebeth sent Pireska and the children with a maid to the room she had reserved for them. "Vlad, Pintea, I apologize, but I have an important visitor, so you will leave the house through the back door. If you want, we can talk tomorrow morning. Ildeko, you come with me."

Both women walked into a large dining room with a round table, prepared to host two people. "Put a cover on and leave us alone," Elsebeth ordered a maid.

"Why did you bring me here?" Ildeko asked, her voice edgy.

Elsebeth slapped her, but it was a gentle thing, just a display of power; Ildeko knew well how tough the Countess could be. "You will not speak like that to me. Did you enjoy Edric in your bed so much that you don't want to be free? Take a chair and sit in front of me." They sat, their knees touching, and Elsebeth took Ildeko's hands in hers. "We need to talk. You will be my secretary. Do you have questions?"

"Yes, my lady."

"When we are alone, you will call me Elsebeth. I always have a close relation with my secretaries, some of them have been my lovers. I have a bad reputation. Some rumors about me are true, some are false. I never strangled three of my maids, but it suited me to let the rumor spread. I did cut out the tongue of a secretary, she was seduced by a man, and started to sell my secrets. The man lost his tongue and his manhood. Questions?"

"Do you think that I am qualified?"

"Not fully, but in those nights we've been together, I made you speak a lot. We were talking or doing ... other things. You preferred to talk. There are many good things in your mind that have no use on a farm. I think that you will enjoy recalling some of your past merchant life."

"Why are you trusting me?"

"You will like the job, and you will have some protection. There is no one to protect you right now; that's why you've landed in Edric's bed." She looked at Ildeko, who nodded. "Would you prefer his protection and his bed? I can send you back."

Ildeko gave it some serious thought, feeling that this might be the hardest decision she had taken in years. "I would like to stay, if... If you do not make me your lover."

"You are a free woman. Now, we have a guest. You will not say anything about what happened today. You will not make hidden signs. I don't like to be upset. You wouldn't like it either."

There was noise of footsteps on the corridor, and the door opened. Seeing Ildeko in the room, Codrin stumbled in the doorway. Elsebeth smiled mischievously at him. During their last walk together, she had invited him to her house, and Codrin was allowed to leave the palace's precincts for the first time. There were five Palace Guards waiting outside. "Your sister?" he asked, struggling to hide his shock; Ildeko should have been with Pintea right now.

"Do you think that we are alike?" Elsebeth asked and gripped Ildeko's shoulder, pulling her until their heads almost touched.

"Not much."

"Until lunch is ready, let's talk on the terrace," Elsebeth said and walked away. In the middle of the terrace, she turned abruptly toward Codrin and Ildeko. They were not trying to speak to each other, and she smiled at Ildeko. "We are not in the mountains, and the view is not what you are accustomed to. Is that not so, Ildeko?" She did not wait for an answer, and her forefinger moved to trace the scar at the base of Codrin's jaw. "Have you ever seen a scar like this?"

Ildeko looked desperately at Codrin, who replied, "Yes, she has seen one."

"Then we have the same level of understanding now. Almost." Feeling Codrin's struggle, Elsebeth placed a palm on his neck, playing with her thumb on his scar. For the first time, she used consciously her Light on him, a slight touch, and she waited patiently for some reaction. *He did not feel my Light.* "We still need to learn more about each other."

"Perhaps we should go slowly with the learning." *I am like a ship without steer, and the current is pulling me in uncertain waters.* Codrin fell silent, looking thoughtful; a part of his resentment had vanished suddenly.

"We will find our rhythm. Lunch is ready." Elsebeth gestured toward the door of the room, where a maid was now standing.

At the end of the lunch, Elsebeth sent Ildeko to her room, and took Codrin on the terrace again. She sat on a sofa, and patted the place next to her, making Codrin sit closer. "What happened to my husband?"

"He tried to rape Ildeko."

"He had such habits, but it doesn't answer my question."

"He is resting in a grave. Does that answer your question?"

"Yes. Irvath considered himself a tough man. It seems that he was wrong. I suppose that the other three, who were with him, are resting too." Her fingers again touched the scar on Codrin's jaw. "It gives you a mysterious look. A small scar like this enhances a man but diminishes a woman."

Mara... Codrin thought, recalling that she had told him the same.

"It seems that I am not the first woman to tell you this. How many women have there been in your life?"

"Not many."

"There is a kind of royal expectation regarding us, and I suppose that things are easier for me than for you, despite the unfortunate fact you killed my husband. It was a political marriage." Elsebeth shrugged and moved her fingers down his neck, using her Light on Codrin again. "My understanding is that Alfrid wants to chain you with a wife and a title. There have been many marriages in the past that started under similar auspices. Some of them went well. Some didn't. Did they pressure you?"

"A little." Codrin took her hand away from his neck and held it in his.

"I don't think pressure would work well with you, but everyone has a weakness. Or more than one. Calista is interested in your youngest son." Elsebeth thought about her Vision, and how much she could tell Codrin without it being obvious that she had the Light. "She had an intuition or a Vision, that Ioan is your son. Today, I confirmed to her that Pintea is Theodrick and the ... father."

"Thank you." *Why did she help me? Is she helping me?*

"It suited me. Saliné does not know yet, but I've already agreed to our marriage, and I will work for it. I see no reason to hide this from you, though things are now very different between us. For me at least." She smiled and gripped his fingers gently.

"And what will you do if things do not go as you want? Would you use my ... weaknesses against me?"

One's weakness is other's gain. Are you my weakness? "You mean, Ildeko and your child? But you don't see it?" Elsebeth turned toward him, and placed her free hand on his shoulder, her fingers touching his neck again. "Once I said to Calista that Pintea is Theodrick, I forfeited my chance to use this weakness." She pushed her Light on him, trying to stir the desire for kissing.

Codrin blinked at her, before whispering, "Things are taking a toll on me. It will be difficult but not impossible to use my son against me."

She pulled his head closer to her. "Difficult, if you want. But why should we talk about things that keep us apart?" *Kiss me, Codrin,* she said in her mind, letting the Light carry her words to him. It was her strongest display of power, and she felt that it was the right time. She moistened her lips, so close to his, and let her mouth slightly open. No one had resisted before. This was the way Count Irvath married her without knowing why.

A time gone memory came to Codrin: Elsebeth and his twin sister talking at the wedding. Then came the memory of kissing her at dusk, in the park. He recalled in the slightest detail the touch of her lips, blinked at Elsebeth, and felt the urge to kiss her again. Placed an arm around her shoulders, pulling her against him, so he could not see her face. Or kiss her. It was a gentle move. He felt a sort of power in this woman. Something dark. And something sad. There was also the image of that young girl, and the feeling of something good. He felt both the need to confront and to protect this woman. He felt confused.

I don't have much power over him, but Codrin did not feel my Light. I can hide it even from the Seer. Why do I have this power? "There are things you need to learn. My past is not clean, and I want to avoid being blackmailed against you. Calista knows some things about me. She is a tough woman. A bitch. A powerful bitch."

"Elsebeth, that girl I kissed at the wedding, when did she ... change?" Codrin held her chin between his fingers and turned her head toward him.

"When I was fifteen, but I am not ready to talk about that." Elsebeth's voice was even, and she turned her head so he could not see her suddenly weary face. *I will never be ready to talk about what happened when I was kidnapped.* She reached for anger and revolt but found only fear. Her free hand started to shake slightly, and she pressed her nails into her flesh.

"We have time." Codrin stroked her hair. "Can we talk about Ildeko?"

"She will be my secretary. Nothing else. If you want to see her, the maid will help you find her room." Unable to recover, Elsebeth felt fragile, and afraid that Codrin was able to sense her weakness. All her adult life she had worked hard to be a tough woman. And to hide what had happened to her.

Codrin spent an hour with Ildeko and his son. Elsebeth did not disturb them and avoided to meet him again. Leaving the house, he was followed discreetly by the five guards who had come with him from the palace.

Chapter 23 - Codrin / Saliné / Elsebeth

An escort of six guards dressed in ceremonial uniforms escorted Codrin to Saliné's office. It was late morning. Cernat, Jara and Dochia were there too, all struggling to hide their tension. Instead of taking a seat, Codrin went back to his old habit of leaning against the window. With guarded eyes, they looked at him, trying to read his mind. It was sunny, and warmth passed through the glass. He shivered. Dochia went into the Light, trying to read Codrin's future. Nothing came to her. She was expecting it but was not less disappointed.

"Today is the ceremony," Saliné smiled. It was a large and warm smile, used to soothe Codrin and hide her sadness. This was a game he did not deserve. She did not deserve it either, but there was no other way, and she believed in what she was doing, keeping the peace, and keeping both fathers of her children alive. Once or twice, that insidious thought, which had been seeded by the Empress in her mind, came to her: to take Edric and Codrin as her lointain lovers. She rejected the idea; Codrin could no longer be hers, but he was unique to her, and he would remain unique.

"Today is an ambush," Codrin said, flatly; for him things were simpler. And more painful.

"This is the first step in your path to find a place, a home and a new family. Elsebeth is both beautiful and intelligent." *Strange this feeling of jealousy rising in me. If I feel like this, how is Codrin feeling about Alfrid?* "I know your tastes." She forced another unfelt smile onto her lips. *That was not the best idea*, she thought, seeing Codrin's fingers gripping the edge of the sill.

"I wouldn't mind knowing her better and telling you my opinion in a few months." Codrin's brow arched, though whether in agreement, disagreement, or some refined irony no one was sure.

"You will have all your life to know her."

"Perhaps as much as you wanted to know Bucur."

"I can't deny that we have a political situation too, but it's not the same."

"At least Bucur negotiated," Codrin shrugged.

"And I negotiated for you." Her voice toughened a little. "You will be a Duke. Elsebeth is a fine woman. Why don't you want to see the good part in this? Everything was negotiated to make a new start for you. And to keep peace."

"The same way the Circle negotiated a new start for you. You just replaced a raw rope around my neck with a silk one that can be pulled more gently. The effects are the same." Codrin touched his neck.

Saliné's smile lingered only because she forced it to stay on her lips. "I am not the Circle. I grew up without a father, and I know how hard it is. You know it too. I want my children to grow up *with* a father. I know that it's not easy for you, but please don't refuse this; I worked hard to make it happen, and the next ceremony is in six months. This is the only path which keeps everyone safe." Her voice became firmer and sharper with each word. "Alfrid agreed that you would take over Sittgart after the Winter Solstice party. Three and a half months pass fast." Saliné did not tell him how hard she had fought so he could leave Muniker after the party. Alfrid insisted on the end of the next summer.

"My impression is that my son will grow up with a dead father and an indifferent mother."

Pain and irritation growing inside her, Saliné closed her eyes and dug her nails in her palm, trying to find an answer, when the page entered.

"Your majesty, everything is ready for the ceremony. We should go now."

She gestured at him to leave the room, stood up abruptly and faced Codrin. "Our son *has* and *will* have both mother and father. Let's work together for that." For the first time since Codrin returned, she touched him, clasping his hand. She flexed it and took him by the arm. That brief touch stirred both, and she released his hand slowly while his thumb lingered on her skin. Both avoided looking into the other's eyes. "Let's go now." Saliné – and the Queen – spoke in that moment.

"Silence!" the Chamberlain of the court shouted and hit the ground three times with his staff. The Queen and the King entered soon after the third stroke and sat on their thrones.

"This is an important day." Alfrid smiled broadly, sweeping the court with his eyes, one thousand people looking at him. Waiting. The throne hall was full. Most of the Litvonian Dukes and Counts were there, and some representatives from Frankis. He had taken great care to ensure they were there. Couriers had gone back and forth for weeks. The Guilds of Muniker were present too, led by Movil, the Caravan's Inn keeper. They would all witness a great moment; the Seer would bend his knee to the King. "At the end of the ceremony, we will have a new Duke and five new Knights." He waved his hand at both Codrin and the Chamberlain.

"Sir Codrin, please step forward," the Chamberlain said, walking to a designated point, twenty paces in front of the King.

Followed by one thousand pairs of eyes, Codrin walked as slowly as he could toward the spot. A page came with a square red pillow and a small scepter. He placed them halfway between the King and Codrin. Like a breeze, a wave of whispers passed around the hall. They stirred Saliné's and Alfrid's attention. They came to Codrin too. Nothing was reflected on their faces, resembling some living statues of different stones and textures.

This will be the hardest thing, Saliné thought, forcing herself not to look at the pillow where Codrin would have to kneel in front of them and pay allegiance. She did not want to attract

Codrin's attention to it right now. He was looking up, above her and the King, his head slightly tilted on her side. *Please Codrin, you must accept, it's the only way to keep everybody safe.*

Codrin saw the pillow too, and like Saliné, he forced himself not to look at it. *They want to make me kneel. They told me nothing about that.*

Mimicking an old statue of the last Empress, Alfrid raised his left hand to enhance his speech. "We are here to express our gratitude to the man who saved my life and my kingdom. From today, Codrin will become the Duke of Sittgart and the Pillar of our kingdom. My queen and I have also agreed to the marriage between the Countess of Baia and Codrin. Their wedding will be announced soon, and Codrin will become part of the royal family. You all know my cousin, Elsebeth; she is as beautiful as she is intelligent."

The Chamberlain came and nodded to Codrin to advance to the red pillow, and he obeyed, moving slowly again, followed by the old man.

"Codrin, will you accept the titles of Duke of Sittgart and the Pillar of our kingdom?" the King asked, and Saliné smiled encouragingly, her eyes locked with Codrin's.

"Your offer honors me, Alfrid. As you all know, I am the Seer of the Realm, and I returned here after three years spent in ... deep solitude. There is a reason for my return from that far place: the nomads will invade Litvonia again. I was sent back by Fate to help you survive the next attack." His pause was punctuated by a heavy silence at first. A wave of, "Oh," followed and the collective thought that he had returned from death to save them again. Many women in the hall covered their mouths. "This is my fate, and the only title I am allowed to bear is Seer of the Realm. I have to decline your gracious offer. Elsebeth is a fine woman, and I thank you," he gestured at both Queen and King, "and her. We will make an official announcement about the marriage at the Winter Solstice." *You set a trap for me. If I pay allegiance to you, everybody will think me a traitor when I claim what was mine. If I live long enough to make the claim.*

Saliné's mouth was frozen, her lips still forming a smile that no longer existed. She wrenched her eyes away from Codrin, feeling that she would cry. Her face did not reflect anything of the storm inside her.

Slowly, Alfrid stood up, his face red and angry; he was about to speak, harsh words gathering behind his lips, when Movil whispered a few words to the three girls standing in front of him. "Seer!" their crystalline voices cried, and they were heard by everyone in the hall. There was a moment of silence, and more women cried the same, then more, then some men. When the cries ended, Movil bowed to the Seer, and all the people from the Guilds bowed too. Then the nobles.

Livid now, Alfrid kept his composure and waited for the moment to consume itself. What had happened weighed on him, and he decided to swallow his anger and choose his words with care. "I wanted you to be my Duke, but I will not force it on you. Chamberlain, bring the first man to receive his Knighthood."

Coming to Codrin's house, Saliné did not know what was stronger, her bitterness, her sadness, or her anger. "I worked hard for that solution, Codrin. You know that this is the only peaceful solution. I thought that you understood it. Is war the only thing you want?" Cernat and Dochia were silent witnesses to her question.

"Give Frankis and Cosmin back to me and stay here with your beloved husband and son. This is a peaceful solution too."

"An idea becomes a solution when it has a chance of being fulfilled," Cernat said. "Alfrid is now the King of Frankis, and he will not let it go. He has the power, Codrin, not you. The Circle and the Wanderers are on his side too."

"Then everything is about Saliné's power: kingdom, husband and son. You talk peaceful solution; you think power and land."

"What chance would you have?"

"Small, but did you consider it?"

"No," Saliné said, flatly. "I want no war. What I planned was the best solution I could see. Why was it so hard for you to accept? Going to Sittgart would have both freed you and given you status. A new life. A new family. You can't live in the past."

"How was I supposed to go there? In a coffin?"

"It's not a coffin that worried you, Codrin. You did not want to pay allegiance. You can't see yourself as anything less than a king. You endanger all of us with your pride, but mostly you put yourself in danger." Her brows drew down in thought, but for the first time, she lost control. Her voice was loud and cracked, and her hand gripped the edge of the table.

Codrin was equally angry. "I was born the son of a King. Against all odds, against the Cirlce and the Wanderers, I built the Frankis Kingdom. For both of us. It is not Alfrid's kingdom. Don't talk to me about danger when your husband only thinks about how to kill me. He is the danger, not me. And don't tell me that you are not aware of that. I will never kneel in front of the man who tried to assassinate me and stole my wife after I saved his life and his kingdom. I will never kneel in front of the woman who betrayed my son and me. Never." Without realizing it, Codrin used a sharp tone of voice he had not exercised for a long time, a time when he was still the King of Frankis.

Saliné stood up abruptly and left the room like a storm, pain and anger reflected in her eyes.

Cernat followed her calmly and glanced back at Codrin from the door. "I don't know where the path you have chosen will take you, Codrin, but I hope that you are sure of it."

"To the grave, perhaps, but at least it will be my path, not the one you've made for me."

Speaking to no one, Saliné went directly to her room and locked the door. She threw herself in her bed and embraced a pillow. And she cried. *Why, Codrin? Why did you refuse? It was the only way to keep everybody safe. I don't know what to do now. I don't know what Alfrid or Calista will do. I must find a way to help Codrin.* She jumped out of the bed and walked in circles around the room. She did not open the door when the maid called her for dinner and, at midnight, she was still walking. It did not help her.

"That was unnecessary," Dochia said to Codrin when they were alone.

"You should leave too."

"If you don't mind, and whether you mind, I will stay. At least you refused Alfrid in a diplomatic way. I wonder why you couldn't use the same diplomacy here. Well," she shrugged, "that's you now. You played that card well with the *return from death*, though you did not say it directly. Some girls almost fainted in the hall." She looked at Codrin, who just shrugged. "If wasn't a bad strategy, but you hurt Saliné, and she was well intentioned."

"She is no longer my wife."

"Finally, you observed that. She is Alfrid's wife now, and that can't be changed."

"What do you want, Dochia?"

"You need to apologize to Saliné. She leaned hard on Alfrid for that deal to protect you."

"Everything she tried to sell me suited Alfrid. Everything was just a game. The Duchy of Sittgart was just a ploy. It's a city without walls, a city that can't be defended. I asked for Arad. They pretended to not hear. So much for negotiations."

"It was Saliné who negotiated for you because you have no power. And did you really expect them to give you Arad?"

"What exactly she has negotiated for me?"

"Time. A family. A Duchy."

"Time for Alfrid to plan my assassination. He will not stop until he kills both my sons and me. That's the man you put on the throne; another Bucur to please the Circle and the Wanderers. Once I agreed to pay allegiance to him, I was as good as dead. Saliné would have looked the other way at my death, would have cried for Cosmin and forgotten him, and been relieved when the son I have with Mara was killed too. Alfrid requested embassies from Frankis to see my submission. That would have been my end."

"That would have gained you time."

"Once I paid allegiance, I would have been one of his many subjects. There is nothing to protect a subject from the will of an evil King. The Seer may have a chance. Your Wanderers and the Circle want me gone. Don't deny it; you know it's true. This charade with Alfrid had nothing to do with unifying the continent peacefully. It has everything to do with your own desire for power."

"The Wanderers and the Circle were created to unify the continent. There were hiccups, but they are finally doing it. I know that is unfair to you, but there is nothing personal in this. Frankis, Litvonia were unified peacefully. Silvania will follow soon."

"And Arenia? There is no peaceful way to take Arenia with Alfrid, and that war would be worse than the two I needed to take Litvonia and Silvania. I am the only one able to claim Arenia and have a chance of a peaceful takeover. Do you think that the Wanderers or the Circle will throw Alfrid under the carpet and put me in his place? No. They will suddenly forget about peace and find that war is the only solution."

"It. Doesn't. Matter. This is the political landscape now. You can complain to me, or to that tree there." Dochia pointed through the window. "It won't help. Alfrid rules in Muniker, and he has the Wanderers and the Circle behind them. You have no one."

"He rules nothing. Behind the scene, it's you who lead. The King Circle and the Wanderer Queen. That's what was all about from the beginning. You are on the other side," Codrin gestured toward the palace.

"We tried to help, but we can't force you."

"If you had helped, I would have been free now."

"That couldn't be allowed without the allegiance. Alfrid has tightened the guard around you," Dochia warned him and stood up. "Your situation is not improving."

"Perhaps," he said, coldly. "But at least I know now who I can count on." *Almost nobody.*

"Alfrid will not try something right now. People are still impressed by your speech. Try to not provoke him, though."

"Tell that to Saliné. Or to the Wanderers, your sisters; they came with the plan to kill me."

"Codrin, I have to leave Muniker for a while. Whatever you think of me, at least be careful. This is not your kingdom. It belongs to Alfrid and Saliné."

ᨒ

A few hours after the ceremony, Elsebeth found Codrin sitting on a bench in the park, an isolated place behind his house, which was not frequented by many people. Elbows on his knees, and head in hands, he was looking at the grass under his feet.

She stopped in front of him and placed her fingers under his chin to lift his head. "You look weak and lost for the mighty Seer of the Realm who made a thousand people bow to him in the throne hall."

"There are battles you win, and battles you lose."

"No one won today, and we will not know for a while if there were losses. And whose. That was between Alfrid and you. It seems that there was a game involving me too."

"I apologize if I have offended you. This is not my game, and I didn't want to play."

How many men would apologize to me in such a case? Perhaps Count Joachim. And Duke Homburg...? "Yet you played. What do you want to announce at the Winter Solstice?" She lifted his head further and played a hand through his hair.

"I don't know," he sighed.

"That would mean only one thing: you hope to leave Muniker by then." Elsebeth lowered her head and kissed him. It was a brief thing.

Slowly, Codrin pulled her on the bench next to him, and turned toward her. His face was inscrutable. His mouth was stretched with a hint of a smile. And his eyes were searching.

"Which girl do you see now? The one you kissed at your cousin's wedding, or the one you discovered in Baia?"

"Both, I think." His palm went up, his thumb caressing her cheekbone. "Your eyes are almost the same." *There is a darker shade in them. It comes from inside.*

"I am not talking about my looks."

"It's part of you. An eye is a mirror. It reveals things." He paused, still caressing her face, his eyes attentive. "Most of the time, I see the woman in Baia. At this moment, I see a small part from the past."

Feeling the need to free herself from his stare, Elsebeth closed her eyes, and she realized that she had not tried to use her Light on him, not even for a moment. "Codrin, I know that you still love Saliné, and that you like Ildeko. And I know that you are trying to avoid a political marriage. But ... if, for whatever reason, you have to, I hope to be the one. You already know that. I may be able to help you build a strong house, and you may be what I need to bring the little girl back. You did not know, or perhaps you knew, that the little girl felt in love at that wedding."

"And this woman?"

"This woman doesn't feel much in general, and it's mostly hate and pleasure. I am not trying to fool you. You don't have many friends here. Many admire you, and that may help in restraining Alfrid's hand, but it won't help you escape. I can't help much either, but I can send Ildeko and your son away, when the time comes. Of course, there is a catch in accepting my offer; you will reveal your plans to me."

Codrin looked at her, and a little grin flashed across his lips. "Thank you for thinking to help me."

Elsebeth smiled too and pushed him with her shoulder. "You were not King for nothing."

"There is a thing I need to tell you," Codrin said, hesitantly, and squeezed her shoulder gently. "You will have a child in ... less than two years. I don't know who the father will be."

"I can't have children." Elsebeth's voice went suddenly cold, and she pushed his hand away from her face. "At first, I thought that Irvath was the problem; he had no bastards from his mistresses. I tried other men, but it did not help. Our marriage is supposed to make your son, Ioan, Count of Baia. He was born there. I was planning to tell you that later."

"I know about your... issue, that's why I've told you. There will be a daughter in your life; it was a clear Vision. Let's walk." He patted her hair gently and stood up, then extended his hand to help her stand.

"Thank you," Elsebeth whispered. Her legs buckled, and she embraced him abruptly, struggling to hide her weakness. Gently, Codrin put his arm around her waist, to support her body. After a while, she leaned her head back until their eyes locked. "Few people have seen me like this, but I don't care." She smiled. It was a genuine smile, the first one in years.

"You are a strong woman. Why should you care?"

"If one looks weak, people will try to take advantage; you have no idea what sort of life I've had. It's not the same for you. You know...?" she said after a brief pause. "There is a thing that you should learn." Her green eyes twinkled as his eyebrows arched expectantly. "You should learn when a woman needs to be kissed. The moment has passed." She laughed and moved away from him. Slowly. Her legs were still weak.

They walked arm in arm, in a sort of studied silence, before Codrin said, "That part of the park is less frequented," pointing to their left.

"You must read the Manners Book of Muniker." Elsebeth turned her head toward him and smiled at his arched eyebrow again. "If you want to give the impression of a certain decision to be taken at the Winter Solstice, you have to parade me on your arm to the bystanders and be very warm to me. In half an hour, both Saliné and Alfrid will be informed. Do you?"

"Muniker." Codrin grimaced but changed their course toward the most crowded part of the park.

Chapter 24 - Codrin / Saliné

It was noon and hot, and most people were hiding inside, trying to escape the scorching sun. *The summers are hotter here*, Codrin thought. He was hiding too, on the small terrace of the second floor. *They are more like Arenia than Frankis*. Absently, he stretched his hand for the carafe of water. He drank a little and shook his head. *It's already warm*. He poured some water into his palm and splashed his face. *Better*. His mind turned back to his escape plans; with Vlad's help, they were slowly taking shape. He had not told Cernat anything because he wanted to take Cosmin with him. *Maybe I should tell him, but I don't want Saliné to know.* Just thinking her name hurt his mind, and he shook his head. *I did not think that this could be so painful. I need to separate myself from her. She has already done so. She has her own life, and I am not part of it. Everybody has betrayed me: my family, the Empress, the Wanderers. Saliné says that we can live in peace, Alfrid and me kissing each other. She doesn't understand what forces are behind Alfrid; how he was conditioned to think that he should have been the Seer of the Realm, not me. That Wanderer, Calista, is worse than Drusila. She even mocked the Empress. I wonder if she knows about that. They only saw the power of the Seer; they never saw the responsibility. The only time I used that power for me was to find Saliné, and the Empress knows it.*

Eyes closed, he tried to think about something more pleasant or about nothing. He could not, and hearing a bird, he opened his eyes, trying to find it. That brought some distraction. It was a small bird, and he forced himself to follow its swift jumps between the branches. At the corner of his eye, he caught some movement, far away, in the park. He tried to ignore it, until he saw the horse, the young boy on it, and the man behind. The man slapped the mare. Codrin jumped from his chair and went down the stairs, taking four or five steps at a time. In a few moments, he was out of the house, running like a storm.

Pain ran through the back leg of the mare where the man had knifed her, and she sprang, fear overriding her training. At first, Cosmin enjoyed the ride, but soon he found that his mare could no longer be controlled, and he leaned forward, clinging to her mane. He started to cry.

The Royal Council was close to its end when Saliné felt something uneasy, a heaviness filling her mind. Followed by Alfrid's inquisitive eyes, she went to the window and opened it, in need of air. It was hot, and that did not help her feel better. "Cosmin!" she cried, and turned away from the window, running out of the room. Alfrid followed her, followed by the councilors.

Codrin was running like he had never ran before, trying to anticipate the path of the frightened horse. There was at least a stroke of luck. Cosmin was leaning a bit to the left and that made the mare gallop a curve that brought her closer to Codrin. When the man knifed her, he took care that she was riding away from Codrin's house.

That day, Cernat had skipped the council, to receive an old friend. They were together on a terrace, under the shadow of some small, ornamental trees.

"I still remember your first visit in Litvonia," the man across the table said. "You were fourteen and fell in love with my sister, who was three years older."

"Yes, she liked to tease me," Cernat laughed. "I was one more admirer in her wake, and she had quite a long wake. I went home upset by her game. In two months, I found another great love."

"Cosmin!" Saliné cried, bursting out of the palace and, without thinking, Cernat jumped over the edge of the terrace and ran toward her. Alfrid came out of the palace a few moments later. Both vanished around the corner, and Cernat tried to run faster. After turning the corner, he could no longer run, but at least he could see. Cosmin was traversing the park in a kind of diagonal path, slightly curved. Saliné was running after him, followed at some distance by Alfrid, and Codrin was running from the opposite direction. Feeling his age, Cernat leaned against the wall, breathing hard.

Trying to keep pace with Saliné, Alfrid cursed the heat. He was not a fast runner and being a bit corpulent made him sweat hard. *If that little bastard doesn't die now, there will be no easy chance to eliminate Cosmin and his bloody father.*

Codrin started to think that he might have a chance; he was now only seventy paces away from the mare and they were on a collision course. *She must slow down*, he thought, seeing the small artificial hillock, twelve feet tall, made of mountain boulders. It hosted some alpine bushes with the white, perfumed flowers that Alfrid's grandmother liked so much. She had died five years ago, but her grandson kept her preferred flowers. Codrin arrived at the hillock almost at the same time as the horse. Instead of slowing, the mare stopped abruptly, and Cosmin flew over her head. Codrin jumped, stretching his hand to protect his son's head. He reached the ground head first. Pain exploded in his mind and darkness embraced him. Before he lost consciousness, he felt his palm touching something soft. *Cosmin.* His last thought.

Saliné, Alfrid and Cernat stretched on their toes, trying to see over the mare, which was hiding both Codrin and his son. *I think Codrin caught him*, Saliné thought, starting to run again, annoyed that the mare was still hiding them. *Fate, please save them both*, she pleaded.

Alfrid followed her, panting more and more, until he was no longer able to run. *If that man arrived in time. He jumped... This stupid mare is blocking the view, and I still must run through this heat.* Resigned, he bent, resting his hands on his knees, trying to catch his breath, his eyes fixed on Saliné, who had just arrived at the hillock.

Codrin woke up alone in his room. It was almost dark, and pain filled his head and body. *What happened?* He touched his head and felt the large bandage. It was wet. *Cosmin. Where is Cosmin? Did I save him? Why there is no one here?* He flexed his fingers, the memory of touching his son, when he jumped to save him, coming back. Half convinced that his son was safe, he tried to stand, but that only made him lose consciousness again. A few hours later, he woke up again, and spent the night half sleeping, half delirious until, close to the morning, he finally fell into a heavy sleep, the only thing which could heal and keep him alive.

༺༻

Cosmin's governess was crying when Saliné and Alfrid met her a day later. "I am sorry, your majesty," she cried, "I should not have let Cosmin go to the stable."

"It's not your fault," Saliné said, pain throbbing in her voice. "Tell me what happened."

"It was... It was... Sir Codrin came to take him for a ride. We were in the park."

"Codrin?" Saliné frowned.

"Yes, your majesty."

"Why did you not tell me as we agreed?"

"I sent the courier, your majesty. I sent him to you, but you were in the council, and the guards did not let him in. I know that it was not the usual day for riding, and I should have stopped him. I am sorry."

The courier was not allowed in the council. That was the unexpected thing Grandfather warned me about. I can't blame anyone for this. It was my failure. "It's not your fault," Saliné repeated and turned abruptly, leaving the room.

"Saliné," Alfrid said gently when he joined her. "There is more to this. I know it's hard for you, but you need to know everything. The guards at the gate between the park and the stable told me that Codrin went to talk to a woman just after they entered the park. He stayed there, with her, while Cosmin rode alone.

Countess Elsebeth told me the same. I am sorry, my love." Stunned, Saliné was not able to react in any way, and he embraced her gently. "Let me take you to your room." He placed an arm around her shoulders and guided her like an adult guides a child.

"I want to talk with them," she said, steeling herself, just before entering her suite.

Alfrid led her to the council room and called the guards and the stablemen there. They all confirmed what Alfrid had already told her and, when they finished, Alfrid finally convinced her to return in her suite. Then Elsebeth came too, and she confirmed Alfrid's version too.

How could Codrin do this to our son? Saliné asked bitterly leaning her head against the window.

Jara and Cernat arrived at Saliné's room a few minutes later.

"She wants to be alone," Alfrid said flatly, stopping them from entering. *She needs to think alone about what Codrin has done. You may put some bad thoughts in her mind.*

Cernat frowned, but he saw that Alfrid was blocking the way and decided to come back later. Her legs weak, Jara took his arm, and they both walked away, followed by Alfrid's wicked eyes.

Saliné came out from her room faster than Alfrid would have liked. "My love, you should rest more."

"I can't. I want to see my son."

"Maybe you should wait a bit longer."

She did not answer and, followed by Alfrid, she walked toward the funeral chamber, where the body of her son was laid. There were five women there, keeping the candles alight. "I want to be alone," Saliné said. The women went out quickly, but Alfrid tried to stay. "Alone," she repeated in a hoarse voice, and he left too.

Her legs buckled, and she had to lean on the wall for a few moments. Closing her eyes, she breathed deeply. Once. Slowly, as if her legs were made of lead, she moved closer to his small coffin. Her hand touched the hard wood, then crept forward. Before touching him, her hand retreated. "My poor son. My beautiful son. You have left me alone." Finally, she found the strength to touch him. "I will never hold you in my arms again. I will never kiss you again. I will never see your beautiful smile again. Why, Cosmin? Why did you have to ride? Why did you have to leave me?" She burst into a silent sob and kneeled in front of the coffin.

One hour later, Cernat found her still kneeling, leaning her brow against the coffin, holding Cosmin's small, cold hand in hers.

"Saliné," he said gently. "You need to sleep."

"I can't."

"At least let's find a chair." He went to the near wall, where many chairs were lined up, and brought two with him. Slowly, he raised her in his arms and seated her. Jara joined them too, and Alfrid, and they stayed there through the night, in total silence.

When the first rooster announced the coming of the day, ignoring her complaints, Cernat took Saliné by her arm. Alfrid joined them and both forced her to walk away, toward her room. They laid her in bed, and the healer gave her a glass of water. There was a potion mixed in the water, and she fell asleep in less than a minute.

Saliné woke up at noon and found Jara sleeping across the bed over her legs. There were two servants in the room too. She tried to move and that stirred and woke Jara up.

"You need to eat something," Jara said, nodding at the women, and one of them came with a small bowl of warm soup.

"I am not hungry. I will go to see him."

"Please," Jara said, and caught her arm in hers. "Just a small bowl, and then we will go together."

Saliné looked at her mother and saw her swollen eyes. Crying, she embraced her, leaning her head on her mother's shoulder. It took her a while to calm down, and like in the far past, when she was a still a small child, she let Jara feed her.

"I want to see him," Saliné repeated when she had finished the soup. She stood up like an old woman, and Jara took her right arm. They walked slowly and met Cernat when they were leaving the room. Without a word, he caught Saliné's left arm. None of them spoke while they walked, and none of them spoke when they entered the funeral chamber. As was the custom in Litvonia, five women were present there, watching the dead and keeping the candles alight.

This time, Saliné did not ask to remain alone. She just sat on a chair and stared at her son, and she did not leave until the afternoon came. Jara forced her to go and eat something. It was not permitted to eat in the funeral chamber.

"How is Codrin?" Saliné asked after finishing, her voice cold.

"He is wounded badly, but he is alive," Cernat said. "He broke his head, broke his left upper arm, and his left shoulder was dislocated."

"Does he know?"

"Not yet, he was unconscious. Perhaps it is time to go and see him."

"I don't want to see him," Saliné said bitterly, and told them everything that Alfrid had told her, and she had verified the day before, talking to each witness.

Both Jara and Cernat listened to her, though they already knew everything; Alfrid had taken care of that.

"Saliné what do you feel about this?" Cernat asked.

"What feelings can one have, losing a son?" she asked.

"I am sorry for not asking a better question," Cernat said gently. "I was thinking about everything we've heard about Codrin."

"You heard. Codrin was careless, but at least he tried to save my son."

"Maybe we should go and see him."

"Fine," she barked and stood up abruptly.

They found Codrin lying in bed, one arm tied in a sling around his neck. He was still trying to understand what had happened. Alfrid had come just an hour before and told him about Cosmin, but nothing about the story they had fed Saliné with. There was the pain, and a fog in his mind that did not help. Entering, even Saliné gasped, seeing how much his head was swollen. With the bandages, it looked like a large, red spotted ball.

"You know," Cernat said, seeing the pain reflected in his eyes. "I am sorry, Codrin. You did everything you could to save him."

"I told you that Alfrid would kill my son. You did not listen to me. You did nothing."

"Our son died because of your negligence, Codrin," Saliné said, coldly.

"What?" he growled, trying to stand, but he was too weak for that, and for a few long moments his vision blackened.

"Rosine, the governess told me that you came to take Cosmin from her. The men at the stable told me that you came with him to take his horse. And in the park..." Saliné breathed deeply, unable to continue. "In the park you let him alone to talk to a woman. Countess Elsebeth has confirmed that too. It's not my husband who killed Cosmin."

"I did not take him, and I was not..."

"We have the governess from Frankis, since the day my son was born. You chose her, and she is a woman both of us trust. Why would she lie to me?" Saliné cut in.

"Because your bloody husband coerced her to lie. And your bloody husband coerced the stablemen too, and that bloody Countess. It was his brother, Edric, who took Cosmin for a ride and left him alone. He even slapped the mare to scare her and make her gallop." *And Elsebeth... Ildeko and Ioan are in danger.*

"Edric is not in Muniker, and there are too many people who say the opposite, and they have never lied to me in the past. I know that you did not want this to happen, I know that you tried desperately to save him when you realized what happened – I saw you running, through the window, and I followed you in the park – and I know that you are upset too, and people in such state of mind try to absolve themselves, but it changes nothing. We've lost our son, the only link that still existed between us." She turned abruptly and left the room, leaving Codrin unable to speak.

Cernat walked quickly after her. "Saliné, please keep what Codrin said to yourself."

"Why? Codrin accused my husband of something *he* is guilty of. Our son died because of his negligence." *Yet it was Alfrid who gave the horse to my son. Against my wish.*

"Let's think that maybe what happened to Cosmin, and the wound, have affected Codrin badly. He is not himself right now. Let's not poison the atmosphere until he recovers, and we may be able to learn more about what happened."

"Fine, but if he repeats that accusation to me, I will not be able to cover him anymore."

"Thank you, Saliné," Cernat said gently and embraced her; then he returned into the house to find Codrin unconscious, and Jara on the edge of the bed, taking his pulse.

"He is alive," she said, relieved, and caressed Codrin's hand. "What do you think about the whole thing?"

"Codrin would not lie, but we have to take into consideration his mental state. I have never seen a head swollen like that. He may be affected in a strange way by the wounds, by grief, and his mind was not yet fully recovered from the wounds he suffered three years ago."

"I would like to talk with the governess."

"Yes, I was thinking that too."

Codrin woke up hearing the door creaking and opened his eyes on Countess Elsebeth. It was almost dark outside. "Get out," he snapped, and his vision blackened from the effort. When he was able to see again, she was sitting on the edge of his bed. *Ildeko and my son are in danger. How could I have trusted this woman?*

"We need to talk. Later. Now, stay calm." She placed a palm on his brow.

Codrin tried to stand and throw her out. Pressing a finger on his wounded shoulder, Elsebeth pinned him back in bed, and he gasped from the pain.

"I didn't want to hurt you. Listen to me and stay calm. You will feel even more pain, and you may faint again. Just don't move; you are a warrior, not a weeping girl." She frowned in concentration and her hand glowed white. The Light moved into his head from her palm. He gasped, then clamped his mouth shut. There was a burst of pain, his head was burning, and he fainted. Eyes closed, Elsebeth moved her palm around his head for more than ten minutes, feeling where the worst parts of his wounds were. *It's worse than I thought*, she thought, and forced more Light into her hand. After a while, she started to breathe heavily, and Codrin woke again. Then she stopped her hand, and the Light vanished. "How could you have hurt your head so badly? It's broken in three places."

"There were several stones where I hit the ground. You have the Light. What are you doing?"

"Healing you. Don't you feel anything mending in your head?" She smiled wryly. "I am tired. I need to sleep. The door is locked, so no one will disturb us." She lay beside him, over his healthy arm, but there was not much space between Codrin's body and the edge of the bed, and she leaned her head on his chest. "Don't let me fall," she whispered and fell asleep instantly.

Codrin said nothing, only nestled her body in the crook of his arm. From time to time, he bit his lip, forcing himself to stay awake. He tried to think, but the fog in his mind was even thicker than before, though the pain had subsided. There was a sort of drunkenness, making his mind numb and free of grief. And, perhaps, free to think. *Jara told me that Vio has the power to heal too. She is Aliana now... So many things have changed.*

Elsebeth woke up after an hour of heavy sleep. "It's always like this, when using the Light for healing," she said and yawned, stretching like a large cat. Her hand glowed white again, only a little, and she moved it slowly over his head. "It's better, but I still have a lot of work to do. Tomorrow, I don't have enough strength to use the Light right now and, anyway, you should not heal abruptly; it will raise questions, even if one can say that it was the Seer's work," she laughed briefly, then became serious again. "Codrin, no one else knows that I have the Light."

"I understand and thank you," he whispered. "But why did you tell that lie to Saliné?"

"Because my dear aunt Calista and cousin Edric asked me to, in the name of his majesty, my other cousin. There is no way to refuse a king. The price of this little affair was Passai, a rich city, a port on the Dunaris River, and almost as large as Baia. It fits well among my other possessions. I still can't be a Duchess, but that should be solved with my next marriage. Saliné hates you right now, so I doubt that you will receive the Duchy of Sittgart, or anything else. I like the confusion on your face." She laughed and touched his cheek. "I should not have laughed. I am sorry for your son."

"They killed him," Codrin said, taken by a sudden burst of anger.

"There was something strange about it, if not I wouldn't have received a city for my generous help. I would advise to keep those thoughts to yourself. Nobody will believe them, with so many witnesses against you. Such words against the King may affect your health even worse than the wound in your head."

Codrin tried to speak, then closed his mouth shut, and tried to use the Light to feel her mind, though he was still weak. It shocked him to feel a sort of amusement. Unfortunately, the Light could not reveal thoughts.

Elsebeth looked at him again. "Let me see the rest of you." She pulled his blanket away and gripped his healthy arm.

"I am naked," Codrin whispered, trying to pull back the blanket.

"It happens that I have seen a good number of naked men, and I can say that few of them had your body." She used the Light to lower Codrin's will, then moved her hand over his chest and ribs, tracing the bruises. Then she touched the large bluish lump on his hip. "This is ugly; the bone must be damaged, and I can't do anything now. Don't walk, or you may limp for the rest of your life." She placed her hand on Codrin's chest again and spread her fingers. "Did you eat?"

He grimaced, realizing how hungry he was, and Elsebeth went to the kitchen to bring food and feed him.

“I will come again tomorrow.” She stood up and went away. From the door, she turned her head back toward him. “Ioan and Ildeko are safe.”

Chapter 25 - Codrin / Saliné

"He was a nice young man," the King said, standing by the grave, "intelligent, pleasant, full of life, and I liked him. He so closely resembled my beloved wife. Our lives will be poorer without him. It's such a pity that Fate took Cosmin to her so early, and it's a pity that everything happened because of negligence but, at least, Saliné's son is now in a better world, and from there, he will look at us, and he will be content that we will always remember him. Let us pray for Cosmin."

Standing beside Alfrid, Saliné was dressed in black, only her porcelain face evident underneath the ample veils. She was so pale that the contrast was striking. There were dark circles under her eyes; evidence that she had not slept.

Codrin could barely walk, and came to the funeral by sheer will, leaning on a cane; no one came to help him. Looking around, he thought that this was a good moment to kill Alfrid. He could hear Saliné's faint sobs, and he forced himself to ignore them. The King's guards were two paces farther from him than Codrin. Slowly, he straightened, and leaned the cane against his leg. *I must not fall. And not fail.* He reached into his pocket for one of his throwing knives. Feeling his hand tremble slightly, Codrin tightened his hold on the blade. Before he could move further, Cernat gripped his elbow; despite his age, he was still a strong man.

"Don't move," Cernat whispered, without looking at him.

When the last prayer ended, Alfrid took Saliné by her arm and escorted her toward the palace. She wanted to stay longer at the grave, but she was too weak to oppose his will. At the last moment, he threw a veiled, amused stare at Codrin.

There were around fifty people gathered at the funeral meal, but no one tried to speak. Wanting to increase the pressure, Alfrid took care to spread the word that his wife wanted a silent ceremony.

His place set at one end of a secondary table, far from the royal family, Codrin took a few bites of *coliva*, a sort of boiled wheat mixed with sugar and cinnamon and decorated with raisins. It was an Arenian meal for the dead that had spread over the continent during the migration that had happened more than eight hundred years ago. Absently, he looked around and, involuntarily, his eyes locked with Saliné's. She pretended that it had not happened, and he returned to his meal. *Most people eat a lot more food at funerals than at weddings*, he thought, seeing the silent eaters around him. After one more spoon of coliva, he stood up and left the hall, walking hesitantly, followed by Alfrid's amused eyes.

Soon, Saliné stood up too, and Alfrid led her toward her room. "I want to be alone," she said when he tried to enter.

"I understand that, my dear, but you can always count on me." He embraced her and went to meet Calista in her secret room, in the left wing of the palace, which belonged to Edric. She had returned to Muniker, the night before Cosmin was killed, and only a few trusted people knew that she was there. The same day, Edric had left Muniker, and returned during the night, dressed like a common soldier. After he had negotiated with Elsebeth and the governess, he left again.

"It ended well. Saliné no longer cares about Codrin," Alfrid said.

It went wrong, Cosmin was not supposed to die. Things are more difficult now. They had planned a riding accident to wound the child and create a rift between Saliné and Codrin. Alfrid had his own plans, and Calista was too confident on her lead to consider that. She forgot that he had the Light too, and once he hoped to be the Seer of the Realm. His Light was diminished when Codrin became the Seer, but it did not vanish. "Your plan was good, Alfrid," Calista said. *But as always, you could not finish it by yourself. You are helpless. We had to negotiate everything with the governess and Elsebeth. And you have chosen that soldier who resembles Edric to kick Cosmin's horse.* She had a Vision about that man, but it came too late to change something. *You will be even more helpless from now on, as Saliné will start to dislike you. She will remember soon that you gave the horse to Cosmin against her will. I will take care of that, and I will make you pay for the game you played on Edric.* "But we still have work to do. Tomorrow, I will arrive in a hurry because I had a Vision about Cosmin's death. Just to keep Saliné tense."

"I don't want her harmed," Alfrid said.

Calista was consumed by her own thoughts; death had made everything more difficult and dangerous. Saliné was in despair, Codrin in rage. There was no more chance to work with him for the Realm now; she was convinced that he had seen the man who resembled Edric and kicked Cosmin's horse. There was no Vision to confirm that, but it was not needed; she just knew. Her careful made plans needed a swift reshuffle. She hated to act in haste. "Of course, I will not harm her, but after a few weeks of talking to her, she will be fully your woman." *She will be Edric's woman.* "I will erase any trace of Codrin from her mind, any trace of good she still remembers of him, and place only bad things there. Then we can get rid of him. In a few months, we take Silvania, and with three armies, you should be able to repel the nomad attack that will happen in four years." She paused, recalling one particular Vision. "We have another problem. There is a nomad raid happening right now; they will cross the border in two days. It's a small horde, just ten thousand men, and they will attack the area north of Ratisbau. You need to raise the army."

"I will send Edric."

"Alfrid, you have to go. You will have twenty thousand men and an easy victory. You need to show strength and leadership."

"I can't leave Saliné alone now."

"You must." Calista's voice became suddenly harsh, and she used her Light on Alfrid. "She will understand, and I will take care of her." *Edric will take care of her.*

Alfrid frowned but nodded.

In the morning, Cernat met Alfrid in the wide corridor to which most of the suites were attached, including the Royal Suite, and the small one where Cosmin had lived until a few days ago.

"Looking for something?" Alfrid asked.

"The governess, I want to ask her something."

"About Cosmin?" Alfrid asked, feigning indifference.

"There is nothing more to ask about my poor great-grandson. It's about someone in Arad. My memory is no longer what it was."

"Unfortunately, she can't help you. I sent her away this morning. Of course, I gave her a good amount of money for ending her service."

"Why?"

"Her presence was upsetting Saliné. She needs to forget. I know it will not be easy, but I am trying to help her as much as I can."

"Thank you, Alfrid, you are a sensible husband." Cernat returned to the suite shared with Jara and took her to see Codrin again.

"Do you still believe that story?" Codrin snapped, the moment they entered his room again. Pain went through his head, and he pressed a hand on his temple.

"Let's discuss this calmly," Cernat said, his voice flat. "We have eight witnesses. Four stablemen, we don't know if they can be trusted, two guards who also may or may not be trusted, Countess Elsebeth, who, I think can be trusted, and the governess, who, as Saliné said, is a woman all of us trust."

"I don't care how many witnesses you listen to. They are Alfrid's people, even the governess is his now. If you want to believe him, because it's he who is speaking through the witnesses' mouths, then leave me alone."

"We need to reconcile two positions that are opposed right now. Talking will harm no one," Cernat replied in a soothing voice, seeing Codrin's livid face. "You were wounded badly, trying to save your son. We all saw how hard you tried to save him. Are you sure that you remember everything properly?"

"Yes. I was on the terrace and saw what happened. Edric slapped the horse and returned to the stable. From my terrace, I had a good view of the gate between the stable and the park."

"I never was on your terrace. Would you mind if I go and see it?" Cernat asked gently, and Codrin nodded, his mouth set tight in a grim line. Cernat was the first to go out, then Jara.

Codrin said nothing when they returned, waiting for them to speak.

"You are right," Cernat finally said. "You have a good view from there."

"Then you believe me."

"For the moment, we only know that you have a good view of the gate from the terrace. In time, we may be able to learn more. We will let you rest now."

Codrin frowned and wanted to curse them and curse everything. *I need to calm myself.* He inhaled and exhaled slowly, seven times, the Assassin Cool for calming a troubled mind.

"Codrin," Cernat said, looking at him, and their eyes locked, "please keep everything to yourself. You may be upset by my words, but it's hard to convince anyone about your version when there are eight witnesses against you."

"Saliné already knows, so Alfrid will know soon."

"She promised to say nothing. And she will keep her word," he added before Codrin could protest. "We will go now. Eat, rest, and get well. You need it. One more thing; the fracture of your arm was clean, the bones did not shift, and it will heal well."

"I need to speak with Vlad." *And tell him about Elsebeth. I still don't know if I can trust her.*

"He is not allowed to visit you."

"The Pig King," Codrin whispered. "Tell Vlad that a woman he knows is in danger. I ... had a Vision about her."

"I will speak with him," Cernat said, and closed the door behind him.

The same morning, three soldiers escorted Rosine, Cosmin's governess, toward the gate. She knew none of them, and even with the pouch of gold she had received from Alfrid hanging heavy at her waist, she was scared.

"There is a carriage waiting for you at the southern gate, and your brother and sister are waiting for you at the crossroads," one man said.

"I thought they were still in the city, and we would leave together."

"Don't worry, we will escort you to meet them, and take care that nothing happens to you."

"Are you leaving the city too?"

"Yes, we have finished our ten-year period in the army, and we are going home."

I don't like this, she thought, *and I am an inconvenient witness. If only my brother had not done such a stupid thing. They blackmailed me with his and my sister's lives, and her three children too. I hope that her majesty will find the letter which I hid in her jewelry box. I explained everything there. And I hope that she will forgive me.* They were now closer to the gate, and fear mounted inside her. A flash came to Rosine, the moment Edric took her to the window to show her a man holding a knife to the throat of her six-year-old niece. That was the moment when she agreed to lie about who took Cosmin from her, even when she could not remember what happened. *They will kill me.*

One of the three soldiers escorting Rosine felt her uneasiness and took her by the arm. "The carriage is there." He pointed to a black vehicle that looked old and decrepit, about one hundred paces from them.

"I will go to clear our exit with the gate," another man said, and left them alone. He returned with the captain of the gate.

"Rosine, are you leaving?" Lisandru, who was the captain that day, asked, a gloomy smile on his lips. Her presence recalled Cosmin's death.

"Yes," she said, her voice sad, "there is nothing left for me here. My brother and sister are waiting for me at the crossroads."

When did they free her brother? "Are you sure that he is there?"

"Yes, that's what the men helping me said." Her foot touched a stone on the road, and she stumbled, nearly fell, her body leaning on Lisandru. "Help me," she whispered. "I apologize," she said loudly. "I don't feel well."

❧

"My dear Saliné," Calista said, "I am glad to see you again." The Wanderer embraced her and whispered gently, "I am sorry for Cosmin, he was such a nice child. This must be an awful time for you." They were on Saliné's terrace, the day after the burial, and Edric had come with the old woman. It was late in the evening, the sun no longer visible over the hills.

"Yes," Saliné nodded, fighting her tears, "he was a wonderful child."

"Saliné," Calista said, thoughtfully, "I returned here as fast as I could, because of some Visions I had, one of which was about Cosmin. It was too late, unfortunately, and I am sorry for that, but I was far from here. Fate sometimes mocks us with our Visions."

"How much did you see?" *If she confirms the truth about Codrin too...*

"Only the end. I did not see what happened before." *My dear girl, this game is more complicated than you think. There is no need to confirm, through an invented Vision, everything you already know. It would be too obvious and make me less credible.* "Let's forget about that, as we need to discuss things of great importance. I know that it's not the best time for you. Unfortunately, it can't wait. We may have a much worse problem here." She leaned toward Saliné and placed a palm over her hand.

"You know that I love you like the daughter I could never have, and I need you to listen to me very carefully. We have to talk about Codrin, and it will not be easy for you." She gently grasped Saliné's hand, who nodded, trying to keep her calm.

"Codrin is a great man, perhaps the greatest of our times but," Calista said, sadness filling her voice, "a more accurate way to describe him is that he *was* a great man. Once I heard that he had returned in such a strange way, there was something that stirred in me, a premonition, and I searched in some old books about a certain disease. Yes, I know that this will upset you, but it's a disease. It happens when a person loses too much blood, and the brain suffers. He recovered only partially, and I think that you already know that. Unfortunately, this disease has no cure. He seems well right now, but his memories will vanish completely at some point and, after that, they will never return, and he will probably die in one or two years. Even now, he may have episodes when he forgets who he is, or what he is doing. Like what happened when ... when your son had that accident, because this is what I think happened. Alfrid told me about the woman who kept him busy when ... the accident happened. Codrin was careless, the other Codrin; the one we knew in the past would never have done such a thing. You should not blame him, as he was not himself. He simply forgot who he was for a brief period, and Alfrid told me that he tried desperately to save Cosmin when his memory came back. As I said, don't blame Codrin; he needs your help."

It makes sense, Saliné thought. "Thank you, Calista. That explains everything. Codrin was careful with every child, and even more so with Cosmin."

"I am glad that you understand the situation. The worst thing now. There is a deep sense of guilt in Codrin right, and a sense of denial too. This is partly justified, as he lost his awareness for a while, and he doesn't remember leaving Cosmin to talk with that woman. He needs to blame someone and, I don't know for what reason, he has chosen Edric. Perhaps because he feels that Edric is like him, the strong man behind the throne. I heard it in my

Vision, but I don't know to whom he was speaking." She looked for a few moments at Saliné.

"No, he did not tell me," she whispered. *Yes, he did.*

I was expecting Codrin to be in a rage and demanding Edric's head. He seems able to contain his anger. That may complicate my plan a little. She thought again. *No, Saliné is covering him.* "I am sure that he will tell you at a certain point, and it's bad that he picked someone from your family to blame. We both know that Edric was not in Muniker that day. Now," she took a deep breath, "last night, on the road, I had another Vision." Calista took both Saliné's hands in hers, looking sadly at her. "You must be brave."

"Codrin will die," Saliné whispered.

"No." Calista shook her head, and gripped Saliné's hands stronger. "He will try to kill Arnis. He wants to punish your family for his own loss."

"Oh, no," Saliné breathed.

"You must be brave, Saliné," Edric said, embracing her gently from behind, "and we must be prepared."

"Do you know when it will happen?" Saliné asked, looking at Calista.

"Only that it will be at night. My Vision was limited."

Saliné pondered for a while before saying, "We must enhance the guard around Codrin's home during the night."

"Alfrid has already done that," Edric said. "And, discreetly, we have set more sentries during the day too. We can't move openly against him, at least not yet. He is still revered by our people for defeating the nomads, and the loss of ... Cosmin created more sympathy." Edric turned Saliné slowly and held her tight in his arms.

"Could you use the Light to learn more?" Saliné looked at Calista again.

"What I've told you will not happen tomorrow, perhaps in a month, or even later. For the moment, we only need to be careful. Each hour I try to learn more, but I have no other meaningful information right now." Calista stood up and walked away, leaving them alone.

"It's my leman day," Edric said. "Perhaps we can go to the park; it's a nice day. You have not slept for three nights."

"I can't," Saliné whispered. "I can't meet people; they will only stare at me and say kind words that are not true."

"Then we will stay on the terrace." Edric led her to the small sofa, seated her, and took her in his arms. Until midnight, he held her attention with many old stories, and he felt that, at times, she was not hearing his words; her mind was split between two worlds.

When Edric left, Saliné walked her way into her bedroom like an old woman. Closing the door behind her, she felt the need to lean against it. *Fate, what have I done that you punish me like this?* It took her a while to dare to walk again. Edric made her feel a little better, but she still could not sleep during the night, and in a semi-conscious state, her thoughts revolved around Calista's words: Codrin will try to kill Arnis. Deep in her mind, from time to time, Calista's words of praise for Codrin lingered too, and they did not seem truthful to her. In the morning, the dark circles around her eyes were even darker.

"Calista you were wonderful," Alfrid said cheerfully when she came from Saliné and told him everything. "I think that in a month we can finish what we started three years ago." He returned to the table with a bottle of vintage wine and two gold cups. "That medical book you found was very useful," he said, filling the cups, and giving one to his aunt. "Salute." He raised his own cup and drank it in one shot.

You are disgusting. It's one thing to plot a crime because of necessity, and something different to enjoy it. She had a second look at him. *Did he plan to kill Cosmin, or it was just an error of execution?* "Don't be silly, Alfrid. There is no such disease or old book; it was just convenient for us to create one. When you come back after defeating the nomads, I will give you a potion, which can erase one's memories." Calista looked at him, their eyes crossed and Alfrid burst into laughter. *You are disgusting.* "You just need to pour a few drops in his wine and bring Saliné to see him, one hour later."

"You are really the most cunning woman I ever knew. Now I must see my soldiers, then Saliné. Tomorrow morning, I will leave for Ratisbau."

"It's better to see her in the morning. Saliné needs some solitude right now." *She needs Edric.*

For more than two hours, Codrin sat at the table, a glass of wine untouched in his hand. The wound on his hip had worsened after going to the funeral. The upper half of his leg was now black and swollen, and he could barely walk a few steps with a cane. His son was gone and buried, and the pain was too strong inside him. Caught in his grief, for a few moments, he did not acknowledge the translucent figure seated across the table, staring at him. He raised the glass to drink, and finally eyed the Last Empress. Deliberately, he ignored her and sipped some wine.

"I am sorry for your loss," the Empress said.

"Why? Your plans worked well. You planned this from the moment you sent me to defend the noble King of Litvonia against the nomads."

"You did not defend Alfrid; you defended the Realm. You were the Seer. It was your duty."

"And you took from me the power of the Seer, arranged for me to be killed and gave my wife to the noble King of Litvonia. How innocently you talked about my duty that day, knowing that I would be killed by your Wanderer tools, three days later. Now you have had my son killed. In the long term, he was a danger to your plans. So am I, so you are now planning my death again."

"I never planned to kill you, Codrin."

"Of course not. I just dreamed that your Wanderers advised Alfrid to kill me and take my wife. In the past, you warned me about some things that would happen. This time, you let me die, and you let my son die. Like a tool, I was used and discarded, at your convenience."

"The Wanderers saw an opportunity to unify the kingdoms, and they took it. That was a good political move. There was no war, everything was peaceful. I can't condemn them, and I saw no reason to interfere. Killing a single man to obtain such a high goal *is* a noble thing. You also planned to unify the continent through *war* and that meant killing a lot of people. What happened looks unjust to you, and it is, but it's just for the many who will not die in the wars you planned for the same thing."

"What threat was my son to your great plans, Empress?"

"They were not my plans, and he was no threat. Not now. He could have become one in the future, and you know it."

"Ah, that's why you killed him, for a better future."

"I don't kill people," she repeated. "I killed a long time ago, when I still lived, but not now."

"This is why you created the Wanderers, to kill children? And why did you let them spread the lie that I killed my son?"

"You are not a child. You must defend yourself; I can't save everybody. Not all the Wanderers are kind women, and there is no need for them to be. At times, tough decisions are needed, if you want to build something. You had your share of such decisions too, in the past, and people died. There is no plan or organization without failures, but we now have two unified kingdoms, and Silvania will follow soon."

"What kind of Empire will you build with a man like Alfrid?"

"He is not a weak man and has Saliné and Edric on his side. She knows how to set the course right, if he goes wrong, and she will. She has done a lot of good things, some of them being your ideas, so you had a role to play too. Your part is not yet finished."

"There is no honor in your new Empire. It's rotten from start, and it will crumble from inside faster than the other one." Codrin closed his eyes, and his hand tensed until the glass broke between his fingers. The shards cut through his skin, and wine and blood spilled over the table. There was no way to distinguish one from the other. He ignored what happened, and he ignored the pain in his hand. A thin ribbon of blood ran down his face; one of the wounds on his head had just reopened. He ignored that too. "And I will never play your roles again, Empress," he said icily. "I know that I will die soon, but I will take your King with me. Perhaps you will be able to stop me, but perhaps you won't. Now, leave me alone and build your Empire over mine and my child's bodies." His voice was loud and cracked; in his inner world, which was not mimicking reality too well; things looked blurred, but sounds were accurate.

"There is too much anger boiling in you. I don't blame you for that, but decisions made in such a state are usually poor."

"I don't care."

"You still have two sons. They need their father."

"Alfrid will not stop until he kills the son I have with Mara. You know it. And you have accepted it. Ioan will perhaps escape because only Vlad and Elsebeth know that he is mine, if you don't tell your Alfrid about him, of course. Or Elsebeth will not betray me again. Killing Alfrid will help my sons survive, and I will do it. I don't care that I will die, and I don't care about your wishes anymore. My only disappointment is that I can't kill a few Wanderers too."

"Which Wanderers? The ones who saved you in the forest?"

"They did not save me; they only took me away, so my scouts could not find me. And they erased my memories. I was supposed to recover them, in seven years, just in time to save your noble King from the nomads again. I am sorry to disappoint you and come back earlier."

"Why should I be disappointed? They were not my plans, and plans are made and changed, anyway – they are living things. I am only an arbiter, not a real player. My time is as limited as yours, and I can't be everywhere. That day, Alfrid's soldiers were closer to you than your scouts, and all your guards were already dead. You were alone and badly wounded. Thais' motivations did not match yours, but those two Wanderers disobeyed their orders to save you, and chose to make their own plan, which half failed, as you recovered your memories four years early. You are here because of their actions. Like it or not, you still have a role to play."

Suddenly, Codrin felt his mind wandering, and he recalled a Vision. "I should have guessed," he whispered. "The next nomad invasion will come earlier than your Wanderers are thinking. That's why I recovered my memories earlier." *They will come next year...* After his previous vehemence, his voice was now surprisingly bland. Unknown to him, the grief and everything that had happed after his son's death, even this visit of the Empress, concurred to restore what was still affected by Thais's potion. Almost everything; but nothing essential was missing.

"Do you know when the nomads will come again?" The Empress also felt the invasion was coming earlier, but there were not enough clues.

"You have an army of Wanderers to look into the future. This time don't count on me, Empress. You have thrown your lot in with Alfrid. Let's hope that you have chosen right."

"I chose nothing." She looked at him, and their eyes locked. They stayed like this for more than a minute. In the end, Codrin disengaged, and looked away. "For the people in Frankis, you are still the Seer of the Realm, and more so for those in Litvonia. In Muniker, they all think that the Seer returned from death to save them from the nomads again. You made them believe that. You own to them. A Seer may lose his powers, but he will always be the Pillar of the Realm. It's his duty to save the people."

"Ah, Codrin, the Great Seer, coming back from death. Empty words to make me feel proud. Your charm is no longer working, Empress. Three years ago, you made your decision. You must learn to live with your decisions. We all must. I've made mine. You will know it soon. If you don't mind, I want to be alone with the memory of my son." He closed his eyes and leaned his head back against the chair.

"It's good to learn that you can make decisions again, perhaps it's the right time to recover from your self-indulged pity. Prepare yourself. The burden of the Seer is for life. You will learn that soon."

Mechanically, Codrin raised his hand, to sip some more wine. When his eyes moved away from his empty, bloodied hand, he found an empty chair across the table. He felt suddenly weak and leaned his head on the table. The world around him became black.

Chapter 26 – Codrin / Saliné / Elsebeth

Alfrid left Muniker at noon. Saliné did not leave her room. She did not let him enter either. They did not meet. When Alfrid was gone, she opened the door and let Jara in with some food. Close to midnight, Saliné reached over and unlatched the window. It was made of stained glass, etched wonderfully with the image of a blue sky and the sun in the right upper corner. She looked at the glass, seeing nothing. That was her fifth night almost without sleep. The breeze came in, and through the window she let herself be embraced by the gentle light of the full moon. Absently, her gaze moved slightly, without interest, from where she'd had it focused for several minutes, to another point that she would ignore for a few more minutes. She heard the door opening, and turned her head to see Edric coming in. She said nothing and turned her head back to the window.

Edric embraced her from behind, and they stood like that for a while. She felt calmer in his strong arms. "Saliné, you need to sleep."

"I can't," she said edgily, and let him turn her until they were face to face. A few tears ran down her face, and he traced them gently with a finger. She swallowed hard and closed her eyes.

"Cry," Edric said, "it will help you feel better."

"I can only cry," she sobbed. "There is nothing else I can do for my poor son."

"Tomorrow, I will take you for a walk in the garden. It's my leman day. You must come. Please." He smiled and lifted her head a little, then kissed her lips, which were wet from her tears. Saliné cried even more, but she laced her arms around his neck, comforted by his touch. His mouth and hands became more demanding, and she abandoned herself to him. "You have to sleep," he said again, when they tried to recover their breath, and he started to undress her slowly.

"I can't," she said, but she did nothing to stop him. Absently, she found herself lying in bed, Edric close to her. Saliné made love in a strange way that night, keeping her arms above her head, as if they were pinned on the bed. Her head moved left and right, in Edric's slow rhythm.

When their hearts calmed, Edric took her in his arms, and she instantly fell asleep, leaning on his chest. She would wake up the next day in the afternoon.

They became lovers again, but Alfrid returned after an absence of only two weeks, the nomads were already gone when he reached Ratisbau. Riding from dawn to nightfall, Edric's courier came with the news.

It was their last night together before Alfrid arrived, and they were lying on the tiger fur in front of the fireplace. The flames were playing gently on their naked skin; Edric's hand moving gently along her back. "Would you consider me as your lointain lover?" he asked.

Eyes closed, Saliné let her mind wander for a while. *How the world has changed with the death of a child.* She forced herself to ignore the pain in her heart; there were two children to think about, and she rubbed her belly, trying to get some comfort from her unborn daughter. *I will always love him, but I must let Codrin go.* A lone tear ran down her face, and she bit her lip. *In mid-autumn when no war can start. We will have six months to negotiate a sort of common future, and I need to control Edric.* "Yes, Edric." *The Silvanian King is ill and, at his death, Silvania will come to us. I don't think that his illness is natural. The Circle and the Wanderers are hastening everything because Codrin returned when everybody had thought him dead. Until spring, I hope Codrin will understand what forces are working to recreate the Empire. It's not fair to him, but when was life fair? When Father was killed? When I lost Codrin? When I lost my son? Life is never fair.* "We will become lointain lovers at the end of spring." Her voice trembled a little.

"I understand." Edric stroked her hair and embraced her tighter; the announcement could be done only nine months after Cosmin's death. "And until then?"

I feel better now, and Edric has helped me recover. Then why do I trust Edric less than before? I will allow him once a week until my pregnancy... "During our leman days, things will continue as they are now, with the necessary discretion, and we will have only one leman day each week." *I no longer trust Codrin as before; he let my son die. I can't trust Alfrid; he gave my son that horse against my will. Who can I trust if even Edric can't be trusted? Calista? Why should I trust a Wanderer after everything that happened in Frankis?* "Yesterday, I learned that Alfrid's secretary is watching us."

"He is a suspicious man, even when I am always leaving the castle in the evening before coming to you. If you agree, I am planning to set a sort of trap."

"You want to involve another woman."

"That's why I am asking you. The Duchess of Henver. She is known for not respecting the rules."

I am talking with my lover to conceal our liaison behind another woman. "And her husband is known for his assassins." *I can control Alfrid, but Edric is like Codrin. I never tried to control Codrin; we were a sort of ... twin souls. I* will *control Edric.*

For ten days, Codrin stayed mostly alone, only the healer and the maids with the food visiting him. Saliné did not want to see him. Waiting for Saliné to recover, Jara fought hard to hide her illness, but now she was restricted to her bed, and Cernat stayed with her. Vlad and the other men from Frankis were with Alfrid, chasing the nomads.

Four days before Alfrid's return, Elsebeth entered his room, late in the evening, and Codrin did not know if he should curse or thank her. He had slowly realized that the wounds on his head were too hard for a common healer to mend. He would have survived, perhaps, but his mind would have been affected. An experience he did not want to repeat.

"Ah," Elsebeth laughed, feeling his indecision, "you wonder how to push me away. But you are limping too much. Let me see you." She sat on the edge of his bed, and their eyes met. "Don't look so hard." This time she spoke gently, and her hand started to glow white. She moved it for a while over the bandage around his head and kept it one minute on his most severe wound. "It feels well; I don't think that you need that bandage anymore, but let the healer do what he wants. Now let's see your shoulder." Her hand moved again. "It's going well, and the arm had a clean fracture." She pulled the blanket from his body and felt some resistance from him. "I already saw you naked and praised your body. That looks bad." She grimaced, touching the lump on his hip; it was larger, and half of his leg was dark blue. "I told you not to walk."

"I didn't. Only at the funeral..." Remembering, Codrin lost his voice and, eyes closed, he stayed silent.

"This will need a lot of Light. I am a little tired, but I will stay here overnight. Move to the other side of the bed, so I can sleep well after trying to heal you." Elsebeth waited for him to move, then undressed. She laughed when Codrin looked away from her. "Am I so ugly? Shall I weep?" She blew out two of the three candles in the chandelier at the head of the bed, then lay beside him, and covered them both with the blanket. "Let me feel you; the better I know your body, the easier it is to heal you." She stroked his hair, moved her fingers over his face, touching his nose and lips, then went down on his neck and chest.

"Is this really necessary?" Codrin asked when her hand slipped down his navel.

"Yes, now be quiet, I have to concentrate." Her hand moved further down, until Codrin's body arched, and his jaw tightened. His heart was beating faster against his will. She kissed him on his mouth. He did not move. He could have withdrawn, he thought afterward, could have turned his head. He did not respond, yet he did not dislike it. She didn't seem to care. Appeared to find it amusing that he felt rigid and perhaps weak.

In the flickering light, he saw her smile, even her perfect teeth. A wonderful woman, like pale ivory, resembling those knives made for cutting paper in Ately, where they crafted things that could work well on both paper and flesh. There was a scent on her. He could sense it, and an undercurrent of intoxication went through him. Codrin knew the perfume, mountain meadows and southern gardens. He could not recall its name.

"The reaction in your body is encouraging," she said, and looked at him, amused and inquiring. "It's a sign of healing, and that I am not that ugly. Perhaps I will not weep this night." She laughed at Codrin's embarrassment, then leaned her head on his shoulder, placing her left hand behind his neck. Her hands glowed even more, and the sudden burn made Codrin arch while his head turned left and right. The burning moved into his bones and went up through his spine. It reached the head, and his mind darkened.

When Codrin woke up, the pain in his body was bearable, and his hip felt lighter. Elsebeth was sleeping. *What kind of woman is Elsebeth?* He hated her for what she had told Saliné, and for what she had done to Ildeko in the past. He was in her debt for healing him, and he had seen the effort that had taken her. She was now sheltering Ioan and Ildeko. *Elsebeth may sell them, the same way she sold me. I need to talk with Vlad when he returns. What kind of woman is Elsebeth?* He fell asleep before he could find an acceptable answer. He woke up late. Elsebeth was already dressed and eating at his table.

"The maids came with the food. They were surprised to find me here, but I told them that I came early in the morning. Fortunately, the night guards were already gone. You need to eat." She gestured at the food. "There is not much left, I was starving."

"How are Ioan and Ildeko?"

"In a good state. I was away for ten days, but Vlad left three of his own guards to watch them. I had to be in Baia with Horwath, during the nomad raids. My Uber Captain, you know him. Most of my dear husband's soldiers, my soldiers now, are cowards. They would have opened the gates of the city, begging for mercy, instead of fighting. Our walls are not impressive." She shrugged.

"Would you consider telling Saliné the real story?" Codrin asked, and felt that it was a stupid question, even before he'd finished.

"But I told her the *real* story. How can I change it now? I will lose a rich city, and I may have an unfortunate accident. You were King once; you should know how these things work. I heard that you used the gallows for people you did not like."

"You've heard wrong; I never killed people without judgment. And gallows were only for assassins, rapists and traitors."

"And what do you think Alfrid would consider me if I changed my testimony, a trusted cousin or a traitor? Come and eat, I want to see how you are moving."

Codrin shrugged and stood up naked, then limped toward the chair where his clothes were hanging.

"Come toward me." Elsebeth flexed her forefinger, and he shrugged again, then walked toward her. She touched his hip, her hand glowing white. "It feels better, but don't force your luck. If you have a cane, use it, even in the house. Now, let me dress you, it must be hard with only one hand." She pointed at the cast on his arm.

"I can manage." Codrin shook his head, but she pulled the clothes from his hand and helped him to dress.

"It's not really my business, but I don't think that your life in Muniker will be easier from now on. When Vlad returns, make plans to send Ildeko away. I will help him, without asking if you want to escape too; it seems that you don't trust me much. Don't worry, I don't feel offended." *Or perhaps just a little; you should understand that I had no choice in what I told Saliné*. "This would be my second gift to you. At a certain point, I will ask for something in return."

"What do you have in mind?"

"I will tell you at the proper time." *You will be the gift, Codrin. I think that you already know.* Her eyebrows arched swiftly, and the tone changed – again. "I have to leave now. Don't walk." She pointed at his hip.

In the evening, Elsebeth did not need to use much Light on Codrin, only his hip and fracture still needed it. She was lying beside him in bed now, leaning on her elbow, keeping her hand on his broken arm. "I must heal it in four days. You need to start training, though you must keep the cast on. I can't see anything in your future, but I have a bad feeling." Now and then, her hand glowed white, and moved slowly over his body. After the first healing, Elsebeth found that she had gained some control over Codrin with her Light.

"I need to leave Muniker," Codrin said, suddenly.

"You've started to trust me," she chuckled.

"As much as I can trust Alfrid's cousin."

"At night, there is no way to leave the house; there are five guards at the door, and twenty on the walls of the park. The barracks of the Palace Guard is close. There are three hundred soldiers there. During the day, it's even worse. So, how do you want to leave?"

"I was planning to run with ... my son, during a riding session." Codrin swallowed hard. "I need to find something else. This time, it must be at night. I was thinking to put some sleeping potion in a bottle of wine and give it to the guards, but one or two of them may fall asleep earlier, and the others would raise the alarm."

"Poison?"

"It would be the same thing, and I prefer not to use it. I can kill the man in my way, but not with poison."

"Touching. Yesterday, I met an old man, close to his eighties, perhaps. A long while ago, he worked in this house. A lady was kept here, he could not remember for what reason. But he remembered..." Elsebeth paused. Their eyes locked, and she smiled at his frown. "He remembered that there was a small, hidden lover's room in the attic. It seems that the lady was still young and had needs to be fulfilled."

"Hidden..." Codrin said, thoughtfully. "There must be an entrance somewhere."

"In this room." Elsebeth pointed at the ceiling, a point above the door.

"Do you mind if I look now?" Codrin asked.

"No." Elsebeth stood up and walked toward the heavy table. "Let's hope that we can carry it, together. You must not force your hip." Codrin grimaced a little, but they were able to move the table, and placed it in front of the door. "I will climb the table," she said. "One needs two arms to check the ceiling. Just keep me safe, I wouldn't like to fall from there." She went up on the table and raised her hands until she was able to touch the wood above. Unwillingly, Codrin had a good look at Elsebeth's naked body. She tapped the wood with a knuckle. The sound was muffled and then it was not, and she knocked faster, discovering a rectangle, two feet long and one wide. She pressed up, but the wood did not move. "It's here, but I can't find how to open it, and I am freezing."

"You have to warm me." Shivering, Elsebeth went under the blanket. Hesitantly, Codrin embraced her with his healthy arm, pulling her against him. "What are you thinking about?" she asked, in a mischievous voice.

Your naked body, and you know that. "It's hard to think much right now, but there must be a way for the man to reach the hidden room, from outside. I have walked a thousand times around the house, trying to find something. I found nothing, and I could not find the entry here either. But I did not look too hard at the ceiling."

"It's always easy to distract a man, and you feel very distracted." She chuckled, then her face went serious again. "I don't know how much time you have; Alfrid came back today. It was a glorious return; hearing that he was leading the army, the nomads ran back over the border. He will pay at least ten troubadours to praise his great victory."

Elsebeth soon fell asleep. Codrin could not. He thought about some fragments of his life. The moment when they met for the first time at his cousin's wedding; her behavior when they met in Baia. Until a month ago, he considered her treacherous, violent and without character. But she had healed him, sheltered Ildeko, and now there was this thing with the hidden room. *She lied to Saliné. Is she just setting a trap for me?* He let his mind into the Light. It came back empty. *She has the Light, and there must be a reason for her to appear in my life again. I feel that she still has a role to play. And her daughter... Her daughter is important. I wish I knew more,* he thought before falling asleep too.

A day later, Elsebeth entered just minutes before the night guards came to close the main door. Codrin was almost asleep when she sneaked into his bed. Saying nothing, she leaned on him, then placed her glowing hands on his body.

"Today, you should be almost healed." Elsebeth let the Light into him, her hands moving over his skin. It did not take long, and she did not feel tired. "I think that it's done, but I will check again in the morning. You still must keep the cast and the bandage on your head; I've left a bit of skin unhealed. Did you find out anything about the room?"

"Yes."

"Do you have a plan for escape?"

"No."

"You still don't trust me. Tomorrow, Ildeko and her family will leave my house and Muniker. Vlad will take care of them. I don't know where he will send them. I did not ask."

"Thank you, Elsebeth." Codrin felt embarrassed by his mistrust and, unconsciously, stroked her hair.

She raised her head until their eyes met. "What do you see now? The girl at your cousin's wedding, or the woman from Baia?"

"I think that I start to see the woman who that girl should have become."

There was a sudden lump in Elsebeth's throat, and she stared silently at him. Her hand gripped his shoulder, and she did not realize that her nails were digging into his skin. Codrin felt both his and her pain and, unable to find the right words, pulled her head slowly down and pressed his mouth on hers.

"Well," Elsebeth said finally, "you've learned when a woman needs to be kissed."

"Would you tell me what happened to that girl?"

Elsebeth closed her eyes and opened them filled with anger. She moved abruptly, trying to leave. She could not; Codrin had anticipated her reaction, and his arm was tight around her waist. "Let me go," Elsebeth hissed, and slapped him. She slapped him again and again until his arm moved up to her shoulders and pressed her against his body. She wrestled hard to escape. Surprised by her strength, Codrin used his wounded arm, finding that he could move it easily. He raised his knee just before her knee could go into his groin. His arm tightened hard around her waist until she gasped from pain and lack of air. Let me go," she breathed. "I won't hit you again, just let me go."

"I won't. Elsebeth, listen to me, you need this." Slowly, Codrin lessened the grip of one arm, and stroked her hair until she went still. "I think that no one knows what happened, not even your parents. Now, tell me. You have to let it go."

That old, black fear mounted in her again, and there was a sudden need for relief. And hope that this man, who the little girl loved a long time ago, could help. Her breath was ragged, and her voice was hesitant and edgy. "They kidnapped me for three months." She dug her nails into Codrin's skin and paused for more breath. "Two men and a woman, siblings. The Duke's children. They used me in every possible way. So many dirty things..." Elsebeth's voice faltered, and she sobbed silently, crying for the first time in many years. "I was fifteen. A month later, I had a miscarriage and was bedridden for two more months. I barely escaped alive. Perhaps it would have been better if I died."

Miscarriage after rape, bedridden, and fighting for her life. Like Saliné... She was sixteen when Bucur... "It was not your fault, Elsebeth." He could feel her warm tears falling on his chest. He could remember Saliné's fight for her life in the smallest detail. It made him want to soothe Elsebeth even more. It stirred his desire and, and feeling her body relaxing slowly, he kept her tight in his arm, unwilling to disturb her.

There were a few minutes of silence until she found her voice again. "My father exiled me because of the pregnancy. After that, I did only bad things, but at least I did not kill anyone."

Bad things... This is the difference between you and Saliné, but she had the support of her family. And mine. Now, I am more like Elsebeth. Lost everything in my life. For the second time. "You were not yourself. I am not absolving you. But now, you have started to be yourself. You must be yourself, Elsebeth. You deserve to be yourself." Running his hand through her hair, Codrin kissed her tears. He tasted salt, then her lips.

Elsebeth drew back for breath, then lowered her head again. She bit at the corner of his lip, and whispered in his ear, "Today, you no longer have that lame excuse that your hip is hurting." There was soft laughter, the breath warm against his skin. It was scented with mint.

"The cast is impairing my movement," Codrin said in a serious voice. In the half-darkness he tried to see her eyes but could discern only her face and the curtain of her heavy hair.

"Men are so weak these days." Elsebeth laughed and rose over his body.

Codrin let himself be taken by the slow rhythm of her and lifted one hand to trace the outline of her face in the low light, then her neck, sliding further down.

In the morning of their third night together, Elsebeth was awake, looking through the window at the pink sky in the east. *The guards will leave soon. I have bad feelings.* Leaning her forehead on the cold window, she waited until movement could be seen outside, and walked toward Codrin. Sitting on the edge of the bed, she stroked his hair. *However much I wish it, you were not meant for me, yet you were my gift. You were right about my daughter. Our daughter.* She laughed quietly and recalled that pleasant Vision; her daughter would be born in nine months. "Codrin." She shook him gently. "I have to leave; the maids will come soon. I can't see your future, but death will visit this place. And something wicked... I don't know exactly what. Be careful." She had a last look at him and stood up. "At noon, I will leave Muniker. Calista will want to see Ioan again, and I can't explain to her why I sent him away."

"Thank you, Elsebeth." Codrin stood up and embraced her.

"The future feels like trouble; you feel like trouble. I don't know if we will see each other again. I have something to tell you. Nothing unpleasant." She pulled abruptly from his arms and went away. From the doorway, she turned back to look at him, just before closing the door. "That girl you met at the wedding... She is back. Thank you, Codrin." *The girl who loves you.* Elsebeth closed the door fast, and leaned against it, a few tears running down her face. She let her Light search into the future, but nothing came to her, only a bad feeling from the past. She shook her head, trying to avoid the unwanted memories. They clung stubbornly to her, and she gasped, a moment of sudden understanding: The Light came to her in those ugly months when she was kidnapped. *Was there any reason for this? Of course there was, but what? And what need was there for so much suffering? Or was it the suffering that brought the gift of Light to me?* She straightened and walked out of the house at a brisk pace. *I will have a daughter. The next Countess of Baia. Or Duchess.*

Calista's potion was similar to what Thais had used on Codrin, but much weaker, able to obliterate memories for only a few hours or weeks, depending on concentration. Five drops were placed in Codrin's wine by one of Alfrid's trusted servants, pretending to work in the Royal Cellar.

"I wish we could use more than five drops; that would have erased his memories completely," Alfrid said to Calista when the servant returned with the news that Codrin had drank two glasses of wine.

"Alfrid, you never think of consequences. We need to test the potion first; I never used it until now. Too much may kill him, and we don't want people to accuse you of poisoning the ... Seer. Did you find out who is spreading this story that he still is the Seer of the Realm, and that the nomads will attack Muniker next year?"

"Everybody," Alfrid shrugged. "People saw him coming to Muniker, and many thought that he came back from the dead because the nomads will attack us soon. They think soon means next year. It seems difficult do to stop this."

"You can't fight against a legend." Calista shook her head and grimaced. "Don't interfere, let them talk; it will stop after a while. At worst, they will stop this nonsense next year when the invasion doesn't happen. What did you tell Saliné?"

"Just that we need to evaluate Codrin's health and talk about his plans. I let her think that it is about his plans for Arnis, even when I did not use my son's name."

"You should go now; the effect of the potion will start soon. It's better if you arrive before that, so Saliné sees the whole transition."

Codrin felt a little dizzy when they arrived and sat at the table. His room had never been so crowded. Alfrid brought his brother with him, and Saliné brought both Jara and Cernat.

"How do you feel?" Alfrid asked as he sat. He pointed at Codrin's bandaged head.

"It could be better."

"We need to talk about your future in Muniker."

Codrin's dizziness increased abruptly, and a black fog covered his eyes. He moaned and took his head between his hands.

"Codrin?" Saliné asked.

Head in hands, he moaned again, and Jara came to him and placed her palms over his. "Codrin," she said gently.

He finally opened his eyes and glanced around. "Where am I?" he whispered. "And who are you?"

"You are in my house," Alfrid said. "Do you know how you arrived here?"

"No. Who are you?"

"I am Alfrid, and this is my wife, Saliné."

"Where is my wife?"

"Do you have a wife?"

"Yes. Where is she?"

"Do you have children too?" Alfrid's gaze steadied, with an eyebrow arched in inquiry.

"Yes, I have two children, but one of them belongs to her first husband."

"What happened to her first husband?"

"He was killed."

"You killed a man to take his wife." Alfrid pointed with a finger at Codrin, looking at Saliné.

"No. How did I arrive here?"

"Where is your son?" Alfrid asked, a little too eager. Unconsciously, he leaned forward.

Codrin frowned and, for the first time, he looked meaningfully at the man in front of him. He did not like the man, and he struggled without great success to adjust his thinking. *This man feels like Count Irvath... My son may be in danger.* "In my house."

"Where is your house?" Alfrid asked, irritated, without noticing Cernat's eyes fixed on him.

Saliné saw it, and she frowned, then tried to interject. Jara touched her arm, stopping her.

"I don't remember," Codrin said.

"Codrin," Saliné said, her voice was gently. "Who wounded you?" She pointed at his bandaged head.

"Who is Codrin?"

"You don't remember." Saliné looked away from him, her eyes glimmering sadly. "Who are you?" Under her apparent calm, she was shocked by two things: the state of Codrin's mind, and the apparent fact that he had a wife and child. Deep inside, she still believed that Codrin belonged to her.

"My name is Tudor." Codrin tried to say more, but the potion made by Calista exhausted him, and he leaned his head on the table, falling asleep.

There was a long moment of silence until Alfrid broke it, looking at Saliné. "It seems to me, my love, that Codrin has tricked us, hiding the fact that he has a wife and ... children. All those things about the Seer returning from death, and the nomads invading us next year, are just a ploy. I think that he is planning to take the crown and make that woman his queen. He is a dangerous man. And deceitful. I fear for our son."

Unable to speak, Saliné looked at Codrin. Looked at Alfrid, then back at Codrin; her head moving slowly, left and right. She stood up abruptly and left the room in haste, followed by Alfrid and Edric.

Codrin woke an hour later and found Jara and Cernat looking at him. "What happened? Where are the others?"

"What do you remember?"

Codrin frowned, trying to gather his thoughts and ignore the throbbing pain in his head. "Oh, no," he moaned, "I told Alfrid about my other son. He will kill him too. He tried hard to make me tell him where my son is now."

"You remember what happened," Cernat said, surprised.

"Yes, I think that I lost my memory again."

"Does it happen often?"

For a long moment, Codrin had to struggle to control his anger. When he'd replied, it was in the best effort he could manage to speak without growling. "This is the second time. The first one was when the Wanderers fed me a potion. They hoped to make me forget everything for seven years, but I recovered faster than they expected."

"You said that the memory loss was because of the wounds."

"That was what I thought first, but then I remembered."

"No one gave you any potion now."

"Is any Wanderer here?"

"Calista."

"That bitch, she was the one who advised Alfrid to kill me. I suppose that they fed me a potion in my ... I suppose it was in my wine. And they did it just before bringing you and Saliné here. The Pig King is playing another dirty game." Codrin looked at Cernat, seeing that he was thoughtful. "I should have realized. You are on Alfrid's side."

"No, it's just that the situation is bizarre. You had a lapse of memory, and now you talk about some magic potion, which no one has heard of before. We need to know more. It's too strange."

"Perhaps. I told you about Edric killing my child; you asked for proof. Now, you are asking me again."

"It's normal..."

"No, it isn't. If you gave me your word about something, I would not ask for proof. That was before, now I don't care much about your word. You should leave now."

"Codrin," Jara said gently, "you have to understand. You need to overcome eight witnesses to make things clear. We must take everyone's opinion into account. I am Saliné's mother. We need to find a middle way between her family and you."

"I don't care about the Pig King and his wife. I asked *you* to believe me, but you are their family, not mine. I understand that now."

"Let's say that we believe you," Cernat said, "how do you plan to...?"

"There is no *let's say*. Leave now." Codrin stood up and went on the terrace, and they had no choice but to leave the house.

"I was tactless," Jara said on their way back. "My words made sense for a neutral person. Codrin can be anything but neutral in this. Yet... I was ready to believe him about Edric, but after this story with a magic potion appearing from nowhere..."

"We should let him calm down and come again tomorrow. Now, I want to hear what Saliné has to say about this. But magic potions..." Cernat shrugged.

"Codrin did not lose all his memories," Calista said, when Alfrid ended his story, and started to pace around the room. *Memories*, she thought. There were already so many layers of interwoven memories and intrigues, so many echoes. *I feel danger.* "Codrin..." She murmured his name, and he let her mind into the Light, trying again to feel him, to learn the tiniest bit of his future. She failed for the hundredth time. "Codrin's mind somehow reverted to the time he spent I don't know where, before...." *Before recovering his past memories? Did someone use the same potion on him? But who could know about that old Talant book? Thais? She was sent there to watch, and she confirmed his death to our Council; he was hit by five arrows, but she had to leave the place in haste because of some unknown riders. Did she lie to us? The healer who treated him after Cosmin's death confirmed that Codrin had five wounds, which seemed to be from arrows, all on his back, as Thais had said to us. One of them traversed his body and almost killed him. And a sixth scar from a spear, which looks old. And several small cuts.* "Where did Codrin hide all these years?"

"I don't know, he refused to say."

"Where did he hide?" she repeated, expecting no answer. *I am speaking to a child. That was the most important thing to know.* She let her mind wander into the Light again. She used no trigger this time and let herself be led into the unknown. A figure came to her. *Ildeko's child...* Then the hand of the man training him. *The wedding ring... It's unremarkable, but elegant in its simplicity.* There was something in this ring, and she forced her mind to remember. She remembered Codrin's ring. *I can't see the man's face... Codrin will train the child. Why is this child so important? I feel him as I feel Saliné's unborn daughter.* Calista frowned, trying to deal with what she had just learned. She went to the table and poured some wine in a glass, then moistened her lips in it, without drinking.

Alfrid's patience ran out and he said, his voice suddenly thin, "Codrin has another son, and we have to take care of him, too."

"Forget about that; the child is a toddler. We have more important things to do now, and I have to figure out why he did not lose all his memories."

"Why is it so important?"

"It's always important to understand what doesn't work as planned." Her voice held a faint irritation, and she sipped some wine.

Edric entered her room that moment. There was tension there, he could sense it, and he was not accustomed to seeing Calista let her feelings be known. He went to the table and filled two glasses of wine and walked toward Alfrid. "Perhaps you need this." Edric gave him the wine, then looked at Calista, whose eyes were even darker than usual. "The potion worked in an unexpected way," he said, carefully.

"Yes." Calista shrugged. "Codrin's memories did not vanish completely. It would have been useful to learn something from them."

"Saliné knows now that Codrin was married and has a new son. She did not look happy, and she left the room abruptly. That suits us. There was no time to ask more questions, and even if she had stayed..." He paused briefly in thought. "Jara and Cernat were listening carefully. You seemed too eager to learn more about Codrin's son." Edric looked at Alfrid. "We need to ask the right questions when Codrin is alone with us. Can we use the potion again?" He looked at Calista this time.

"Not yet." Calista set her glass down on the table. "There are things to be done first." *Tomorrow, I will go to see Ildeko and her son. I will bring them to see Codrin. There must be a reaction, something...*

"Good," Edric said, laughing out loud, and his laughter melted some of the ice in the room. "I now have enough time for another night with my little Duchess."

"You should marry him off soon." Calista looked half amused at Alfrid.

"Calista, I already know that I will marry that *beauty* from Silvania. My dear brother still doesn't understand how lucky he is to have Saliné. The Silvanian beauty was supposed to be his wife, before your new arrangement, so please allow me some liberty. Mr. Duke, the old husband, is out of Muniker for a week, and I intend to use this time in a very judicious way."

"That's why the servants cleaned the old pavilion in the park." Alfrid laughed, his voice still a little strained.

"What could be more romantic than making love with another man's wife in the midst of nature?" Edric laughed too. "Now please excuse me, I have just enough time for a bath. She wants me to be pure. I am afraid that I only partially fulfill her desire for a pure love."

"Be discreet, the Duke is not an easy man, and he employs one of the best assassins in Litvonia."

"That's why I chose the park. She will not enter the castle. The old man has spies here." Edric shrugged. "Three days ago, she had another lover in her bed. I am covered."

"Edric," Calista said and fell silent, looking at Alfrid, who understood the message and left them alone. "Why are you doing this? It's dangerous; because of the Duke, and because you are breaking the rules of courting. Muniker is all about rules."

"For Saliné. We are lovers now, but she will announce me as her lointain lover only in spring. Because of her son's death." Edric turned his palms up. "I have the feeling that Alfrid knows about Saliné and me, so I just want to keep him distracted."

Another broken rule, but at least I can't complain about this. "Saliné may learn of the Duchess too."

"I've already told her. Not everything, of course. She understands that it's only a ploy. Unfortunately, she stopped me seeing her for two weeks until she learns more about Alfrid. When Alfrid was away, his secretary set some spies on us."

"This," Calista said thoughtfully, "started before Alfrid went away with the army. Things are going the wrong way, and we may need to act against Alfrid earlier than I thought. I did not want to tell you, but," she shrugged, "we need to adapt. Do you remember that young soldier who looks like you?" She glanced at

Edric, who nodded. "He was the man Alfrid sent to kick Cosmin's horse in the garden."

"What?" Edric emptied his glass in one shot. "He did not kick the horse; he knifed it. That's why it went wild. It was supposed to be a little accident, not..." He paused, struggling to contain his anger, and filled the glass again.

"Codrin saw him, and he thinks that it was you who killed his son. I think that he complained to Saliné, but she chose not to believe him, and *not* to tell us. The good thing is that she knows about the man, and a week ago, I took her to see him, but he had left the army. I assume he is dead. It doesn't matter much; I've settled some vague ideas in Saliné's mind." Calista tried to sip some wine, only to find that her glass was empty, and she gestured to Edric. Her glass filled, she took her time. "In the worst case, we will accuse Alfrid of killing Cosmin. It seems to me now that he did want to kill the boy, though we planned a mere accident. In that case ... we must act quickly to silence him." Her voice carried a tone of sadness.

"Open a bottle of Tolosa wine," Alfrid said and waited patiently until his servant obeyed. "Go and fetch Gerd here." Lips pursed, he inclined the vial and let twenty drops fall into the bottle, then put the cork back. *Codrin should lose his memory for two or three weeks.*

The door opened and another man came in. Tall and slim, he did not look like a servant, though he was dressed in royal livery. Few knew about him in the palace, and even fewer that he was an elite soldier Alfrid used for dirty jobs.

"In the evening, place the bottle in Codrin's house, like you did it last time. You know what to tell him." When the man left, Alfrid sat in an armchair, leaning his head back. *Once I finish with Codrin, I will have the Duke of Henver informed of his wife's lovers. He will know that I was the one who... Calista thinks that she can play me. She forgets that I have the Light too. The next nomad invasion will be smaller, and with three kingdoms under my crown I should be able to repel it.*

&

They were in Saliné's office, Cernat and Jara. He had made plans for this morning, but they felt weak and unbalanced. Everything felt unbalanced. "Strange those new Visions from Calista," he said, finally. "About Codrin, and everything else.

"Yes," Saliné sighed. "Some things are strange. I am not talking about my son's..." Her voice broke, and she breathed deeply to recover. "It's that all these things, Visions, loss of memory, sickness appeared out of nowhere, and everything is converging in the same direction: Codrin."

"What sickness?"

"Codrin is sick, and that explains his memory loss. It seems that he will not survive more than a year or two. Alfrid promised me to keep him safe. He no longer sees a rival in Codrin as he is sick."

"Who told you this?"

"Calista, she recognized the disease in an old book."

"Can she give me that book?"

"I can ask if our library has it. She read it in her Hive."

"Codrin is not sick, his memory loss..."

"He lost his memory because of his wounds," Saliné cut in, nervously.

"No, Saliné, two Wanderers gave him a potion, trying to keep him away for seven years until the next nomad invasion. They were opposed to Calista, who wanted to kill Codrin, so Alfrid could marry you."

"But Calista found that book about the disease and she had the Vision about..." She stopped abruptly, shaking her hand in a nervous discharge. "See? This is what I feel wrong. Too many things are suddenly pointing at Codrin. We have that old saying in Frankis: when everybody looks right you go left."

"Do you think now that maybe Codrin is right, and it was Edric who released the horse?"

"I can't think that without a proof. My feelings are no proof either." *Edric would not do such a thing to me. Why did Calista take me to see that young soldier who resembles Edric?* Saliné stood up and paced around the room, trying to recall, before saying, "The day when my son ... Edric was not in Muniker. I am sure about that."

There was silence, and Cernat followed her, trying to understand her struggle. For the wrong reason he asked, "Will you help Codrin to escape?"

"I can't work against my husband. I hoped to convince him to let Codrin leave, but now... You don't really need my help. In a month, send him away, and even if I learn something, I will pretend ignorance. That I can do. In a month." She looked at Cernat. "I don't want a war this autumn. We need time for some kind of negotiation."

"Let me undress you, my dear," Edric whispered in her ear. "I like to explore you." Slowly, he unlaced her bodice, and his forefinger touched her lips, then went down her chin and neck and played around a breast that bounced slightly when he let it free. "What a pity that I can't see you, but light would attract more than insects here." *Saliné will be upset if this would spread, and the Duke of Henver is a man of temper. Calista was right, he likes to use paid assassins, and he has enough money to find skilled men.* He shivered and shook his head. *There are four sentries around the pavilion and twenty on the walls surrounding the park.*

"I can play the game too," she said, not understanding his sudden lack of motion and interest, and her hand plunged into his pants.

Edric gasped, and any thought about her husband and his paid assassins vanished from his mind. He undressed her fast and she helped him. They crashed into the bed.

Hidden behind the tree, the shadow listened to the faint moaning coming from the pavilion. Through discreet and patient observation, the shadow knew that there were four soldiers around, and their locations too. Only one could pose a problem, the one in front of the tree behind the pavilion. *The sentries are listening to the lovers too. That could be an advantage.* Moments before the thought ended its course, a small chuckle came from the closest sentry. *It's time.* The shadow moved out from behind the tree. In three large steps arrived behind the sentry who was slightly bowed, to hear better what was happening inside. A faint moan which did not resemble the ones coming from the pavilion was heard, and the sentry found a better position in the grass. Standing still, like the sentry before, the shadow listened to the night: crickets and moaning. He moved with quiet steps toward the back of the pavilion, and from there, behind the bed. Dressed in black, including a balaclava over his head and face, the shadow melted into the dark blue canvas wall behind the bed. The space was just wide enough for a man to sneak in. In the low light of the moon coming through the door on the opposite side, the small difference of colors did not matter much, and anyway the couple wrestling on the bed did not have eyes for the canvas or for faint color differences. *I arrived a bit earlier than I wanted, but no killing goes fully as planned. I like her perfume,* the shadow sniffed quietly. *Is it her husband's favorite? I like the noise less. I am aroused.* The shadow fought a sudden desire to laugh at the peculiar situation – he had never killed before while wanting to lay a woman.

With a last grunt, Edric ended his assault and rolled, satisfied, on his back. *She claims pure love, but she is skilled in bed. I guess she did not learn that from her decrepit husband.* He half turned, and his hand followed the curves of her body. After a while, it settled on her breast. "My dear, you offered me a wonderful night. I misspoke. You offered me the start of a wonderful night."

"That sounds better," she chuckled. She felt both tired and well and, eyes closed, she forced herself not to yawn. *Edric is better in bed than Larsin, but tomorrow I will be with Albart. I've heard that he is the best lover in Muniker*. "Are you hungry?" she chuckled, wakened from her half sleep by the strange noise coming from his stomach.

I am afraid that it was not the stomach, the shadow thought, cleaning his dagger on the sheets.

"You did not answer," she said, jokingly and turned toward Edric. *He fell asleep*. "I don't like sleeping men." This time, she was annoyed and pushed him. Her hand slipped on something wet. Before she could scream, a fist thumped into her head, and the Duchess of Henver passed out.

The shadow left the pavilion the same way he had entered and walked fast toward the stairs on the wall surrounding the park. At its foot, he picked up a coil of rope, hidden behind a small bush, and looked at the wall. *Another sentry comes. Complications. Always.* He leaned against the wall and listened to the night. On the rampart, a pair of feet were padding almost noiselessly, but he could feel both the sentry's rhythm and the change in position. A minute. Another minute. He calculated. Quietly, the shadow climbed the stairs until his head went a little above the wall, and he stopped there, a darker spot against the dark sky; the sentry was coming. In front of the stairs, the soldier turned, ready to walk back. Silent, the shadow followed him. A dark hand covered the soldier's mouth at the same time a dagger slid across his throat, and he was dead before understanding what had happened to him. Standing still, the shadow listened to the night again. *All clear*. At leisure, he bent and grabbed the rope, walked twenty paces further and uncoiled it down the wall. It was long enough to be passed, at its middle, around a merlon, both hanging heads touching the ground. Keeping both strands of the rope tight in hand, the shadow climbed down into the street, outside the Royal Palace's precincts. He pulled one head of the rope, and the whole thing fell on his head. *Sometimes, plans don't work as planned*, the shadow almost chuckled, working to coil the rope. When all was done, he vanished into the night.

One minute later, a woman's scream pierced the night. It was strong enough to chill all the sentries in the park and wake up some bad sleepers in the palace.

I should have hit her harder, the shadow thought. *But I could have killed her, and that would have been bad. I need to walk faster, and the moon has just vanished.* The street was still empty and silent, and that brought some calm in him. *I don't know this part of the city well, but it must be here.* Fifty feet tall, the outer wall of Muniker was just in front of him. *The stairs must be close.* One minute later, the shadow climbed the stairs, and everything was only a repetition of the previous encounter with a sentry. There were some differences, though: the shadow tied one head of the rope to a merlon, relieved the soldier of his coat, tied the rope around his waist and slowly let him down outside the wall until the rope tightened. *It did not touch the ground, but it must not be far from it. I hope that I calculated its height well.* Free to survey the night again, he heard faint cries coming from the park. They belonged to men this time. *I should have been already away from the wall by now. Why did they place more sentries than usual? If they know something...*

At the first scream, the sentries around the pavilion froze, and they could not move even after the second or the third. "Alarm! Sound the alarm." One of them finally woke, and from the walls more soldiers came down, one of them with a torch in his hand. The woman was still screaming.

In the palace, Saliné was awake. After Cosmin's death, she could not sleep more than three or four hours. She preferred to read, to keep her mind busy, away from that avalanche of bad thoughts tormenting her mind. *Did someone scream?* She raised her head and listened. The palace had a shape resembling a letter E; her suite was in the middle, and the pavilion was not visible from her window. She stood up and, opening the door, went out onto the terrace. This time the screaming was clear. *A woman.* "Guards!" she shouted. "We have intruders in the park." *I hope it's not the Duchess. Edric...* She pressed a hand to her mouth. *Fate, no, not another death. Please.*

Twenty minutes later, surrounded by ten guards, Alfrid arrived at the pavilion. He would not have come, but many in the palace knew that the scream was related to his brother. The captain of the night guard was already there with ten soldiers.

"I am sorry your majesty, but your brother is dead," the captain said. "The Du... The woman is still alive, but I was not able to extract much from her. Maybe your majesty can calm her."

"Raise the alarm in the garrison and set patrols on the street. No one is allowed to leave the city, now or tomorrow morning. Call both Chiefs of the Guards and all the captains to the palace."

"Should we search the house of the Seer too?"

Alfrid was annoyed by the Seer word, but kept it hidden. "Bring me one of the sentries at his door. Did Codrin leave the house?" he asked when the man arrived.

"No, your majesty. He tried to leave late in the afternoon but returned in the house after a few steps. He did not feel well, and walked badly, as if his sight was blurred. He even me asked me who I am, even when he knows me well."

"Let him sleep. He still suffers because of his son." *Well, I showed some humanity, and they noticed my goodwill toward the Seer. Calista's potion works, and I don't care about her worries. Tomorrow, I will parade Codrin in front of the whole palace. A mindless man. His aura will be gone.* Alfrid ducked his head and entered the tent.

If not for the large pool of blood, under the torches' feeble light, Edric looked asleep; his death had been too quick to alter his features. *You died earlier than I had planned, brother. You should have been more careful. We all know that Duke Henver is a dangerous animal. I can't even punish him. Unless we can catch the assassin. I want to catch the assassin, but I won't punish the Duke. He will be in my debt.* "My dear," he addressed the Duchess, "I see that you are well. I need some information from you, and then I will send you discreetly away."

"I know nothing."

"Please try to remember; even the smallest detail may help us."

"We were almost asleep when I heard a faint noise. I asked Edric what happened, but he did not answer. I shook him and found blood. Before I could scream, the assassin hit me, and I lost consciousness. I think that he was between the bed and the wall of the pavilion. When I woke up again... I screamed."

"Thank you, my dear." *The assassin spared her. Duke Henver spared her. I may guess why.* He looked at the woman who did not realize that she was half naked. "Let me take you away from here."

When the King returned to the palace, Vlad, the Chief of Muniker Guard, Alois, the Chief of the Palace Guard, and their ten Uber Captains, who were not in charge with a gate, were already in the main hall waiting for him. "Where is Lisandru?" the King asked after a brief search. Frinz, Pintea and Lisandru were the most important Ubers in the Muniker Guard.

"He left Muniker five days ago, to bring his wife back," Damian, his brother, and an Uber Captain too, said.

"Vlad," the King turned towards him.

"Ten patrols are already on the street, and another ten will follow. In fact, they should already be there by now. Any man wandering on the streets will be sent to the barracks. We will question them there."

"My brother was killed. Find the assassin."

"I am sorry, your majesty. We will leave no stone unturned."

"Alois," the King turned toward the other Chief.

"The palace is sealed, your majesty, and there are twenty guards in the Royal Suite. Her majesty the Queen is there with the prince and her family. We considered that the assassin may try to hide here, instead of leaving, and our guards are searching every room."

"That was a good idea."

"It was Vlad's idea, your majesty."

"You two are working well together. Where is Aunt Calista?"

"In her room; she refused to go to the Royal Suite. There are five guards with her."

"Sir Vlad!" one guard shouted, entering the hall in a rush. "We discovered that the assassin left the city by climbing down the western wall. He killed one of our sentries, before going down. Your majesty." He bowed, finding himself in front of the King.

"Keep a few patrols inside, but send most of them out of the city," Vlad ordered. "Frinz, go and make ready ten more men for each patrol that goes outside."

"Bring me some good news," the King said, struggling to keep his calm; there was less chance now to find the assassin. "I will go to see my wife and son."

The patrol led by Pintea was the third one to leave the city. Through some large gaps in the clouds, the moon provided enough light for a low-speed ride on the road, which was well maintained. The patrols set on the meadows around the city were not so lucky, and they mostly had to walk, horses at halter. Ten minutes later, they arrived at the first crossroads, and Pintea left five soldiers to guard it. The next crossroads was three miles further south, and from there they turned back, leaving three more men behind. The moon was now hidden behind the thick clouds, and their road back was slower.

When the moon appeared again over the crossroads, the men left at the crossroad pushed their horses to ride south. "Let's go, Zor," one of them said, "we have a long way to Poenari, but at least you should be proud that for an hour you served in his majesty's patrol, which was searching for me."

"Sometimes, you have a strange sense of humor, Codrin," Lisandru laughed, followed by the third man. "But you are still wearing a Muniker guard's coat."

"This is the second one. The first one I took from the sentry on the wall was too small. The second one, I grabbed from a guard at the stable, when I fetched Zor. He was there for his horse too. At least the second man was lucky; I did not kill him. There are men from Frankis in Vlad's Guard. He could have been one of my men in the past. I would have hated to learn that later."

That's why people are loyal to you, Codrin, you care about them. "At the next crossroads, ten of our best men from Frankis are waiting for us. They have just resigned from his majesty's Guard."

"Tell me about weird humor," Codrin mused. "Thank you, Lisandru."

Riding freed Codrin's mind, and his thoughts recalled the day before. Recalling every aspect of the escape plan, he was walking through the park, between the old trees, when Saliné came and joined him. Neither of them spoke, and they walked together for a minute. With no warning, she turned toward him, and touched his face, like so many times in the past. Saying nothing, she let her fingers trail down toward his chin until they left him. Eyes locked, they stared at each other in silence, and the last sunshine enhanced her fair face. As abruptly as before, she turned and walked away.

She knows that I am leaving, Codrin thought, staring at her walking away, and he was strangely calm that she knew about his escape, planned to start in a few hours. This was always Saliné's way of saying farewell when he had to leave for a long time. Hoping to make her turn and see her face once more, Codrin let her take a few steps and said, "The nomads will invade next year. I had a Vision." He had missed that view in Muniker, he will miss it even more in Frankis.

"Thank you, Codrin." Saliné turned her head and their eyes met again. There was a small, worried smile on her lips.

Shaking his head, Codrin came back to the road in front of him. *Only the kiss was missing,* he sighed. *Saliné has the Light too; did she know about my escape from a Vision or from Vlad? Or did she ask Vlad after having the Vision?* His thoughts swayed again, and he recalled the death of his son. For the rest of the night, Codrin rode without saying a word.

Lisandru felt his uneasiness, and stayed silent, watching the dark road.

❧

Saliné could not sleep. She walked around the room for the hundredth time and went to the window. There was a tall, burning candle not far to her left, and by its light someone watching could have seen a taut anguish to her beautiful face as she listened without hearing. There were torches burning in the park. Her gaze went beyond them, to the south, a doomed look. There were stars above Muniker in the clear night. They blurred in her sight as she stood there, holding memories of love and death. *I am cursed*. Tears blinded her. Unseeing, she looked outside until her grief expended itself into nothingness. The dawn found her still in front of the open window. The shadows of the night morphed slowly into trees and people running around. She did not see them. When Alfrid came to take her to the council, her face was white, her grief hidden deep. Outside, the light was still feeble. It did not matter to her.

"Did you find Edric's assassin?" Saliné knew the answer, and she asked only because she needed something to extract herself from that dark lethargy.

"We are still searching. Let's go now. Vlad will give us the latest news." Alfrid lent her his arm, and they walked out together.

Neither of them spoke, not even when they entered the council room. There was no visible tension there, only tiredness and a degree of disbelief. They would grasp everything later, and many kinds of fear would visit them. Only Calista and Saliné were partially able to see into the future, to understand the yet invisible storm this night had brought to them. Alfrid felt strange; he was half faking his grief, half of his mind in the room, half caught in a pang of fear that he could not understand.

Before Vlad could make his report, the day captain entered in haste, and stopped in front of the long table. He opened his mouth, then clamped it shut. Opened it again, all eyes on him, everyone expecting him to say that the assassin had been caught.

"The Seer escaped." His voice was weak, the voice of a man speaking against his will.

"He is no Seer!" Alfrid shouted and banged his fist on the table. It sounded like thunder in the sudden silence. "What did you say?"

"The... Sir Codrin escaped, your majesty." His voice was pitched so they all had to lean forward to hear.

Yesterday, I said farewell to him, Saliné thought. *He took advantage of the trouble. Did he know that Edric would be killed? A Vision?*

"How...?" Alfrid tried to speak calm and royally. The voice filled the quiet room with a whimper.

The captain moistened his lips. "There is a room... A hidden room in the loft. It can be reached from the bedroom, through the ceiling."

"And you did not know," Calista said, feeling pity and derision for Alfrid, who could not manage to speak or to close his mouth, his restless tongue visible, red in the gap of his white teeth. Her voice was a shade less controlled than usual. Her dark blue eyes were burning, that kind of smoldering a coal has before it bursts into flames.

No, the captain shook his head. "The hidden room had a window, and..."

"And there was a rope hanging there, I know, and you did not know. Who was the last one to see Codrin?"

"Gerd, my lady. We interrogated the guards. He went inside with a bottle of wine. He returned after ten minutes and bragged that the ... that Sir Codrin shared the wine with him. This morning..." He moistened his lips for the tenth time. "This morning, we tried to interrogate Gerd, but he seems to be ... mad. He doesn't recognize us. He doesn't speak. He cries."

"Codrin poisoned him to escape," Alfrid snapped.

"Poison kills," Calista said, coldly. "He must have been hit on the head. Perhaps he fell on the stairs, thinking of the Seer's wine. Head wounds sometimes present in such symptoms. Tie him to his bed. He will recover in a few days. Or he will die." *Idiot. You tried to give Codrin the potion*. She glanced sideways at Alfrid. "You may go, captain." She glanced at Saliné this time and saw her frowning. *Does she realize what happened to Gerd? No, Codrin's reaction to the potion was too different. Alfrid used more of it.* "Vlad." She nodded at him and closed her eyes. *Did Codrin kill Edric? But he was not fully recovered, and assassination attempt needs planning. A Vision?*

"Codrin killed Edric," Alfrid said, before Vlad could start to report.

"I think that Codrin and the assassin were different people." Vlad spoke slowly, weighing his words; it was hard to reconcile positions that were too far each from another.

"Why?" the King asked, displeased. *I need a way to put the killing on Codrin.*

"Two of our guards were attacked, and their coats were taken, so two men needed cover to escape. In the beginning, we thought that the assassin had a helper."

"The assassin escaped over the wall, and Codrin with our own riders," Saliné said, thoughtfully.

"I think that both went out with the riders, but we don't know with which patrols. The land was rocky at the foot of the outer wall, where the rope was tied, and the rope was too short. Anyone climbing down there during the night would have broken his neck. And two horses are missing from the stable. I apologize, your majesty, but it seems that my negligence made possible their escape."

"There was no way to foresee this," Saliné said and, morose, Alfrid nodded too. "At least we know that the assassin is no longer in the city."

"Two missing horses and coats are not enough to confirm that Codrin did not kill my brother." Alfrid stood up, walked a few steps, then sat back. "We will spread the news that Codrin killed Edric. It may even be true."

"I don't see a reason to do this," Saliné said.

"I don't see it either," Calista interjected before Alfrid could protest. *It might be true, but with Edric gone, only Codrin can save the Realm from the nomads.*

"We can close the council." Alfrid stood up abruptly and went out without waiting for Saliné.

"Vlad, please walk with me." Saliné placed her hand on his arm, and they went out from the palace, together. "Did Codrin work alone to escape? I can think of both, a lucky shot or friends' help. It will stay between us."

"I helped him, your majesty," Vlad sighed. *Please don't ask me who killed Edric. I have the feeling that it was Codrin.*

"Well, I suppose that you were not the only one. And I told you to call me Saliné when we talk like now. You did that in Frankis."

"We are no longer in Frankis."

"You are still upset at me because I did not take your advice to refuse the marriage with Alfrid."

"That was just an opinion; it was not my marriage."

"I should have listened. Thank you for being open with me." *My son would have been alive. Edric would have been mostly unknown to me, but alive.*

Calista was alone in the funeral room; she had sent away the five women taking care of the candles. Silent, Saliné came and sat in a chair next to her. She placed a hand over Edric's cold one. *He looks like he is asleep.* Unwillingly, she compared his face with her son's. Even in death, Cosmin's face carried the fear of dying. Edric seemed serene, his lips stretched in an approximation of a smile. Her mind recalled his devilish, handsome smile that had charmed her so many times. Her world was poorer again. She turned her head and met Calista's intense eyes. "You think that it's my fault." *In a way, it is. Edric was with the Duchess to protect me,* she thought, and her tongue was bitter in her mouth.

"It doesn't matter." Calista shrugged. *Each has their own weakness. Yours is Alfrid. You should have made Edric your lointain lover a long time ago.* "Let the past rest; we are sailing through uncertain waters. We have enough time to talk about them." She smiled sadly and placed her hand over Saliné's, which was still over Edric's. *It feels like a blood bond. There is so much blood between us. Edric's... Cosmin's... Codrin's... Could I have done things differently? There was no way to foresee this.* She shrugged and ignored Saliné's glance. *I must think about Saliné and Codrin. A hard task. There is no other way, but I have until spring.*

In the evening, the Royal Council met again, and Alfrid looked at his brother's empty place. *You wanted a Duchess; you got the Duchess of Death. You wanted my wife too. And my crown.* Together with Saliné, he was the last to arrive, and seated himself in his chair. She placed her hand gently over his, under the table. The council was smaller now.

Calista was there too, and the old Wanderer looked even older; she was in a shock she had never felt before. In the morning, the flurry of news and orders and plans of action helped them. There were urgent things to do, and their minds were working, sometimes more than was needed. Now, it was different; excepting Alfrid, every person in the council feared that the kingdom had lost the only man who could save it.

Saliné seemed oddly focused inward, her mind preoccupied with understanding things that could not be understood. The cycles of her life; they came and went in a strange way, alternating. There was a time of bliss, then a time of loss and sorrow. Her Father. The bliss, loss and sorrow repeated with Codrin. It repeated with her son. Then with Edric. *This time, I've lost a son and a lover. If it continues like this, there will be no more people to lose. And no life to live.*

Alfrid looked at the people in the room and made his announcement. "I've decided to call the army. In a week, we will move into Frankis."

Abruptly, Saliné retracted her hand from his, struggling to hide her surprise, which did not escape Calista. She paused to think. When she looked back at Alfrid, there was something sharp and searching in her gaze. "You can't send an army to Frankis without my approval." Her voice was as sharp as her eyes.

"I am sure we will have it. We need to react fast and catch Codrin." A feeling of childish sullenness was visible on Alfrid's face. He grimaced and passed a hand over his scalp.

"We may decide something today, but I have not given my approval for the army to march into Frankis. Until then, there will be no army going there. We can discuss the necessity and see what's next."

"Of course, we must send it. I have put out a call for forty thousand soldiers. Codrin is the *necessity.* We must catch him before he becomes too strong. We will bring him here. He will stay here until he accepts our suzerainty and that bloody Duchy he refused." Alfrid became nervous, and his voice became thin. "No, a ducal title is too much for him now. We will make Codrin a Count."

You will never win a battle against Codrin. I can't use this argument... "He will go to Arad or Poenari. Most probably Poenari. How do you plan to catch him?"

"With forty thousand soldiers, we can take Poenari, before Codrin is able to gather an army."

"Did you ever see Poenari?"

"It's a fortress. Any fortress has its weakness. We will block all the roads and prepare for a hard siege. A hundred catapults and three hundred assault ladders."

"Assault ladders are useless. Poenari's walls are a hundred twenty feet tall. No one ever succeeded in a siege there, even with larger armies."

Alfrid's mouth opened, then closed without a sound. He looked like a cornered animal. A stubborn one. "It doesn't matter, with a full siege and all their roads cut, we can take it in a few months, half a year. I don't care, but I want him here." His voice was tight and angry.

"Alfrid," Saliné said and paused. In contrast with his agitation, her voice was almost gentle. Her eyes were not. "Winter is coming soon. The army will make the journey to Poenari, find that it can't be conquered and come back with several thousand soldiers fewer. We will not send any army. We need a negotiated solution. As we are hemmed in until spring, Codrin is hemmed in too. I want to send a courier to him."

"And what solution do you have?"

"None." Saliné swallowed with difficulty; her mouth was dry. She closed her eyes for a moment, hearing her own word as a distorted echo inside her skull, and she hesitated, then opened her eyes abruptly on Alfrid. "We must stay in contact with Codrin and find one by spring. I will send Pintea with a letter." She looked at Count Joachim, and said without waiting for an answer from Alfrid, "Joachim, cancel the call for the army." Her voice was now flat and precise, carrying the tones of a commander of men on a battlefield.

For the second time, Alfrid opened his mouth and closed it without a sound.

When the issue with the army was resolved, Saliné said what would be the most controversial thing in the meeting: "The nomads will invade us next year." The meaning of her own words came like a revelation. *Codrin will keep the peace until after the invasion, that's why he informed me.*

"Codrin's lies!" Alfrid shouted, and banged his fist on the table, in a strange repetition. It felt childish and forced. "The invasion will be four years from now. All the Wanderers know this."

Saliné smiled wryly at him. "The nomads will invade us *next year.*"

"I will not..." Alfrid said.

"Yes, you will," Calista cut in. "Did Codrin have a Vision about this?" She looked at Saliné, who nodded. "The Wanderers knew that they would come earlier. Codrin may be right or wrong but, next year, we must be prepared to fight the nomads. That brings Silvania into the discussion. Alfrid, be ready to go there in three weeks. You will take ten thousand soldiers with you, to make sure that no hothead will reject your claim. The Silvanian King is dying." *See, Alfrid? This is the effect of poison.* She looked at Saliné, who nodded, and both waited until Alfrid gathered himself and ordered Joachim to call ten thousand soldiers for Silvania.

Calista nodded to Saliné to stay with her in the room. "What are you planning to ask Codrin?" she asked when they were alone.

"Truce until after the nomad invasion. Later, perhaps, we can find some sort of arrangement." *We must find one, there has been too much death already.* She found herself rubbing her thumb against her first two fingers, as though feeling the texture of a piece of fabric.

"I think that Codrin had the same thing in mind, telling you about the invasion." Calista fell silent, trying to sort several strings of thought coming to her without order or reason. "It's hard for me to tell you this, but..." She paused and turned her head to meet Saliné's eyes. "Alfrid is not the best future for your children." She pointed at Saliné's belly. "We need Codrin's help. Do you still want to keep that name for her?"

"Are you thinking to change her name to Edrica?" *No, my links with Codrin are deeper.* "I will keep the name."

"It's your choice, not mine. I am simply curious why you chose that name."

"Ioana was Codrin's twin sister."

"Oh," Calista said. "That makes sense. It makes even more sense now." *This is Fate's hand. Destiny. Ioana and Ioan, the makers of the new Empire. It's clear now. In the evening, I will go to see the boy. Codrin must train him. We will find an understanding.* Eyes closed, she let her mind wander into the Light. A Vision came to her, and she opened her eyes abruptly. *I am a stupid old woman. Ildeko and her son are on the road toward Frankis. That means... That means only one thing: Codrin is the father. Thais used the Talant potion on him, and he lost his memories. For three years, Codrin found shelter in Ildeko's house. Thais tricked everyone, even the Empress. And Elsebeth tricked me. Why?* "In the Alban Empire, in hard times, they had Viceroys. We can have one for Frankis, and your unborn daughter can be the link we need to have Codrin on our side. You know what I mean."

ঌ৩

"I am sorry, your majesty," Rosine cried and felt to her knees. "I lied to you. It was not Sir Codrin who... Edric and Calista threatened to kill my niece... I left behind a letter in your jewelry box." She lost her voice and continued to sob.

Jewels ... what woman needs jewels after a son's death? Her eyes blurred, Saliné looked at the woman at her feet, a mound of nebulous contours and colors. Like her mind. She looked up at the sky. It was clear, the world lighted by a bright sun. It looked like a yellow spot to her. She sobbed and pressed a hand to her mouth. *Edric... How could he do this to me?* "Vlad, take care of her. Keep her in your castle and tell no one about her."

"Apart from us," Vlad gestured to include Cernat too, "only Lisandru and Pintea know about her. Lisandru saved Rosine when two former soldiers tried to kill her. Unfortunately, we had to act fast, and they were tough soldiers. They died in the fight. We don't know who paid them to kill Rosine."

"We can guess... She was an inconvenient witness," Saliné whispered, and walked away, ignoring the woman still kneeling in the grass. She could not look at her. Not yet. Later, she would interrogate Rosine again, but not now. She could not think clearly. She might want to kill the woman. And Edric, if he were still alive.

"Perhaps we should go back," Cernat said; he had tricked Saliné into taking a ride on the hills around Muniker, saying nothing about Rosine.

In her room, Saline found Rosine's letter, then another one, waiting on her table. It was from Idonie. A small text written in large red letters: 'Don't let Cosmin ride', and a long explanation written in normal size and ink. *It came too late*, Saline thought, throwing the letter away, without finishing it. *Fate is just laughing at me.*

Three days later, on the same hill, Saliné interrogated Rosine. The day Cosmin was killed, the woman was drugged and woke up alone in garden. Calista and Edric came to her the next morning and made her look through the window: there was a man in the garden. He was holding a knife at her niece's throat. Her six-year-old niece.

Back in her suite, Saliné locked the door and sat on the tiger fur. She took a knife and pierced the fur a few times. The place where Edric's head used to rest. Calm again, she lay on the fur and started to think. In the evening, people came and knocked at her locked door. Then they spoke to her. Alfrid. Jara. Cernat. She did not answer until their voices became worried. "Leave me alone!" she cried, and her world became silent again.

Calista was found dead in the morning. There was a flurry of soldiers running back and forth in the corridors. People were shouting. Guards were placed at each intersection, and in front of each important suite. There were more knocks on Saliné's locked door. Then voices.

"Leave me alone!" she cried.

Late in the evening, Cernat threatened to break the door down, and she finally unlocked it, allowing him to enter. Alone.

"We need to do something about your protection," he said, worried. "Calista was killed last night, and," he chose his words with care, "we have a security issue right now. I am not sure if Alfrid is able to fix it. He seems lost. All day, he stayed in his office doing nothing. Count Joachim is running the palace."

"You are wrong, Grandfather, I just resolved the last security issue." There was a biter grimace on Saliné's lips.

Cernat froze for a few moments, stared at his granddaughter, then he smiled briefly. "You know, Saliné, here you found an oasis of happiness again; Alfrid was a surprisingly good husband to you. Arnis was born, and you thrived again as a mother, yet you were not the same person as in Frankis. People change, and anyway they were small changes. In the last days, I recognize again the Saliné I knew, the one who fought in Severin when Aron kept her prisoner. You have brought justice. Do you have thoughts about Alfrid too?"

"I don't have any proof that Alfrid was involved in Cosmin's death, and he is my husband. Little Arnis needs a father. My unborn child needs a father." She pointed at her belly. *Though she may be Edric's daughter. That night with him... I still don't understand that night. We were no longer lovers. There was a sort of premonition, a sort of need, enveloped in a strong surge of Light. It never happened before. It never happened again after. Fate.*

"Do you want to talk?"

"I want to eat. Then I want to talk."

Saliné was hungry and ate everything that was put on her plate. Her gestures were mechanical; her mind was not there. She tasted nothing. She did not speak. Her eyes were fixed on a point on the wall in front of her. At the end, she took the glass and drank the wine in one shot. She filled it again. This time, she sipped slowly. "Now, I want to talk." Only Cernat and Jara were with her in the room.

"You feel sad and angry because of Edric." Jara walked behind her, embraced her, and leaned her head on Saliné's.

"Yes, I do. He was my lover; he did bad thigs, but it was not him who frightened the mare to... To kill my son."

"Codrin saw him with Cosmin and the horse." Jara's brows arched slowly, questioning Saliné.

"This time, Codrin was wrong. Last night ... when I returned from Calista ... many things came to me. My mind was not yet ready to understand. Perhaps it did not want to. The evening before he was killed, Edric told me that Cosmin's mare was knifed, and that was what made her gallop like a crazy animal. And Edric was not in Muniker that day. That means..." Saliné paused thoughtfully. "That means that he wanted to absolve both Codrin and himself at the same time. Perhaps he had a premonition of his death, or perhaps he was just making an overture, trying to inform me step by step. It was not easy for him. It was not easy for me." She paused again and sipped some wine. "A few days ago, Calista reminded me about a soldier who resembled Edric. We were walking in the park, and she made me walk toward the stables to see him. She said that she wanted to make a joke. The soldier was gone."

"You think it was him who..." Cernat asked.

"I think so, and I assume he is dead. The same as Rosine should have been dead by now."

"Do you think," Cernat asked carefully, "that Cosmin's accident was planned by Edric and Calista, or they just took advantage of what happened?"

"It's only a guess, but I think that they planned a sort of a minor riding accident. One that could be used against Codrin. It went wrong. It no longer matters." She shrugged and struggled to control her wandering thoughts. *I was harsh with Calista, but she used my son as if he were a toy. And Edric...* "What matters now is that an unknown party interfered and send *that* soldier to scare the mare. And to kill my son. He was chosen for his resemblance to Edric. That party wanted Edric dead, and I think that it was Codrin who..." Saliné stopped for a few moments and moistened her lips. "Who killed him. I doubt that we will ever know who sent the soldier to scare the mare." *I am not sure that I want to know.*

The news about the death of the Silvanian King came to Muniker a week later. Joined by Joachim and ten thousand soldiers, Alfrid went to Silvania to claim his new crown.

Chapter 27 - Codrin

Four groups of people arrived at the bridge over the Rhiun River almost at the same time. Codrin and his men were two hundred paces from the riverbank when they saw a small band of riders, led by two women, already crossing the bridge from the other side.

"Let them pass," Codrin said, and moved his horse out of the road, signaling to the incoming riders that he had no intention to harass them. *Wanderers?* He watched the women's silhouettes becoming clearer. There was also a large Mounte with them, whose horse was probably unhappy. Suddenly, Codrin pushed Zor and met them at the exit from the bridge. He dismounted abruptly, and caught the first woman in his arms, even before she was fully dismounted, then turned her twice in the air.

"You did not forget how a warm greeting should be." She laughed, and he put her down.

"Strange," Codrin said, with a thoughtful look, unable to fully hide the glimmer in his eyes, "I have the impression that something has changed since the last time we met. Perhaps you have grown."

"A little. Perhaps."

"From here to here." Horizontal with the ground, his palm moved from his breastbone to the top of her head, which was at the same level as his mouth. "Not very much, indeed."

"We are all like this, in my family."

"Yes, you are," Codrin said, and a hint of bitterness touched his voice.

"You know what happened. I am sorry."

"Yes, I passed through Muniker, but why should you be sorry?" Codrin ruffled her hair, and his bitterness faded. "Where are you going? We can stop here for the night. There are many things to talk about."

"It's only afternoon. Why stop so early?"

They must have an urgent errand. "Well." Codrin shrugged to hide his disappointment. "Where is home for you now?"

"Poenari."

"Then we may meet again there. We are going to Arad and Poenari. To ask... Well, I don't really know how things will work for me after all these changes."

"I know." She laughed. It became contagious, and the people behind her looked amused at Codrin. "That's why we are here, though I have to say that our Visions were strange and blurred, and you were never present in them. We've guessed from other people's actions. Poenari is waiting for you. It's a sort of an ... isolated island in Frankis. Saliné has allowed that. I'm monopolizing you; there are more people waiting in the line." She gestured behind her.

Codrin let her go and looked around. In front of him, Amelie was in Lisandru's arms, but she pulled herself away from her husband and came to meet Codrin. "Another girl who grew in my absence," he said, embracing her, then turned toward the largest Mounte he had ever met. *Strange,* he thought, *I've met four young girls in my new life in Frankis. One of them became my wife; the other three became my friends. At least my friends did not betray me. Or perhaps I am too harsh with Saliné. Am I?*

"I think that I did not grow too much since you left." Boldur laughed, towering over Codrin, as they clasped hands.

"Perhaps it was not needed."

He knew all the men, and their friendly greetings warmed Codrin. It took them a while to move again. The long bridge toward Frankis gave Codrin the shivers. Not because it was the longest bridge in Frankis and Litvonia. Not because in the middle it narrowed as one pylon had collapsed, and there were no longer masons with the skills of the old ones, who died hundreds of years ago. The bridge had been repaired – it was too important to let it fail – but it was narrow in the middle. *This is the third time I have crossed the Rhiun*, Codrin thought, *and each time, something new came into my life. The last time, it was a sort of death which came into my life. Isn't that strange?* He let Zor choose his pace and was soon engulfed in the midst of the riders. From time to time, they looked at him and worried for the inner struggle reflected on his face, yet they did not disturb him.

At the other end of the bridge, there was a kind of repetition; three men were waiting patiently for the larger group to pass. One of them carried the Primus Itinerant of Frankis insignia. He smiled broadly as the group approached. "I did not know that so many people from Poenari went to Litvonia. Is there something I missed?"

"Perhaps," the first woman said.

"Aliana, did you see your sister? There are some rumors related to the next nomad invasion."

"I wasn't in Muniker. That's your destination, not mine."

From the corner of his eye, Verenius caught the next incoming rider, but his attention was still on Aliana. The fleeting image returned to him like an afterthought, and he turned his head abruptly, his lower jaw dropping. He blinked like a man confronted by a ghost.

"Are you hungry, Verenius?" Codrin asked, without stopping.

"This is not..." Verenius turned his head toward Aliana, and he read the contempt in her eyes. "Your majesty," he breathed.

"Thanks to your Circle and the Wanderers, I am no longer the King of Frankis," Codrin said without turning.

"Everything that happened was a mistake, but we could not know. We thought you were dead." Verenius pushed his horse until he was riding parallel with Codrin.

"You wanted me dead. The Circle tried to kill me. The only mistake was that you failed."

"That's not true," Verenius said, speaking fast, almost like a child caught cheating, and Codrin did not bother to answer. "Or at least I was not aware of it. If that's true, Maud will pay. And the situation we have now is now even worse than what we had before you unified Frankis; it's a disaster. All the things that were done in Frankis and Litvonia will unravel."

Apart from a fleeting glance when he left the bridge, Codrin never looked at Verenius, but his stare got colder. He kept his anger inside. They had created this situation. It was not his failure or his fault. "Perhaps. We will know next year."

"Whatever you think of me, I acted in the interests of the Realm. I was proud of unifying Frankis and Litvonia peacefully, the same way I was proud when you unified Frankis against the Circle's will. Now, I have to eat my pride."

"Be careful, it may be poisonous."

"It's bitter, for sure. You will always be the King of Frankis for me. I am your man. Let me come with you."

For the first time, Codrin really looked at the Primus Itinerant. "Then come with me, Verenius. Taking back the crown of Frankis again may be even more poisonous than your pride."

"Curse me, but we have to work with the Circle and the Wanderers."

"Do you really think that I can work with those who tried to kill me?"

"The Realm is weaker now. We need to find a solution. We can't find it without them."

"Like killing me again? This time properly?"

"I still don't know what happened to you. You vanished for more than three years..."

"You will learn all in Poenari. I hate that story. Don't ask me to tell it three times a day."

A few minutes later, led by Pintea, the fourth group caught with them. "I have a letter from Saliné," he said, before dismounting.

"Will you return to Muniker?" Codrin asked.

"In a month or two. I was not given a date to return, and I want to see Poenari again." Pintea winked and laughed.

"Then I will read the letter in Poenari." *It will be good to have Pintea there.* "There are other people you know in the group."

Pintea looked at Aliana, and his eyes brightened. "You must be ... Aliana. I apologize for this direct approach; it may be that you no longer remember me."

"Should I?" she asked, thoughtfully, a little glimmer in her eyes. "You resemble a skinny boy who pestered me when I was alone because this man there," she pointed at Codrin, "was too busy with his protector of caravans games. And my sister was some sort of a prisoner in Severin. His eyes were always dreaming about a girl, though I never knew who she was."

"Was he that transparent?"

"Men are transparent to women in general, and even more to those who have the Light."

"Yes," Pintea said, a touch of melancholy in his voice. "The Wanderers have the advantage of the Light."

"Pintea, I am no longer a Wanderer."

Then there may be some hope for me, he thought, meeting her eyes.

"And I think that I deserve a warmer greeting from an old friend who ran with me through all the forests around Severin when I had nothing to do." Aliana laughed and embraced him, and they stayed like that a little longer than was needed for a simple greeting.

In the evening, close to the heart of one of the three fires, Codrin took Aliana's hands in his. "Aliana... I am still not accustomed to this name, but I was told that you no longer use the old one. We need to talk about something that happened six years ago." Unaware how focused Pintea was, looking at them, Codrin pulled her hands closer to him. "It's about a strange Vision, in which I was not alone."

"So, it happened. I thought that I was dreaming."

"Everything was blurred and fragmented. I could hear only one word in two. The only thing I could understand was that a girl had been kidnapped by the Wanderers. There was no name. It took me a few days to decide to visit Alba Hive. On the road, I was turned back by the Empress, who told me that Aliana had already taken the Oath, and she was on the road toward Nerval. Then Drusila brought me a letter from Dochia. I turned back. I am sorry. I should have been more..."

"They were right; it was necessary to go to Nerval. You know why."

"Yes, you saved the Realm, but I did not think those two women could be so wicked not to let Jara know that you were alive."

"I did not even know that I was *dead*."

"I may forgive Drusila for trying to kill me, but I will never forgive her for what she did to you and to Jara."

"Drusila? I understood that the nomads attacked you."

"Those who tried to kill me were Alfrid's men. And everything was instigated by the Wanderers and the Circle. I am not yet sure how much was Drusila involved in this. We can talk about this later. In Muniker, they are no longer my family, but they are still your family, and they love you."

"I love them too, and each time they get out of Litvonia I will run to meet them. It has never happened though since I left. But I will never return to Muniker. I have even more reasons now. And perhaps I am little upset at Mother because she pushed things in the wrong direction with the marriage. That does not absolve Saliné."

"They are your family, and Jara was always a practical woman."

"Sometimes, that had unintended consequences."

Soon after their talk ended, Aliana sat next to Pintea, their shoulders almost touching. "I still don't know who that girl you were dreaming of was," she said, her voice rich and warm.

"Does this answer your question?" Pintea asked and took her hand in his.

"It does."

A day later, they reached the carriage with Ildeko, Pireska and the children. Codrin embraced them all. "I will explain everything in Poenari," Codrin said, seeing the mute questions on the faces of the people who rode with him. "The only thing you need to know now is that they saved my life, and that the little one is my son."

Suddenly, Aliana frowned and went in front of Ildeko, who was holding Ioan in her arms. She touched the boy's hand, stretching her mind into the Light. No Vision came to her, but she felt something strange in him, something that it would affect everybody's future. Her eyes met Codrin's. "There is something in Ioan's future. Nothing bad, but I have to learn more."

Once they arrived in Mehadia, old memories started to haunt Codrin. These were places that he knew, places where he fought and won battles and cities. He felt defeated now. *Mehadia belongs to Devan now. I was close to losing Saliné to his son. Then to Bucur. Then to Eduin. I lost her to the Pig King. I need to forget this. Here, I met Mara, and I have a son with her. I have children from two women I like, but I was not married to. I no longer have a son from the woman I was married to, and I loved. I did not think it would be so hard to lose a child. I still love her, and that's what makes everything so difficult, but there are other links between this land and me than Saliné. I have deep roots here. This is my kingdom.*

Codrin thought about the subtle irony of life, and its forks, more numerous than could be found on the longest road and asked himself how one could trace back to see where the fork that had led to a specific event appeared. Some lines were so long that they became lost memories. Some questions could never be answered.

In Poenari he found his people, twenty-seven days after leaving Muniker under the cover of night. Mara and their son; Vlaicu who had come from Arad; Varia and her daughter, Livia; Sava and Julien; Valer. Only old Bernard was missing; he had died three months earlier, and that's why Amelie, his granddaughter and Lisandru's wife, was there. There was a bit of strangeness and warm memories resurfacing, when Mara embraced him, but then she presented her husband, and Codrin felt a sort of relief. His son, Radu, was now ten years old, and Codrin realized that he considered Mara's husband more a father than himself. *Things will change in time*, Codrin thought. *If I stay alive.*

❧

After a week in Poenari, Codrin started to feel at home again. He felt a stranger too; so many things had happened while he was away. It would take time to learn everything. Sava entered Codrin's office and placed the papers on his desk. "We have an unexpected visit. Darkness and Shadow honor us. Should I prepare the gallows?"

"I can say many things about them, but at least they don't lack courage." The door opened, and before the young page could ask, Codrin said, "Let them enter."

On the surface, nothing could be read on Drusila's and Maud's faces; they were women of power, able to hide their worries, but the thoughts and feelings swirling in them were more like a storm than a breeze. Codrin raised a brow at them; gestured toward some chairs on the other side of his desk.

"Your majesty," Drusila said, echoed by Maud, and she was the first one to sit; then she waited, her fingers drumming softly on the table.

Skimming through his papers, Codrin ignored them for a few minutes. "What brings you here?" he asked, eventually.

"I couldn't miss seeing my sister," Drusila gestured at Maud, "being hanged with a 'traitor' placard tied to her body. I suppose she could not miss the same thing happening to me."

"Did you have a Vision about your hanging, and come to advise me on how to proceed? Preferences? Silk rope? Perfumed soap?" Codrin asked, still looking into his papers.

"Do we need one?"

"A Wanderer taught me once that a Vision opens a way into the future. Why did you come here? I am tempted to hang you for trying to kill me. Or are you a step ahead of me, and you've brought the poison that killed the Dukes Stefan and Manuc?"

"We never tried to kill you."

"Then everything was just a nightmare. I am still the King of Frankis. My wife was not sold to the Litvonian King. My son is still alive, playing in the garden."

"We work for the Realm. So do you. There is no need to tell you why all this happened, you already know; I talked with the Empress before coming here. We accepted the plan of the Litvonian Wanderers and Circle, but we never tried to kill you. No one from Frankis tried to kill you, and no one will try. And I am afraid that the nightmare has just started."

"Ah, yes, my being alive is a nightmare for you. Did you bring the poison? Calista thought it could cure your nightmare. It seems that she was wrong. I am still alive. Her death saddened me. I am no longer able to hang her for killing my son, but at least I killed Edric. He organized my assassination three years, and he killed my son. You came here only because your wicked plan, which began with the assassination attempt against me, has started to unravel."

"We did not know about Calista..." Drusila's voice broke a little, but it recovered fast. "In a few weeks, Silvania will be unified with Litvonia and Frankis. It's one more step toward unifying the continent. It's what the Wanderers, the Circle and the Assassins were created for. It's what you planned as the Seer of the Realm."

"And what do you want from me? My blessing? I am no longer the Seer. The Empress took care of that; she was afraid that I would learn about your attempt to assassinate me."

"The strongest Litvonian Wanderer died. Their best army commander died. Next year, the nomads will invade the Realm again. The burden of the Seer is for life. You are the Pillar of the Realm now."

"You must lead the army against the nomads." The translucent silhouette of the Empress appeared inside his mind, together with Drusila and Maud.

Codrin stretched his mind until he broke free from that inner world. “Sava, there is a new Wanderer that has joined us inside our minds. You can’t see her, and you will not be able to hear us from now on. I may behave strangely at times, because I will not be able to see well or fully control my body. Neither will they.” He gestured at Drusila and Maud, who were still talking to the Empress.

“Then I should leave.”

“No, I need you to watch and memorize everything. How we move, or how our faces and bodies react during the conversation. You have a keen sense of observation.”

“My sense makes me itch to strangle Drusila.”

“Don’t, she will look better hanged.” Codrin blinked and went back to his inner world.

“You must lead the army against the nomads,” the Empress repeated.

“Whose army?” Codrin asked.

“The army of the Realm.”

“You are avoiding my question.”

“No, it’s you who is avoiding your duties. You must defeat Baraki and allow the full unification of the continent. That is what it means to be a Pillar. And the Pillar is meant to serve the Realm.”

This pause was longer than the one before, and when Codrin spoke again his voice was different somehow. “Baraki killed my family and tried to kill me. Alfrid killed my son, ruined my family, and tried to kill me. But at least Baraki is a strong man, and he became King by his own actions. Alfrid is just a puppet in your hands. I had a Vision before leaving Muniker: the Silvanian King will not die naturally. He will be poisoned, so that your puppet can inherit a new crown.”

“It’s Saliné who will lead the Empire.”

“And that should make me feel better?”

“We are talking about unifying the continent, and making the Realm safer, no wars, no more nomad invasions. Are you too weak to pass over your feelings for your lost wife? We are trying to build..."

"You have already failed. There is no foundation under your building. You took a stone from Frankis, gave her to a mud-man, and asked her to build in a swamp. Muniker is a swamp. It was like this since you built the Litvonian Kingdom, Empress. The Alban Empire was created by tough men and women. It became weak in time and vanished. Muniker is as rotten as the Alban Empire became close to its demise. You know that. I've already made my decision. You will learn it soon." Codrin stretched his mind to break the grip of the Empress's own mind and went back into the real world.

Drusilla leaned forward, hands on her knees; the inner world was a blurred copy of the real one, and something flickered in her eyes, a distant horizon, a movement of things across an imagined future. There was something in her Vision, yet there was nothing. "Empress, don't ask us to kill him. I won't do it."

"When did I ever ask you to kill somebody? You poisoned Dukes Stefan and Manuc because your plans needed it. I did not ask that, though I agreed with your plans. The Litvonian Wanderers took the decision to kill Codrin, and I agreed with that too. I always agree with a coherent plan for the Realm, which has a good chance of success. Codrin was planning to take Litvonia too, and he would have defeated Alfrid, but asserting authority over a larger kingdom takes years. I feared that he would be too weak to face the nomads and the Arenian army led by Baraki during the invasion. I assumed that we would have three kingdoms united under Saliné's and Edric's rule. Yes, Alfrid would have been replaced by Edric on the throne; that was Calista's plan. In some ways, Edric resembled Codrin. You don't know, but Saliné had already realized that, and she was slowly being prepared by her entourage to accept him as her husband."

"Three years ago, Codrin had accepted to postpone the invasion of Litvonia until the nomads would have been defeated."

"Yes, but the plans were already in motion, and it was an issue with his son, Cosmin. He was too weak to keep the Empire and unable to have children. We could not afford another civil war at Saliné's and Codrin's death. It would have ruined everything."

"Our plans went a bit awry."

"It happens sometimes. We have one year to find a solution. My feeling is that Codrin will take a decision, which will allow him to postpone the real one. Well," the Empress shrugged, "we will learn that soon." And she vanished, leaving the two women a little bewildered, feeling that the rope was tightening around their necks. The Empress was up there; they were living in the real world. At times, that could be dangerous.

Codrin ignored them when they returned from their inner world, and both women left the room, unwilling to stir another discussion that could bring the gallows back. "Well?" Codrin looked at Sava when they were alone.

Words did not come easily to Sava. There were things to consider, and he had the feeling that his answer might change the fate of Frankis and more. His first answer was only to buy time. "Maud looked like a dead fish. She did not move at all. Without her breathing, I could have thought that she was some piece of exotic furniture that you brought from Litvonia."

"She was just a witness."

"Drusila has the cold mind of a snake, and knows how to hide her thoughts, but somehow she lost control over her hands. They were restless, wriggling or drumming the table with her fingers. In more than twenty years, I've never seen her acting like this. I could feel her fear, yet I don't know what she feared. She did not seem too impressed by the threat of a rope around her neck, so it must be something different."

Yes, Codrin nodded.

This will be the most important thing; Sava thought and moistened his lips. "You were uneasy, as if you were forced to take a decision and feared its outcome. Yet a decision you must take. Your people are uneasy too, and they are waiting for you to decide their future. Your future."

"Tomorrow, I will decide," Codrin said and, eyes closed, he leaned against the backrest of his chair.

The next day came sooner than Codrin had wanted, and all his important people were gathered in the Council Room, including the Dukes, who had come in haste just the evening before. Codrin glanced away and exhaled, hard, fighting an inner voice brining a stern reminder that lost opportunities have a habit to take revenge. "I am the right ruler of Frankis, and I intend to *rule* it, but I will not claim the crown now." His voice was grave, and he enunciated each word slowly and clearly. "Alfrid is stupid enough to send an army here in spring before the nomad invasion. I will claim the crown after the nomads are defeated."

There was a long moment of uneasiness around the table; some people were hoping for an earlier claim. Under his calm voice, they felt Codrin's indecision. They knew him too well.

Suddenly, Drusila sprang to her feet and bowed deeply. "Thank you, your majesty."

"What are you thanking me for? I have said nothing yet about the gallows."

"I will thank you for that too, if you choose not to build one for me. You took the right decision for the Realm. Few people are able to retrain themselves when power is involved." There was a sudden surge of Light in her, but no Vision came, only a vague intuition. "It may serve you better than you think now."

That evening, Codrin finally opened Saliné's letter. He was not surprised to read that she asked him to do what he had just done, to postpone his claim on Frankis. One reason was the nomad invasion, the other was asking for some sort of negotiations to find a compromise.

We know each other well, but what kind of compromise can be found between a man who still thinks that he has a wife and kingdom, and the woman who thinks different? Codrin twirled the letter between his fingers. *Yet I have the feeling that some sort of understanding may be found. Perhaps I am just fooling myself. Or perhaps not.*

Chapter 28 - Saliné / Codrin / Alfrid

In mid-spring, Vlaicu arrived with ten thousand riders in Muniker, and Count Joachim led them to their reserved place in the camp in front of the main gate. It was a calm day, if not for the agitation of the men. There was more stir than was normal in a camp of such size. And more fear. Even the rats running between the tents knew that. From the camp, Vlaicu went directly to the palace, to the throne hall, where all the commanders were gathered in front of Alfrid and Saliné.

"Your majesties," Vlaicu bowed. "I have brought ten thousand Frankis soldiers with me."

"I asked for twenty thousand." Alfrid glared at him, his narrow lips pressed together in an angry line.

"My orders come from the Seer, your majesty. That was the number he considered appropriate for this war. The new nomad army has a hundred fifty thousand less soldiers than the previous one. The Arenian army will be delayed and will not be able to join the nomads in time. I was charged to tell you that the danger is smaller."

Alfrid snapped his head, struggling to find a crushing answer, but Saliné was faster. "We have to thank you for coming to our aid, and for the information, but the nomads are still stronger than us." She placed her palm over Alfrid's. *Why doesn't he see it? Codrin came halfway and sent the army as the Seer, not the King of Frankis. We must leave the door open for negotiations.*

"We are leaving in two days. Prepare your men," Alfrid said abruptly. He did not address Vlaicu in particular, and stood up, followed by Saliné.

The day before leaving Muniker, Alfrid took captain Roderick aside. "I will promote you the second commander of the Palace Guard, but Alois will come with me. You will stay to guard my family. You will receive two more companies of archers. The ones you used four years ago to kill Codrin. You failed then, and Codrin remembered that he was talking to you just before he was shot, and his men killed. He may arrive in Muniker to take the city while I am away. He will try to trick the Queen to let him enter. Then he will try to occupy the palace and the throne. Here is a paper that gives you authority over the Royal Guard too. All the commanders and soldiers from Frankis will come with me. Frinz will command the Royal Guard during my absence. Take care, Roderick, that man in Frankis is dangerous. For both of us. This is the paper." Alfrid extended his arm and gave it to the new commander.

"I will not fail you again, your majesty."

Unknown to Alfrid, Vlad had sent twenty guards from Frankis on patrol in the south. They returned three days after the army had left Muniker and put themselves at Saliné's disposal.

Vlaicu and Joachim worked well together and chose the battlefield and the strategy. They were able to arrive before the nomads at the position their scouts had marked on the maps. It was a good position, large enough to let their army use its full power, narrow enough to constraint the larger nomad army. A copy of Codrin's strategy. Behind them, there was a small ridge with a two-hundred-foot gap in the middle, and five hundred archers were placed on it. In front of their army, there were now a hundred fifty thousand nomads. Alfrid's army had sixty thousand men. The ratio was better than during the first nomad invasion, but Alfrid was not Codrin. Every soldier knew that. The ratio should have been even better, but the Silvanian army had to counter a column of ten thousand nomads at their northern border and was delayed by two weeks. Hunkai, the nomad commander, was a clever man; with only ten thousand light riders, he had kept the heavy Hussaris cavalry of Silvania out of the main battle.

As in the previous battle, the nomads were let to make the first attack. Twenty thousand riders from their right wing moved like a wall across the field. Alfrid's left wing was ready to charge and meet them. In the middle of the battlefield, the nomads gradually altered their course, moving left. They looked like one body, twenty thousand riders moving with a precision and synchronization that would have shamed a flock of crows. They rode in parallel to the center of Alfrid's army, and a cloud of arrows darkened the sky. The nomads were trained from their childhood to ride and shoot at the same time. Half of the arrows fell short. Half of them fell on soldiers. Alfrid felt a sting in his left upper arm. The arrow had passed through his ring-mail. It cut his skin, going an inch deep. For a hardened soldier that was only a scratch.

"I am wounded," he cried and turned his horse abruptly. Joachim tried to stop him, but Alfrid cried again: "Get out of my way, I am badly wounded."

His hundred strong Guard followed him, and in two minutes they were out of sight. Then five hundred riders more turned their horses and ran. Then one thousand. Then more. There were no more than thirty thousand soldiers still standing. Ten thousand of them were from Frankis, the only army that did not try to run. From Litvonia, Count Joachim, Duke Homburg, Duke Drasdin, and Vlad's Royal Guard stayed, but they were no more than twenty thousand men. Like one single body, the nomad army moved up the plain. They did not hurry, trying to build more pressure, waiting for the enemy army to disintegrate from fear.

"We must retreat!" Vlaicu shouted. "Orderly! Start from the left. Vlad, take every archer you can find and place them on the ridge behind us, to cover our withdrawal. Duke Drasdin, you will move back first with your spearmen. Be ready to close the gap when the last rider pass. This will turn ugly."

Two-thirds of the Litvonian and Frankis soldiers were able to leave through the gap behind before the nomads finally reached them. It was a swift clash, between a running army and a confident one. Joachim was gravely wounded. A curved nomad sword hit his helmet and bounced off to cut into his shoulder. His right thigh was already wounded, and he lost control over his body. He lost the halter. Half conscious, he leaned on his right and started to slide.

Boldur lunged with his long arm, and his sword hit the nomad in his chest, throwing him from his horse. He picked Joachim up with one hand and laid the half-conscious man on his horse, in front of him. "Try not to fall," Boldur said, and parried another sword attack.

Vlad's archers started to shoot, and the nomads decided not to follow the running army. They were men of swift action, and the battle had ended with less than a thousand dead on their side. They were thinking now about the coming pillage. About the blonde women they would rape in the undefended villages. They liked the blonde Litvonian women. They were thinking about the slaves they would capture. The Serpent had brought them great luck in this invasion. It did not look at all like the previous disaster.

Hunkai, the nomad commander, had his own dream. It involved taking Muniker and spending his nights in the Queen's bed. That would enhance his fame. There were many tales about her beauty, and he had seen the woman in Arad, before the first nomad invasion. Hunkai's mother was a blonde Rosin, and he inherited his looks from her. Unlike his hapless brother, who commanded the last invasion. He was a good spy and had learned many things on his trips, though he could not find the red-haired woman called Vio. He was sent by Baraki to kill her, but she was already dead. *Saliné ... She has red hair too,* he thought. It was a known thing that a red-haired woman makes a man stronger in bed. *I will light a hundred candles in her bedroom to see her hair while I have her.* It was also a known thing that Baraki wanted the

Queen for his son, but Hunkai was within his rights. If he was able to take Muniker, the Queen was his plunder. He would have her for two or three weeks, then give her to Baraki's son. Perhaps she would become pregnant and give him a red-haired son. It was within his rights to get the child, though Baraki's son would get the woman. That would enhance his fame even more. It was a known thing that red-haired warriors are fierce in battle. *Perhaps I should declare her dead and take her with me. I am more a man than her husband or Baraki's son. Her King ran away from battle.* He spat in disgust; the thought that a man could be such a coward enraged him. *It may be dangerous to kidnap her, but I am dangerous too. Saliné... I don't like that name. I will find another one. The Red Moon... It fits her better.* Hunkai was a determined man. His older brother had lost the previous war and his life. He would win this one. Unknown to Baraki, he had started the invasion ten days earlier, trying to take Litvonia and prove himself. There was the consideration about the pillage too. After the victory, Baraki would become Emperor, and Litvonia his land. Pillage would be forbidden. *War without pillage is a tree without fruits, a waste of time and men.* He looked at the tough men around him and said only one word: Pillage. The nomads cheered him in one loud voice.

Codrin avoided Muniker on his route toward the north-east of Litvonia. It was not a long detour, only twenty more miles. In Poenari he had a Vision about the battle; it was a blurred thing, and he did not know the outcome, but he saw Alfrid running away. His Vision came late, and they rode like madmen across the roads in Frankis and Litvonia. They still arrived twelve days after Alfrid had left his city. At the crossroads north of Muniker, Codrin found a small army camped on the plain, and he stopped his march. The scouts returned with the news that five thousand Litvonian soldiers were ready to join him.

"They are led by Count Ulmas," the lead scout said. "He is waiting to meet you at the crossroads."

Recalling what happened after the first nomad invasion, Codrin took two hundred soldiers with him. At the crossroads, he found ten guards, the Count, and two women twenty paces in front of the men.

"The road through Muniker was shorter," Saliné said in a bitter, yet calm voice. Her face was white, and she was lacking sleep; there were blue circles around her eyes. She knew that Alfrid had run from the battle, and the army crumbled because of his cowardness. She knew that many villages were pillaged right now, people were killed, women were raped, and many more were taken slaves. She knew, and she could do nothing to save them.

"But perhaps not safer," Codrin said, fighting against his own surge of bitterness. It had nothing to do with his safety. It had everything to do with the woman in front of him.

"Would be so hard for you to work with me against the nomads?"

"Yes," he said curtly. "Our views regarding the political situation in Frankis are quite different. We are not on the same side. We are no longer in the same family."

Oh, Codrin, how I wish things to be different. The glimmer in Saliné's eyes became sad, but she said nothing.

"Does it matter?" Dochia asked. "Does it matter when the nomads are so close to Muniker?"

"You know, Dochia? When I first came to defend Litvonia from the nomads, I was thinking like you. We both know what happened. Am I wiser now? Perhaps. We will know in the end."

"You did not defend Litvonia. You defended the Realm. Even without the Seer's powers, you are still bond to the Realm. You are the Pillar."

"Isn't it strange that the Wanderers did not care too much about that bond? Was I not the Pillar of the Realm when they tried to kill me?"

"You are answering wrong with wrong. The Litvonian army was routed by the nomads."

"I know. That's why I came." The scouts had brought him the news of the battle only the day before and confirmed his Vision.

"What can you do with ten thousand soldiers?"

"Dochia," Saliné said gently. "We are all worried, but we can't change what happened. Codrin," she turned toward him, "I brought you five thousand riders. They are not the best, but it was all I could get. There are more than a hundred and fifty thousand nomads, less than two hundred miles away." She gestured toward the north-east, to cover the tremor in her voice. Her upper lip trembled too, and she bit into it. "Seven thousand Hussaris will arrive from Silvania in five days, but I don't know if we have those days."

Looking at her, Codrin recalled the few times when he had seen her so troubled. Saliné was always composed and could hide her worries well. His mind went back in time, to Severin, when they were struggling with Aron's and the Circle's intrigues. "Five thousand soldiers are a good help," he said gently, and stretched his hand toward hers. Saying nothing, Saliné placed her hand in his. "I've heard what happened to Calista; Jara wrote everything to me." *Strangely, now that Calista is dead, I no longer hate her so much*. He gripped Saliné's hand gently, and she answered the same way. "Vlaicu is waiting for me fifty miles north of here. He has ten thousand soldiers from Frankis and twenty thousand from Litvonia. Count Joachim is with him, but he is wounded. Alfrid was wounded too. I am sorry." *A scratch on his arm.* But he could not tell her that.

"I know about Alfrid, he took refuge in Auers fortress. How is Joachim?"

"It could be better, but he will survive. How many guards do you have in Muniker?"

"One thousand five hundred."

"You will take another thousand of those who came here with you. Please do as I say," he added swiftly when Saliné tried to protest, grasping her hand more strongly. Unconsciously, his thumb swept over her skin. “I may be forced to use the same strategy as in Poenari and let them besiege Muniker while we harass them with night attacks. Joachim will come to Muniker too; he can’t fight right now, but he is a good commander, and Cernat knows what to do in a siege. Damian will come too; he was slightly wounded. We may be able to gather more soldiers who escaped and dispersed south of the battlefield. Joachim sent couriers, telling everybody to come south of the Jauras Mountains. My scouts are combing the area, looking for both friends and foes.”

“Is there no other way? The nomads will ruin all the villages on their path toward Muniker. They will kill and rape and take slaves.” This time, it was Saliné’s turn to strengthen her grip on his hand.

Codrin answered carefully. “If we arrive first, there is a chance to stop them close to Ratisbau, in the Jauras Mountains. It depends,” he stopped briefly, “if they’ve already split in many small bands and started the pillage. They have this habit after winning a battle, and that may play to our advantage. I have to leave now.”

Saliné nodded silently, raised her free hand to his face, her fingers touching him briefly. She turned abruptly and went to her guards, leaving him alone with Dochia. Saying nothing, the Wanderer embraced Codrin, then followed Saliné.

Codrin was half right about the nomads. They had split into three equal bands of fifty thousand soldiers and started to pillage the land, on their way to Muniker. One band passed Ratisbau without trying to take the fortress and went further south of the Jauras Mountains. Codrin waited for them to cross the Dunaris River and attacked when two thirds of their army was on his side. Less than a thousand nomads from those who crossed the river were able to run away. Codrin followed them, and occupied the pass close to Ratisbau, waiting for the Silvanian army to join him, then went south, toward Muniker.

On his road south, the scouts came with the news that the nomads were leaving Litvonia. Hunkai, the nomad commander, had tried hard to make them continue the attack on Muniker. He was killed by his own captains. One of their armies was almost destroyed, and the devil with two swords had returned. They did not want to meet him. There was enough plunder to take home, and they did not care much about Baraki, their Khad; they were a loose alliance of tribes, not a kingdom. Khads come and go; the tribes remain. It was like this for thousands of years. The nomads did not like to lose the spoils of war. During his dreams of glory and red-haired women, it seemed that Hunkai had forgotten that.

"Sometimes you need a bit of luck," Codrin said, looking at the map on the wall of the council tent.

"Sometimes?" Vlaicu asked and laughed.

"Well, always, but sometimes you need a bit more." Codrin laughed too. "Send five columns toward the border, different routes, two thousand men in each, to search the land. Put in the lead Litvonian commanders who know the area well. The nomads are usually chaotic when they retreat, and our men may be able to kill more of them and free some people who were taken as slaves."

Two days before Saliné and Codrin met, Alfrid arrived in Auers. It was not a large fortress but, raised on the top of an abrupt mountain, the tall walls were hard to take by siege. He felt secure there. The nomads were not good at taking fortresses. He felt bored too, from being forced to stay in a small room for more than a week, because of his wound. The bandage was as huge as the wound was small, covering his arm from the wrist to the shoulder and neck. The bandage restrained his movements, not the wound itself. A great bandage showed everybody that the King was badly wounded. It was a good strategy, and Alfrid smiled inside. The courier entered the room, and the King nodded absently at him.

"Sir Codrin has defeated the nomads," the courier said, struggling not to look content. After running from the battle because of his wound, Alfrid might be not pleased to hear that his sworn enemy had defeated the nomads.

"Ah, this is good news," Alfrid said to the courier's relief. "I suppose you are tired from the road. Go and rest now." Thoughtfully, Alfrid started to walk around the room. *Now everything is on Roderick. He must deny Codrin entry into Muniker. Soon, Baraki will come with the Arenian army, and Codrin will have to fight. That man killed his family. They will weaken each other. But ... if Codrin pulls a trick and finds a way to enter Muniker, he may take it for himself. Roderick must stop him. Saliné is a clever woman, and she convinced Codrin to postpone the claim for Frankis until after this nomad invasion. Now it's my job to solve the remaining issue. But if Roderick kills Codrin, Baraki is free to invade Litvonia.* Alfrid rubbed his chin, walking around the room. *Five thousand more guards in Muniker, and no one can take it from me. Autumn will come and Baraki will leave.* Alfrid smiled and sat in his chair, then started to write the letter for Roderick, the second Commander of the Palace Guard. There were not many words: He must not enter the city. Alfrid was a clever man. Four years ago, Roderick had led those two companies of archers, which had almost killed Codrin after the first nomad invasion. If Codrin won the throne, Roderick would lose his head too. The archers were in the same situation. Alfrid took care to say to Roderick that Codrin had recognized him and wanted his head. Roderick was clever too, he said the same to his thirty archers, and they were now his most trusted men in Muniker.

Count Joachim, the Duke of Hamborg and Damian arrived in Muniker late in the evening, with five hundred men, all wounded but able to ride. The Count's and the Duke's faces were whiter than the finest paper, and their mouths clenched; they had ridden by sheer will. Dismounting, they almost collapsed and were carried on stretchers to a suite close to Saliné's. There was an experienced healer to take care of them, but Saliné joined her, and several evenings she stayed with them, changing their bandages. Joachim's wounds were bad, but she said nothing to him.

"Your majesty," the Duke of Hamborg tried to protest when she worked on his bandage for the first time.

"I healed my first wounded man after the battle for Mehadia. I was just sixteen at the time, and I learned the trade from Codrin. But if you think that my skills are not good enough..." She smiled at the Duke, and for all his pain, he smiled too.

"I've told you that Saliné is not an ordinary woman," Joachim said to the Duke, when she finally left them alone. His weak voice carried a hint of amusement.

Five days later, Joachim tried to get out of bed; he wanted to check the strength of the Guard. Helgia, the old woman in charge, blocked his way, and with a discreet gesture sent a maid to fetch Saliné. She was not yet sure that Joachim would survive, but she was sure that he would die if he were to leave his bed.

"Joachim," Saliné said when she arrived, "in the healing room, Helgia is the Queen. We all listen to her. My grandfather, Frinz and Damian are supervising the guards. Don't worry; your time may come sooner that you would want. Men are always eager to fight."

"My Queen, I am afraid that I am not one of those men. I hate to fight." Joachim laughed, then he grimaced, as his movement brought up his pain. "If your majesty wants to satisfy a small curiosity of mine, Vlad also told me that he learned how to heal from Codrin. I wonder who taught him."

"I am sorry, but you have to ask Codrin that. It's not my tale to tell."

"I have a feeling that he got the skills from those men who taught him to fight with two curved swords. They know how to kill. They know how to heal. No one can kill better than a healer; it knows where to stab. Or so I've heard."

Saliné smiled but said nothing.

ஒ

Roderick did not feel right in his shoes as Guard Commander. There were too many things to consider, and his mind was restless. Each time a scout came from the outside, he questioned him. Alone. He did not know which of them would bring news from the King or bad news. The news from the King could be bad too. The man in front of him was the tenth scout who had come to Muniker in just three days. There were so many things.

"Codrin will be here in six hours, and he has five hundred soldiers with him. Almost forty thousand more are following him at a slower pace. They will be here tomorrow. The Silvanian army joined him in Ratisbau," the scout said to Roderick.

"Why is he coming here?"

"I don't know. There are rumors of another army coming soon, attacking from the west this time."

There is no other nomad army. He is coming to take Muniker. And to take my head. "Go and rest now." *This time, I am better prepared.*

For the second time in his long carrier, Captain Frinz left the main gate of the city without a captain and went to the palace. The first time was when the Seer had returned from the dead. "Your majesty," he bowed to Saliné, "we have a situation at the gate. Commander Roderick ordered me to close the gate and stop the Seer entering the city."

"Roderick doesn't command you or the Guard of Muniker. He is in charge of the Palace Guard."

"He has a written decree from the King. It puts me under his command."

"I see. Go back to the gate and send a courier when Codrin comes in sight. You will tell no one about this."

"Close the gate!" Roderick shouted, looking at the incoming riders. The last rain had been two weeks ago, and they stirred a lot of dust on the road. They looked like ghosts. "Nobody enters without my permission."

"The gate stays open." Saliné was just twenty paces behind him.

"The King gave orders to let no one inside," Roderick said, his voice low and cornered.

"Commander," Saliné said icily, "you don't tell me what to do. Frinz, when Codrin arrives, give him an escort to take him directly to the palace."

"I apologize, your majesty, sometimes my new position gives me headaches." Roderick bowed, avoiding her eyes. *I need to find another way.*

Roderick was a clever man. In the last letter, the King had asked him only to bar Codrin's entry into Muniker, but he knew how to read between the lines. He would not let the man live again. Codrin was a dangerous man, who liked to kill. Roderick was on his list. The captain enjoyed his life and was starting to appreciate being a commander. He still had headaches from needing to think about too many things at the same time, but he enjoyed his new power. He would take great care to keep it. With five archers, he climbed the stairs toward one of the many balconies of the throne hall. The afternoon sun was halfway down from its zenith, and the light was not great up there. Nobody would see them. Below, on the floor, the light played colored games, filtered by the stained glass. He chose the large balcony in the middle; it offered a good view to the archers and enough space to move without been seen. The hall was still empty, and they sat down on the floor, hidden behind the balustrade.

Saliné decided to receive Codrin in the throne hall. He deserved that, and she was standing waiting for him to traverse the hall. He deserved that too. There were not many people there; she knew that Codrin did not like large ceremonies.

"Be ready," Roderick said to his archers, and they stood up, careful not to be seen from the floor.

Saliné's and Codrin's eyes met, and there was a spark that both struggled to ignore. They were people who knew how to control themselves, and nothing could be read on their faces.

"Thank you," she said simply.

The archers in the balcony nocked their bows. "Be ready at my signal, I don't want to hurt the Queen," Roderick ordered, then turned abruptly as two young women entered the room. There was a moment of silence, and Roderick looked at them, starting with the one who was taller than him. The second one barely reached his chin. *I don't know them, but they are young and ignorant.* He moved to escort them out.

"I think you are tired." Saliné looked at Codrin. "A room is waiting for you, then we will have dinner."

"What are you doing here?" Roderick asked the women. Abruptly, the archers lowered and hid their bows.

"Sir Roderick," the tall one curtsied, "we are lost. It's our first time in the castle, and we want to see the Seer. I thought the view would be better from here." She looked down past the captain and advanced a little. "I was wrong. Is there a lower balcony? We will be in your debt if you can help us." She smiled warmly at him and stepped a little further on, craning her neck to look down. The second woman came closer too, but she was shy and hid behind the first one.

Codrin pondered how he would survive having dinner with Saliné after so long. *Cernat will be there. And Jara. Why did I think that we would dine alone?* He laughed quietly inside, a touch of bitter humor. "Thank you." He tried to say more but found that his mouth was sealed. Or his mind was sealed.

There was a moment of silence, as Saliné did not feel at ease either. "Please follow me," she finally said. It took her a great effort to find even the simplest words.

"There are no balconies on a lower level," Roderick said, struggling to keep his calm. He saw Saliné and Codrin ready to leave the hall. "You must go now." He took the tall woman by her arm and pushed her back toward the door. "You are distracting the guards."

"I apologize," the woman said, still craning her neck, her voice disappointed. "Would you escort us down? I am afraid of getting lost."

"I have duties to perform." Roderick pushed her harder toward the door, and went past the smaller woman, who finally found the courage to move toward the balustrade and look down.

"Get out now," Roderick snapped, and stretched his free hand to grab the second woman. His foot slipped, and he sprawled on the floor. The guards smiled and looked away, pretending not to see what had happened; Roderick was an important man now, and had a bad temper.

The women sprang. Two guards fell before any of the others realized what happened, except for one. It was too late for him; a knife cut his throat. The tall woman's foot went into the stomach of another guard, throwing him down. On her side, the small one killed the fourth guard, then jumped on the fallen man. There were some grunts, and falling bodies, but the guards did not shout. The fight ended in less than twenty seconds. Down in the hall, Saliné and Codrin were leaving through the door. Three or four people raised their heads toward the balcony – there was nothing to be seen.

"This one stained my dress," the small woman said, rubbing it above her knee; her foot was still on his chest. "That's a pity; I was becoming accustomed to wear such expensive dresses. All my clothes together would cost less than this garment." She laughed. "Your sister has good taste. It's a pity that I can't take with me to the Hive. They would kill me for such a dress."

"It happens sometimes during a fight." The tall woman laughed quietly and nudged Roderick with her boot; she thought she had seen him moving. "Dead. He looked taller in my Vision. Such a short man made me climb here. He deserved to die. Now let's go and report to my dear sister. She promised us a place at her table for dinner." She bent to clean her knife on Roderick's shirt.

"Why did you not tell her about your Vision?"

"She had enough things to worry about, but mostly I wanted to protect Mother. She... She has been acting a bit strange lately, I was told."

The royal dinner was mostly silent; none of them seemed to be able to find the right words. There were short sentences now and then, banal things that all of them were trained to say and keep the appearance of a conversation. From time to time, Saliné and Codrin glanced at each other, when the other one was not aware. Or so they thought.

"Before coming here," Aliana said, struggling to stifle a smile, knowing well what reaction her words would stir, "we killed Roderick." *I hope this will make you more talkative.*

"What?" Saliné asked, her hand suspended between the plate and her mouth. Her face went white.

Only one word. Aliana pouted. "And five more archers. They were hiding on a balcony, ready to shoot. They are still there. I had a Vision this morning."

"Aliana, this should have been handled differently."

"You were busy being silent in the hall. You are busy being silent now. I needed to find something to do; Muniker seems to be a boring city. Kasia helped me. They were worse than Meriaduk's guards in Nerval, even Roderick. All they could manage was a pitiful little red spot on Kasia's dress. One man touched her knee as he fell. She is too shy to say, but it seems that Kasia likes your taste in clothing." She looked innocently at Saliné.

"Roderick?" Codrin asked, as Saliné seemed a bit stunned. "The man Alfrid sent to kill me four years ago. Thank you, Aliana." *Is this why she came here? No, her Vision about Roderick was this morning. It must be another one. Something important too, if not she would have stayed in Poenari.* He did not know that Aliana had come only the day before, to heal Count Joachim with her powerful Light; she had the same gift from Fate as Elsebeth. Saliné would need him soon.

"Please," Saliné said, "are no other better subjects to discuss?"

"Are there? I haven't heard any." Aliana laughed quietly.

Saliné smiled. "Thank you, Aliana." She stood up and went to embrace her sister. "You were right, discretion was needed, if not, people would start to worry. Roderick's body will be found tomorrow morning somewhere in the city, close to an inn. Perhaps he was drunk."

The atmosphere became warmer and, at the end, Saliné gestured toward a maid who came with a child in her arms. They were already standing, ready to leave the room. Codrin frowned when the maid brought the little girl to him.

"She has done nothing bad," Saliné said to Codrin. "I just wanted you to meet my daughter, Ioana."

Codrin smiled, sad, for she was another man's child, but pleased to hear the name of his twin sister. "Thank you." He reached out and touched the girl. The Vision came abruptly, and Codrin's upper lip twitched a little.

"That twitch means an important Vision," Aliana said, pointing at his mouth.

"Yes," Codrin said, "Ioana will have an interesting future." A little lost, he became silent, recalling some words from the Empress about the girl's future. *Should I presume that she was half wrong, or that she was half right?*

Codrin left Muniker early in the morning, eager to meet Baraki. He had waited more than fifteen years for this. His farewell was a little strange, but all the time he had spent in Muniker, over the years, had been strange, farewells included. On the road, he still recalled Saliné's hand trailing down his face. Her usual way to tell him farewell. A longer one, this time. *Only the kissing was missing.* Codrin smiled at his thought.

At the head of five hundred soldiers, Alfrid returned to Muniker a week after Codrin went to fight the man who had killed his family. Prudent, he sent a captain with a few soldiers toward the gate, to learn more while he changed his garb. The day before, he had received a letter from Saliné that Roderick was killed. She did not write how or why, but some things could not be delivered through the couriers. He blamed Codrin's spies for the murder.

"Codrin has indeed left the city, and the gate is already open for your majesty," the captain said on his return.

Saliné made Codrin leave; she is a clever woman, Alfrid thought. *He will not enter Muniker again.*

The guards at the main gate lined up to salute him, and Alfrid entered the city riding at a slow pace. In front of the palace, he was greeted by Count Joachim, who was limping a little. Aligned in two long rows, ten feet between them, forty trumpetists played the royal anthem while the King walked quietly. It was the usual protocol. He always enjoyed it.

"Joachim," Alfrid said jovially when the anthem ended, "I am glad that you are almost healed. It's good to be home again. Let's go inside now; I can't wait to see my wife and children." *This will be a wonderful night.*

"Her majesty is waiting in the throne hall." Joachim bowed, and gestured toward the open door.

Alfrid stopped abruptly just in front of the door. "How do I look?" he asked.

"A very refined costume, as usual."

"I am wearing more blue than usual today, but it's such a bright day." Alfrid pointed toward the clear sky and went inside.

Joachim walked slowly after the King while the captain and Alfrid's twenty personal guards tried to follow the Count. "Captain," Joachim said with a severe look. "The Queen and half of our Duchesses and Countesses are inside to greet the King. The Queen and the Chamberlain took great care to make a perfect ceremony. Do you really want to enter dressed like this?" He pointed at the dusty capes and ring-mail of the captain and soldiers. "You deserve to be inside as you have guarded the King. Change your clothes and come back to the throne hall. The ceremony will be quite long. And a little ... boring." He grimaced, making the soldiers smile.

This time, Alfrid walked fast, and found more than three hundred people, mostly men, waiting in the throne hall. Saliné was seated in her place, and in Alfrid's place, little Arnis was sitting on his knees, his back turned to the waiting people and his father, hitting the backrest with a toy, in a rhythmic way. Now and then, he tried to climb down from the large throne, which seemed to be a little boring for a toddler. Down on one knee next to him, the maid was struggling to distract the child with stories or with her hands, making him giggle from time to time. At Saliné's side stood Thais, the Second Light of Litvonia, and Klavis, the Chancellor and Alfrid's uncle. There were many important people there; even the Duke of Hamborg was present, with three men dressed in ceremonial uniforms. He looked a little pale because of his wound.

Hamborg did not come to Muniker since my coronation, Alfrid thought. *Not that I missed the snake, but it seems that he has finally realized his place.* When Alfrid arrived thirty paces from the throne, Saliné stood up, to greet him.

"We are glad that you escaped, and your wound was not so serious," she said, her voice composed.

"Ah, it was a nasty nomad arrow in my upper arm. It's almost healed." He rotated his shoulder to prove the healing, then walked toward her until they were face to face. "It's so good to be home." He smiled and embraced her. Then kissed her. "Second Light." He nodded to Thais when Saliné disengaged from him. "Uncle." He nodded to the Chancellor. "Our little man has taken my place. He seems to be an eager man. This is a sign that he will be a great King." Alfrid laughed and stepped toward the throne, where Arnis, still with his back to Alfrid, was trotting now, delighted by the sound his little feet were producing on the hard wood. There was a pillow there, when he was seated, but now it lay a few feet away from the throne.

"Your majesty," Damian said, "It's a bit unusual, but I have a plea for an unusual case."

Case. What case? I want to eat, bathe, and go in bed with my wife.

"Yes, Damian," Saliné said before Alfrid could make his mind.

Damian gestured toward a veiled woman, who walked in front of them. Slowly, she pulled the veil up, revealing her face, and all the people around stared at her. Saliné's eyes were on Alfrid.

Alfrid's smile became a trifle strained, and after a long pause, he asked evasively, "Saliné, wasn't she one of your maids? I think she left Muniker some time ago. Or even Litvonia."

"Yes, she left after her majesty's son had died," Damian agreed.

"And why has she returned now?"

"She did not leave Litvonia. Vlad took her to his castle. She has a story about the people who killed my son. We need to hear her story."

"My dear," Alfrid turned toward Saliné, "I am sorry that you have to hear such terrible things; I don't know what was in Damian's mind. You are still affected, but it was an unfortunate accident, and we all know who is guilty for that. Codrin was careless... Perhaps this woman was paid by him to give you a false story and stir troubles here. Codrin is a troublemaker; we all know this. In fact, I am sure that she was paid by him. Let's send her back to Frankis. We should not spoil the happiness of being together again."

"I met her when two former palace guards tried to kill her," Damian interjected, and Alfrid threw a murderous stare at him.

"How is she still alive if the guards tried to kill her?"

"Because I saved her," Damian said bluntly.

"We will stop this talk now. Send the woman away." Alfrid's voice was now nervous and rose to a higher pitch. He moved forward to reach his throne.

Saliné stepped abruptly in front of him and barred his path, then gave him a roll with the seals of all the three kingdoms: Litvonia, Frankis and Silvania. "This is our divorce paper. It is all according to the law, and it has all the needed signatures."

Alfrid looked at the paper in his hand, then at her. "I won't stop you, if you want a divorce, but the *King* has the last say in this. I will allow you to return to Frankis as a Duchess. The children will remain with me. We will talk about this tomorrow. I am tired."

Without a word, Saliné gave him a second roll, much larger, bearing the same three seals.

"I suppose that this is your marriage contract with Codrin. It seems to be quite a long document. I don't care what you do. But only after we have a *real* divorce, not this farce." He gestured with the roll in his hand.

"Alfrid," Saliné said, her voice stern and calculated. "With this is the paper, you are deposed." She pointed at the second roll. "You abdicated your duties when you ran from the battle and disorganized our army. We lost many good soldiers there. You hid in Auers fortress because you had a scratch on your arm. You let the nomads pillage the kingdom. Children, women and elders were killed, and many were taken as slaves. You are no longer the King of Litvonia. For the rest of your life, you will stay in Auers. You like the place."

"Enough!" Alfrid snapped and stamped his foot on the floor. "Litvonia no longer has a Queen!" he shouted to be heard around the hall. "She has forfeited her rights. Joachim," he turned toward the Spatar of Litvonia. "The Queen... The *former* Queen and her family will be placed under arrest in her suite until I will sort out this situation. The children will move into my suite. Escort her there."

"I am afraid that is not possible; her majesty has instructed me to escort you to Auers. Please follow me."

"Uncle, this is not..." Alfrid turned toward the Chancellor, who just shook his head.

Saliné came closer, and her voice became a whisper to be heard only by him. "You were my husband, and we have two children together. That's the only reason you will not share Calista's and Edric's fate. I want you to know that I punished Calista myself; I slit her throat with my own hands. Codrin killed Edric."

Alfrid's mouth said a silent oh, and his lips remained rigid, open and round, a red circle, almost crimson. His face blackened. He wanted to cry that his wife was a killer. He wanted to order her seizure. With some effort, he clamped his mouth shut.

"If you are not in Auers in five days, and stay there for the rest of your life, I will forget everything that linked us in the past, and you will end with a rope around your neck. Leave now." She gestured royally toward the door, and turned her back on him, walking toward her throne at a measured pace. She sat with a display of calm that she did not feel and turned toward her son. Then she smiled to calm him. It was a sad smile. The people in the hall realized that, and they bowed to her.

"Alfrid." Joachim gripped his elbow with a firm hand.

Led by the Uber Captain Frinz, three soldiers wearing the colors of the house of Litvonia, and three more led by the Duke of Hamborg, walked behind them. They formed a U around Alfrid, between him and the throne. Then came three men led by Damian wearing the colors of Frankis. A captain and three men wearing the colors of Duchess Maltia. Horwath and three men wearing the colors of Countess Elsebeth, Alfrid's cousin. Then even more came. The ails of the U lengthened, leaving Alfrid only one way out, and he grimaced; in front of him was a map of the strongest houses of Litvonia; even the Guilds of Muniker had sent their men, led by Movil. Shoulders slumped, he tried to say something more, but thought better of it. Pressed by Joachim's steady hand, he moved like an old man.

Chapter 29 - Codrin

It took Codrin five days to lead his army through half of Silvania, toward its eastern border. It was not a large kingdom. At noon, they arrived at a place he recognized – down there, five miles in front of him, was the entrance into the gorge of Neira. His mind wandered into the past when he had passed through that gorge. The fight against Baraki's men. The death of his brother. The death of his mentor, Tudor. The oath he had taken at their graves, to bring justice. *This will be a fight like no other. In two days, I will die, or I will fulfill my oath.* He rose in the saddle and looked around the large valley with his spyglass. Far in front, on his left, he saw the small path that allowed him to escape into the mountains, away from the large road. *Baraki's men followed the road.* From this position, he could not recognize the mountains, but he remembered how the valley looked from up there. "Vlaicu, send men back and tell the army to set up camp well back from the edge. I don't want to be seen from the valley."

In the evening, they had the war council. It was unusual to have one two days before the battle, but Codrin had decided to wait there and plan small things that could decide the fate of a great battle. This was not a battle against the nomads. This was a battle against the best army on the continent. He knew that army well; it had been led by his father once. He had fifty thousand men. Baraki had twenty-five thousand more. On the map, he let his finger follow the gorge, and shook his head to keep his memories at bay. "The scouts reported that there are paths along the gorge, following the ridges. I want all our archers to be place on the ridges, from here to here." His finger slid over the map, starting from the entry point. "Two thousand archers spread over three thousand feet. The other one thousand archers will wait at the other entry point and will start to shoot as soon as the enemy is in range. And they will follow them, continuing to shoot." *It feels so strange to call the Arenians my enemies.* "Following the scouts, the archers will be able to walk along the ridges until they reach the middle of the gorge. From there," he tapped on the map, "they must walk around the mountains to reach our side of the gorge. They may not arrive in time for the next part of the battle."

In the morning, Codrin canceled everything and asked the archers to come back. In the afternoon, Baraki's army started to leave the gorge and slowly filled the small plain.

"Should we attack?" Vlaicu asked when half of the Arenian army was out of the gorge.

"No," Codrin said, his tense eyes fixed on the soldiers in the vanguard.

"Did you have a Vision?"

"No." *I have had no Vision since I went away from Poenari, but I can't tell them that. And Baraki is a Seer.*

Baraki knew that Codrin's army was hidden behind the ridge, five miles away from the mouth of the gorge. He also knew that Codrin's army was not ready to attack. "I told you that he is a coward," he told the men following him out of the gorge. "He is hiding behind the ridge. His army was defeated by Hunkai, and only the nomads' stupidity allowed him to survive. We are not nomads. We will camp here, on the plain, and let our army rest. Tomorrow, we will destroy him and unify the continent under one rule. The new Alban Empire will be born."

On the edge of the ridge, Codrin waited until the Arenian army secured camp and raised the tents. He stretched his mind to feel the Light, but nothing came to him. *I am blind. Why is Fate doing this to me? Or is it the Empress?* There was a small ripple of Light that usually came to him before the Empress appeared. Something was different though. *Baraki... He is using the Farsight. I can't use mine. I can't use what I have lost. Baraki will know now that I am no longer a Seer. Fate,* Codrin shrugged and shook his head. "Vlad, raise the banners." He heard orders being shouted behind him, and the men moving swiftly. He did not turn.

"It's done," Vlad said, and Codrin finally turned.

In front of him, there were three large banners, each bearing two ravens and a crown, waving on thirty-feet-high poles. Two poles for each banner. They were large banners, and the wind in the valley made them flutter a little. *Last time I saw them...* Codrin thought, and memories charged at him like heavy cavalry. *Last time, I saw these banners on the Royal Castle of Arenia. The day I ran away from my own house. The day my parents and twin sister were killed. These are my banners, and I represent the House of Arenia. It will mean nothing if I lose tomorrow.* He took his spyglass and scanned the Arenian camp, less than one mile in front of him. Some soldiers were pointing at his position, at his banners.

At dawn, the drums began to beat in the Arenian camp. Yawning soldiers came out of tents and hurried toward their horses. The drums became more demanding. The lines began to form, slow and steady; they were all men of high discipline. Baraki was still in his tent, the last council before the battle.

"Raise our banners," Baraki ordered, and a courier ran out of the tent. "There is not much to say. The battle is ours to win. Last night, I hovered over the land with my Farsight. They are scared, and the little rat leading them has lost the powers of the Seer. Don't ask me why. I don't know. Perhaps his goddess found him too weak and did not want him to lose this battle in her name. Let's get out and finalize the last details on the field."

Baraki's tent was raised on a small mound, and from outside it, he was able to see most of his camp. "Our lines are almost formed," he said, and looked at the ridge where the enemy was standing. He saw only the three banners and one man on a horse. There was no one else on the ridge. For a moment, Baraki thought to let his Farsight see over the ridge. He decided against it. The use of Farsight weakened the Seer, and he needed his strength for the battle. "I've told you that they are afraid. Some of his men may have ran already. He doesn't dare to show his numbers. We will attack with both wings at once. The middle will ride when our wings engage them." He looked at his own banners, the Stag of his house, and the Horse of the Khad. There were few nomads in his army – they did not get on with the Arenians because of the past invasions – and they were used only for scouting, but Baraki was proud of his dual inheritance, nomadic from his grandmother, Arenian from his grandfather. He raised his hand, and the drums changed tune. The King and the Khad were now at the head of his army.

From his position high on the ridge, Codrin saw the battlefield like a plate, slightly lower in the middle and cut in two by the road leading into the gorge. He saw the Arenian army too. Its discipline. Eyes closed, he remembered the last time he was in the middle of that army. It was just after his father had defeated the nomads. Eyes open again, he looked at the banners; not at those belonging to Baraki. On the left, he saw the banner of Duke Anghel of Debreten, his second uncle. *Anghel must be too old for battle now. My cousin Mesarosh is leading them. I have not seen him since... Since a long time ago.* The drums in the valley changed tune again. *They are ready to charge. Both wings will attack at the same time.* He looked to the right flank. *The Duke of Sucieva. He was twenty-five when I left. I wonder if Captain Ioan is there.* During the night, he was immersed in the past, and several times he recalled a certain evening in the Cursed Forest, every detail, every word. *That was my first job as Lead Protector, and Captain Ioan came into our camp.* In the valley, the drums changed tune again. *They are charging.* Codrin raised his hand, and his drums answered, their beat strangely resembling the one coming from the valley. Then his drums changed tune and became louder. Then louder. The Arenian wings moved. They resembled two slow waves, rising steadily. The waves moved faster, and faster, gaining speed to negotiate the slope toward Codrin. In the middle of the slope, a few hundred riders detached from the main force. They moved toward the middle of the battlefield. The wings followed them. They were soon far from the main army. Codrin raised his sword. From the valley, his silhouette looked strange. A lone man dressed in dark blue, his sword pointing to one of the banners behind him. That was his only gesture, and he remained like a stone, unmoving. The incoming riders merged in the middle of the slope, then they split, ready to surround him. Behind Codrin, a wall of riders came into sight. They were mixed, men from Frankis and from Litvonia. Men from Silvania. Light cavalry and heavy cavalry. There were the banners of the three kingdoms too.

Baraki followed the advance of his wings. When they were close to the end of the slope, he raised his sword, ready to order the charge of his full army. His eyes were glassy, anticipating the victory. *They are almost there*, he thought, and closed his eyes for a few moments.

The Arenian riders seemed to split again, ten of them eager to arrive first. They swerved left in a little arc, then rode toward Codrin. In front of him, they stopped abruptly. The horses neighed, and their echo lingered in the valley.

"I heard the drums calling the men of Arenia to her King. We answered the call," Duke Mesarosh said.

Baraki started when a hand touched his arm.

"Your majesty," the Count of Breila, his brother said, his voice low and urgent. "We have a problem." He pointed up toward the ridge with his chin.

"What?" Baraki snapped, looking at him. Then he looked at the ridge. Then he understood. He wanted to say something, but nothing came.

There was a commotion in the Arenian army, and more soldiers moved away. From the ridge, a mass of cavalry bore down like a storm. Frankis and Litvonian. Silvanian and Arenian. The heavy cavalry was leading them, Hussaris and Teutons, ready to crush everything in their path. Baraki turned his horse abruptly and shouted, "Retreat!" He couldn't believe his eyes; there were only five thousand soldiers with him, and most of his commanders had vanished. Only the Count of Breila and Commander Ioan were still with him.

"Ioan," Baraki said, "you are the only commander of the Royal Guard who stayed with me to the end. And I always suspected you of not being my most loyal soldier."

"I am the most loyal soldier, Sir," Ioan said and Baraki frowned; he was accustomed to being called your majesty. Before he could react, Ioan hit him with the hilt of his sword. "I have always been loyal to the legitimate King. Tie him to the horse," he ordered his men.

There was a sudden commotion, and some soldiers still loyal to Baraki unsheathed their swords. A sword struck Breila's helmet, and he fell from his horse.

"I would run, if I were you," Ioan said and gestured across the field. Codrin's cavalry was coming. "There is no need to tie Baraki anymore, just take his sword."

Three hundred paces from the remaining Arenian army, Codrin raised his hand to slow his men. They gradually came to a halt.

"Your majesty," Ioan bowed when Codrin dismounted in front of him.

"Captain... My apologies, Commander Ioan. We meet again in a most interesting situation." Codrin stretched out his hand and, surprised, Ioan clasped it. "Just a reminder of the time when you left my caravan in the Cursed Forest."

"Your majesty, we have a gift for you." Ioan snapped his fingers, and two men came forward with Baraki.

"Your crimes have come to an end, Baraki," Codrin said, struggling to keep his voice calm. In that moment, long forgotten memories came to him: his twin sister Ioana playing the lyre for the whole family. She was only fifteen when her cousins raped and killed her.

"What differences are there between my crimes and yours, Codrin? You did not come to your position through love and peace."

"No, I fought hard for my place, but I never killed the ones I pledged to protect, and I never killed children, even when they belonged to my enemies."

"That's a poor strategy; let their children grow, and they will kill you. Look at our current situation."

"I will make a note to check later if you were right or wrong."

"I am not a child anymore, so I guess that you will hang me."

"You are an intelligent man, Baraki, perhaps you are even a Seer who can see into the future."

Baraki was hanged. There were no gallows, so he was hanged from a tree, a hundred paces from the graves where Codrin's brother and Tudor rested. Baraki's brother, the Count of Breila joined him on a different branch, a little lower to underline the difference in rank.

Alone, Codrin went and knelt by the graves. “I have fulfilled my oath to bring you Justice. May Fate allow that you rest in peace.” Unmoving, he stayed there for a few minutes, then he stood up and turned toward the men who were bowing thirty paces from him. There were not many, just twenty-three, his most trusted men, and he looked at them, one by one. “One more thing to do, and we can have peace.”

There was a council that evening, and Mesarosh was named regent in Arenia, to rule until Codrin returned. Ioan, the new Count of Breila, and the Duke of Sucieva would assist him. In the morning, the armies split, going west and east. *I still have one more thing to do*, Codrin said to himself, and turned Zor on the road toward Muniker for the second time in his life.

Chapter 30 – Saliné / Codrin

"Who should I announce? The King of Arenia?" The Chamberlain asked, a hint of worry in his voice, looking at Saliné, then at the people gathered in the great hall of Muniker. *One wrong step and my head will fall.*

"The Alban Emperor," Saliné said from her throne, her eyes fixed on the large door of the hall.

The old man nodded and swallowed heavily, then coughed to regain his voice. "I announce His Majesty, the Alban Emperor." At the end of the phrase, he hit the floor three times with his staff. *May Fate allow it to be true. That's a man who deserves the emperor crown, even if he may want my head because I was Alfrid's man. And I invited him to that ball...* The old man's mouth twitched, and he clamped it shut, his teeth clacking loudly.

Codrin walked across the hall, and thirty paces from Saliné, their eyes met. He stopped, and she stood up. The whole hall was blanketed in stillness; not even a whisper could be heard. Then something broke, and the flurry of a fluttering dress was the only thing moving in the stillness. Saliné ran toward him, and her speed was almost as good as when she was a child. Codrin caught her in his arms, and turned her once, as he had done many times in a long ago past that seemed to come to them again.

After seating Saliné on her throne, he approached Thais, the Second Light of the Litvonian Wanderers, who was standing next to her. Their eyes met, and he bowed. "Thais, I have to thank you for saving my life, when Alfrid tried to kill me after the first nomad invasion." His deep voice was calm but loud, reaching everyone in the large hall, and when he paused it was filled with whispers, and many young women pressed their hands to their mouths. And even some older ones. "But I will not thank you for that potion." This time he whispered, so only the Wanderer and Saliné were able to hear him.

"I apologize, your majesty, but the potion had its role. A role that I was not fully... A role that was not clear at all, at that moment. The Vision came to me later. If you trusted me with your life, you must trust me with this too, because I am not allowed to tell you what future that potion created. I apologize for that, but it's a bright future. The day when you establish your successor to the throne, you will remember my words, though I will no longer be alive. And you will know."

Codrin frowned for a moment and recalled a brief Vision. "Yes, you are right, that will be an interesting moment. What was done was done. I want that book with the recipe destroyed. Calista used the potion, on me – twice, though the second time I was able to avoid it – and I don't know on how many others. I believe that her potion was meant to create another future too, but I doubt its brightness. I charge you with the destruction of that Talant book, and whatever copies have been made."

"I did not know about Calista." The Wanderer rubbed her left temple, and lines deepened between her brows. "I should have been more careful. Would your majesty agree to my destroying only the pages with the potion? There are strong healing recipes in the book."

"Do you understand them all?"

"Some of them; others are unintelligible. We know the words, but they are assembled in strange phrases."

"Unknown dangers. Or unknown gifts. Destroy the pages with the recipe for the potion, and lock the book away," Codrin said and walked to his throne. Seated, he took his time to assess the crowd, then Saliné. "So now, it seems you are both a single woman and the Queen of Litvonia. The Queen of Silvania. And ...

the Queen of Frankis." His voice was serious, but his eyes had a sort of devilish amusement. "Would you consider marriage? There is a certain political need for it."

"I married once for love, and once for political need, though I found love again later. I find that marriage made for love has a certain quality that the other lacked."

Codrin smiled, stood up, took her hand, and pulled her up too. "There is an announcement to be made. The coronation of the Empress and Emperor of the new Alban Empire is settled for tomorrow afternoon. Of course, we must be married by then. Chamberlain," he looked at the tall, old man, who tried in vain to become small and invisible, "you served the previous King well. You know your duty. As you know, some things are pressing. Movil, the keeper of the Caravan Inn, will help you in your work."

"Your majesty," the Chamberlain moistened his lips, "we need... We need.... We need time. Three weeks for the wedding, the dress, the hundred maidens who will join the Empress, the hundred young men who will join you. The choir in the church. The hundred-piece orchestra for the marriage feast. The banquet. A new nuptial bed, ebony and gold." As if caught in a trance, he started to speak faster and faster, ignoring every gesture Codrin was making to stop him. "The golden marriage crowns. Wedding rings. The coronation crowns for the Emperor and Empress. The one thousand men in the throne hall during the coronation. The next day's banquet. The five thousand people outside the castle, so you can speak to them after the coronation. We have to do all this. We need three weeks at least." His voice ended in a tenor tremolo, and his hands started to shake. He clasped them tight at his back. His lips clamped even tighter, and he looked as if he was toothless.

Codrin clamped his mouth shut too, struggling not to burst into laughter; the man did not deserve to be shamed in front of so many people. "Chamberlain, look at us. What do you see?" His voice was composed, with only a hint of amusement.

"Our great Empress and Emperor, of course."

"Let's forget about that for a while. What do you really see when you look at us?"

With sudden inspiration, the Chamberlain studied Codrin's clothes, dark blue shirt and pants with not a single gold thread embedded into it and no gold buttons. He wore no jewelry apart from his wedding ring. His stance was that of an Emperor and his clothes were just functional things. He recalled Alfrid, and his vests, yellow, green, and blue things, the gold chain, the long earring, three large rings, and an even larger medallion. His eyes moved to Saliné, her simple dark green dress, tailored to enhance her natural elegance. There were no ribbons, and her only jewelry was earrings and a wedding ring. "Everything will be ready in time, your majesty. May I leave now?" He bowed after Codrin's silent agreement and moved quickly. By the time he reached the back door, he was already running.

Turning toward Saliné, Codrin saw the old wedding ring he had given to her; it had not been on her finger just minutes before. He took her hand in his, and they walked out of the hall.

Appendix

Arad

Codrin, son of the slain King of Arenia and the legitimate King. After his father's death, he finds sanctuary in the former kingdom of Frankis, sometimes using the name Tudor to conceal his real identity. King of Frankis

Saliné, Queen of Frankis

Cantemir, Chancellor and former Master Sage of the Circle

Mara, Vice-Chancellor, former Secretary of Poenari

Vlaicu, Spatar of Frankis (commander of the army). Former Chief of the Guard of Severin before Severin fell to Aron.

Sava, Chief of the Guard of Arad, former Chief of the Guard of Leyona and Poenari

Jara (Stejara), former Signora of Severin, former Grand Signora of Midia. She lost her castle to Grand Seigneur Orban after her first husband, Malin, was slain in battle. She lost Severin to Aron when Mohor was killed.

Cernat, Jara's father

Ban, Chief of the Archers of Arad and Sava's right hand. Former Chief of the Archers of Severin before Severin fell to Aron.

Vlad, born in Litvonia, he followed Codrin to the former Frankis Kingdom. Chief Scout of Frankis

Orban (the Beast), former Grand Seigneur of Arad

Panait, the first Mester of the Merchants Guild in Arad

Vio, Jara's daughter

Veres (Snail), Jara's son

Mark, Jara's and Mohor's son

Delia, Panait's wife

Calin, former Secretary of Mehadia and Mara's father

Pintea, Vlad's brother
Julien, Sava's son and captain

Muniker
Alfrid, King of Litvonia, King Consort of Frankis
Saliné, Queen Consort of Litvonia, Queen of Frankis
Edric, Alfrid's brother and Saliné's lover
Calista, the Second Light of the Litvonian Wanderers, and Alfrid's aunt
Joachim, Count, Spatar of Litvonia
Elsebeth, Countess of Baia
Vlad, Chief of the Royal Guard
Movil, Mester of Muniker Guilds, innkeeper of Caravans Inn
Frinz, Uber Captain
Pintea, Uber Captain
Lisandru, Uber Captain
Damian, Uber Captain
Roderick, captain, charged by Alfrid to kill Codrin.
Maltia, Duchess of Kolugn
Cosmin, Saliné's and Codrin's son
Arnis, Saliné's and Alfrid's son
Rosine, Cosmin's governess
Klavis, Chancellor and Master Sage of the Litvonian Circle, Alfrid's uncle
Alois, Chief of the Palace Guard

Litvonian Forest and Baia
Ildeko, Codrin's new wife
Pireska, Ildeko's mother-in-law
Irvath, Count of Baia, killed by Codrin
Elsebeth, Countess of Baia
Fandras, Uber captain of Count Irvath, killed by Codrin
Horwath, Irvath's captain
Ioan, Ildeko's and Codrin's son
Ferent, Ildeko's first son

Nerval

Meriaduk, the High Priest of the Serpent

Dochia, Frankis Wanderer and priest of the Serpent

Ai, the young, invisible woman helping Dochia in the Sanctuary

Kasia, new Wanderer, Dochia's apprentice

Aliana, Frankis Wanderer

Mira, Dochia's first guard

Irina, Dochia's second guard

Gresha, merchant, Kasia's cousin

Adex, First Vicarius

Krisko, merchant thief

The High Sphere

Dochia, the Last Empress, founder of the Order of the Wanderers

Nabal, the Last Emperor, he joined the Serpent God

Frankis Wanderers

Drusila, the First Light of the Frankis Wanderers

Dochia, the Third Light

Aliana, a powerful young Wanderer sent to help Dochia in Nerval

Satia, Aliana's mentor

Splendra, the Third Light, converted Serpentist and High Priestess of the Serpent in Frankis

Arenian Wanderers

Ada, the Second Light of the Arenian Wanderers, and the strongest Light of all the Wanderers until Dochia emerged in Nerval

Litvonian Wanderers

Elagia, the First Light of the Litvonian Wanderers

Calista, the Second Light

Thais, the Third Light

Yantha, a new Wanderer, Thais's novice

Frankis Circle

Cantemir, former Master Sage

Maud, the new Master Sage

Aurelian, Sage and Primus Itinerant, killed in Severin

Belugas, Sage and Primus Itinerant, hanged by Codrin

Verenius, Sage and Primus Itinerant

Iulius, Itinerant Sage, hanged by Saliné after poisoning Duke Manuc of Loxburg

Severin

Mohor, former Seigneur of Severin and Jara's second husband, killed by Aron

Aron (Big Mouth), Seigneur of Severin after killing Mohor, former Spatar of Severin (commander of the army). Deposed by Codrin, he found refuge in Castis

Bucur, Aron' son, killed by Saliné in Castis

Senal, former Secretary of Severin, killed by Veres

Leyona

Garland, former Grand Seigneur of Leyona

Leyonan, former Grand Seigneur of Leyona, slain in a battle against Codrin

Maud, Secretary of Leyona and the new Master Sage of the Circle

Sava, former Chief of the Guard of Leyona

Bartal, second Secretary of Leyona

Lina, Garland's wife

Farcu, Chief of the Guard of Leyona's castle

Dobre, governor of Orhei in Leyona Seigneury

Peyris

Stefan, Duke of Peyris, poisoned by the Circle

Cleyre, Stefan's granddaughter and Duchess of Peyris

Costa, Duke Consort of Frankis

Nicolas, First Spatar of Peyris

Reymont, former Secretary of Peyris and Hidden Sage of the Circle

Tolosa

Baldovin, former Duke of Tolosa

Leon, the old Duke of Tolosa

Laure, Baldovin's wife, and the real ruler of Tolosa. Maud's daughter.

Marie, the new Duchess of Tolosa

Joffroy, Pierre's son and Duke Consort of Tolosa

Pierre, the Spatar of Tolosa (commander of the army)

Deva

Devan, Grand Seigneur of Deva

Filippo, Devan's son

Balan, the first Mester of the Merchants Guild in Deva and Sage of the Circle

Mona, Balan's wife

Dan, Chief of the Guard of Deva

Poenari

Varia, Governor of Poenari

Boldur, one of the Mountes' chieftains, Chief of Guard of Poenari

Bernart, custodian of Poenari before Codrin took the fortress.

Siena, Bernart's granddaughter

Amelie, Bernart's granddaughter

Assassins

Scorta, Assassin Master, joined Dochia in Nerval

Arenia

Tudor, an Assassin renegade and Codrin's mentor

Ioana, Codrin's twin sister

Radu, Codrin's brother

Baraki, the new King of Arenia, former Chief of the Royal Guard of Arenia

Iulian, captain of the Royal Guard of Arenia

Mesarosh, Duke of Debreten

Loxburg

Manuc, Duke of Loxburg, poisoned by the Circle

Agard, Secretary of Loxburg and Hidden Sage of the Circle

Miscellaneous

Spatar, Chief of the Army

Vistier, administrator of a castle and coin master

Wraith, most successful Lead Protectors (only four in Frankis)

Black Dervil, mercenary captain (only four in Frankis after Codrin killed Sharpe)

Vicarius, the most powerful priests of the Serpent

galben (galbeni at plural), gold coin, ten grams weight

cozonac, cake from Arenia

turn, alternative time unit of measure, equivalent of one hour

Months of the year

Gerar, January

Florar, May

Stove, July

Wanderers ruling councils

Inner Council of the Three

High Council of the Seven